The Gifted Spawn

The Gifted Spawn

R.R. Brooks

Published by Escarpment Press

Indian Land, SC

The Gifted Spawn

ISBN: 978-1-7346750-7-8

Published by Escarpment Press
Indian Land, SC

Also by R.R. Brooks

Justi the Gifted
The Clown Forest Murders (with A.C. Brooks)

Acknowledgements

Pressure from my granddaughter spurred me to complete the saga of the Kingdom of the Zell and the divine gift to mankind that would become conscience. As the story evolved from draft to final form, Tom Hooker, Frank Robinson, Jerry Mandel, Jon Riley, and Lisa Youngblood of The Appalachian Round Table critiqued this story piece by piece and provided a path to improvements. My wife Sherry was supportive, not only in theory, but in practice as well, providing a beta read of the finished work. To fans who read the first part, *Justi the Gifted,* to fantasy writers who wield magic, and to the late David Eddings whose *Belgariad* series inspired this story, I am grateful. I invite my readers to put aside hassles and slide into the world within, where circumstances may differ, but the people are the same.

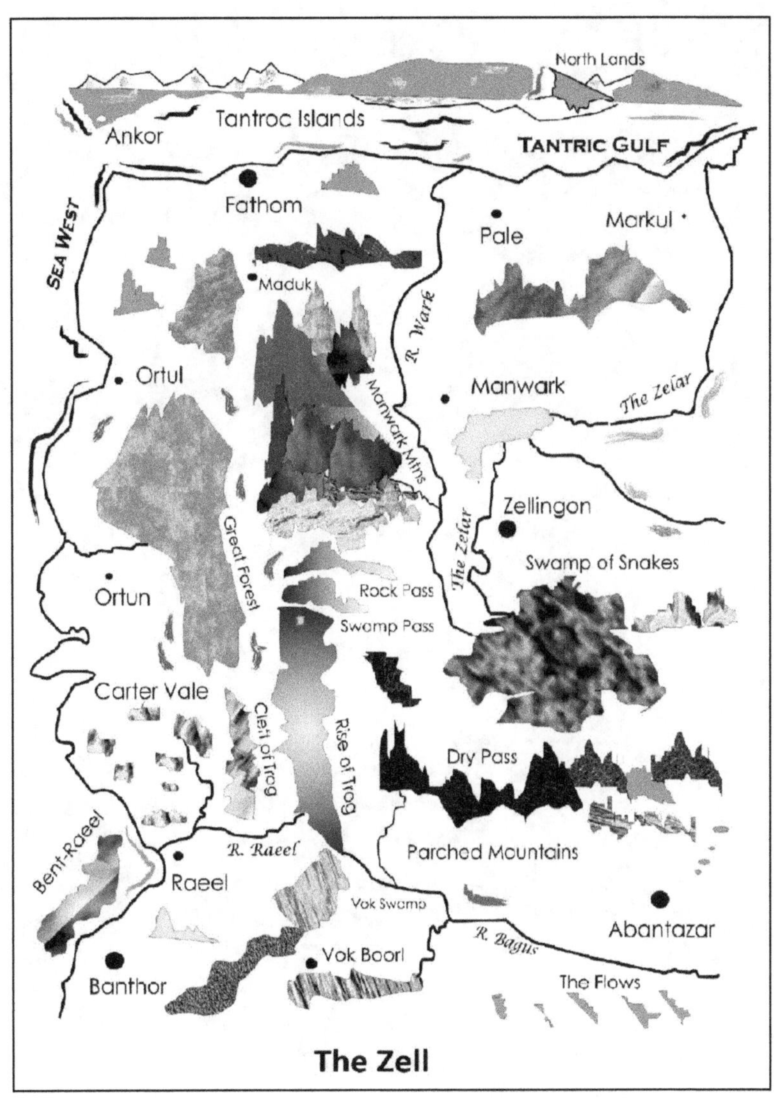
North Lands
Tantroc Islands
Ankor
TANTRIC GULF
SEA WEST
Fathom
Pale
Markul
Maduk
R. Wark
Ortul
Manwark Mtns
Manwark
The Zelar
Zellingon
The Zelar
Great Forest
Swamp of Snakes
Ortun
Rock Pass
Swamp Pass
Carter Vale
Cleft of Trog
Rise of Trog
Dry Pass
Bent-Raeel
R. Raeel
Parched Mountains
Raeel
Vok Swamp
Abantazar
R. Bagus
Vok Boorl
Banthor
The Flows
The Zell

Principal Characters

Adamanti—Angels of Li

Aduk—Tantrocan high priest before Provak

Breel—Healer of Pale, daughter of Credo

Brokul—Tantrocan king

Brosun—Tantrocan prince and king, son of Brokul and Cantor

Caldir—Tantrocan high priest after Provak

Cantor—Consort of King Brokul

Credo—Healer of Pale

Danilla—Princess daughter of Mercerio and Justi

Dar—God of chaos

Entor—Scholar, student of Meligo

Fospe—Ice representative

Irend—Husband of Provani, stepfather of Justik

Justi—Consort of Queen Mercerio, bearer of the Justice Power

Justik—Son of Justi and Provani, wielder of killing flame

Lyra—Lynx host of Marget, guardian of Meru and Danilla

Marget—Male spirit appointed guardian of Justi

Meligo—Zellish scholar

Mercerio—Gifted Queen of the Zell

Meru—Prince and King of the Zell, son of Mercerio and Justi

Provak—Tantrocan high priest, Caldir's teacher

Provani—Justik's mother

Rakur—Ortul seer

Ranera—Tantrocan princess, daughter of Cantor and Brokul, sister of King Brosun

Sathal—Thal's son
Thal—Ice chief

Prologue

In a world created by two gods, two separate peoples dwelled as enemies. The Zellish inhabited the southern continent—temperate and abundant—and worshipped Li, the god of order. Tantrocans occupied the cold northern continent across the Tantric Gulf and honored Dar, god of chaos. Tantrocans believed in slaves and human sacrifice to Dar and saw the peaceful Zellish as suppliers. These people were natural enemies, and the gods fomented that enmity.

"Our clash has created matter," Li thundered as hot gases exploded where his will had thwarted Dar's.

The spirit plane shuddered with the act of creation. Li's angels, spirits called the Adamanti, remained bathed in holy light. Dar's creatures, the Miasma, watched the light about them darken.

Dar gazed on the expanding universe and then at his servants constrained to blackness. "This new matter will coalesce, form worlds, and give rise to creatures with bodies. Let us endow them with souls so that they know their gods. Let these physical beings decide by worship who is the greater god. We shall not further disturb this physical world."

And Li agreed. Neither Li nor Dar would change the material world as it evolved to include humans. Some did good and worshipped Li. Others followed the evil ways of Dar. But evil seemed more attractive than good. And this led to a change in the material world.

Li's gift was immaterial and thus did not violate his agreement with Dar. Li blessed a peasant boy, Justi of Ortun, a village on the west coast of the Zell, with a way of thinking, of being aware of right and wrong. Dar's spirits were enraged and, using the same pathway, divided the gift, scattered it. Justi was left with one component, the sense of injustice. Another human, a girl named Mercerio, was empowered to sense feelings and deliver mercy. The act of the dark spirits caused the unintended material change: Justi obtained a power to do something about injustice. He could cast a shaft of killing flame.

When the Tantrocan invasion gave them control of the northern Zell for ten and seven years, Justi found Mercerio, gained control of his gift, and drove the Tantrocans back across the Tantric Gulf. A fragile, temporary peace ensued.

"The gifts are physical," Li's angel said. "They will not vanish but will be passed on. What powers might the children have? And which god will benefit?"

PART I
Li's Victory

After driving the entrenched Tantrocans from the Kingdom of the Zell, the Zellish celebrated and restored their land. A new queen began her reign and the worshippers of Li and Dar coexisted. Clouds that threatened such tranquility were yet to gather.

1
Provani's Reward

Aduk, the high priest and chief advisor to the Tantrocan king, gazed at the rocky Ankor harbor from his castle chamber. He cursed the biting winds that frothed waves and rattled his windowpane and marveled how a short sail across the Tantric Gulf could grant the Zellish a warmer climate. Motivated by a hunger for riches, slaves, and sacrifices to the god Dar, the Tantrocans had conquered the Zell. Now that occupation was ending.

Aduk, a thin, bird-like man who hated cold, moved before the burning fire and reread the report of how the Zellish army drove the Tantrocans from Zellingon. The one called Justi caused the defeat by using an unnatural power. But there was good news: the Tantrocans had kidnapped Princess Mercerio and taken her to Fathom. That would certainly bring the Zellish army after her but without Justi, who wandered by himself searching for the girl. Both were young and probably had some romantic connection that seemed to give Justi control. Aduk intended to crush the connection between Justi and Mercerio by revealing the boy's infidelity. Justi had spent a night with a courtesan. The high priest sent his agent to bring the Abantazar woman to Fathom to tell her tale to the princess.

Aduk wanted to control Justi's power. Confident of his drugs and mind control, the priest prepared to cross the Tantric Gulf.

Provani had seduced the Zellish champion when he was of ten and eight years. She'd been dragged to Fathom to make Princess Mercerio reject Justi. Without Mercerio, Justi would lose control. Rumor had it he'd killed a friend when distant from Mercerio.

Provani gave a lurid rendition to Princess Mercerio, a graphic exaggeration about what occurred. "Justi led me to the little room. It was his idea. Inebriated, he stripped off my clothes and practically raped me." She improvised further. "He said he much preferred me to you. You should abandon him." Provani's appearance—a pretty face, alluring curves, and long red tresses—gave the tale a ring of truth.

Mercerio listened without interruption, her face composed. Then she said, "I feel sorry for you, Provani, and wish you a better life."

What kind of reaction is that? The girl's calmness confounded Provani—this was not the reaction the Tantrocan commander Karabandor wanted. Mercerio didn't seem to care that Justi had slept with a prostitute. Could there be no close relationship between Justi and Mercerio, no faithfulness to destroy?

Karabandor was waiting when Provani came from Mercerio's room. "I listened to your fornication tale. Sounded genuine. Let's see if the princess now realizes Justi's worthlessness. For your sake, I hope she curses him."

That made Mercerio's reaction Provani's problem. "I've done what you wanted. May I go now?"

The Tantrocan eyed her body, and Provani could sense his thoughts. He wanted her as his bedmate or as entertainment for his officers.

"Not so fast. We will see if you must perform again."

Karabandor left Provani in the locked room, which shared a wall with Mercerio's, and made it easy to hear Mercerio's reaction to Justi's arrival. When Mercerio banned Justi from her royal presence, Provani cheered. Her story was a success. She had earned her freedom.

Karabandor returned and partly agreed. "The princess seems enraged by your tryst with Justi. That pleases me."

"Good, Commander," Provani said, huddled on her cot. "I am ready to leave."

The Tantrocan smiled. "There are further tasks for you here in Fathom. Pretty yourself. I will summon you this evening."

Provani fell onto the pillow and stifled a barroom curse. She pounded the bed and screamed into a pillow. She'd done as told and expected to be sent back to Abantazar, back to the southern warmth and far away from the cold north coast. Now stuck, powerless in a small room behind a solid door, she would become a Tantrocan plaything. She rose and went to the window that faced a cart-wide passage between two large buildings. The drop from the second floor looked bone-breaking.

She heard shouts and watched three soldiers rush down the alley toward the main gate. Fathom was about to become less secure. She pressed close to the pane and eyed the building side. Only the protruding timber ledge that marked the second level provided a perch for foot or hand. *I must escape. Or I'll wind up a sex slave of the Tantrocan.* Provani tied together two thin wool blankets that would be her rope and anchored the lifeline to the bed frame. Provani heard the hall guard shout, his voice fading as feet pounded on the stairs. This was her chance.

The window wouldn't open. She grabbed a stout chair, angled it, and stomped on a leg. It snapped off, sending a splinter into her calf. She yanked the sliver out, swiped the blood away, and bounced the chair leg off the windowpane. The blow stung her hand and left the pane intact. She wrapped a towel around the wood and, with a grimace, smacked harder. The window shattered, sending fragments into the alley. She scraped shards from the frame and laid the thin, straw-filled pillow over the bottom edge.

With a bag slung on her shoulder, Provani squeezed through the tight opening. A glass shard cut her shoulder, and blood stained her thin gown. She cursed. Once outside, she fed out the blanket and slid down to the ledge. She eased her lower body below the ledge and felt blindly for irregularities in the wall, somewhere to place her foot. The blanket half ripped at the window and Provani dangled lower, her full weight on the damaged rope. It ripped the rest of the way and she fell.

The bag slipped from her shoulder and cushioned her impact with the ground. Still, her ankle rolled, and she cursed, then slapped her hand to her mouth. *Now*

I'm caught. But no one came as she limped away, trying to remember what she'd seen of the layout of Fathom. The wounds to her calf and shoulder stung but had stopped bleeding. With the blanket remnant and her satchel held close, she darted across the deserted central square toward the postern gate on the south wall. *If I am lucky, it will be unguarded.*

2
By Foot

Provani crept through the alleys of Fathom. The clamor of the Tantrocan rush to defend the main gate kept her hidden as she slipped undetected to the courtyard across from a small gate. She peered at the door secured by a thick crossbeam set in U-shaped brackets bolted to the frame. The beam would be a problem, but there loomed a greater problem, an oversized, armed guard who held his post despite erupting chaos.

Provani considered using her wiles to bypass the giant and was about to show herself when a voice ordered the big lout to help move something. He grunted a reply in a froggy voice and thumped off. Provani waited until Froggy disappeared, then darted over the pebbled space to the door.

Up close the beam seemed even more massive. She strained to lift the block of wood from its door-side holder but could hardly budge it. Fighting back anger, she gave the beam a smack and it rattled, sliding a bit. *I do not have to fight gravity. The plank is at a slant and loose.* She braced herself at the higher bracket near the portal opening and inched the wood along the metal, first a finger-width and then a finger-length. With new-found strength, she slid the timber until one end fell. The rough-hewn wood hit the ground and scraped against her ankle. Provani yelped. The door was still blocked by the fallen beam but open wide enough for Provani to squeeze through.

"Halt," yelled Froggy, hopping to his post.

Provani sprinted over a hill, stepped into a hole, and fell facedown into a trench. She closed her eyes expecting a boot on her back, a blade in her heart. But only a cool wind touched her and wrinkled grass at her side. At last she raised her head. No guard. In the distance the breeze rustled bushes and lifted branches of beckoning pines. She wrapped the blanket around her shoulders and limped down the sloped field toward the forest.

The trip to Fathom from Abantazar had been hard enough, riding with the brutish kidnapper. She shivered with the memory of wearing but a flimsy shift and clutching a thin blanket. At least with a horse, the journey had been quick. Without a horse, the trip back would be long and arduous. Because weeks had passed and autumn temperatures in the northern regions dropped when the sun set, the journey would be colder. At least Provani had conned a woolen cloak from her besotted guard. *Why didn't I hide food?*

Provani shook off her doubts and reached the forest. Her scratched and bruised feet—one from the beam and one from the drop from her room—needed tending, so she sat against an oak and massaged each protesting foot. And that's when she saw the brown lump beneath a bush.

It was a leather travel pouch that held treasures. Boots and a pair of knee-length leggings, obviously for a man, would keep her feet and legs warm. She stuffed the toes of the boots with grass, pulled the boots on, and tied the legging straps above her knees. She smiled at the warmth.

The bag also contained bread, thick-waxed cheese, dried meat, a skin for water, a flint, a blanket, and, most importantly, a hunter's knife. She gasped at the sight of the blade—she'd seen it before, in Justi's belt when she'd undressed him. This pouch was his.

A rumble in the distance and dust cloud marked the advance of the Zellish force toward Fathom. That meant soldiers who would treat a girl of her profession with brutality. *Time to move. I must make another league before resting.*

She headed deeper into the woods with the sun behind her.

Provani put more than a league between herself and Fathom. As clouds crept over the sun, the landscape grayed, and trees transformed into gloomy sentinels. When the moon rose in the late day sky, the clouds fled, and the temperature dropped. Weary and chilled, Provani stumbled into a small clearing with a central depression. She started a fire and savored the warmth while chewing on stale bread and a piece of cheese, forcing herself to conserve. She would keep her eyes open for late-season berries and planned to snare rabbits.

Provani tossed several thicker branches on the fire and nestled into the blanket. The forest quiet unsettled her, and she forced her mind to wonder how Princess Mercerio had confronted Justi. Given Mercerio's naiveté, she probably attached immense and stupid importance to his bedding another woman. *How silly.* She toyed with the knife from the travel pack, thinking again of her encounter with the blond boy in Abantazar. The memory pleased her, but it was tainted by a sudden, realized truth: the event never should have happened. How stupid of her not to see the strangeness. She'd never heard of Justi and never met him. Yet she'd woken that morning with a clear picture of the youth in her head and knowledge of where he would be. How?

3
By Horse

As the Zellish army attacked Fathom, Justi, the gifted commoner able to cast a killing flame, escaped with Mercerio, heir to the Zellish throne. Mercerio befriended the Tantrocan guard, and he allowed Mercerio to visit Justi's room. They overpowered the man and left.

Outside, the young escapees faced a different problem. Justi had been told that Tantrocan archers would put an arrow in the princess if she tried to escape. "If I see anyone carrying a bow, I will kill him."

"No. You will direct your fire toward the bow and not the man."

Justi didn't like any limitation, but he did what Mercerio wanted. And that is why an arrow struck Mercerio's shoulder. She fainted and Justi picked her up, burned the path clear, and carried her from the town.

In a ravine beyond Fathom's walls, Justi used another remnant of Li's gift, his healing power. He repaired the damage to Mercerio's shoulder and let her sleep. When she woke, recovered from her minor blood loss, he told her they had to flee back to Zellingon while the Tantrocans were under attack and far too busy to follow.

"It is a long trip on foot with meager supplies," Mercerio said. "But we are young and healthy. You have muscles hardened by adventure and battle and can protect me."

Justi liked that description. He led the princess through shoulder-high weeds to the large forest south of Fathom and into the open spot where, days earlier, he'd been discovered by a Tantrocan party and taken to Fathom.

"It would be nice to have a horse," Mercerio said.

Justi peered through the trees at the smoke over Fathom. The muted battle clamor said they were far enough away, so Justi risked a piercing, two-toned whistle.

Mercerio jumped and grabbed Justi's arm. "You could have warned me. What are you doing?"

A neigh, followed by pounding hooves, answered Justi's signal. The white stallion, who had been grazing in a hidden glen, galloped into the clearing. Rested and fit, the horse snorted and pranced, happy to be reunited with his master.

Justi patted the horse. "Glad the wolves didn't get you, boy."

"Wolves?" Mercerio glanced left and right.

"We're not far from the Great Forest. Wolves hunt in packs. They can even bring down a war stallion."

"Why didn't you say we had a horse?"

Justi smiled. "Couldn't be sure. Wolves, you know. But I need to find two bags." He searched the area and uncovered a bag beneath a bush. "Do you see another one?"

"What are you talking about?"

"There's a travel sack missing." Justi searched in a widening circle, his movements mimicked above by a gliding hawk.

"Maybe a raccoon dragged it off," Mercerio said, glancing toward Fathom with a frown. "I see figures coming through the same gate we used. What if they come here?"

Justi watched the men in the distance. "They're heading away from us. But we should move. I just wish we had the second bag and not the thieving raccoon. It had food in it."

"Which is why the raccoon wanted it."

"At least the saddle is here."

A rhythmic thudding from Fathom indicated the siege was underway. Black smoke thickened over the town as Justi mounted, pulled Mercerio up in front of him, and reached around for the reins. The stallion trotted along the path taken earlier toward Fathom and entered the aspen glen where Justi had rested. Sunlight sifted through the tall quaking trees, creating a serenity that beckoned. Justi resisted the urge to stay and headed southeast toward Zellingon.

* * * * *

I am Marget, Justi's spirit guardian, *in the earthly form of a hawk. The high spirit of Li, the Adamanti, assigned me to protect Li's gift. Since the gift had been divided into parts, the power component with Justi and the mercy component with Mercerio, I warded both these humans. I had protected the* *warhorse and kept him near. Now, as I flew above, I sensed that the servants of Dar watched.*

*****

"The army will send the Tantrocans back to Tantroc," Justi said. "I hope it happens with little bloodshed, for I fought alongside many of those men."

"Do you wish you could be there to help them?" Mercerio asked.

"No. They don't need my help to destroy what's left of the Tantrocans. I've had enough fighting and killing."

As the horse set its own pace through the hills toward the River Wark, Justi found Mercerio's form pleasant. Despite their friendship in Abantazar, the march north to Zellingon, and rescuing her before the first time, he'd not felt this close to her before.

"Are you all right?" Mercerio asked. "You seem to be fidgeting."

Justi willed himself to take deep breaths. "I'm fine. It's just the excitement of escape."

"That was an hour back. No one came after us."

"Right. Well, we have ground to cover." He urged the horse into a trot, thinking his dalliance with Provani remained a barrier between him and Mercerio. That bothered him, for he liked the princess. On one hand he wanted to talk about it, to tell her Provani meant nothing, that he hadn't sought her. No money was exchanged until she stole his purse. But another part of him didn't want to deal with the problem at all. How could he explain sleeping with Provani when he himself didn't understand it? Somehow he managed to keep quiet for the next hour, thoughts tumbling in his head.

Mercerio seemed immersed in her own thoughts as they passed the scenery of the Manwark Mountains. She broke the silence when Justi had convinced himself the issue wouldn't come up again. "Tell me about Provani," she said.

Justi sighed. How stupid to think he'd escaped. "Is this really what . . . I mean . . . haven't we already said everything we need to say? Shouldn't we be discussing what you will do when you become ruler of the Zell?"

"My mother rules."

"You'll have many weighty things to think about when you are queen. Shouldn't you get started?"

Mercerio smiled and leaned her head back. "How did you meet Provani?"

As the stallion stepped over a fallen sapling, Justi realized he had to answer. "I'm not sure. By chance."

"Really? Were you looking for her?"

"No. Of course not. It was unplanned, unexpected. Remember when you came into the courtyard and we agreed that we couldn't understand one another. You left in a huff."

"I am never in a huff. That's not how a princess behaves."

"You were, because I didn't want to explain how I felt about killing the Tantrocan who tried to rape my mother. It was late afternoon—after you called me a wild beast and then said I was Justi the Botu, the bird who buries his head in the sand at the first sign of trouble, because I didn't want to discuss what happened."

"Are you still stuck on that? I said I was sorry. Are you blaming me for your, er, adventure, saying our argument sent you to Provani? So it's my fault?"

Justi gazed at a high cloud. "No. I just remember that I was angry. I walked to clear my head and wandered into the marketplace. Found myself hot and thirsty in front of the Abantazar Inn. Perfectly innocent. I entered and sat alone drinking. This girl arrived and could have chosen any of the empty tables. Instead, she sat next to me. As if she'd been sent."

Mercerio held on with her legs as the horse picked his way up a rock-strewn slope. "Maybe it was not a coincidence," she said. "*Someone* knew you in Abantazar. Remember the knife attack with the poisoned blade? Could Provani be a second attack?"

The stallion's ears perked up at a gurgling sound. He trotted in the direction of the water. When he found the narrow stream, he lowered his head to drink. Justi scanned the area. Prints, both human and animal, crisscrossed the muddy bank. Although the water was far enough from the trees to prevent a surprise approach, he was uneasy.

"I see what you're saying about a planned meeting," Justi said at last, "but Provani didn't try to poison my beer. I thought she was just being friendly."

"This is a good place to rest," Mercerio said.

Justi kept his concern to himself and maneuvered the stallion away from the water after he'd had his fill. They dismounted, walked upstream, and sat on a slab of rock. The smell of late-blooming bushes and a warm breeze brought welcome relief after the danger of escape. Even the hawk was quiet as it settled onto a high branch above them.

"I'm beginning to think that bird is the same one I've seen since I was of ten and two years," Justi said, pointing. "It seems to have a bit of white on the wings that other hawks lack."

"Maybe it is the same bird. Sort of your guardian. Too bad it didn't guard you against Provani."

"It may have tried. A hawk at the entrance to the Abantazar Inn did not want me in there. It dived at my head. Twice."

The hawk lifted into the air and swooped over the horse, startling it. The bird circled the area and dove again, screeching. A large black bear lumbered from the forest, its wide grizzled head pointed in their direction. It rose on hind legs and roared.

The stallion backed up, eyes wide. Justi grabbed the reins and, yelling, yanked the horse toward the rock. Mercerio jumped to get on, landing belly down on the horse's back. Justi yanked her upright, and she swung her leg over. Justi leapt up behind her, flapped the reins, and they galloped off. The bear settled on all fours and ambled toward the stream.

"Did you really have to handle me like a potato sack?" Mercerio asked. "How do you know the bear wouldn't go away?"

"Because I used to hunt with my father. The bear wanted a drink, and we were in the way. He was also rather large, in case you hadn't noticed. A big male as tall as the horse when he stood."

"Then we ought to thank the hawk for keeping you out of danger." Mercerio pointed to the sky. "Except for Provani."

Justi squinted at the creature. "Could have been the same type of bird I saw in Abantazar, at least a related southern species."

"So you were sitting with Provani drinking and drinking. Then what?"

Justi groaned. "Why do I have to tell you more? You heard the story."

"Provani may have lied. Tell me your version." When Justi said nothing, Mercerio sighed. "I will explain. You and I are the Children of the Gift. We must be together to control your killing power. I help you dampen your gift. Obviously, I need you for protection. To be close, we must be honest with each other. I like you, Justi, and . . . well . . . feel hurt by what happened with Provani. But I think Provani exaggerated."

"I'm sorry it happened. We had several drinks, all of which I paid for. Now that I think about it, maybe only I was doing the drinking. I'm not sure what Provani had in her mug. I remember feeling fuzzy when she led me to an upstairs room. She said I needed to rest, and I was kinda sleepy. Then things sort of happened."

"Things?"

Justi's face warmed and he reined to a stop where the stream again neared the path. "We need to fill the skin."

The hawk glided down to settle in a maple with a split trunk. Its head twitched back and forth, studying them. The pair dismounted and Mercerio cast a glance at the nearby trees. "I'll be right back."

Justi tried to think of what to say but had nothing by the time Mercerio returned.

"So what happened?" Mercerio demanded.

Justi stood with his back to the princess. It seemed that anything he said would be wrong. "Fine. We wound up on a cot. Without our clothes." The last came out as a mutter. "Wait. I just remembered. The bird screamed outside the window, and Provani went to close the shutters."

"Without her clothes?"

"I suppose."

Mercerio turned abruptly and went to the stream. She seemed intent on studying the flowing water. "Did you see her again?"

"No."

*****

My hawk form makes it easy to watch and listen to humans. *Sometimes I wish I had more power. Guarding Li's experiment can be harrowing—the Miasma modified the thinking of a cat, a dog, and wolves as they tried to destroy Justi. Even a human assassin failed.*

Justi's defeat of the Tantrocans enraged the Miasma. His continued existence thwarts expansion of Dar's influence in the human realm, and that alone fuels their desire to destroy Li's gift. Now I sense a new reason: Justi is of breeding age.

Should Justi and Mercerio mate, any child might also have the Justice Power, perhaps a more controlled version of the gift. The dark spirits will seek to prevent the union and try to find some earthly force to destroy Justi.

*****

Justi wasn't sure how satisfied Mercerio was with his Provani story. An uncomfortable silence settled between them until Mercerio took the conversation in another direction.

"Perhaps we should have rescued Provani," she said, as if they were talking about a pet.

"We were in a bit of a rush, remember. Besides, Provani was not a captive."

"I'm not so sure. I believe she was manipulated into meeting you. And then forced to come to Fathom. This didn't just happen and it wasn't her fault. It's easy to dismiss people who act badly, like prostitutes, but Provani isn't bad. I liked her and hope she's all right."

4
By Boat

After Provani, Justi, and Mercerio fled, the Zellish army attacked Fathom. Toughened and smartened by the siege of Zellingon, the Zellish knew not to use scaling ladders against the town walls. A battering ram pounding the gate was a better tool.

When Karabandor saw this, he tried the same method that had stopped the siege of Zellingon. "Bring the princess," he ordered. "We'll display her on the wall with a sword to her neck. That will stop the Zellish. They revere their precious royalty."

That ploy had forced stealth in place of the frontal assault. Justi led men through a secret tunnel beneath the city walls and saved Mercerio. Unfortunately, as Justi left to assist the Zellish, Karabandor scooped her up and made her a prisoner in Fathom.

The soldier sent for the princess returned alone. "Where is Mercerio?" Karabandor demanded.

"Mercerio and Justi escaped, my lord." The soldier flinched when he uttered the news.

The commander cursed. "Find them."

The battering ram splintered the main gate. Zellish swarmed inside to win the fierce hand-to-hand combat that even Karabandor was part of. The man wielded ax and sword, until he was struck down and captured. Seeing their leader fall, the Tantrocans fled, and a surge of desperate barbarians escaped toward the sea. The Zellish let them go.

High priest Aduk left Fathom as the Zellish drew close. With his young acolyte Caldir toting two travel bags, the bird-like, acerbic cleric exited the south gate and headed to the coast. When they reached the water's edge, Caldir placed the bags on the wooden dock where a small boat was moored. Together, the men waited in silence for Ukor, Aduk's strongman, who would sail the vessel across the rough Tantric Gulf.

The sky held a gray cast, and the wind decorated the dark sea with whitecaps. Aduk did not welcome the crossing but had no choice. The Tantrocans had lost, and after years of domination and exploitation, the taste of defeat was bitter.

Ukor joined them. Leather covered his broad chest and thick limbs, leaving only his head exposed to the wind. Gray streaked the man's black hair. The dark-skinned, tattooed assassin stood a head taller than Aduk and Caldir and had no trouble tossing the two travel bags and his own into the boat, but Aduk discerned a new slowness in Ukor. The man had never really recovered from his confrontation with Justi outside of Ortun. Aduk felt somewhat responsible, but he'd warned Ukor not to get close, to use an arrow from a distance, rather than a close-up knife. Ukor's arrow wounded Justi, and Ukor made the mistake of approaching to finish the job. He was burned and suffered a blow to the head, injuries that kept him hiding on the coast for months.

"Fathom is lost," Ukor said. "The commander fell. If he's lucky, the Zellish may spare his life. They are silly about things like that."

"Did he at least kill the boy?" Aduk asked.

"The princess and her protector escaped. His power maimed three men and started fires. I should have killed him when I had the chance."

Aduk thought it was not a matter of wanting to kill the boy, but of being incapable.

"We cannot tarry here," Ukor said as stronger wind rocked the small vessel. "My departure from Fathom was clearly visible. The Zellish may send a force after me."

The cold gust flattened Aduk's gray robe against his body as he descended the dock ladder into the vessel. He wrapped a canvas about him and thought over his problem as Caldir and Ukor oared the vessel from the dock and set the sail. Thin as a winter reed, old Aduk never felt warm. He accepted the insistent sea breeze as cold punishment for defeat. Not the loss of Fathom—that was inevitable. His failure to gain control of Justi's power irked. He'd used drugs to subdue the boy but learned little. Justi's nonsense about wanting to right wrongs and prevent injustice was pure goat dung. Given time, he thought, I would have brought the boy under control and might have learned to harness his strange power.

Aduk's problem was King Brokul, who would blame him for the defeat. A false accusation, for he had not only warned of the Gifted Child but had even located the boy in Ortun. Yes, Aduk's own killer failed to slay Justi, but that showed the boy's power. Aduk then convinced Brokul to send a large force to Ortun. Was it his fault the soldiers failed to find and capture the boy and let him flee? That failure was not Aduk's.

The little vessel caught the wind and bounced through the choppy sea toward Ankor. Behind him, Aduk saw the smoky haze that marked the loss of Fathom. He wasn't sure how, but Aduk vowed the Tantrocans would return and, when they did, they would have an answer to the unnatural power of Justi. That, surely, was Dar's will.

When they reached Tantroc Island, Aduk told Ukor to beach the craft and avoid the pier where the low tidewater slapped against slippery stones. Ukor complied, and the high priest, impatient to be on land, jumped from the boat into a wavelet that soaked his feet. He stepped onto the stretch of sand over which loomed the great Tantrocan royal fortress, a dark stone edifice with towers. Gulls cruised near the castle walls, adding droppings to white streaks already there. Aduk frowned and turned toward the Gulf to see a dozen vessels on the horizon. They contained, he realized, the meager remnant of the Tantrocan army, something the king would want explained. His thought was interrupted when Caldir grabbed a rope to help tug the boat onto the sand.

"Let Ukor do that," Aduk said impatiently. "Take my bag to my chamber. I will change there and await the summons from King Brokul. Find some decent wine and cheese. I'll eat if I have time and will want meat when I return from the king. Make sure there is plenty of firewood. The chill on the water has settled into my bones."

Caldir tossed the rope to Ukor. He lifted the two travel bags from the boat and dropped them on the sand as Ukor yanked the small vessel out of the water. The acolyte cursed, sick of being at Aduk's beck and call, sick of being the high priest in training. As far as he could see, Aduk had no new knowledge to transmit.

Caldir, handsome with black hair and blacker eyes, thin lips, and sharp features, had not seen three tens of years. Palace women seemed attracted to him, despite his one defect, the eye patch. This son of a palace whore, who imbibed to mask the pain of her existence, Caldir had been injured when his mother flung a glass at her son's face. With unfocused vision and an eye patch, Caldir avoided military service, a fate much less desirable than his current position that afforded power and revealed his considerable talent. Despite this good effect, he never forgave his mother.

Ukor dragged the boat onto the sand. Caldir hefted the two bags and accompanied Ukor to the post above the tide line where the boat was secured.

"The priest is agitated," Ukor said.

Gulls rose from a sand dune and screeched in agreement.

Caldir put down his burden and considered the climb to the castle. "He has his reasons."

Ukor nodded. "Not only will he endure the wrath of King Brokul, who will blame everyone but himself for this disaster, but he is affronted by the power of this Justi. He can't comprehend it and can't abide the idea that there is someone more powerful than himself."

"Are you saying we are defeated forever and condemned to this cold existence? Things change as the sands of time flow. Old strengths wane and new strengths arise. Aduk is already plotting the next move in this game."

Ukor finished with the boat and pointed toward the path. "Perhaps he will include you in that plotting, now that you are his priest in training."

"My training is done."

5
Hot Spring

Justi and Mercerio followed the stream southeast, encountering neither men nor animals. Justi halted the horse, listened intently, and grabbed Mercerio's arm. "I heard something."

"I hear only high limbs creaking, birds calling, and my stomach. I am hungry and tired."

The sun sat on the ridge line of the Manwark Mountains when the companion hawk sailed low over the trees west of the trail. The bird repeated the maneuver.

Justi scanned the area. "Tired. Right. We should be safe if we go into the trees far enough to hide a small fire. The temperature will fall tonight."

"What about eating?"

"We have food, Your Highness," Justi said with exaggerated deference.

Justi and Mercerio dismounted and led the horse up a slope to where the trees thinned around a grassy space. Trees had been felled and chopped. Seasoned logs were stacked near a fire pit.

"Many must know this place if there is firewood," Mercerio said. "Should we stay?"

"I suspect only one traveler uses this place. Maybe a Fathom merchant. That is why it is kept clean and ready. Otherwise the firewood would benefit only the next person to come along. Like us. But I do not think it has been visited in a while. The long grass is undisturbed, and the fire pit has sprigs of new growth."

Mercerio shrugged. "What about water?"

"There must be a stream nearby."

Justi removed the saddle and blanket and let the horse dine on the grass. He left Mercerio to select the food and set off to explore, taking with him several snares. He returned with good news. "I found clean water. And there were rabbit droppings nearby. I set two snares."

Mercerio held up an oilskin and frowned. "We can hope for fresh rabbit for breakfast, but tonight we get stale bread and moldy cheese."

"My other pack, the one we couldn't find, contained the nuts, fruits, assorted biscuits, smoked venison, dried fish, and candies," Justi said, grinning. "All provisions suitable for a princess. And my favorite knife." He carried small branches to the fire pit and assembled a pile with dried grass.

"At least you have the knife you stole from the Fathom kitchen. It is dull, but it works."

"I can sharpen it if I find the right rock."

Mercerio watched the horse paw at a mound of grass. Then she stood to walk a circle around the clearing. "What makes this a favorite place to spend the night?"

"Well it's hidden from the main path and there's water," Justi said. "Could be some other feature, I suppose. There's still plenty of daylight. Want to explore?"

"Yes. Maybe I'll find something like apples to flavor the cheese. Since I have no venison or smoked fish. Or candies."

They followed the stream up a slope some hundred paces to a plateau where a fallen oak allowed the sun's late rays to shine on the water source. A gently bubbling pool surrounded by slabs of rock overflowed at the downhill edge.

"There's steam rising from the pool," Mercerio said, cautiously sticking her finger into the water. "It's warm, but not too hot."

Justi also tested the temperature. "Perfect," he said. "That is what makes this place valuable."

Mercerio touched her long black hair. "I haven't bathed in weeks. The day is still warm, and the morning will be cold. This will do nicely." She dropped her cloak on a rock.

"You mean to go in there? There's no privacy, not even any bushes nearby."

"The water is hip deep and the bottom is sandy. Nobody is around."

"I am around."

"You will be fetching my blanket. It will do as a towel." She slipped off her boots. "And you can keep your eyes averted when you return."

Justi was doubtful. "The blanket will get wet. You need it to cover you in sleep."

"I only want it to cover me while my dirty clothes dry. We can dry things out with a good fire." She began to remove her garment and made a dismissive gesture in Justi's direction. "Go. I need some privacy."

Justi stepped back, then froze in place when Mercerio turned and dropped her breeches to the ground. She bent to remove her stockings and saw him still behind her.

"Are you going to wait until I am unclothed?" she said. "Go. And get both blankets. You need a bath, too."

Continuing to watch the princess as he backed away, Justi felt his face aflame and realized he'd stopped breathing. He darted back to the campsite and grabbed both blankets. When he returned, Mercerio's wet garments were spread across a rock. The princess was submerged in the transparent hot pool, her female form far from hidden. He again seemed unable to move, thankful that he held the blankets in front of his breeches.

"If you would stop gawking and open the blanket, I can get out," she said. "Turn your eyes."

He sort of did as he was told.

Mercerio emerged and wrapped the blanket around herself. "You looked."

His face burning, he replied. "I did not."

"Such an affront to royalty could earn you punishment, like chopping something off. I'll overlook it for the moment. Now get in there with your clothes on and wash them as they come off. I'll spread them to dry near the fire."

"What about my privacy?"

"Boys do not need privacy. I have seen lots of them naked, and one more will hardly matter."

"You've seen lots?"

"Young boys. Hurry before we lose the last rays of sun. And you can use this damp blanket as your towel." With that announcement, Mercerio turned, dropped the blanket, and wrapped the dry one around her.

Wearing blankets as cloaks, the pair tried to gather extra firewood. Keeping covered and picking up logs proved difficult.

"This is ridiculous," Justi said. "Go sit by the fire pit while I fetch the fuel. And take this with you." He tossed his blanket at Mercerio, who smiled and left.

By the time Justi returned with a large load of wood, the princess had constructed a rack from fallen branches and spread their garments on it near the pit. Justi dropped the wood and constructed a small pile of sticks and grass before fetching the flint. He stopped to slap at his neck. "Demon curse. Some kind of insect."

"You are giving them a large target," Mercerio said, grinning.

Justi grabbed his flint and set to work starting the fire. He tried not to glance in Mercerio's direction, but when he did glance her way, she was smiling. Once the fire took, he wrapped himself in a blanket. That action and the smoke from the growing fire drove off the bugs.

"I hope you have seen enough," he said.

"As I said, another naked boy. All the same parts in all the right places. I admit that you have developed some nice muscles for one who did most of his fighting by casting flames."

Justi grunted.

"The fire will dry our clothes shortly," Mercerio said. "We should eat and get ready to sleep. We can discuss those arrangements as we dine. It will grow cool by dawn and one blanket apiece may not be enough. Especially if one is damp."

6
Brokul and Aduk

Aduk donned a dry robe but had no time for a drink before he was summoned. He composed himself and descended the winding stone staircase from his isolated tower, planning how he would diffuse the king's anger.

He used a side door near the front of the great room and avoided the long walk from the main entrance under Brokul's reproving gaze. The immense space used for meals, meetings, and entertainment had a raised platform at the front where King Brokul filled a fur-covered chair. With his broad chest, thick muscled arms, and black, bushy beard, Brokul intimidated when he was content. Today he'd added a scowl. Fires burned in four of the room's ten hearths. Aduk stood near one, absorbing warmth to combat the lingering effects of the raw sea air.

King Brokul gazed at the wall sconces, then examined the high rafters. Finally, he aimed his black eyes at Aduk and waved him forward. "Speak."

Aduk cleared his throat. "As you have undoubtedly heard, Highness, Zellingon was lost to the resurrected Zellish army. Many died. Your men fought bravely but were demoralized by the unnatural power of the one called Justi. Fathom, too, is lost."

Brokul leaned forward, his large fists grasping the chair arms. "And what do you think this means, Aduk?"

The meaning should have been obvious, Aduk thought. The Tantrocans had been vanquished and sent home. But he suspected the king wanted a more philosophical, even theological, interpretation. Aduk spoke the words he had carefully prepared. "Our days of ascendance have passed. We must bide our time."

"You take no responsibility for misreading the prophecies?"

"The prophecies foretold our victories. We were able to rule the Zell and harvest its riches for ten and eight years."

"What of this child of . . . power?"

"Prophecies said he would thwart the will of Dar, and so it has come to pass. We knew of this child, took actions to stop him, and failed."

"If your great assassin Ukor had been effective, this Justi would be dead."

"I do not think that was ordained by the gods. Your troops in the boy's hometown of Ortun did not kill him. They allowed him to escape and join with Mercerio."

"So Dar has no reward for us, his faithful followers in this frozen land?" Brokul slammed his fist on the chair arm. "We are destined to suffer in dark and cold and eat mostly fish. And still provide sacrifices to Dar."

Brokul stood. The elevation of the platform made him a head taller than the high priest who himself was above average. The king stepped toward Aduk, who backed to the nearest hearth. Aduk wondered if he should reveal what he'd thought of on his way down the stairs. His analysis of events was not complete, and, if his interpretation changed, he would appear the fool.

But he had to say something, even if it were conjecture about a piece of old writing.

Brokul glared, his bushy eyebrows low. "What do you make of this dilemma?"

"The one called Justi has a power he wields reluctantly and without much control," Aduk said. "It is possible that, with the Zellish victory, his gift has run its course and may not be used again. It is also possible that Justi's gift will fade as he gets beyond the headstrong, fiery age of his second decade. Thus, time alone may favor us."

"Where in the texts does it say any of that?"

"It is but conjecture, my lord."

"As such, it is worthless. What else do you have?" Brokul demanded.

Aduk did have something else that was based on prophetic texts. He had not finished going over all the documents found in Zellingon, but the new words he'd studied offered some hope. Unfortunately, the information implied that years would pass before the event might take place. Brokul would not be the king to use the information, but perhaps he could convey it to his son, the child expected from his consort Cantor. Not that one could be certain who the father of that bairn might be. Aduk knew the king's consort pleased herself with many tools. "There are passages in ancient documents newly discovered in the library at Zellingon that speak of a child of Dar. Such a child may be our answer for the child of light." The fireplace logs snapped and crackled, sending a shower of sparks at

Aduk. He stepped to the side, swiping embers off his cloak.

Brokul smiled and relaxed his tense posture. But the change was fleeting, and his frown remained. "What exactly is this child supposed to do?" he asked.

"The writings are not explicit on such things. The best one can glean is that the child will oppose the child of light." The text seemed to say, "children of light," but Aduk saw no reason to complicate the story.

Brokul clasped his hands behind his back and traced a path around his chair, walking past the stone wall with the ceremonial sword beneath high windows. He returned to the platform edge and stepped down. "And where do we find him?"

Aduk had not anticipated that question and had no answer from the texts he'd found, so he improvised, "The child may be born here in Tantroc or in the south. We must wait."

"That's hardly an answer. For how long do we wait?"

"Time is of little concern to the writers of prophecy. For all we know, this child may not yet be born. Or he could have been born the same time as Justi."

Brokul visited the lit fires, pausing to study the flames, and returned to his throne. "If we had such a child and could control him, then we might again conquer the Zell. The southern lands are filled with riches, including slaves. Just the thought of that makes me impatient."

"Yet patience is called for, Majesty. Our army has suffered grave loss of men and arms. Now is the time to replenish ourselves while we await the child of Dar."

Brokul tented his fingers. "It would behoove you to alert your web of spies to be on the lookout for such a child, for any hint of a power to confront this Justi."

"Of course, my lord."

Aduk left wondering how long the king's patience would last.

7
The Power

Southern air warmed the night, so Justi and Mercerio slept cozy with single blankets. Justi rose in the middle of the night, stoked the fire with a fresh log, and found the clothes had dried. At dawn he woke in dim light to bird sounds. Mercerio did not stir, so he added wood to the fire, dressed, and went to check his traps.

He found two rabbits and returned to clean and spit them. Mercerio, up and dressed, took over the task of roasting the catch. By the time the sun peeked over the eastern hill, they could enjoy roasted meat for breakfast. Neither traveler had much to say, something Justi was content with after the previous day's uncomfortable conversation. As they finished one rabbit, a sudden change in the weather gave them something to talk about. First, the tops of tall trees swayed, and then the temperature dropped. The breeze gusted and leaves blew to the ground.

Justi eyed a mass of clouds over the peaks of the Manwark Mountains and sniffed the air. "We are about to lose our pleasant fall weather. Those clouds are full and moving swiftly.

Mercerio did her own assessment. "I smell snow and would prefer to be in Zellingon before it arrives."

The campers prepared to travel. Justi whistled for the horse.

Three highwaymen who preyed on travelers between Zellingon and Fathom had wandered close enough to their campsite to smell the fire and hear Justi's whistle. The men's proximity did not happen by chance. The servants of Dar had watched Justi and Mercerio turn toward Zellingon from Fathom and directed the men. Dreams were a favorite Miasma method for molding humans to their will.

The leader, a hefty man—with more fat than muscle—and a spotty black beard believed in omens. When he envisioned two young people and a large white horse without a guard, he took the vivid vision as a guide. The Miasma encouraged that interpretation and sent the notion that there was profit to be made: the horse would fetch a handsome price and the girl might be sold in the right market. Hefty Thief woke with a notion that he should quickly kill the worthless man.

The robbers knew the place—they'd camped there before. When the smell of roasting rabbits reached him, the leader whispered to his companions, "Perhaps we'll find more than firewood and a chance to bathe. Be silent and be alert."

The two companions were wiry, one without hair on his head or face and one with orange hair and a wisp of beard on his chin. All three had large knives in their boots. Scents of food and smoke drew them close enough to hear Justi's voice.

The leader whispered to the one with orange hair, "Bok, make your way around to the back of the little circle. Stay hidden until I call you." To the hairless one, the leader said, "You stay with me and move when I say so. Don't make a mess. We want the girl unharmed."

Bok disappeared into the trees. Hefty waited a few moments before pushing into the bushes, his bald companion a step behind.

When something snapped in the forest, Mercerio startled. "What was that?"

Justi grabbed the kitchen knife and stood ready when two men emerged from the trees. A big, bearded man came first, followed by one with no hair. Both wore dirty, loose clothing and had a rough appearance that announced danger.

"Well, what have we here?" the bearded one said as his gaze checked Justi and then lingered on Mercerio. "Is that rabbit I smell? Might ye have more? Surely you would be willing to share."

The bald one eyed the princess. "All the leftovers," he said.

Mercerio edged closer to Justi. "You are welcome to the remains of our breakfast. We were just leaving."

"Now that is rude. We would enjoy your company for a while." The speaker had an ugly scarred face beneath the sparse beard. His face twisted into something even uglier when he tried to smile.

"You will have to excuse us," Justi said, grabbing both bags and stepping toward the path.

When the strangers pulled out large knives, Justi dropped the bags and showed his own blade.

"A foolish thing to do, boy. There are two of us, and our weapons are more suited to slicing throats than bread. Why don't you save your life by fleeing? We will take care of the girl." The leader and his companion stepped apart.

"Where is the horse?" Hairless asked.

"We'll find it."

Justi saw the fat man leer at Mercerio, and his mind filled with the memory of his mother's near rape that had led Justi to kill the man. Mercerio faced the same fate, and this should have sparked the Justice Power. But Justi felt nothing but panic and grasped the knife more tightly.

The hawk swooped and screeched. Hefty yelled a man's name and sprang forward, faster than a man of his size should move. Justi relied on his reflexes that war had honed. He leapt to the side and slashed the attacker's knife hand. The man dropped his weapon but in a fluid motion yanked a dirk from his belt. Justi danced back and felt a surge of heat. His hair grew brighter, his body became taut, and his mind focused. The pent-up energy of the Justice Power released with a dull boom, and a white flame arced from Justi's outstretched hand into the belly of the beefy man. Hot light slammed into his assailant, searing fat and muscle. The man spasmed and one hand slapped against his stomach wound. A gurgled moan escaped his mouth as the thief fell, spilling entrails.

In tending to the first attacker, Justi lost track of the second man. The bald one had circled and grabbed Mercerio. He held a large knife at her throat.

"Drop your weapon," the man barked. "Or the girl bleeds."

Justi's mind raced. So much for wanting nothing to do with killing and war, he thought. Perhaps that was not his decision alone. He dropped the knife, wishing for his sword, aching to blast flame along the blade with the precision that would spare the princess. He gathered himself, willing the power into his hands, and stepped forward.

As he did so, Mercerio twisted and thrust her elbow back and up, catching her captor high on the rib cage. He grunted and brought his knife across her arm, slicing deep. He shoved his hostage to the ground and lunged at Justi. A white beam slammed into his chest, through his filthy shirt, and lifted the man into the air. Silent, eyes wide with a smoking hole in his chest, the thief hit the ground dead.

Justi breathed deep and felt the power drain away. A twig snapped and brought a new rush of tension. Justi whirled, ready to kill, expecting to face another enemy. He saw only Mercerio, who lay on the ground, moaning, her hand clutching her arm. Blood seeped between her fingers. Justi ran to her and lifted her hand. "The cut is deep, but it does not gush. That is good."

"How can a knife wound be good?" Mercerio gasped.

Justi tore off his sleeve, bunched it, and pressed it on the gash. "Press this against your arm." He closed his eyes, willing the other component of his gift to manifest but fearing it might be lost. But with his hand on her bare arm, he quickly sensed the sliced muscle and vessels. He began to orchestrate repair, joining severed fiber to severed fiber, sealing blood vessels, and closing the skin. When he was done, he lifted the cloth and saw that the bleeding had stopped. The skin was closed in a red line. There might be a scar, but he thought the damage would heal.

Mercerio moaned, "We must run. Others may come."

As if summoned, a man emerged from the trees. Justi turned, prepared to fight again, and stopped, his mouth open in surprise. It was his stepfather, Rocley, the lean and fit man who'd raised Justi, a veteran hunter and Zellingon military scout. His tanned, friendly face radiated intelligence and concern. Behind Rocley stood the white stallion, eyes wide, a hoof scraping the ground.

"Well, 'tis a good thing I decided to follow you," Rocley said. He smiled and embraced Justi. "Seems I timed my arrival perfectly to put a bolt in the ruffian you did not see, the one about to sail a large knife at your back."

"Father! How did you find us?" Justi asked, embracing the man.

"Later. What is Mercerio's condition?"

"Her arm was cut by the robber's knife. I repaired the damage."

Rocley knelt and examined the princess. "She is very pale. We must get her back to Zellingon where a physician can do more." He helped to get her onto the horse.

"What about those two?" Mercerio asked.

Justi considered the dead robbers. "We can pray to Li their souls will have some comfort. As to their bodies, let the vultures feast." He picked up a knife used by the attackers. "This might be useful."

On the path toward the Manwark road, Rocley said, "When you were not in Fathom, I figured you'd escaped. The cook said she saw you fleeing as the battle began. There were singed buildings away from the battle area that made your path easy to follow. Once I discovered that you had mounted a horse, the trail you left was obvious."

"Is that how the thieves traced us?" Justi asked.

Rocley shook his head. "I saw no evidence of that. It might have been coincidence. You were able to take care of two, but you must pay attention to what is behind you."

"At least there was no poisoned knife," Mercerio whispered.

"What happened in Fathom?" Justi asked.

"The Tantrocans fled. Karabandor is now a prisoner."

"There was a thin man in a gray robe. Seemed to be in charge. Did you see him?"

Rocley shook his head. "No one like that was captured."

They made progress toward Zellingon, with Mercerio on the horse and Rocley and Justi walking on either side. After several hours, they had to stop. Mercerio lapsed into unconsciousness and slipped from the horse. Justi caught her.

"She feels warm," Justi said.

Rocley touched the princess's brow. "A fever. We are near Manwark Lake. You must cool the princess with lake water, and I will go on to summon help."

8
Starving

Provani trekked south from Fathom and arrived in Maduk, a town that had never fully recovered from the Tantrocan occupation. She saw no women in the streets and few merchants that might have food. The taverns were filled with surly men. She chose the inn, which had retained an air of decorum and claimed to serve food. She found the innkeeper, a rosy-cheeked, plump woman. "I am a refugee from Fathom, traveling south and must beg for any spare food you can offer."

The innkeeper raised an eyebrow. "Times be difficult with all this fighting going on. Farmers deliver little to Maduk markets, and what they do bring is dearly priced. I cannot be giving away what I have to serve my guests."

"Have you something not good enough for your customers? I would take anything." Provani still had food in the travel pack but thought it wise to augment supplies while she could. The journey to Abantazar would be long.

The woman brushed imaginary crumbs from her smock and studied Provani. "Ye seem comely enough. Perhaps you could trade something for your food."

Provani surprised herself with her answer. "I am not in that business. If you are so ungenerous with your stale bread, so be it. I will leave before your good guests arrive and expect me to be part of their entertainment."

The woman's cheeks grew even redder. "I meant no offense," she said, holding her hand up. "If you would sweep this floor, I have old bread and cheese for you. Leaving would not be a bad idea. The men in this town are not kind or generous and see women as prizes."

Provani tidied the dining room and then stuffed stale bread, goat cheese, and two apples into her sack. As dusk claimed Maduk, she traveled back streets to a town gate and left. Her route took her east toward the River Wark.

For days she hiked alongside the Manwark Mountains where grassy areas housed rabbits. She managed to trap only one, but it was fat enough to last two days. Her food supply, meager to begin with, was soon exhausted. Having cut back her daily ration, Provani was weak and unable to cover the distances she needed. She crossed the River Wark with a notion that towns existed to the east, but without a map or knowledge of the area, she wasn't sure where.

Tired and disheartened, Provani made camp in a thicket and wondered if this was to be her final resting place. A numbing fatigue gripped her, as if a parasite were sucking away her energy. *Without food I cannot go on. Perhaps it would be best to lie down, sleep, and never get up.* She idly poked at the pitiful fire, trying to ignore stomach pangs and thinking how to soften acorns, when she felt a presence. At first she thought it was hallucination, a prelude to death, and dread crept over her.

"Might I share this camp with you?" a female voice asked.

Provani jumped. In the shadows stood a girl not much older than herself, dressed in a loose robe the color of summer moss. Her face, surrounded by cascading black hair, seemed pleasant enough, but her dark eyes were intense, assessing. What most caught Provani's eye was the visitor's backpack.

"Who are you?" Provani asked, her hand grasping the knife.

"I am called Credo and am a scholar traveling from Pale to Zellingon. I smelled your fire from the road and, seeking a place to rest, thought I might find company."

Provani relaxed. "I would welcome your company. You are bold to approach a traveler on this route. Men treat lone women badly."

"Some do. But I can detect their thinking and sensed no man here."

Provani ignored the claim. "Do you have food?"

Credo shrugged the pack from her back. "I have biscuits, dried meat, and fruit and would share them with you in exchange for conversation and warmth." She settled on the fallen tree trunk near the fire and produced food that Provani consumed ravenously.

Only then did she realize she hadn't provided any conversation. "I am sorry, but I haven't eaten much more than a few berries and stale bread in the past two days."

"You are pale and thin," Credo said, handing over an apple. "How do you come to be here without supplies?"

"I am traveling from Fathom to Abantazar and had little chance to prepare."

"So you flee the Tantrocans." Credo gathered fallen branches, snapped them into smaller pieces, and fed them to the feeble fire. They caught and she added two larger logs. The fire brightened and radiated more warmth. "Abantazar is many days distant. You will not make it without food. I am heading to Zellingon, for I have heard that the crown city has been liberated with the aid of a gifted warrior."

Provani had heard no such tale. "Who?"

"Justi of Ortun."

"You'll not find him in Zellingon. He is in Fathom and may not be free to leave."

"You know of this Justi?"

"I met him once."

Credo dragged a branch from beneath a tree and pulled a knife from her bag. The serrated blade divided the wood into arm-length pieces that she set aside. "These will keep the fire going as night falls. Predators avoid fire."

Provani smiled and, as a draft sent glowing embers aloft, pulled her cloak closer.

"This Justi is said to possess power to cast fire, a talent that slew many barbarians and turned the tide in favor of the Zellish. Did you see him wield such power?" Credo asked in an excited voice.

"No, that is not the power I saw in Justi."

Credo's face betrayed her disappointment. "Well, I will still go to Zellingon to learn what I can and to acquire supplies for my healing potions. Why don't you come with me? It is safer to travel as two. Even if

Zellingon is not your destination, you can obtain food there."

That prospect seemed dim to Provani, for she had no money. If she found a job, it would delay her. Warmed by the larger fire, Provani yielded to her fatigue. In an area cleared of rocks, she'd spread pine boughs. Now, with the bag as a pillow and her blanket, she reclined on the ground. "I will think on it, Credo, but now I must sleep."

Credo watched Provani for some time before adding a large chunk of wood to the fire and finding her own spot to bed.

Birdsongs woke Provani from a dream in which she saw herself tending to a baby. She shook the image away and rose. The morning chill pierced her garment, but the rising sun promised warming. Credo came back from the woods and announced breakfast of bread, smoked fish, and elderberry tea. After her own visit to the trees, Provani ate, trying to decide whether she should go to Zellingon or Abantazar. Mercerio had hoped Provani might find a better life than that of a prostitute. That sentiment weighed on her. If such a life existed, she could probably find it in Zellingon. Probably more easily than in Abantazar where her professional activities were well known. Although she had no real ties to Abantazar, she was a girl of the south and that was where she wanted to be. Somewhere dry and warm.

"Have you made up your mind?" Credo asked. "The road to Zellingon goes east from this one near Rock Pass."

As if seeking an answer, Provani faced the rising sun. "Your offer is kind and appealing, but I must continue south. I don't know exactly why." She turned to find Credo staring at her with a frown. "Why are you looking at me like that?"

Credo circled her. "You are pregnant."

"That cannot be. And you could not discern it under this cloak."

"Yet I do. Not by seeing but by sensing."

Provani thought of her early-day queasiness and her fatigue and realized that Credo's words might be true. This woman had called herself a scholar. Perhaps she meant seer. Provani tried to think who the father might be but realized she could not be certain. "So why do you frown?" she asked.

"A darkness lies over your womb."

9
Caravan

Pregnant. Darkness. The thought chilled Provani. She refused to accept the darkness part of Credo's words and didn't want to hear more. "I must continue on my journey south," Provani announced, "and will leave you at the Zellingon road." She stuffed her blanket into the travel bag.

Credo regarded Provani for a long moment, then picked up her staff. She circled the campsite, thumping as she walked. At last she said, "If you insist on continuing alone, I have another suggestion. On the morrow a caravan will leave Manwark and travel the Zellingon road south in the direction you want to go."

"How do you know this? More sorcery?"

Credo smiled. "Hardly. The trader called Hillus travels regularly from Vok Boorl to Pale to deliver wool and acquire salted fish. I know his schedule. Half of the fish will be dropped off in Manwark in trade for metal goods."

"Why would this Hillus want a passenger?" Provani asked.

"Because he owes me a favor. I cured the man's son Irend from a fever not long ago. As for being a passenger—"

"—I could be more than a passenger. I can cook and tend horses." Provani got to her feet slowly, feeling better than she had in the past few days.

"The men would welcome a cook, for I suspect they subsist on dried lamb and bread, more intent on feeding the horses than themselves. The caravan will protect you from robbers, starvation, and perhaps boredom."

Provani debated whether one could trust lonely men even if Credo called the trader trustworthy. *Why am I even concerned about men? Have I not welcomed strangers to my bed for years?* She wondered again if Mercerio's influence were to blame for her feeling. She weighed the danger of walking alone and vulnerable against the safety and food in a group. I can't go on alone. "Fine. Where do we meet this caravan?"

"At the Zellingon road near the River Wark. There is grazing for the horses and a stream. We can be there today." Credo scooped dirt onto the fire and picked up her pack. "The day promises to be most pleasant, and the chittering squirrels want us to be on our way."

Credo's friend, Hillus, a man of fifty and four years, agreed to take Provani along with him. He was rotund, almost as wide as tall, with a round face elongated by a short beard and a spike of hair on his head. Both beard and hair were mostly gray.

"You can cook?" Hillus asked, a gleam in his eye.

Provani nodded and the deal was struck. She would earn her keep by doing the cooking for the seven travelers: Hillus, his two sons, and four shepherds of Vok Boorl. The unrelated men were ten years younger than Hillus, bearded, their faces tanned by lives in the southern sun. The sons had no facial hair. The younger, called Timo, was a slight boy of ten and five years.

Irend, tall and muscular, was Provani's age and seemed pleased to have her join the group. He smiled and offered to show her the victual wagon.

After Credo left, the caravan traveled southward, stopping near Rock Pass. Hillus placed root vegetables and salted fish in front of his passenger and pointed to a well-used grate set up over the welcome fire. Provani boiled and seasoned the vegetables and soon served a tasty meal, which she finished off with pan-roasted apples sweetened with raw honey.

"Well done, Provani," Irend said as he finished eating. "Not raw, not overdone, and not regretted, as when we cook for ourselves." He sat back, contented.

"Best meal I've had since Manwark," Timo said, eyeing the empty pot.

Other men grunted in agreement and began fussing with pipes. After the meal, Hillus posted a guard. Provani noticed that the traders all kept swords near them, even as they ate.

"The Tantrocan control for almost twenty years has made many men outlaws," Hillus said. "They may have been merchants or farmers, but the barbarians changed that. Now they make their living robbing people like me."

Provani slept in the cook wagon, cramped but still better than the bare ground. Having someone keep watch is a comfort, she thought. Her comfort vanished when the posted guard yelled and was the first to go down. Moonlight showed attackers with knives that slashed two additional men from Vok Boorl. But Hillus, despite his shape, was quick, and he, Irend, and another fended off five robbers, killing three with sword thrusts that changed the odds. The last two ran.

Strangely calm during the melee, Provani had hidden behind a wagon. After the fight she ran to the wounded watchman. Hillus' son Timo moaned and bled from a slash across his ribs. Provani grabbed a bottle of spirits and dumped it on the shallow wound. She contained the bleeding with a strip of cloth. She did the same for a second trader with a sliced arm.

"You did that well, Provani," Irend said, his face creased by worry. "Will my brother be all right?"

"The cut will heal, but he will not be riding a horse," Provani said. "He will have to remain quiet in the wagon."

"Pray Li that he survives. This was his first trading trip and should not be his last. Now we must bury the dead and leave."

Provani gazed at the dead bodies. *That could be me if I were traveling alone.* That forced her decision. She had intended to leave Hillus and the men when they reached the River Bagus and take the route along the river to Abantazar, a road notorious for robbers. That alone said she must stay with the caravan. But two other items influenced her thinking. Mercerio's words about finding a better life had begun to make her yearn for such a thing, something that she would not find in Abantazar. Then there was Credo's announcement of her pregnancy. *I can't just think for myself. I must stay.*

The caravan, now manned by only five including a woman and a wounded boy, resumed its journey an hour later with Provani and the sleeping Timo in the wagon driven by Irend. Hillus drove another, trailed by horses left by their attackers. The other survivor rode a horse. They traversed east of Swamp Pass and west of the Rise of Trog. Days later the diminished caravan reached the outskirts of Vok Boorl with Provani wondering about her future.

10
Caldir

Caldir served food and drink when Aduk returned from his meeting with King Brokul. Twice Aduk cursed the one called Justi, and Caldir decided he needed to know more about the Child of the Gift.

"What power does this Justi possess?" Caldir asked as he served wine.

Normally closed-mouthed, Aduk seemed willing to talk, becoming more so as he drank the Maduk red, a pleasing mix of berry flavors. "He is the one who drove us from the south, the one who thwarted Dar's will. His power flows like lightning bolts from his hands. The light sword he wielded against our soldiers burned flesh from bones. He slew hundreds in driving us from Zellingon. Never underestimate this boy."

"Did we know of this champion when we invaded the Zell?"

"I have shown you the texts that speak of a Child Gifted. This must be Justi. I knew of the prophecy that said a child of light would oppose the servants of Dar, but the text did not say when or predict an outcome. Therefore, I supported the invasion of the Zell. But I was vigilant, seeking signs of this child."

"Did you find any?" Caldir asked.

"I tortured information from a trader, who reported an unusual child in Ortun, a village on the west coast. There was a report about an Ortun woman who burned a Tantrocan to death with magical power." Aduk shook his head. "The Ortun connection was too much coincidence. I believe that woman was Justi's mother."

"What did you do?" Caldir added wine to Aduk's cup.

"I sent Ukor. He failed to kill the boy and was injured in the process."

"Ukor has not spoken of it."

"He is ashamed of his failure," Aduk said, regret in his voice. "I convinced King Brokul to dispatch troops. They too failed."

Aduk's words slowed and his eyelids drooped. Caldir put his mentor to bed and left, mulling over the tale of a humble peasant boy who held great power. It made him think of his own origins in a region far east of Tantroc. He and his mother had been captured and dragged to Ankor as slaves. He remembered Aduk examining the men, women, and children and later heard Aduk's explanation.

"I hunted for unusual minds," Aduk had said. "You were a dirty urchin, but you held me with a bold, challenging gaze. That demeanor impressed me." Later, Aduk admitted more to himself than to Caldir he wanted a spark of will, an intellect. Perhaps even a psychic ability.

Caldir chewed on this memory as he stood in the cold hallway before his chamber gazing at the sculpture at the end of the passage. A fierce-faced, legendary seer, rumored able to be a mind reader, grasped a naked woman's head. Surely the woman was thinking she was cold. Aduk claimed psychic ability, but Caldir laughed at the notion. Aduk had the mind-reading skill of a toad, he thought.

In his chamber Caldir stoked the fire and thought of Patch, the servant whose disappearance opened Caldir's path to becoming a priest. Patch also served Ukor and would entertain by removing women's robes slowly, fondling the revealed flesh, and on Ukor's command, taking the women. Then Patch became too fond of Ukor's favorite. Aduk had surmised that Ukor killed Patch, probably by accident, trying out some new form of persuasion.

Caldir smiled to think that his opportunity arose from the demise of one who tested women. *But I alone grasped the opportunity.* At the age of ten years when Aduk took him on, Caldir proved more than a house servant. He grasped all aspects of Aduk's schemes, including the priestly rituals and the political ploys. By his mid-teens, with muscles from the better food and with the eye patch thanks to his mother's drunken rage, Caldir announced he wanted to become a priest.

The high priest had not laughed at the request but warned that studies for the priesthood were arduous. "You have much to learn, Caldir, to become a priest of Dar," he'd said. In the end Aduk agreed to take on Caldir as his student.

After the fire conquered the chill in his bedchamber, Caldir donned his sleeping garment. But he wasn't prepared to rest, and his mind roamed over his history and the notion that this was a key moment. As Aduk's acolyte, he'd studied ancient texts and politics. More recently Aduk lectured on techniques of mind control and its assistance by certain potions. At one point, after commenting on strong and weak minds, he mentioned wanting to use his techniques on Justi of Ortun. That was the first time Caldir had heard the name.

The high priest had his chance to examine Justi in Fathom. Aduk had drugged Justi and probed his mind, and then complained that he'd learned little about the power, for the boy seemed to invoke the flame in a random fashion in response to what he perceived as injustice. What can a toad learn? Caldir thought.

"Justi lacks control," Aduk had said. Yet the man wanted more time with the gifted Zellish youth, sure there was gold to be mined.

Gold mined by a toad.

Caldir resented that Aduk kept Justi to himself. The Ortun boy was an obstacle to be overcome. Politics and power—the affairs of King Brokul's court—consumed Caldir. More than priestly chanting. It galled him that, as the Tantrocans regained their strength, they focused only on the threat posed by Justi and were held back by poor leadership, a lack of will and boldness. Old King Brokul was content to enjoy his new children, his half-naked wife, and his immense banquets. His fire had banked. Nothing Aduk said moved the king.

If I were high priest, things would be different. This Justi is not insurmountable. I would spur the king to act.

11
Zellingon

Credo's knowledge of medicine came from her mother, who taught her to treat certain maladies, especially blood disorders. Whether her skill was natural or magical was debated, with some scholars suggesting that Credo had received some component of Li's gift to Justi. Credo could only say that she sensed illness and knew how to treat it. When she heard that Zellingon was freed, she traveled from Pale, a small town on the northern coast, to buy medicinal supplies. Her dream of being needed by a special patient forced her to travel sooner than expected.

Credo had left Provani safely with the caravan near the River Wark and west of Lake Manwark. Alone, Credo should have turned toward Zellingon. Instead, a strong impulse drove her to Manwark, in search of a special patient. Credo knew it wasn't Provani. Their meeting seemed fortuitous, but the woman was not sick, just hungry. She'd acquired a few bruises escaping her Tantrocan captors, but they needed no treatment. Provani was blessed to make it out of Fathom alive and to encounter someone with food when starving. Twice blessed. No, thrice, for the caravan might not have been passing at the right time. *Provani couldn't be the special patient, but what of her unborn child?*

The Manwark Road was empty, except for occasional deer. Once, Credo glimpsed a red fox darting after a rabbit. When the hawk appeared in the sky the third time, always in front of her, Credo took it as a sign.

West of Lake Manwark, a feverish Princess Mercerio lay barely conscious. Justi bathed her brow to no avail. Rocley built a fire for warmth and to dispel the gloom. He fed the blaze with treefall and got ready to leave.

Smoke led Credo to the site where a young man knelt near a sleeping woman. Her approach startled an older man, who ordered Credo to halt. She introduced herself as a healer from Pale.

Justi lifted his hand from Mercerio's cheek. "You are a physician?"

Credo nodded.

"I am Justi and this is my father Rocley. This is the Princess Mercerio. She was cut by a knife and burns with fever." He waved Credo closer. Justi told how Mercerio received the knife wound as Credo knelt and felt Mercerio's brow and examined the wound. The gash was almost healed, but the surrounding red skin meant infection.

"How long ago did this happen?" Credo asked.

"This morning," Justi said. "The wound was deep, but I have healing power myself. I closed it."

The knife wasn't clean," Credo said.

Minutes passed while Credo held Mercerio. Finally, the healer breathed deeply and opened her eyes. Mercerio lifted her head, perhaps seeing the campsite for the first time. She seemed more alert than any time since slipping from the horse. Credo went to her bag and gathered several vials. She spoke to Rocley. "Can you heat water for tea?"

Justi frowned. "The princess suffers. This is no time for tea."

"The tea is for the princess. She has blood sickness—from the foul blade. I have arrested it. We must apply a poultice to continue the healing." Credo searched in her pack and produced three packets. She handed one to Justi. "This one makes the tea."

Credo fire-cleaned a blade, pierced and drained the wound. She applied salve and a bandage. With the treatments, magic and otherwise, Mercerio was able to take sips of the tea, and her fever eased by dawn. Credo ordered Justi to let the patient rest for the entire day before continuing the journey.

When they reached Zellingon, Justi and Mercerio were embraced by mothers, advisers, and teachers. Queen Melsin explained that she had ordered repairs for the walls and guards for her daughter. "Mercerio will never be kidnapped again." She declared.

Rocley hugged his wife Arturi and left to consult with the chief guard. Melsin and Mercerio retreated to the queen's apartment, leaving Justi to face his mother.

Arturi hugged him and then stood, arms folded. "Why did you disappear from Zellingon without saying anything?"

"I had to go after Mercerio. There was no time to explain."

"You should have taken men with you," his mother said. "What happened?"

Justi admitted he went south—in the wrong direction. "My favorite seer Rakur found me near the Swamp of Snakes and pointed me north. Days later I made it to Fathom."

"How did you get into the town with Tantrocans guarding the place?" Arturi asked.

"Four Tantrocans brought me in."

"Why?" Arturi held her hand up when someone knocked on the door.

Goren, the Ortun seer, now middle aged, rotund, and white-haired, entered, and Justi repeated his story. "Why did the Tantrocans leave you unharmed?" Goren asked.

"A tall, bird-like man wanted to know about my power, why I had it, and how I used it. I think he drugged me. He was unhappy about my answers and wanted to question me again, but he didn't get a chance. When the Zellish attack began, Mercerio and I fled. Father found us when we were a day's ride from Fathom."

Goren's eyes grew larger as Justi spoke. "The one who questioned you, that sounds like Aduk. He is King Brokul's high priest and fancies himself a mystic."

"That was it? Just some questions from this priest?" Arturi asked.

"When the Zellish army started its siege, we escaped." Justi told about finding his horse, saddle, and bag, avoiding a bear, stumbling into a hidden campsite, and the attack. "Mercerio developed a fever from the knife wound. We camped west of the Manwark Lake. I bathed Mercerio, but the fever did not abate. I think our fire caught Credo's attention and brought her to us."

"What happened then?" Arturi asked.

"Credo introduced herself as a healer from Pale and treated Mercerio. Her skill with medicines saved the princess."

Goren tapped his index finger on the arm of the chair. "Medicine and more. Even her presence was beyond coincidence. You and the princess are the Children of the Gift. Credo could have been brought to you because you needed her."

Justi shrugged.

12
Credo

For saving Mercerio's life, Queen Melsin named Credo the Queen's Healer, a title that assured access to medicinals and inclusion in the college of healers. Credo stayed weeks in Zellingon consulting with the medical society, both learning and teaching. During that time her need to be in Pale grew. She couldn't see why, but it became an irresistible urgency. On a cold day, she took tea with Princess Mercerio.

The two sat at a round table at a window overlooking the plaza in the palace forecourt where sunlight gleamed off the central pool. Children splashed as two dogs barked from the edge, and a middle-aged man berated his mule for dallying over a drink from a trough.

"I am grateful for your hospitality," Credo began, "but I must return to Pale. You have several healers here, and even you and Justi possess powers to mend the body. Pale has me. My friend Marek will worry at my long absence. Indeed, I should have been back a week ago."

"I sense there is more to this sudden departure."

"You are right. I feel I am needed for something important back in Pale. But I cannot say what."

"I am not one to ignore such feelings," Mercerio said. "But this pleasant weather is about to change and make travel difficult. If you insist on leaving, I will have one of my men accompany you."

"That is not necessary, Highness. I made my way here alone and can abide a little cold weather on the trip back."

Mercerio shook her head. "The highways are still infested with villains. A woman as young and comely as you would be vulnerable. Furthermore, you will be carrying botanicals and potions that thieves would find valuable."

"Very well. But can you spare a guard for such a trip?"

"I have someone already charged to deliver royal orders to the Pale town council," Mercerio said. "Panthis is a skilled warrior, big, strong, and handsome, and enjoys the company of women. He will find you pleasant to behold. If you do not wish his attentions, tell me and I will instruct him accordingly."

Credo pondered this new information and then smiled. "I cannot say anything about intentions from some man I have not met. But I assure you, Highness, that I am capable of handling men."

Panthis was about Credo's age, tall with blond hair and a ready smile. As predicted by Mercerio, he seemed aware of his attractiveness and expected women to fall under his spell. Credo resisted. Their trip to Pale was conducted with dispatch, and she gave him no opportunity to be affectionate. In fact, to control his spirited nature, she served him tea with herbs known to deflate temporarily the lust of the male.

As they traveled, Credo lost the sense of urgency that drove her from Zellingon. Curious, she thought.

When they reached Pale, Panthis said he enjoyed Credo's charms and wanted to visit again. He then went to consult with the town's leaders about a coastal early warning system in case the Tantrocans decided to return. Credo wondered what the man meant by charms.

Days after returning to Pale, Credo finished tending a young child with a mild fever and promised that both the child and the distressed mother would improve. Wrapped in a wool cloak, she walked home in a brisk wind from the Tantric Gulf and her sense of having some important task returned. At home she questioned her roommate Marek, who served as surrogate for Credo's mother who'd died. "Has anyone called for me? Am I forgetting anything?"

Marek frowned and continued serving tea. "No one has summoned you. Calm down. Rest before dinner."

In her room Credo brushed her long blue-black hair, trying to relax her mind and figure out what was so urgent. Then she wondered what had become of Panthis, who'd promised to stop by before he left for Zellingon. Had he already forgotten her charm?

Marek announced that dinner was almost ready, and Credo went to the kitchen table. Her thoughts returned to Panthis, seeing his handsome face and strong hands. Marek started her litany, topics that needed attention like a sore toe. One of her favorites already occupied Credo. "Have you looked around since we last talked?"

"Looked around? I always take pleasure in our environment."

"You know what I'm talking about. You are of breeding age, Credo, and have a beauty that attracts men. It is time that you became serious about one and gave your own heart the medicine it needs."

Credo thought of Panthis. *Hardly suitable for marriage. Too stuck on himself.* "No one has caught my fancy." Was that the truth, she wondered?

"You are too choosy. The seasons come and go, and women do not retain their figures and unlined faces forever."

"Be not concerned, Marek. I am quite content. When the right man appears, then I will become serious."

Marek frowned. "What about the man who accompanied you from Zellingon? You said some interesting things about him."

"He was . . . tolerable."

"Tolerable. Will you see him again? He is still here in Pale?"

Credo wanted to see Panthis again, but she didn't need to tell Marek that. "I don't know his affairs." She left Marek to finish the meal and smoothed her gown over long legs, thrust out her chest as if to say she still had her figure, and left to fetch water and wood.

A day later as dinner was served, a knock at the door surprised Credo and Marek. Credo answered and returned with Panthis. He greeted them most warmly, praising the smell of the food.

"It is just something I put together," Marek said, basking in the complement of her cooking skills and smiling with extra color in her cheeks.

"I'm about to start my journey back and had to bid farewell until we meet again in Zellingon. When you visit as the Queen's Healer."

Credo found her emotions bouncing from joy that he remembered to say goodbye to unhappiness he was saying goodbye. Then back to joy at the notion of seeing him in Zellingon. "Thank you for calling, Panthis." That sounded cold, she thought.

"You can't be starting a journey in the dark," Marek said. "You must join us for dinner. I've prepared enough grazebeast roast and potatoes to feed even more than three."

Panthis accepted. As he ate, he confessed to liking the taste of Marek's cooking even more than the smell. Marek blushed. After the repast, she suggested that Panthis spend the night and begin his trip on the morrow. When he did not object, Marek disappeared to prepare the guest chamber. Credo gave Panthis a long look and invited him to the rear room. She lit two lamps, brought tea, and let Panthis begin the conversation.

"I am glad I got this chance to get to know you, Credo. I find you delightful."

"I thought I was charming."

"That too. I want to know more than I learned about you on our trip."

"What else could you wish to know? I am a healer," Credo said, thinking Panthis seemed to have developed even larger blue eyes during his week in Pale. *It is just the lamplight in place of sun.*

"What else do you want to be?" Panthis asked.

"What do you mean?"

"I mean, do you want to be a wife?" Panthis asked with a smile.

Credo held her cup halfway to her mouth. "Are you asking to be my husband?"

"Would you say yes?"

"This is silly. We hardly know each other."

Panthis lost his constant smile. "You are right. Since our trip, I have not stopped thinking of you. We have known each other for a short time, but there is a connection between us. I want us to be together."

"How can that be?" Credo asked. "I live in Pale and you in Zellingon."

Panthis rose and knelt before Credo, taking her hand in his. "I am sure I can arrange an assignment here, a permanent assignment. The kingdom needs eyes on its northern shoreline to guard against the Tantrocan return."

Credo bit her lip, looked away and then back at her guest. "I admit I am attracted to you, Panthis, but this is so sudden. We should know more about each other. Surely there is time."

"Time is something to be enjoyed now. None know how much time is given them."

The conversation continued in this vein until Marek announced that the guest bed was ready. Panthis seemed too serious when he wished Credo a good night filled with the most pleasant dreams. Credo retreated to her room.

In the middle of the night, Panthis found his way into Credo's bed and was not rebuffed. He soon had her nightgown off and took his time exploring. When he removed his clothes, Credo saw that there was no lingering effect of the herbs she had placed in his tea during their journey. Their lovemaking was not entirely quiet and went on for some time. Credo was sure that Marek would have some new verses in her favorite litany.

Panthis left in the morning with the promise to return. He never kept that promise for he never made it to Zellingon. Queen Mercerio sent a messenger to Pale to ask if Panthis was still there. Credo told when Panthis began his trip, and a search ensued, but no trace of Panthis was found. His disappearance remained a mystery.

When Credo discovered she was pregnant, she knew who the father was. Only later did she realize that with Panthis' departure she lost any sense of having a task that needed her urgent attention.

13
Coronation

Queen Melsin was worried. Mercerio had moped around the palace since the return from Fathom. At first Melsin thought it was the knife wound, but Mercerio was fully recovered. The queen found her daughter in her bedchamber. "Mercerio, you do realize you will soon turn ten and eight years?" Melsin asked. "That means you will become queen as the daughter of King Bronte. As the king's commoner widow, I can only serve as queen until you reach maturity. That is about to happen. It would behoove the future leader of Zellish people to embrace her role. A people's spirit often reflects that of its leader. They have sacrificed a lot to restore this kingdom. Your coronation in a lavish ceremony is their reward."

"I know, Mother," Mercerio sighed. "I have just had a lot on my mind."

The queen waited. When her daughter remained silent, Melsin asked, "How are you and Justi getting along?"

"Fine." Mercerio went to her dressing table.

"Really? You've hardly seen him since he rescued you. Has he done something?" Melsin put her hand on Mercerio's shoulder. "Tell me."

A tear formed on Mercerio's cheek, the first drop in the flood. She hugged her mother and sobbed the story of Justi and Provani. She was in no way forgiving of Justi, but Melsin read between the lines.

"And did you believe this Provani?" Melsin asked, pulling a brush through her daughter's hair.

"I have no doubt that Justi slept with her, but I suspect Provani targeted him. I like Justi. I thought he liked me. It's like he betrayed our love. This is a barrier between us."

Melsin thought a bit. "You must realize, Mercerio, that men can separate the physical from the emotional. Not that men aren't capable of great emotions, but they can act without thinking, especially when manipulated by a pretty girl. I presume this Provani was someone whose appearance would attract a man."

"Quite," Mercerio said, staring into a looking glass. "Tall and slender with a pretty face and long red hair. Add a smile and drinks and she'd be irresistible."

That description surprised Melsin. She turned Mercerio around to face her. "Justi has been a true champion for the Zellish, and some would cheer a union between you two. But it may not be the marriage for you. Justi is peasant-born and uneducated. And you are about to become Queen of the Zell."

"What am I supposed to do?"

"Make him act the way you want."

"I'm not sure how."

"You'll figure it out."

"But what about Provani? How am I to think of that?"

"Think of it this way. In a depressed state, after several drinks with a willing and alluring beautiful girl, Justi followed his nature and went to bed with her. He did not know her and has not seen her again. You are hurt by this, of course, but that is part of growing up. Boys are in many ways weaker than girls, subject to forces we don't understand."

Mercerio wiped her eyes. "I think he likes me."

"Maybe. It is best to proceed as if this never happened. Put him behind you. There are many fine young men lingering in Zellingon. Just move on."

The crowning of Mercerio as queen confirmed the peace for the inhabitants of Zellingon. The throne was moved outside to accommodate expected crowds. The stones of the courtyard had been swept and scrubbed till they gleamed in the bright noon sun. By that hour, the temperature had recovered from a morning frost and become mild. Even the early breeze had stilled.

At noon trumpeters in red and white livery sounded to announce Princess Mercerio's presence at the palace doors. The princess, clad in a rich gown of cream and gold, appeared on the steps of the palace. She sniffed the pleasant smell of incense burning in ceremonial pots and nodded to the guard captain her readiness to proceed. Commanding everyone's attention, including Justi's who watched near the palace, she descended the steps and proceeded slowly through the crowd at a stately pace set by a group of drummers. Six armed guards walked alongside and behind. Mercerio climbed the steps of a platform on which Queen Melsin and the chief cleric waited.

The priest pronounced the words of coronation and placed a gold crown on Mercerio's head. He stepped to the side and Queen Mercerio settled on the red cushion of a gilded throne. She accepted a golden scepter that embodied the power of the Kingdom of the Zell, and the crowd roared. Mercerio smiled and waved to her subjects.

"Where did they find the crown and the scepter?" Justi asked a soldier. "Wouldn't the Tantrocans have stolen those?"

"The crown jewels were hidden somewhere only the Queen Mother Melsin knew of."

Mercerio stood, adjusted her crown, and addressed her subjects. She spoke of a new age of Lihoch, meaning the spirit of righteousness, and pledged to defend the kingdom from any new Tantrocan incursions. She dedicated her reign to King Bronte, her dead father, and to the cause of justice.

Justi waited for Mercerio in a quiet meeting room, thankful to escape crowds of people he did not know. Zellingon was filled with citizens from all over the kingdom. Visitors jostled in the streets, filled every inn, and imposed on residents' hospitality. Wealth and status meant guest quarters in the castle. Additional staff was employed to serve travelers who required too much attention and too much food. This invasion of strangers alarmed Justi. He sensed danger.

Justi was admiring swords on a side table when Queen Mercerio arrived, still in her coronation garb, including the gleaming crown and the large official amulet with the gold-encircled sapphire dangling from her neck. Sparkle, an orange-on-black cat that had been her pet in Abantazar, greeted her with a meow.

Justi smiled. "You look especially . . . lovely . . . Royal, I mean."

"I am royal. You should have bowed when I entered," Mercerio said with a wag of her finger.

"Sorry. Sparkle distracted me."

"You are forgiven," Mercerio said, smiling. "You have seemed distracted and distant this past week. Why?"

Justi really had no reason to alarm Mercerio. He'd been thinking of assassins often used by Tantrocans. If the northerners wanted revenge for their defeat, what could be better than killing Mercerio? He shook off his disquiet and said, "I was thinking of my village now that the war is over. My parents will return to Ortun to settle affairs with the family store and see if my grandfather is all right."

"Is travel safe?" Mercerio sat at the table and pulled the centerpiece vase closer.

"The army will ferret out any pockets of Tantrocans to the west until the entire kingdom is clear." *Then why do I feel this way?*

A servant knocked and was admitted. The small man with blond hair and pale skin wore loose clothing. "Highness, the refreshments you ordered."

"Are you new?" Mercerio asked. "I don't recognize you."

"I'm just here for the coronation, Highness."

The man placed two mugs of a dark liquid and a plate of pastry on the table. "The beverage is a southern fruit juice." He bowed and backed away.

Justi felt heat spread in his chest. Then his ears burned. He studied the servant, unable to shake the sense that something was wrong. There was no reason for a new man to attend the queen. And when do servants linger if dismissed? Mercerio raised a mug to her lips. Justi placed his hand over the top.

He motioned to the servant. "You will consume this."

The man's eyes darted from Justi to Mercerio, and then he danced. In one fluid, practiced, continuous motion, he pulled a knife and sailed it at Mercerio. Justi shoved her aside and the blade thudded into her chair. Mercerio heaved the vase at the assassin. The man ducked and pulled out a second weapon, some sort of flat disk. The blade whirled when he released it toward Mercerio. The queen screamed.

From Justi's hand flew a blinding white flash, and the air thrummed with the sound of a great bow. The fiery lance drilled a fist-sized hole in the knife-thrower's chest. His body flew back and rattled against the door, and a whiff of cauterized flesh and expelled feces tainted the room. Two guards shoved open the door, sliding the dead body along the stone floor.

Mercerio stood eyes wide, her hands cradling the amulet on her chest. The jewel held the sharp disk in a groove of the wide gold setting.

"Do not touch that," Justi yelled. He unclasped the amulet and lifted it away. The disk came free and clanged on the stone floor. Justi put his arms around Mercerio, who seemed to have lost all color. "Take the refreshments and dispose of them," Justi said to the guards. The liquid contains poison. Find out who knows that man."

The smaller guard picked up the food and drink and the assassin's blades, and the larger one dragged the body off.

"That was the danger I sensed," Justi said.

"Why did you not speak of it?"

"It was just a feeling. I did not want to alarm you."

Mercerio frowned. "You should have told me. Now you have killed him."

"He tried to kill you."

"Why did you not grab him before he went for his knife? You are bigger and stronger and had the opportunity. I thought my being near you gave you control of your power."

"We have talked of this before. Nothing has changed. What are you really asking, Mercerio?"

The queen grabbed the table edge. "I am concerned that your power controls you. That it will destroy you. Not all killing is justified. Your power is wild and dangerous. You have used it in the cause of justice, but that may not always be."

Justi felt the sting of Mercerio's intense accusation. But it was one he had levied at himself. "I have used my power to protect the innocent, and more than once that has been you," Justi said stiffly.

Sparkle jumped onto the table. The queen frowned at both the cat and Justi. "I fear the power, Justi, for it lacks an ingredient to make it truly a thing to serve Li."

"And what is that?"

"It lacks mercy. You lack mercy."

Justi had hoped to tell Mercerio how he felt about her. Instead, unfairly accused, he was angry and was about to say so when Sparkle placed his paw, claws out, on Justi's arm. Justi swallowed his words.

PART II
Genesis

Children appear to advance the causes of both Li and Dar in the realm of men.

14
Vok Boorl

Provani's pregnancy couldn't be ignored. Mornings she suffered an uneasy stomach and could hardly face cooking the early meal, let alone eating it. This day, as the caravan skirted the Swamp Pass and rumbled along the Rise of Trog, she vomited. Missing her time of month confirmed the diagnosis. She did her best to hide her condition and thought she succeeded, but Hillus gave her some odd looks. By the time the wagons reached the River Bagus, she felt better. Timo, the wounded son, also regained strength. His ribs grew less tender and the wound healed.

The days grew sunnier and warmer as the caravan skirted a large swampy tract. Forests yielded to grassy plains, and at last Provani spied the village of Vok Boorl perched beside a large lake where small boats plied the placid blue water. Vast fields, some with houses, spread beyond low village buildings on the shore. Sheep and goats eyed the passing wagons.

The older Hillus son Irend must have seen Provani admiring the landscape. "Those herds are our wealth," Irend said, a flash of pride in his dark brown eyes. "We are all herdsmen and some are traders. Those fishermen are just taking the day off."

Provani had grown used to Irend's open and easy style. He seemed to anticipate her questions and offered answers without being asked. She perceived his frequent and long glances and welcomed them. This was quite different from the treatment she received from men at the Abantazar Inn where her services were bought with a coin.

The wagons pulled up to a many-roomed fieldstone house. Hillus' wife Myrene greeted her husband with a warm embrace. Provani was introduced. Myrene did not seem happy to learn that Hillus had acquired a young female cook along the route. But she mellowed when told how Provani cared for Timo. Myrene did not want Provani to stay in her house with two sons who couldn't keep their eyes off her.

Myrene sent a message to Olinie, a widow neighbor, who offered Provani quarters in exchange for help. With little choice, Provani accepted. She cooked, cleaned, cared for goats and chickens, and sold the eggs, milk, and cheese. Olinie, a large woman with a ruddy complexion and gray hair, could have handled the work by herself. Provani's real job was listening to the widow, who wanted an audience for her constant chatter. Goats were not good conversationalists.

But Provani's mind was elsewhere. She knew that being pregnant was a problem best solved by having a husband. She assessed her prospects. There were several, but her eye settled on Irend. His strength and quiet ways attracted her. She liked his smile. What's more, she suspected she had a head start with the man.

"What do you know of Irend, the first son of Hillus?" she asked Olinie.

The woman smoothed her hair back and cast an appraising eye in her servant's direction. "He is available for marriage, if that be your meaning."

Even though the woman surely knew that a successful courting of Irend would mean the loss of her servant, Olinie agreed to invite the young man for dinner. Her round cheeks and dimpled chin lit up as she agreed to teach Provani how to prepare a well-seasoned goat roast.

"This will surely please Irend. It has done so for any man I've used it on."

"You mean your husband?"

"Any man."

On a warm day a week after her arrival in Vok Boorl, Provani delivered the invitation to the Hillus ranch. She brought a berry pie whose preparation was orchestrated by Olinie. Perhaps "dictated" was a better description. Irend was off shearing sheep, but Hillus, seemingly flummoxed by the unexpected development but mollified by the pie, promised to convey the message. Myrene frowned.

Irend replied in person that same evening. He seemed eager to pursue Provani and came for dinner several times, always bringing flowers, complimenting her on her beauty, and then on the food. She wasn't sure which attracted the man more. After the third meal, Provani decided to move things along. Olinie had gone off to a neighbor's and promised to be quite late. Provani took Irend to her room and, as she had done to Justi, bedded him. The rancher, like Justi, was obviously inexperienced, but proved to be a fast learner.

Hours later Irend stopped talking about sheep breeding and said, "I have thought of you every night. I have thought of you each morning. Only my shyness kept me from coming here sooner. You are beautiful, Provani, and I am happy in your company. I believe we should be more than just friends sharing food and . . . well, this."

Provani touched his bare arm, as if to agree. Then she kissed him, which led to further lovemaking. Somewhere in the middle of that, Olinie came back to the house and wisely did not say goodnight.

In the hour before dawn, Irend said, "My father has given me my share of his vast farm, and I would have you for my wife."

Provani pretended to be surprised while rejoicing at the early success of her plan. It would not matter now if her pregnancy showed. She should have answered immediately but did not. For some mysterious reason, her condition held her tongue. Her mind revolted against the deception. Irend deserved better. That she should even think such a thing surprised her. When her brother pushed her to have sex with his friends for money, she learned to distrust and hate men, including the sorry examples in Abantazar. Perhaps Princess Mercerio had somehow altered her thinking.

It made no sense, and she couldn't understand why she did it, but the truth tumbled from her mouth. "I would be honored to be your wife, Irend, but there is something you must know. It will cause you to take back your words." She sat on the edge of the bed, her bare back to the man.

Irend put his hand on her shoulder and let it trail down. "What is it, Provani? Nothing you say can change my love for you."

Provani breathed deep and collapsed onto the pillow, still facing away. "If you do withdraw your offer of marriage, I will understand and honor you."

15
Irend

Provani hesitated, waiting for some reaction. As she related her past, Irend maintained his usual unperturbed state and said nothing. Provani slid her legs over the edge of the bed and sat up. She finished her confession with "I am with child."

Irend maneuvered to sit beside Provani and took her hand. "I will be honest with you."

Provani tensed. She cast her eyes to the floor, expecting scorn and rejection. That was what men used to put women in their place. Men could have sex freely, but women who took men to their beds became objects of derision. And woe to the woman who gets with child. Scorn and rejection. She raised her chin, defiance on her face.

Irend rested his chin on her shoulder. "Your life has been a hard one, lived in tough places. I am not the one to judge you. My feelings remain the same. I love you. Your child will be our child."

Surprised and pleased, Provani wriggled free, kissed this man, and pushed him back onto the bed. They made love for the third time. What Irend lacked in skill, he made up for in enthusiasm.

When they emerged from the bedchamber the next morning, Olinie presented a hearty breakfast of eggs with sautéed vegetables and goat cheese served with bacon. Provani was almost getting to like the raw milk drunk at every meal in Vok Boorl. She didn't know if

Irend ate more heartily than usual, but nothing went to waste. He departed with a kiss for Provani and a sheep-need-tending farewell.

When the herdsman had gone, Olinie cleared the table. When the plates were stacked in the sink, she asked the question. "So?"

"So what?"

"Have you solved your problem?"

"What problem is that?"

Olinie stood arms akimbo. "You cannot fool an old woman. You are pregnant."

"How—?"

"You act so—how you walk, what you eat or don't, how you fuss over the toy dolls in the bedroom. So did he ask you to marry him?"

A smile flooded Provani's face. "Yes, yes. Oh, yes."

Apparently, ranchers did not abide delay. Within the fortnight Provani married Irend before a priest in a small wooden building that served as a temple of Li in Vok Boorl. Hillus was happy for his son and gave the couple a house near the main one on his farm. Irend was even happier than his father, and Timo was glad to have a new sister. Myrene was the holdout. She congratulated her son, had no words for Provani, and managed to excuse herself early.

A month later Provani revealed her pregnancy. It progressed without incident as she learned the herder life and found she liked it. She rose and went to bed with the sun. While Irend was out managing the animals, Olinie showed Provani how to create mouthwatering food that would do more to cement a marriage than good lovemaking.

Irend never failed to appreciate his new wife and brought her gifts from his trading ventures with his father. He also brought news of the reestablishment of the Kingdom of the Zell under Queen Mercerio. Provani again wondered how the princess could have so changed Provani's life. She refrained from asking about Justi.

* * * * *

After seeing that Justi and Mercerio were safely back in Zellingon, *Li's angels directed me to check on Provani. I flew southwest from Zellingon, battling contrary winds rolling off the Rise of Trog and evading larger hawks who resented incursion in their territory. I arrived in Vok Boorl after Provani wed Irend.*

I had witnessed Justi's encounter with the redheaded Abantazar girl and feared it might destroy his relationship with the princess, a relationship demanded by prophecy. When Justi left Abantazar with Mercerio as the Zellish army marched north, I thought that was the last I would see of Provani. Now I was being sent to check on her, and the reason was one I'd overlooked until Credo's pronouncement. If Provani were indeed pregnant, that child might be the next bearer of the Justice Power. Wouldn't that be good? It would confer Li's gift on a new generation. Why then had Credo said she sensed darkness lingering over Provani?

16
Justik

Provani gave birth in the spring and named the child Justik. Irend accepted the name, perhaps thinking it derived from the kingdom's legendary hero, Justi. Little did he realize how close he was to the truth. The boy's face, hair, and icy blue eyes made it clear to Provani that this was Justi's child.

From the beginning, Justik was different. He seemed to dwell inside himself, accepting the care of parents as his due. He never laughed. His personality was mercurial: he could be content one moment and fly into a rage the next.

Irend kept cats in the barn, and they became a source of entertainment for Justik in his sixth year. The cats were never his pets and, in fact, learned quickly to avoid the boy who seemed to delight in pulling tails, pelting them with rocks, and in one instance maiming the smallest cat with a stick.

When Provani discovered what had happened, she chastised her son. "You have done a bad thing, Justik. The poor cat will never walk right again. You are forbidden to go near them." Provani dared not physically correct her child. He would react with a fit of rage, pummeling her, spouting hate. His reaction was more animal than human.

Justik stared at his mother as if trying to understand what she was talking about. He seemed unfazed by the incident. In fact, he glowered at his mother as if she were the wrongdoer. He endured her words, then turned and stomped off. "It was a bad cat. It tried to lick me."

* * * * *

Angels saw this behavior as typical of uncontrolled human children. *But the high Adamanti became alarmed and told me to watch the child. Although Justik was Justi's son, he seemed evil. How could that be? I surmised the reason: Provani was under the influence of the dark spirits when she conceived, and their foul influence controlled the child from the onset. The angels of Dar had not noticed the boy, as far as I could tell. If he exhibited any power, they surely would.*

* * * * *

Justik killed his first animal when he was eight. By that age he had learned to make animal traps and a squirrel became his victim. After setting the snare and waiting patiently for hours, Justik watched the poor animal step in the loop near the free food. The trip sprang and the loop tightened about the squirrel's hind leg. It leapt and danced to no avail. Justik came from his hiding place armed with a knife and began poking the tip into the squirming victim. This continued for some time until, tiring of the game, Justik stabbed the squirrel through the neck. The unfortunate squirrel quickly bled out while Justik watched with a morbid fascination. He could have claimed the prize as evidence of a successful hunt, for squirrel was an edible game. Instead he buried his cruelty.

Irend rarely hunted and never for squirrel. Justik understood that a hunter does not prolong the death of prey and does not bury his catch. But Justik was not a hunter. He was a torturer. The only power revealed in Justik was the power to be cruel.

He began playing with fire when he was nine and became quite skilled in starting a fire almost anywhere. Once he decided, on a cold day, that the barn would be more comfortable with a small fire in the middle. Only the fact that Irend was nearby prevented loss of the whole structure.

The boy did not have friends, for it did not take any child long to realize that this grim creature was unlike them. They avoided him, and Justik did not seem to much care about his isolation. When he was ten, he did seek out other boys, but his purpose seemed to be to challenge them and defeat them. At first it was in sports, then in dares of varying sorts, and finally in fighting. He beat them, often severely, stopping only when bigger boys intervened. He used no special power in these fights, just his fists.

As it had with his father, Justik's power emerged with puberty.

17
Proposal

The queen mother told Mercerio to get over Justi and find love elsewhere. "It is your responsibility to ensure the future of the Kingdom of the Zell by producing an heir. Without a royal heir, conflicts will arise that will weaken the Zell and invite Tantrocan invasion."

"That makes me feel like a brood mare," Mercerio said.

"Find someone less complicated than Justi."

Mercerio couldn't do that. She now viewed his dalliance with Provani as unfortunate, something to be forgiven and forgotten. Maybe Provani and Justi were victims, manipulated by Dar. She knew having a child was her duty, and for that she needed a husband. Justi would do wonderfully. Mercerio loved Justi and wanted him close. She wanted him to say he loved her, but how to make that happen vexed Mercerio.

Justi's turmoil had a different flavor. Without a battle to fight he felt useless. When he wasn't wondering what he should do with himself, he thought of Mercerio in the hot pool that first night out of Fathom. The image filled his mind with fantasies. Circumstances dictated their openness with each other, but Mercerio pushed the boundaries, seemed to enjoy his discomfort. Did that mean she loved him?

Even hunting deer with his stepfather Rocley, focused on scat, bent branches, and hoof prints, did little to calm him. He enjoyed Mercerio's company and wondered if he should tell her how she affected him. That's what she wanted, he suspected, given her flirting, keeping track of him, and grilling him on how he felt about things.

Mercerio borrowed a hooded cloak from a maid, escaped the royal guard, and went to the house Justi shared with his parents. She found him packing his parents' belongings. Mercerio hung her outer garment on a wall peg and stood before the fire, eying the jumble of clothes, jewelry, and kitchen implements. "What are you doing?"

Justi continued working. "Where are your guards?"

"I gave them a rest. A woman needs privacy, you know. Our conversations are for us."

"I'm getting my parents ready to return to Ortun. Mother and Father will travel soon if the weather stays warm."

"Where are Arturi and Rocley?"

"Shopping. Won't be back for hours."

Mercerio counted the trunks and travel bags. "Will you be going with them?"

"I haven't decided. There is nothing holding me here." He wanted to take back the words as soon as they left his lips.

"But if there were, you would stay?" Mercerio asked.

Justi imagined some new task he would not do correctly and then be compared to some animal that wasn't smart. When she'd asked him to chop carrots for dinner in Abantazar, and he did it wrong, she'd called him a Botu, the head-in-the-sand bird that hid from trouble. No, he was a Botu because he didn't answer her questions about using his power the right way. "Like what?" he asked.

"A task, a role. Have you forgotten the ancient words about two children of the gift who must stay close? We are those two. When we are near, my power helps control yours. Well . . . it could. When we are distant, it gets out of control. That is when you killed Gralil."

Justi paled. He didn't need to be reminded of Gralil's death. Perhaps he'd have had better control if Mercerio were near, but she was busy being kidnapped. "The fight is done," he said. "I will never use my power again."

"You can't know the future."

"You are speaking like a foolish girl," Justi said, biting his tongue immediately.

Mercerio folded her arms and glared.

"I'm sorry, Majesty," Justi said. "I forgot my place. Such a comparison could never be applied to a royal."

"You were rude and out of place," Mercerio said and then added in a softer tone, "but sometimes even a royal can be foolish."

Justi picked up a pile of Rocley's clothes and placed them in a worn leather travel bag. He thought of his biological father. When Valego's spirit appeared to him and when Mercerio's father, King Bronte, showed himself as a ghost, they delivered a clear message. They had to be together to complete his gift.

"We should not stay together because of some vague words of prophecy."

"There was nothing vague about our fathers' words," Mercerio said, as if she'd read his thoughts. "They said we had to meet and work together. These are not words to be dismissed."

"That could simply mean we had to unite to save the Zellish people from the barbarians."

"War is over, yet our gifts persist. Saving us from the robbers shows your gift has not vanished."

"I suppose," Justi said. "So what is this task you've found for me?"

What Mercerio said convinced Justi once again he didn't understand women. Instead of telling him his task, the queen frowned and said, "Foolish girl? Is that what you think of me?"

"I thought we were finished with that. I already apologized."

"Answer the question."

"I think of you all the time and not as a foolish girl."

Mercerio's hand lifted to her mouth and she studied the plank floor. "Would you say we are close friends?"

"Very close friends." Justi stepped closer to Mercerio.

"We should be, for you have seen more of me than any other man, save the court physician."

Justi turned a color that had nothing to do with the Justice Power. He looked at Mercerio as if she had just stepped from the hot spring. "What I mean is that there is a much better reason why we should be together."

"There is?"

Justi hesitated as if he'd forgotten how to form a sentence. Finally, he muttered, "I love you, Mercerio."

The smile on the queen's face chased all gloom from the room and Mercerio said, "I love you, too."

They kissed. When she pulled away, the queen's eyes were wide. She yanked him back and this time she did the kissing. Finally, Mercerio separated them and straightened her gown.

When his heart slowed, Justi said, "Too bad I am so common. I'm sure there are rules governing who you can love."

"Are you saying you want to marry me?"

Justi frowned. "I am sure that there are even stricter rules about who the Queen of the Zell can wed. I'm sure your mother wants you to marry someone rich and powerful. For political reasons."

Mercerio leaned forward and kissed him again. "As your queen I have the right to choose my consort and my husband. I would choose you, Justi, but only if that is your wish."

"But what about your mother?"

"I'll handle my mother," Mercerio said. "But you must tell me your feelings in this matter, for I cannot read minds."

Not so sure of the mind reading, Justi said, "I love you, Mercerio, and would gladly be your husband if you would have me."

Mercerio's eyes moistened as she studied Justi. She flew into Justi's arms and kissed him. He encompassed her body with his arms. Before the kiss morphed into something more intimate, they heard voices and footsteps. Justi went to the window. "Visitors," Justi said. "Demon curse. I guess this is not a good time for proposals."

"It has been a perfect time," Mercerio said.

18
Wedding

A gust of chilly air brought in leaves along with Goren and Meligo when Justi opened the door. Goren, the seer from Justi's hometown, seemed oblivious to the invasion of nature, but his student Meligo grabbed a broom. Meligo, a young man with dark hair that burst from his scalp and flopped to his shoulders, had organized the Zellingon library and updated the catalog while Goren taught him the scope and meaning of prophecy. Goren seemed impressed by the boy's insights. Now Meligo, the budding scholar, swept leaves out the door.

Goren in a white hooded robe puffed himself up and said, "Sorry for the intrusion, Highness, but we have made a discovery."

"How did you find me?" Mercerio asked.

Meligo answered as he replaced the broom. "Surely you must know the queen is protected at all times," Meligo chirped, replacing the broom. "I only had to ask the guards where you were."

Mercerio frowned. "I thought I'd outwitted them. What is this discovery, Goren?"

"An ancient scroll has been discovered in the palace library. The Tantrocans largely left that room alone. Only a few of the items had been examined, most likely by Aduk, the high priest."

"He's the one who questioned me in Fathom," Justi said.

Goren nodded.

"The scroll, Goren?" Mercerio prompted.

"Yes, well the scroll—Meligo found it—speaks of a Child of Darkness. He or she will arise after the Child of Light. That being you, Justi."

"Both of you," Meligo added, bowing to Mercerio.

"How does this affect us, Goren," Mercerio asked.

"It implies that the battle between the forces of Li and those of Dar is not over."

"I think we know that," Mercerio said.

"Specifically, it means the Tantrocans will view their defeat as but a setback in the war," Goren said. "They can rebuild and return. If they have a Child of Darkness with powers comparable to Justi's, things may not go as well for us."

"When is this dark child supposed to arise?" Justi asked.

Goren drew a big breath. "The ancient document says only he will come after you. Could be almost your age."

"Or not yet born," Justi argued.

"Thank you for this, Goren," Mercerio added. "It would help to have another document to elaborate on this lone text. Maybe your friend, Rakur, could help. Aren't ancient texts his hobby?"

Goren sighed. "He's disappeared. Left without a word."

Not long after the recapture of Zellingon and the crowning of Mercerio, the Zellish had another occasion to celebrate. Their queen took a husband, and her happiness radiated to all her subjects.

The marriage, an elaborate ceremony in the great temple of Zellingon, was witnessed by friends and subjects alike, including the Queen Mother. Justi's parents and Goren returned from Ortun for the event. Even Rakur, the seedy seer of a coastal village near Ortun, reappeared, arriving just in time to be the cause of the one glitch in the proceedings. His dog Foot skipped past the guards and charged down the center aisle of the temple, a guard in pursuit. Foot darted onto the raised platform where the wedding party stood. And surveyed the frozen group. He spied someone he knew and leaped into Justi's arms, planting a kiss. Rakur grabbed the overenthusiastic animal and took him off, leaving the groom's wedding garb wrinkled.

"Animals seem to love you," Mercerio said as the dog was led away.

"It has to do with my healing power. They seem to sense it. Foot is still thanking me for fixing his lame leg."

Mercerio huffed and turned back to the priest. "We can proceed."

The high priest finished the ceremony and pronounced the pair man and wife. Trumpet blasts filled the temple. Great cheers erupted. The queen mother congratulated her daughter and new son-in-law and said she hoped this would ensure the kingdom's future. A line of guests offered similar sentiments. At the end of the temple ceremony, the crowd went into the castle for a great party. Wine and new beer flowed freely. Platters of roasted grazebeast, smoked venison, and baked fowl accompanied cheeses and early vegetables imported from the southern regions. Music and dance followed. Justi had been tutored by a court attendant on how to dance. He became competent and spent much time dancing with his wife and then a cluster of older women—wives of noblemen—he met for the first time. He was sure they took his measure from both his words and dance steps.

Justi removed his bride's garments and they kissed. "I have thought of this for a long time, Mercerio. You are the most beautiful thing I have ever seen."

"Even more beautiful than Provani?"

"I was so filled with fermented honey that I have no memory. But I will remember you and these moments." Justi distracted the queen with a kiss and kept her distracted as their union was sealed. The couple slept, woke, made love, talked about nothing, and slept again.

Mercerio woke first with a new inquiry. "I wonder if I shall become pregnant."

Justi sat up, his hands scrunching the blanket, pulling it from Mercerio. "Perhaps. It is in Li's power now, but the possibility worries me."

"Why?"

"It is hard to explain. But I worry what any child might face, given a father who wields a killing power and a mother who has other powers. What if he inherits some distorted mix of the two? As a prince he would have dominion over people, and that would make it more difficult."

"We cannot know such things. And I should not be worrying on our wedding night. Now lie back down and hold me.

Justi did as he was told and was about to sleep again when the queen said, "What if Provani became pregnant?"

Justi's lidded eyes snapped open. He did not speak for a full minute until he sputtered, "You saw her in Fathom. She wasn't with child."

"She could have been. It would have been early, only weeks, right?

Another long silence. "Such women do not get pregnant."

"Really? How do you know?"

"Men know."

Mercerio took her hand from Justi's thigh and placed it on her belly. She closed her eyes and seemed to be trying to hear a far-off wind. She heard something, perhaps a flutter of owl wings in the rear garden or of bat wings near the roof. "I wonder what became of Provani."

The sound of breathing was her answer. Other than that, only silence came from her husband. Justi lay face down, fast asleep.

19
Zellish Births

During her pregnancy Credo continued to serve as a healer, and her mysterious power to diagnose and treat seemed to grow stronger as her pregnancy progressed. Her diagnoses became more accurate, her remedies more focused, and her insight into ailments clearer. With a sharper mind, she caused the blood to flow, to cleanse, to heal.

A young patient, frail and underweight and prone to every contagion that entered the village, had seen more than her share of Credo's healing. She'd been treated for cough and fever at the beginning of the healer's pregnancy and barely responded. Months later, at the time Credo felt her child's first movement, the girl suffered a repeat affliction and had difficulty breathing. Credo was able to detect and correct a sluggish response of blood cells to the invaders that attacked the patient. She enabled the cells to seek out and destroy the invaders. Within a day the girl lost her bluish hue and her fever. The patient became stronger, ate better, and stayed well.

The different response of her patient at two times planted a notion in Credo's head: her powers were magnified by her yet-to-be-born child. Her abilities grew along with the baby. Did this mean her unborn child was in some way gifted?

Gifted or not, the child took its time arriving. Credo's due date came and went, and she waddled around for an additional week before the birth process began. Marek would have nothing to do with the notion of going it alone and had a midwife standing by throughout the long labor. After a night without sleep, Credo gave birth to a healthy girl whose lusty cry woke a nearby rooster and a neighboring dog. A warm breast quieted the child, who then allowed her mother to sleep for an hour or so. When it was time to nurse again, Marek was there for diapering, burping, and cleanup.

"What will you name this girl?" Marek asked.

Credo did not respond at once but stared into her daughter's large black eyes. Her face was narrow with a small nose and lips. Her hair, just a layer of fuzz now, would be black. She will be beautiful, Credo thought. As if in agreement, the child stretched her fingers.

"I will name her Breel, after my mother." Credo had inherited her abilities from her mother, a woman with remarkable healing skills. If Credo's child helped her heal even before birth, she merited her grandmother's name.

From the start Breel watched everything around her. Serene, she soon found ways to tell her mother and Marek what she wanted and was content to observe as they tended to her needs. She smiled, full of contemplation.

One afternoon months later as they discussed whether Breel showed any of her father Panthis' features, Marek remarked, "She seems to know what we are saying."

"Far too soon for that. Just likes the sound of our voices."

The next year Marek repeated her comment with a slight modification as Breel was acquiring her first words. This time Credo was not so dismissive. "Perhaps. More than once Breel has reacted as if she gleaned what I was about to say. Surely that is my imagination."

When Breel progressed to using full sentences, Credo recalled her thought about Breel's mind-reading. The child was rejecting some food that Credo insisted she eat before she received a treat. Finally, Breel said, "I see how your mind works."

"What do you mean?" Credo asked.

"You think this green stuff will taste better if I think of the cake. You're wrong. The green stuff is still yucky. I don't just pretend to hate it so I can be in control. You don't like it either. You wish Marek would stop making it."

Credo's eyes grew large, for these were her thoughts. Was Breel just clever—too clever—or lucky, or did she have some gift of clairvoyance? Perhaps from Panthis?

Mercerio had been Queen of the Zell for less than a year when she went into labor on a late summer day. The court physician checked her status and announced that everything was normal. Royal midwives scurried about for the first few hours, but when it became evident that nothing was amiss and that the labor would proceed at the slow pace of a first child, things quieted both inside and outside the palace. The waiting began.

Melsin, the queen mother, immediately dispatched a messenger to find Justi and Rocley. They had chosen this time to go hunting, sure that Mercerio was weeks from giving birth. At Mercerio's insistence Justi had provided precise information about where he would be. The messenger found them, and the pair returned to Zellingon with haste, arriving well before there had been much progress in producing the royal heir.

"You shouldn't have gone off," Mercerio said.

"The physician said your time wasn't—"

"What does he know?"

Justi squeezed his wife's hand. "The important thing is that I am here with you. We will share this blessing together."

"If you really loved me, you would have stayed here."

"I do love you."

"I was about to send the entire guard after you," Mercerio panted with a sheen of sweat on her forehead.

Justi wiped her face with a cool cloth. "The scout was sufficient. He knew exactly where we were hunting. You made very sure of that before I left."

Mercerio groaned through a contraction.

Perhaps as a distraction, Justi said, "To tell the truth, I suspected something was happening when we were screeched at several times by that hawk who seems to live forever."

"The hawk? What are you babbling about?"

That took Justi by surprise, but he suspected Mercerio wasn't really hearing what he said, for they'd often spoken of his mysterious hawk. As the queen lay back with her eyes closed, he said, "There can be no doubt that Goren's interpretation is correct. The Ortun seer has always insisted that the bird is a guardian of some sort, surely sent by Li because I hold the Gift of Justice."

"Don't puff yourself up so. You only have part of it." Mercerio screamed at a strong contraction.

A flurry of activity ensued with the return of midwives who had been waiting outside the royal bedchamber. The chief nurse examined the patient. "Summon the physician," she said.

Justi retreated from the royal bed chamber into the hallway where he began pacing.

A baby boy was delivered as the sun set. The child had Mercerio's black hair and dark eyes. The queen's labor was not done, however, and minutes later she delivered the second child, a girl with Justi's blond hair and blue eyes. The physician pronounced both children healthy, but to Mercerio's mind, spent too much time examining her son.

"What is wrong? Why do you poke at him so?" the queen asked as she held her daughter, who'd not received so much attention.

The silver-haired doctor handed the boy to his mother and smiled. "Nothing is wrong, but his right hand seems stiffer than his left. That may correct itself over time."

Mercerio touched her son's hands. The left one almost managed to grasp her finger, but the right did not try. Her daughter was able to wrap both hands equally well about an offered finger.

"Do not worry, your majesty," the physician said. "I will monitor the prince as he grows." The doctor gave instructions to the nurse and left.

Mercerio summoned her husband.

Justi kissed Mercerio and examined his new children. The queen told him to hold his daughter, which he did with some reluctance and great joy. The girl watched him with wide eyes and stretched as if searching for something. When he returned the princess to her mother, Mercerio handed him his son, who seemed quieter.

Justi returned the prince and said, "I know that look, Mercerio. You are worried. What is wrong?"

"There may be a problem with his right hand," Mercerio said.

"What?"

"Some stiffness. But the physician claims it may pass as he gets older."

Justi considered his wife and the child. He examined his own right hand, the one from which issued the Justice Fire. It too felt a bit stiff, probably due to grasping a bow string on the hunting trip. He could not remember it being any different when he was younger. Perhaps the difference in the infant's hand indicated he'd inherited the gift. Then Goren's words about the Child of Darkness who would come after the Child of Light filled his mind. The prophecy said the Child of Darkness would come *after.* That could mean the next generation. What if his son had inherited the gift, but it was perverted, evil? He dared not voice such an idea to Mercerio.

"No need to worry," he said a bit grimly. "His hand may strengthen in time. We must be patient. The more important thing, at least according to your mother, is to provide him and his sister names. She is anxious to announce it to the crowds that have gathered."

"I am content with what we have already decided. I see nothing to change it. We shall call him Meru, meaning wise."

"What of the princess? Shall she be referred to as the girl?" Justi asked, grinning.

Mercerio smiled at the light-haired child who seemed about to cry. "We did come up with a girl's name even though you were convinced that your child would be a boy. This is Princess Danilla."

With that pronouncement, Danilla let out a strong cry that woke her brother. Meru echoed his sister in a weaker voice, and Mercerio felt a strange sensation. The nurse came close and told the queen it was time for feeding. Justi kissed Mercerio and backed away as his children drank their first meal.

As the months went by, the physician encouraged Mercerio to give the prince opportunities to use the hand. Danilla needed no such prompting. She was the first to roll over, first to crawl, first to walk. Her hands were in everything. She decided which toys were whose and was ready to enforce her decision with a poke at her brother. But she never did. A toy might have to be removed from Meru's grasp, but it was done gently, almost apologetically. By the time both children were walking, Danilla was always the leader, and Meru seemed content to follow. Mercerio and Justi came to see their children as the doer and the thinker.

20
Tantrocan Births

Tantrocan spies kept King Brokul informed of events in Zellingon. News of Mercerio's coronation reignited his anger over losing control of the Kingdom of the Zell, and he again blamed his priest Aduk and military leaders for the defeat that expelled them from the land they'd occupied for years. From his chamber he gazed glumly to the beach below where frothy waves pounded the sand. Icy winds further darkened the king's foul mood.

Aduk should have dealt with the Child of Light predicted in his opaque ancient texts. The man could have killed the one called Justi when he had him in Fathom. That would have cleared the way for a second invasion. The priest's notion of harnessing the boy's power and using it against the Zellish was folly.

Brokul understood his forces stood little chance against Justi. Their reign in the Zell ended when the child matured enough to use his power. His existence was their bane, thwarting a second invasion. In his heart, the answer was obvious. Justi had to die.

Cantor, Brokul's consort, distracted him from sour thoughts about affairs of state. At least for a time. The dark-haired, mysterious woman with large, obsidian eyes had been Brokul's companion for years and continued to kindle his lust.

Cantor believed sleeping with the Tantrocan monarch solidified their relationship. When she was being honest, she enjoyed the swift roughness of the sex. There were many ways to control a man, she thought, and this was one of the most effective. Let a man think he was directing things, and he was likely to do what she wanted.

A month after one of their more enthusiastic encounters, Cantor realized she was pregnant. Her pregnancy surprised her, for she had concluded that Brokul was unable to generate a child. The timing meant that the child could only be the king's. As she debated ending her pregnancy, Brokul discovered her condition, not something he was perceptive enough to detect on his own. That left either Aduk or one of her maids who told Brokul.

"It is about time you produced a child," he said. "Too long have I suspected you were barren and would have to be replaced."

Chilled, Cantor forced herself to mimic the king's enthusiasm. "I am also pleased, my lord." She thanked Dar she was with child, feeling stupid to believe that she could go on as the king's plaything. If Brokul had not impregnated her, she would have had to bed a partner who resembled the king. Without a child, she would be replaced, probably after an unexplained death.

"You will remain close until the child is delivered," Brokul said. "Pray to Dar it is a boy."

Cantor spent nine months under guard. There was no opportunity for amusing assignations. Her sexual appetites found satisfaction in the rutting of the king until her size became the only thing that concerned her.

Brokul's prayer to Dar that there be a boy child was answered. In fact, Cantor gave birth to twins, a boy named Brosun after his father and a girl named Ranera after Cantor's gypsy aunt. Scholars speculated whether birth of twins for both Queen Mercerio and Cantor was a sign—perhaps Li and Dar were manipulating things to serve their own ends.

As his offspring grew, Brokul still regretted losing the fruits of the warmer lands, including the slaves and sacrificial victims, and he remained fascinated by the Zellish use of unnatural power. He reread reports of the killing flame Justi used against Tantrocan soldiers. Those who died immediately were fortunate. Those who survived the flame lived burned and maimed. Why would Dar permit this to happen? he wondered. These thoughts perturbed Brokul even as he watched his son Brosun grow, but over time he accepted reality. The older he became, the more he relished his comfort and realized that waging war was not a path to comfort.

Ranera and Brosun grew up in the harsh Tantroc environment. Children are more tolerant of cold and ice, but one winter after months of snow, after they learned the history of when the Tantrocans controlled the rich, warmer region to the south, the twins decided the Tantrocans should have those treasures again. It was their destiny.

From the time he was five, Brosun fell under the influence of Caldir, the acolyte to Aduk, who served as teacher of the king's children. Caldir saw himself as the high priest one day and perceived that Brosun could make that happen. The teacher encouraged his student to think of himself as king. When the prince developed the notion that he was a mystic like his mother, Caldir joined in the fantasy, knowing full well that the manipulator Cantor had no such talent. Brosun convinced himself that he could communicate with the spirits who serve Dar, and Caldir suggested that Dar wanted a new high priest. Who else would Brosun pick than his apparent friend and teacher?

Caldir's lessons prepared Prince Brosun to replace his father. By the time the prince was ten and three years of age, he was burlier than his burly father. Brosun embraced the notion that his people had the right and destiny to reconquer the south. Caldir encouraged that thinking.

Tantrocan kings ruled for life. As long as King Brokul remained alive, Brosun was fated to be prince, the one who waited. Caldir chose to instruct Prince Brosun with a history lesson on certain kings of Tantroc. The lesson unfolded in a small room with a view of the gray rocks that descended to the shore, a bleak scene well suited to tales of regicide. Caldir paced the plank flooring and told of cases in which a son was suspected of killing the reigning king.

"After the taster sampled the meat pie, the prince added the herbal mix as he passed the plate to his father," Caldir said in a matter-of-fact voice. "The king argued with his adviser and did not notice. No one noticed. Three hours later, the king was dead, and the prince assumed the throne."

Brosun's eyes widened as the tale unfolded.

"Regicide is what it's called," Caldir said. "The son then becomes king." He related tales of a hired assassin, a fall from a parapet, and a stabbing. Brosun was fascinated. Caldir ended the lesson by saying, "There have been many cases where a prince assisted Dar in providing us with a new and vibrant king."

"Were these murderous princes not punished for their deeds?" asked Brosun, eyes narrowed.

"Sadly, they were not." Caldir suppressed a smile.

Ranera's blue eyes, blond hair, and athletic figure gave her a northern beauty, and her personality made her a charmer. Unlike her brother, she did not worry about the spirits and stayed grounded. Her mother informed her she would not be ruler, unless her brother died early, but she could wield power either in Tantroc or another kingdom if she knew how to act. Cantor taught her by example to be an opportunist.

Ranera fantasized about a more comfortable life across the Tantric Gulf. She grew up convinced that the people of the Zell were her enemies who had only driven out the Tantrocans by what she saw as trickery. She dreamed of the day she and Brosun would again occupy Zellingon.

Caldir taught the princess, feeding her resentment of the tradition that made her twin brother the king. "I understand your wanting power. That is natural. Keep in mind that there might be a chance to rule in a neighboring kingdom."

When Ranera became a ten and five, a new lust for something besides power emerged, namely a love of the flesh, something her mother taught her without trying. Ranera's mother had little to do with the twins' upbringing after they reached five. Teachers took over their care, leaving Cantor with abundant time to resume her hobby of bedding an assortment of men. This continued for years as the princess and prince grew into their second decade. Ranera took to spying when Cantor had a guest and observed her mother's techniques for controlling men and pleasing herself in the process. Once she watched how a large military man was played by Cantor. He seemed very willing to do whatever her mother demanded. That amazed Ranera who had grown increasingly interested in the young men in the king's court. They never ignored her but did not always behave as she wanted. Now she knew that variety meant excitement and men were different. These episodes prepared the princess for womanhood. She found herself assessing palace boys in a new way, checking their physical builds, their muscles, their actions and what that might promise for the part she could not see.

She had inherited Cantor's hobby of luring boys first, and later men, to her bed. Ranera used Caldir to suggest and arrange for visitors to her bedchamber. The priest was happy to serve the princess, for he had in mind how she might be used to further his plan for Tantrocan conquest.

PART III
Dar's Breath

Events unfold that presage renewal of the great conflict.

21
Childhoods

At the lake where village kids swam, Justik found three boys his age. They ignored him. When Justik didn't take the hint, Kamo, the largest boy, challenged, "Who invited you?"

Bigger than Justik with arm and shoulder muscles honed by shearing sheep and hauling hay, Kamo annoyed Justik. "I invited myself."

"We don't want you here," Kamo said.

Justik scanned the mostly vegetated shoreline, and then glared at Kamo. "I don't think so," he said. "I'm staying and there's nothing you can do about it."

"Maybe there is," Kamo said and moved closer. "You'd better run or that pretty face of yours will get messed up." Kamo clenched his big fists.

The pair circled, getting ready to exchange blows. The witnesses shouted insults and encouragement. The slap of water on the shore accompanied the dance. When a goose landed noisily, Kamo lunged and punched. Justik stepped to the side and the blow missed. Justik caught the boy with a glancing blow to the ear. Kamo stumbled back. a hand on his reddening ear, his face contorted by the sudden pain.

"You're a bastard," Kamo said. "What did you put on my ear? It burns."

Justik had to admit his hand felt warm. "You're a sissy. You act like your father's pig."

"You don't even look like your father," Kamo yelled. "Bastard."

Justik knew he was different from his father but wasn't sure what that had to do with being a bastard.

"Irend is ruddy, but you're as pale as a baby's ass." With that remark, Kamo thrust his boot-covered foot out and pounded Justik's thigh.

Justik grunted with the pain and fell. As Kamo delivered the next kick, Justik rolled away and scrambled up. He charged and landed a rib punch. "So what," he said. "Your face is piggish, and your father looks like a horse."

Kamo reddened. "Irend has brown eyes, and your mother's are green. Yours are sky-blue. Neither Irend nor Provani have your stupid yellow hair. Know what that means, pretty boy?"

Finally, Justik began to understand what Kamo was talking about. He wasn't sure if the color of his parents' eyes and hair meant he couldn't be Irend's child, but he didn't want to hear any more. Kamo, however, had the last insult already out of his mouth.

"Your mother is a whore," Kamo said, "and you're her bastard son."

Justik, swinging at a frenzied pace, pounded Kamo, at last landing a punch on the larger boy's face. Blood spurted, and Kamo ran off whimpering and clutching his nose. His friends went with him.

Justik had time to think of what he'd learned as he walked back from the lake. He had to admit that, not only didn't he resemble Irend, he didn't feel like Irend's son. Resentment of Kamo and his friends grew until he hated Kamo for saying it, his father for lying, and finally his mother for hiding the truth.

He found his mother in the kitchen adding carrots to a stewpot. He marched in, slapped the table, and said, "You lied to me. Who is my father?"

"Irend has always been your father," Provani answered mildly without turning from the stove.

"I don't mean who is your husband, the man who has always played father to me. I want to know who my real father is."

"Why are you asking this now?" Provani said to her red-faced son.

"Because I just figured it out. I'm not like Irend. I have blue eyes and neither of you have that color. I have the right to know who my real father is."

Provani did not answer immediately. After a moment's thought, she said, "Your real father was a good and powerful man. But I cannot give you his name."

"Why not? I should know who my father was and what he is like. Is he dead?"

"We met in Abantazar, and he is very much alive. But you don't need his name."

"I want it. Why can't I know?"

"Because it would be dangerous for you to have that information. There are some who might harm you if they knew. Understand that what you don't know can't be taken from you." Provani crossed her arms and thinned her lips.

Justik kicked at a kitchen chair and stomped from the room. He had no idea what his mother was talking about.

Justik's power emerged fully when he reached the age of ten and seven. That's when he could no longer contain his curiosity about the opposite sex. He had to explore, whether the girl was willing or not. One girl had caught his eye, and he could see no reason why he should not see her blossomed body. He knew what went on between men and women and wanted to explore.

The girl, of course, did not see it that way, although she was attracted to the village rebel precisely because he had such a reputation. Late on a warm day, Justik lured the buxom girl into the walled garden behind his house. He started with kissing, which the girl tolerated, maybe even liked. That went on for a while as the sun set. As it grew dark, Justik's excitement grew, and he maneuvered them onto the ground, covering her leg with his own, and reached into her loose white top.

"Stop it. Don't," she said in too-loud a voice and struggled to get away. "Leave me be."

"I want to see you and feel. Don't pretend you haven't done this before," Justik said in a husky voice.

"I haven't. Let me go." The girl tried to cover herself, but Justik was stronger.

With one hand over her mouth, his other roamed over her body, pushing aside garments or ripping them in his quest to see and feel. As his prey squirmed and tried to breathe, Justik touched first breasts and then inside undergarments. The girl managed to get free, scrambled to her feet and headed to the courtyard gate. Justik caught her, punched, and slammed her against the wooden barrier.

"We can do it this way instead of on the ground," he said, and slapped her.

The girl screamed, and Provani, who'd just returned, heard the cry. She called from beyond the closed wooden gate. Justik, who wasn't finished, muttered a curse and punched his victim. He threw the stunned, half-naked girl over his shoulder and ran through the house and away. Darkness had left the street deserted, and Justik had no trouble carrying the unresisting girl to the reeds near the lake.

Once they were hidden, he proceeded to remove the tunic from the dazed girl and spent some time touching her breasts. The girl seemed only vaguely aware of what was happening, but when he started to lift her skirt, she recovered enough to strike her assailant. The blow caught Justik on the cheek, her nails drawing blood, and that caused him to transform from a lusting predator to something more.

The power he'd sensed in hitting Kamo appeared in full. His hand heated and his yellow hair brightened. When he shoved the girl away, a light beam erupted and burned into her chest. A scream caught in her throat, and in a second, she was dead. Justik backed away stunned at what happened. He had not wanted to kill this girl, but she had resisted, even hurt him. She deserved what she got. He felt no sympathy.

Justik jumped when an owl hooted. But he was alone. The half-naked corpse was the turning point, something he could not cover up, a crime not to be excused. He realized his reputation meant he would be accused, judged, and punished.

He dumped the body into the bushes and headed back home. It was time to flee. He gathered a few things, including the purse his father kept hidden in an old boot, and began his journey under moonlight. He knew where he had to go.

Far north of Vok Boorl in Pale, Credo's daughter Breel had grown tall with an elegant bearing and sure and measured actions. She developed the kind of beauty that caused people to linger, as if they were trying to understand what attracted them. It may have been the ready smile or the large, dark eyes that seemed to glow, penetrate, and perceive. Breel was striking and memorable.

She had inherited her mother's power of healing, but it was not the same. Credo could correct any imbalance in body fluids and strengthen defenses against unseen invaders. Her skill saved Mercerio.

Breel's talent was diagnosis and treatment of mental problems, a power that came to light with a patient Credo could not cure. A village girl refused to leave her house, expressing great and irrational fear at being outdoors. Credo could find nothing wrong with the girl, and Breel took to visiting her, just to talk, often holding hands. As they spoke, the girl became calmer about the prospect of leaving the house. Finally, one warm day when the sky was clear and the wind but a gentle breeze, Breel said, "You must leave the cabin that has become your prison. The golden day calls you. I will help."

Breel led her to the door, encouraging, describing again how safe it was, how there was nothing in Pale that could harm her. Insisting Breel stay at her side and clearly nervous, the girl seemed ready to bolt. When the healer took her hand, however, something remarkable happened. Breel felt the girl's fear and was able to take it into her own mind. At the same time, she changed how the girl thought. Bit by bit, the girl calmed.

"The trees are beautiful," the girl said. "They seem peaceful, welcoming."

By the time they returned to the house, the girl was relaxed and joyful. She said she would walk by herself the next day to visit Breel. And she did.

Perhaps that same power gave Breel a special connection to the dog she adopted. The black animal, clearly young, arrived at Credo's house hungry, thirsty, and timid. Wary, the dog eyed Breel, as if she were the one he'd been seeking.

"Mother, we must adopt this poor animal," Breel said.

Credo examined the visitor. "It sems fed. Somehow it has found food, judging by its coat. But it hardly seems suitable as a pet. It cringes whenever anyone gets near it and only eats when we move away. Of what use would such an animal ever be?"

"I think there is a reason he is here," Breel said, not knowing the dog was the son of the wild dog that had saved Breel's father Panthis from a hoarwolf. "He's frightened, but that will pass." She squinted and circled the dog. "It will take work, but Bib may become my protector."

"Bib?"

"We'll call him Bib because he has a white patch on his chest."

The dog remained skittish and avoided human contact. Only by slow movements and patience did Breel eventually get close enough to lay a hand on his back. The animal whined. In ten minutes of petting and talking, Breel entered the creature's head, sensing the panic there. Her gift took the fear into herself, and the dog visibly relaxed. When the mysterious process ended, Bib was transformed. He became what a guardian should be: alert and protective. The puppy in him made him bold and exploring.

Bib grew to be a credible guardian, one whose mere presence would keep village boys distant unless approved by Breel. Standing waist high next to Breel, the dog followed her everywhere. When Breel touched Bib, she sensed the dog's mind and was amazed how intelligent a canine could be. He soon responded to both voice commands and gestures.

As Breel traveled with her mother to northern villages, her reputation as a healer of the mind grew. She fixed cases of anguish even after traumatic events like the loss of a child. A depressed farmer who'd lost his wife found peace and strength after talking to Breel and feeling her touch. One young boy was a fanatical collector of pebbles, filling his room with the small rocks, which had to be stored in precise arrangements or he panicked. Breel was able to change his thinking and behavior so that he not only stopped adding to his collection but began to dispose of it. She could even feel the pain of animals and told several owners of beloved dogs that it was time to let them go. Not everyone appreciated that advice, but many agreed.

Bib came in handy when Breel faced her greatest challenge as a mental healer: the hermit possessed by demons. This was the diagnosis of his neighbors who shunned him. They blamed demons for the man's slovenly appearance, his unkempt beard and hair, his emaciated appearance, and unpredictable eruptions of rage. The hermit roamed the village at night, howling until men drove him off with clubs and threats. Breel approached this sorry victim with care and Bib accompanied her. The man had to be coaxed to open his door and at first refused Breel entry. Until Breel spoke in a soothing tone. Her words probably mattered little to the hermit, who backed into his shack and sank onto a pile of rugs. Bib woofed as gently as his mistress spoke, and together, they approached the man. Not sure what she would feel, Breel put her hands on the dirty cheeks.

"No," shrieked the man and batted Breel away.

Bib growled and the man covered his head with his hands. Breel said soothing words and grasped the man's arms, feeling a swirl of fear and chaos, a fevered brain. Breel maintained contact, willing calm and absence of pain. Slowly the man's tension eased, his cheeks softened, his eyes lost their fevered brightness. A croak became a sigh, and the man sank onto the rugs. He slept.

When Breel left the man was awake again, coherent, and obviously embarrassed at the mess in which he lived. Over the next few days, he changed profoundly, became normal. Eventually he was accepted as such.

Breel's reputation as a mental physician was firmly in place.

Prince Meru avoided childhood sports and preferred reading, which he learned to do at an early age. He consumed manuscripts on every topic from nature to religion to history. Tales of the Tantrocan invasion intrigued him, especially ones that foretold the restoration of the Kingdom of the Zell aided by the god Li himself, using a great power entrusted to Justi, Meru's father. This assertion seemed odd to the prince, for he had never seen his father use any power. In fact, Justi avoided confrontations and served the queen by mediating conflict. But the history texts claimed he'd turned the tide of battle. Possibly exaggerated, Meru thought, especially the story claiming his father sent killing fire from his right hand.

When the prince began his lessons in swordplay, he had to use his left hand, for he lacked strength in his right. It seemed weaker than ever. The condition of the crown prince became known among the populace, and he earned the nickname, The Withered Prince.

Princess Danilla had no concerns about how her body worked. She was healthy and confident, fond of dragging her brother from his studies for adventures and exploration. It was on one outing that she gained a companion.

On a fall day the prince and princess were in the woods west of Zellingon. It was a patch of forest patrolled regularly by Zellish guards, so was considered a safe place for the royals to roam. Danilla's target was the lake in the middle of the forest. They followed a narrow path bordered by thick bushes that curtained the trees left and right.

"Why do you want a turtle?" Meru queried, ducking branches in the shadowed expanse.

"I want to put it in the castle pond."

"That's stupid. It would be happier here."

"You don't know that. There could be predators out here."

"Like what?"

"Like wild dogs. Maybe a wolf."

The trail opened on the lakeshore. Sunbeams bounced off the placid dark water as Danilla signaled they should stop and be quiet. She scanned the pond edges without seeing her quarry. Meru had just suggested they give up when a twig snapped in the trees behind them. The twins turned. From the thicket came one of the creatures Danilla imagined could threaten her turtle. The wolf stared at the humans, growled, and bared sharp fangs.

The sudden danger immobilized the children, but an observer would have noticed a change in both. Meru seemed to turn pale green and a haze rendered him less distinct. Danilla seemed brighter, even a bit yellow. The wolf stepped forward as a scream came from above. A diving hawk, talons extended, scraped the canine head. The wolf snapped at the hawk and missed, probably thinking appetizer. The bird flew to a branch and screamed. The wolf bristled and glared at Danilla and Meru, who backstepped into a rhododendron.

"I can throw the box at him," Danilla whispered.

Meru pushed his sister behind, offering himself as the meal to satisfy the predator. When the wolf took another step forward, the hawk dove again and raked the wolf 's head with talons. Something strange occurred. Prince Meru lifted his hands, palms outward, and expanded his chest. He also turned a bit greenish, and an azure mist billowed from his hands. The mist enveloped the wolf. The animal sniffed and acted confused. It stood taller, then crouched down. It licked its lips and squinted. Then the eyes closed.

"We should leave," Danilla urged, pulling her brother's tunic.

When the prince and princess took a quiet step to the side, the wolf's eyes snapped open. Although the green mist remained a cloud over the beast, it could see its prey clearly. But it did not act as if Meru and Danilla were prey. The wolf yawned and shook its head. It stood, stretched, and turned toward the lake.

"What happened?" Danilla asked. "That green mist. It came from you. What was it?"

"I don't know. I just raised my hands to block the wolf."

"Well, the green stuff did something. It seemed to put the wolf to sleep and then change his mind about eating us. We better ask someone."

"Or we should keep quiet about it and how you dragged me out here to turtle hunt. We are done, right?

We must leave the forest and hope we meet no other creatures."

*****

As a hawk, I could watch over and warn Justi's children, *but I needed another form to protect them from such dangers as wolves. The forest provided a solution. Near the lake a feline slept in a patch of sunshine. It was a large, five times the size of its barn-dwelling relatives, a creature humans called a lynx. I didn't relish it, but I knew what I had to do. I abandoned the now-comfortable hawk and thrust my spirit into the dozing cat. The bird shuddered and flew off, and the cat woke with a twitch and spun around with giant eyes. It took me a moment to master control of the beast, and then I trotted after the prince and princess.*

*****

Meru stopped. "The wolf would have eaten us," Meru hissed. "And so will the cat."

"It does not seem interested in eating us," Danilla soothed.

"How can you tell?"

"By the eyes. And it is sitting and licking its paw."

"Maybe it is washing before eating."

The cat finished the licking and approached the motionless prince and princess. When it reached Danilla, it sat close enough for Danilla to reach out and touch. She did and the animal closed it eyes. More touching and a loud purr began. Danilla forgot about her turtle and settled for a cat.

The children started back toward the town wall and the cat followed. Meru seemed alarmed, but Danilla was content to go directly back to her secret exit through the town wall. Once back in the palace, Danilla rewarded her protector with a chunk of left-over deer roast, and with that gesture, the cat became a royal pet.

"I will call you Lyra," Danilla said.

Lyra was beautiful, made striking by oversized paws and a golden-brown coat marked by spots and a white belly. Her broad head featured long whiskers and pointed ears tipped in black. The cat learned to abide all members of the royal household, but always wanted to be close to Meru and Danilla. She seemed partial to Danilla and slept in her room.

* * * * *

I decided to remain in the form of the cat. *It gave me added ability to protect the children of Justi and opened the castle interior as my domain. It took time to adjust to a new species, and I missed the ability to fly, but if necessary, I could find another bird to inhabit. Having regular food without having to hunt meant I was always near my charges.*

* * * * *

Meru sat in the royal garden wearing a glum expression. The warm day encouraged the birds to visit a feeder in waves, new arrivals pushing off those who'd had their chance. Not far from Meru, Lyra hid under a bush and watched the feathered show. She also watched Meru.

Queen Mercerio arrived, causing Lyra to lift an eyelid. "What seems to be bothering you?" she asked her son.

It took a moment before she got an answer. "I wish I had two strong hands. I wish people didn't treat me as if I might break. I wish I had power like my father."

"Li gives each of us the power we need to play our role. You have a good heart, and that is what you need to one day be king."

"But the teacher says father could fight. Isn't that something a king needs?"

Mercerio considered how best to answer her son. "We have been blessed by almost two decades of peace. A king must now keep the peace between disgruntled lords. If there is fighting to be done, you will have an army. A king should not be caught in battle. That is what killed your grandfather King Bronte."

Meru sighed, obviously not satisfied. "Did you ever see father use his power?"

"I did several times. I was always fearful, for a flame capable of killing another, even many others, is unnatural. It was a time of great conflict, however, and I have to believe that Li entrusted your father with his gift to protect us."

"I have heard how you escaped from Fathom and how the Justice Power cleared the way. Did father ever use his power after that?"

"Once."

"When? Why?"

Mercerio remembered the campsite attack but wasn't sure how much to reveal to her son. "It is time for dinner and the cook likes to serve when the food is fresh from the oven. Go find your father. I will consider answering your question when we have more time, and you can understand the circumstances that made it necessary."

Meru sighed again and headed inside. Lyra rose, sniffed at Mercerio, and trailed after the prince.

As the prince and cat disappeared, Mercerio wished for a way to get help for her son's hand.

22
Abantazar

Provani said she'd met his father in Abantazar but wouldn't give his name. Justik intended to learn of his mysterious sire, dangerous or not. He followed the little-used route west through dry empty lands, plagued by heat, insects, and hunger. Eating rabbit and squirrel left him unsatisfied and forced him to beg at the occasional farm. Late one day he approached a fenced, isolated house and pushed through the gate. Dogs barked and a young couple emerged from the front door.

The big, muscled farmer loomed a head taller than Justik. "What be your business here, stranger?" the man asked, his hand on the large knife at his belt.

"I must have food and drink," Justik said.

The farmer assessed the visitor as he might a horse. "I suppose we could provide a meal in exchange for work. The barn needs mucking out."

Justik eyed the large structure near the house. He knew what mucking involved and wanted nothing to do with it. "I need to eat first."

"First the barn, then you eat," the man said.

Justik considered his chances of disarming the sour-faced farmer, but the man's size made that too dangerous.

The young wife intervened. She placed a hand on her husband's arm. "We can give him some food. He will have strength if he's fed." She retreated into the house.

The farmer frowned and pointed to a table near the barn. "You can sit there. There's a pump and cup. Your labor will pay for the food."

Justik ate the scant, tasteless food and fought to keep his anger in check. Control was important, especially after killing the girl in Vok Boorl. He remained calm as he raked and shoveled manure and straw and then spread new hay. He laid a bed of straw for himself and was ready to sleep when the farmer arrived.

"It's warm enough to sleep under the stars," the man announced. "I want you off the property."

Justik cursed and stumbled away into blackness. The color of his thoughts matched the night. He felt humiliated, used, and belittled. When he did lie down in a copse, he realized there was a better way to get what he wanted and deserved—if only he could summon the flame. The moon cast enough weak light to give Justik a view of his hand. He willed it to ignite, but nothing happened, then wondered if he could burn only if he were struck.

The answer came the next day when he encountered a young merchant enjoying a midday meal in an isolated clearing. The fellow sat on a log and regarded his visitor with dark, unfriendly eyes beneath thick brows. "You will not have my food, beggar," he said and rose to stand. His hand moved to the sword on his belt. "You are a fool for traveling without provisions."

Justik wanted food, not a lecture. When the merchant drew the sword and threatened to use it, anger enveloped Justik and his face and hands warmed. The merchant flinched, for he saw reddened cheeks and too bright hair. When the man pointed his weapon, Justik raised his fist. The merchant lunged as flame leapt to his sword arm. He gasped, swiping at the burning fabric on his arm, then cursed and swung the blade, slicing the loose tunic. Justik's second lance of flame found the man's chest, leaving the smell of singed cloth and charred flesh.

Justik rationalized that he'd acted in self-defense, but whether warranted or not, the attack did not much upset him. He enjoyed the dead man's food. Now he knew he could call on the flame without being touched. After that, killing became routine when provoked or someone was slow. More than one farmer and his wife welcomed him in for a meal and a bed, and then found themselves his victims. Justik took pleasure threatening his victims with death. Driven to greater and greater depredations, from simple killing, to torture and killing, to mutilations, Justik saw himself as a powerful creature destined for something great.

* * * * *

Although I was busy in Zellingon as the spirit guardian *of Justi and of his children, my ability to monitor Dar's servants revealed their interest in Justik. I watched them touch Justik's mind and stoke his dark impulses, obliterating human mercy. The Miasma touch fed the blackness Justik felt, and the more he gave in to evil, the more control the dark ones gained.*

*****

From Vok Boorl to Abantazar, Justik left a trail of obscenities, dead bodies all marked by holes burned into flesh. Although Abantazar served many merchants and hosted regular caravans, it had no wall. Hot and tired, Justik entered after dark and found the Abantazar Inn, the very place where he had been conceived years before. Men quenching thirsts at end of day occupied a few tables, and a young woman sat alone at another. Justik invited himself to join her.

"I am new to Abantazar, but your beauty makes me feel welcome," Justik said.

"That may be so, stranger, but I am not to be long alone at this table. I await someone." Dark-skinned with braided black hair to her waist, the woman wore a tan, low-cut gown.

"Maybe you need to rethink that. I sit where I like, and your presence makes this the best spot in this miserable place." Justik waved a serving girl close and ordered drinks for both. "Your expected guest is obviously not here. So we will enjoy this time. Maybe you will grow to prefer me. What is your name?"

The woman made a motion to leave, but Justik clamped his hand on her arm. She did not try to rise again, perhaps convinced by the strength in his grip and the stare of his icy eyes.

"Your name?"

A stern voice growled behind him. "You will have no use of her name, fool. Unhand her and find somewhere else to drink." The speaker towered with bulging muscles and scarred forearms. A scar reddened one cheek. Eyes of coal fixed on Justik.

The size and strength of the bearded man made Justik cautious. The power warmed his hands, but he fought to contain his anger. He could not show his power in so public a place.

The giant grabbed Justik and half-dragged, half-carried him through the entrance door. Justik found himself in the air, smelling garlic and sweat, then flying. He hit the ground and his attacker planted a wide boot in his ribs. Justik sucked air, twisted, and let his rage explode. The flame burned the man's calf.

The stunned giant howled and backed away, grasping his leg. "Dar's spawn," he spat. "What kind of djinn are you?" A hefty knife materialized in his hand, the wide metal blade gleaming in the lantern light.

Justik scrambled to his feet, his hands glowing, his eyes narrowed in an inhuman glare. His opponent thrust the knife, but the younger man danced to the side and punched the giant's midsection. The man grunted, swung a sledge-hammer fist at Justik's cheek, and prepared to impale his opponent. Justik took a glancing blow that stunned. Staggered, he brought his hands together and aimed at the giant's gut. Flame cut into flesh, the man dropped the knife and spasmed. He wailed and went down, his hands grabbing blackened cloth and entrails.

A gathered crowd of drinkers and the giant's woman gasped as the foul stench of burnt cloth and flesh rose over the writhing man. Justik turned to the group his fist still aglow. The half dozen spectators backed away.

Hours later, hungry and thirsty, Justik hid in an abandoned building on the outskirts of Abantazar. He crouched in a dark corner surrounded by baskets, broken crockery and baled rags wondering what he could have done to avoid the fight. It was stupid to reveal his power. He thought he'd learned better control. Something thumped in the dark and Justik tensed, thinking of a desert rat. From the gloom came light, then a short, fat man in white robes with a lantern. He held up his hand, apparently a sign of peace.

"I mean you no harm, stranger," he said. "Your fight this evening drew my employer's attention, and he would like to meet you."

"Your employer?"

"Yes. He runs certain operations in Abantazar, and the man you fought was his employee, who now lies on a bed and may die. I will let my boss tell you what this means. He invites you to join him for dinner."

A high wall of dun-colored stone embedded at the top with spikes shielded a large residence. Justik handed his knife to swarthy guards, menacing men who said little. His escort led him inside a marble-floored villa and introduced him to a handsome, light-skinned man of medium height in white breeches, a broad black belt, and a soft, shiny, cream-colored shirt. He dismissed the escort.

"Welcome. I am pleased that you decided to join me," he said. "I am Farsik." The well-spoken man exuded civility belied by ruthless eyes. He swept his hand toward two cushioned chairs.

"I am called Justik. Why am I here?"

Farsik's mouth opened when he heard the name, and he took a moment to answer. "To enjoy a fine meal and wine. And talk. When I learned you defeated Gror, my personal guard, I knew you must be someone special. Gror has never lost a fight."

"He was not very friendly. I was defending myself."

"That is of no consequence," Farsik said with a wave of his hand. "Only results interest me. So tell me about yourself and how you managed to avoid death at Gror's hands."

Justik saw no reason to reveal his origin to this man. "I come from the west. I am just traveling to see the world. As for taking down that giant, I used my speed and his carelessness."

"And extraordinary skill. One might call it a talent. Gror was burned. That did not come from speed, and you had no weapon to cause such damage. A rumor has spread in Abantazar about other deaths from burns along the route from the west. People say that a djinn or Dar-mon is on the loose. Perhaps you know something of this demon." Farsik's eyes gleamed in the light of an oil lamp.

Justik shrugged.

Farsik nodded as if the two had reached some agreement. "This talent of yours reminds me of another's," he continued. "In the great war, the Zellish army was led by one with the ability to burn, even at a distance. If one is to believe the reports. You seem to have a similar gift, and I want to employ it."

"How?"

"I supply services of various kinds. We provide women and other diversions. We offer protection for merchants and caravans. We collect fees and taxes. For these enterprises, I need men who can convince the reluctant to cooperate." Farsik leaned forward and smiled. "And I pay well."

Farsik rose and led his guest into a private dining room. A polished dark table with two place settings was lit by candles and oil lamps. The men sat and a servant appeared with a platter of southern meats and vegetables. Justik tasted a flavorful red wine and enjoyed a meal he would call a feast. Justik asked what the job entailed.

"You must be willing to twist arms."

When the meal ended, Farsik sat back. "Think on this opportunity, Justik. I have excellent guest quarters and would be pleased to have you use them."

Justik realized how tired he was and accepted this offer. A woman glided in wearing a white, low cut gown that left her arms bare. When she stood before the candelabra, her pleasing form was revealed through the translucent garment.

"My colleague will see to your comfort," Farsik said with a smile.

The woman took his hand as Justik rose and led him toward one of the exits.

As they were about to leave, Farsik said, "There is another interesting aspect to the story about that warrior who defeated the Tantrocans years ago. It's his name."

Justik stopped and eyed Farsik. "What about it?"

"It is almost yours. He was called Justi."

Justik filled in the gaps. If he had a similar name and a similar skill, could not this Justi be his father? In the morning, after his bed companion provided food and drink, he walked to the Abantazar Library and asked the keeper what the origin of the Zellish army was. The man said it assembled in Abantazar when the Princess Mercerio had been revealed and called for a fighting force. The princess led half the army, and the other half was commanded by one called Justi, chosen because he possessed a talent.

"What talent?" Justik asked, wanting to hear another account.

Awe filled the keeper's face. "Justi could sense wrong and bring forth a flame to punish the wrongdoer. The Tantrocans were the ultimate wrongdoers of that time, what with slavery and sacrifices to Dar. This Justi faced them in battle and destroyed hardened soldiers with sweeps of flame. Scholars still write accounts of the battles that restored the royals to Zellingon."

"When did this happen?"

The keeper squinted at his questioner. "Before you were born."

"How old was this Justi?"

"Why . . . your age I would guess. You appear something like him. Only darker."

Now it all made sense. His mother worked here in Abantazar as Mercerio formed her army. Justi too was here and had opportunity to meet Provani. The timing was right.

23
Dark Power

Caldir arrived in Provak's small chamber to find the priest huddled near the lit fireplace. Caldir wondered how the diminutive high priest could be cold, given his rotundity. Surely, he had the blubber of a fur seal to keep him warm. Even his head should be warm enough with its thick, black hedgehog hair.

Provak pointed to a nearby chair. "Caldir, I know you are unsatisfied that I was chosen to replace Aduk after his mysterious death. Perhaps he led you to believe that you were ready, but that was not true. Besides, the king selects his own chief priest. You were not Brokul's choice."

The death of Aduk was no mystery to Caldir. He knew the insufferable old bird had been poisoned. As for his disappointment, he let that be Provak's conjecture and waited.

"It is time to focus on the future. Our people deserve victory over the followers of Li in the south. That is Dar's will. The gods tend to even things up in the human realm. That has occurred."

"Meaning?" Caldir asked.

Provak raised his hand. "The Child of Darkness may already be with us."

Caldir wore a stunned expression. "What are you talking about?"

"My spy in Abantazar reports a young man with power to kill by a shaft of flame. Even his name is similar: Justik."

Caldir stroked his chin. "Interesting. That cannot be a coincidence."

"You will find him and bring him here." Provak tossed a bag to Caldir. "That gold will convince him to come."

Caldir glanced in the bag. "What happens if he is recruited?"

Provak leaned back and folded his arms. Sea birds screeched over the sounds of surf breaking on the rocks and sand below the window. "I see Dar's followers overrunning and enslaving the minions of Li," he said. "We shall rule the Zell."

Before he set off for Abantazar, Caldir handled an important task. He had become Prince Brosun's confidante and risked instructing the prince on how to become king. Brosun was not interested in waiting until nature took its sweet time to do away with his father. He had no love for the man and welcomed Caldir's counsel.

"Here is what you will need," Caldir said to the prince when they were alone, handing the boy a packet of green-tinged powder. "It is called kingsbane."

Brosun examined the gift, picked it up with two fingers, and placed it in a wooden box. He closed and locked the lid. "So how is this bane used?"

"It dissolves in water and mead and has no odor. It is slow acting. A sufficient dose causes no immediate effects, but within three hours there are odd rhythms of the heart, brain convulsions, and then death."

"Sounds like the symptoms reported for my father's former high priest. His servant found him clutching his chest, spasming, and foaming at the mouth," Brosun said.

"I have heard the same story," Caldir said, smiling. "Now, I'm showing you this only as part of your lesson on the natural world. Whatever you do with this material is your own business. I do not want to know." The teacher held his student's eye for a moment before he turned and left.

As Farsik's enforcer, Justik had little trouble convincing the man's customers to pay for every service provided. Justik acquired wealth and rewards, including women. He should have been content but wasn't. He was Farsik's tool, his lackey. What was his real destiny, his purpose?

Caldir visited Abantazar taverns and paid to learn where Justik often drank. Late on his second day in Abantazar, the Tantrocan entered one such loud, busy place where Justik sat alone. Caldir introduced himself and offered to buy the drinks.

Justik eyed Caldir, wary he might be an assassin hired by one of the foolish merchants who resisted paying for Farsik's protection. But nothing about the stranger seemed threatening. "Why would you do that?"

"I have heard of your talents and am intrigued. You seem quite special. I have a message."

Justik decided he could abide some fool's chatter in exchange for drinks and compliments. When he studied Caldir's unpatched eye, he decided the man was no fool. The host delivered cups of mead and Justik did most of the drinking and in the process told his story. He wondered about the purpose of his power and was happy to listen to Caldir's answer. The priest told of the Tantrocan conquest and subsequent expulsion and of a Zellish hero who caused Tantrocan defeat with a power like Justik's.

"I believe that was my father," Justik said, slurring the words. "He had a great purpose and so should I. I should go to Zellingon and find Justi, to see if we have a connection."

"That might not be wise," Caldir warned. "Your power could be viewed as a threat to the kingdom, and you could be imprisoned."

"I would not allow that. No man could stop me."

"Be not so bold, Justik. Even this Justi was said to be struck down by a poisoned knife. The toxin almost took his life. And neither he nor you would survive an arrow in the heart."

"I wouldn't give them the chance," Justik said and drained his mug. He stopped the servant girl passing with a tray of drinks for others and grabbed one for himself. The girl did not protest.

"If you were to confront Justi, you could have a younger, less developed power than the Zellish champion. It's possible you would be vanquished."

Justik laughed. "But the younger power could be stronger."

"Risky notion. Going to Zellingon now, alone, is foolish. I have another proposal that will get you there in a stronger position."

Justik took another swallow of his mead as a nearby table erupted into a loud argument. When one of the drinkers stood, cursed his companion, and stormed from the tavern, quiet returned. Justik turned back to Caldir and said, "I'm listening."

"The Zellish used unnatural power to defeat us. If we had a countervailing power, namely you, we could vanquish them, for we are greater warriors, not held back by the silly notions of mercy. We would imprison the queen and her consort and rule the kingdom. And you would share in our power."

Justik wanted power and recognition. Caldir's offer got him what he deserved. He would visit Tantroc and take a position of importance in the Tantrocan court. Justik was tired of Abantazar.

Not long after Caldir left for Abantazar, King Brokul had his last meal. It was the usual feast of game, roasted roots, and drink that went on for hours. The king left early, claiming he wasn't feeling well. He made it to his chamber and did indeed sleep, but only for a short time. He awoke in great distress, sweating, clutching his chest, and convulsing. Cantor watched the symptoms progress until the king lapsed into unconsciousness. Only then did Cantor summon the court physician whose only job was to pronounce the king dead.

Prince Brosun was crowned the next day. The prince commanded his sister Ranera to attend both the coronation and the celebration that followed.

When they were alone in the private area of the castle, Ranera could not contain her resentment. "How fortunate that father died in the prime of life. I still wonder how that happened. Do you have any theories, my king?" The princess said the last with a small, feigned bow.

Brosun glared at Ranera. "What are you saying? That I had something to do with his demise? I would watch my tongue if I were you. Accusing your king of a crime is treasonous, and I would have no problem punishing you."

"Oh, I don't doubt it, but it was only a question."

Brosun stepped closer. "You don't fool me, Ranera. I know you wish you wore this crown. You lust for power more than you lust for bed partners. If you were strong enough, you'd probably try the obvious way to gain power: kill me. But that is not your style. Besides my sudden death would be followed by your sudden death."

"But that would end the royal line."

"If I be dead, what would I care?" Brosun considered what had been said and ended the conversation. "Just be content with your status as princess. I'll handle the power, and you can pursue your hobby. A princess can be a valuable commodity in negotiating treaties and alliances. Perhaps I'll find you a husband."

Ranera stood open-mouthed as the king left. Then she fumed, considered how she might engineer her brother's death by a plausible accident, and came up with nothing. She grabbed a figurine of a nude male and smashed it against the fireplace.

Caldir and Justik headed east from Abantazar on horseback and turned north through sparsely populated eastern wastelands, avoiding Zellingon and at last reaching the northern coast at Pale. There they found Caldir's boat and crew waiting to ferry them across the Tantric Gulf. The sea was smooth, the wind moderate, and the air warm. They arrived at the main Ankor dock where a messenger took Caldir aside and spoke at some length.

Justik surveyed the austere setting and wondered whether he could tolerate much time in this cold climate. Caldir finished his conversation with a smile and motioned to Justik. The pair climbed the stone steps to the palace overlooking the sea. Caldir took Justik directly to King Brosun, making sure his guest understood how important he was to gain immediate audience. The large timbered throne room was occupied by a dozen armed guards who eyed Justik and seemed ready to act if he were to venture too close to their king.

"I just learned of your father's sudden death, King Brosun," Caldir said. "My condolences to you, Princess Ranera, and your mother."

"Yes. Thank you. It was very unexpected," Brosun said, holding the priest's eye. "But we must carry on. Who is with you, Caldir?"

"This is Justik, my king, a man of power to serve our cause in honor of Dar."

"Power? What sort of power?"

"The same power that defeated your father's forces at Zellingon and thwarts our rule over the Zell."

"And do you offer this power to our cause, Justik?"

Justik decided that this was the cue for him to establish his position and make his demands. He had no fear of these fierce warriors, for his power through practice could be called forth at will, and would, if he so desired, kill every man in the chamber. "I will use my power to destroy the Zell. They are soft and weak and have rejected me. But it will be on my terms, and I will reap the rewards of your conquest."

"You demand much, yet we have only rumors to substantiate your power. How do we know what you offer?"

Caldir held up his hand and spoke to the guard at his right. The soldier disappeared and the king glared as they waited. Moments passed before the jailer dragged in an emaciated man in rags. A prisoner of some sort, Justik imagined.

Brosun nodded and said, "I have condemned this wretch to death for thievery that left his victim dead. Save us the trouble of hanging him."

The man's head did not rise from his chest and he seemed only half conscious, possibly because of torture. Justik waved the guard away and raised his arm. A boom sounded and simultaneously a beam of flame erupted from his hand and struck the man in the chest, penetrated, destroying tissues and instantly stilling the heart. The unpleasant tang of burned flesh made Brosun flinch. The prisoner uttered no sound, fell back, and was still.

The king jumped to his feet, amazement on his face. "Very well, Justik, we must ponder this power you have displayed. Please be comfortable as our guest."

Caldir played the host, finding Justik quarters. He ordered wine and the pair sat as Caldir related the plans developed by the Tantrocans to reestablish their presence across the Gulf. The southerner was not much interested in details but focused when Caldir let slip that the king would ask the High Priest Provak his opinion of Justik. It angered him that his value should still be doubted.

"Do you see Justik as our champion?" Brosun asked Provak.

Provak could have said that Justik's power assured Tantrocan victory. Instead he asked, "Can Justik be trusted? He is Zellish and has no connection to Tantroc."

Brosun frowned. "Gold will be his connection."

"He is dangerous. Your own person is at risk."

"I will make sure I am not in his presence."

"But— "

"You seem to be against the invasion. Do you not believe the old prophecies you are so fond of quoting?"

"I am saying we should be cautious. We have delayed the second invasion for two decades. What is the rush?"

"Your caution irritates me. We will reclaim the Zell."

Mobilization began immediately. But Caldir had another component of his plan that delayed an invasion. He needed allies. Caldir mentioned an alliance with the Ice, a people to the east, but all Justik heard was that Caldir's scheme would delay things.

Justik welcomed the extra time, for he was not sure his heart was committed to Caldir's notion of gaining power by conquest. He worried about Justi of Ortun. Their similar names convinced him Justi was his father. Justik did not care about how that happened, but that meant both Justi and Prince Meru, the son of Justi, could kill him. He wanted time to learn what he could of the boy who was almost a year younger than he. He might also find power in Zellingon by demanding recognition. Without telling Caldir, he decided to travel there.

24
Expulsion

In his castle chamber, an unshaven Caldir in night garb concentrated on the task that would spark the invasion of the Zell. As he took another bite of egg pie, sun from a narrow window splashed over his worktable and a map of Tantroc and the northern Zell. A half-composed letter lay near an ink pot and quills. He cursed, pounded the letter, and set it aside. What he'd said about the king's sister was not quite diplomatic. The priest took a fresh palimpset, inked a quill, and was about to start again when a knock interrupted.

Justik entered and planted splayed fingers on the tabletop. "I am leaving Ankor."

Caldir froze. "Leaving? Why?"

"For a short trip."

"Trip? Where? How long? And why?"

"Frown not, priest. My journey will not interfere with King Brosun's plans. It would be prudent for me to see where we will be fighting before winter sets in. I will return after you have readied an invasion."

Caldir sat back and glanced first at the map and then at Justik. "Could you not just study this map? Leaving would be dangerous. You could be injured or killed."

Justik smiled. "Not likely. I will just be a traveler, a citizen of the Zell. It's not as though I resemble a Tantrocan."

Caldir shook his head. "No, but you will be a stranger. You won't fit in. I don't like this and forbid it."

"It is not a matter of your liking or forbidding."

Resignation clouded Caldir's face. He drummed his fingers. "You must take bodyguards."

"Do you really think I need guards?" Justik picked up the egg pie and turned toward the door.

Caldir clenched his fists and watched his champion leave.

A hired boat ferried Justik across the Tantric Gulf to Fathom. From there he walked in fall sunshine to his real destination, Zellingon. He encountered travelers who told stories of the restoration of Zellingon, of their champion, and of rebuilding the kingdom. Nice history, but he wanted to know what was happening now. He reached the royal city without incident, planning to observe and learn firsthand about who might be his father and possess his killing power.

Tavern patrons fed him information. He heard the history of Justi from residents who'd witnessed driving the Tantrocans from Zellingon. Some claimed to have seen Justi in battle and confirmed the Justice Fire. In one establishment Justik found a war veteran whose face was marred with a splash of red, smooth skin. An old burn, Justik thought.

"I'm new here, friend," Justik said when he joined the man at a scared wooden table. "May I join you in drink. I'm buying."

"New, eh? From where?"

"Sailed into the gulf from the west," Justik said, a partial truth.

"Mighty dangerous this time of year," the man said after a sip of beer. "There's a sea monster in the gulf that moves west in the fall. Called the Megadarch, a creature larger than any small boat. Some cross between a reptile and a giant squid. Said to grab ships in its tentacles and sailors in its maw. A fishing boat went missing in the past fortnight. You could have been another."

Justik took this as imagination and alcohol talking. "Good to know. I'll be careful. But tell me about your face."

"It was an accident. I got too close to the enemy when Justi attacked."

"Sounds as though this Justi didn't have much control," Justik said.

"Sad but true. Once he was isolated in a back lane of Zellingon away from the main conflict. He had just dispatched two Tantrocans when a comrade erred by approaching him from behind. It is said that Justi whirled around and, not recognizing his friend in the heat of battle, killed him."

So my father is easily distracted, Justik thought. In another drinking place, Justik found a porcine fellow as bright and cheery as the establishment, a rotund man delighted to imbibe and talk of any topic that came his way. Justik steered him to current affairs, and the fat man told stories of Queen Mercerio, of Justi becoming her consort, and of their son, Prince Meru.

Justik asked, "So how does this Justi appear?"

Relaxed, with a half-drained tankard, the man squinted, bloodshot eye. "In fact, by Li's breath, I would say that years back he seemed exactly as you do today. But without that scraggle of beard on your face. Yes, you've got the same hair and eyes."

Boss Farsik had given that same answer. Justi's appearance years ago would bear on the father issue. His demeanor now might reveal whether he retained any power.

"Maybe not so strange. But what of today? Has he not grown old?"

"He is yet a handsome man with a square jaw, blue eyes, and thick hair as blond as summer straw." The fat man took another swig of beer. "Strong, too."

Justik also possessed great strength. Perhaps he shared this with the most important man in the realm, the great hero, his sire. "What about Prince Meru?"

"Well, he be different. He has his mother's dark hair and, well, a delicate look. Then there's his hand."

"What about his hand?"

"You've not heard of the Withered Prince? That's what they call him because of weakness in his hand. Oh, it appears normal enough but has no strength."

After sharing another brew, Justik left thinking he only had to be wary of his father. His half brother was no threat.

Justik got his own view of Justi a few days later in Zellingon's main square. A ceremony honoring donors to the royal museum drew a small murmuring crowd. A woman with a gold pendant, a man with blond hair, and a younger man of Justik's age arrived to a trumpet fanfare. The queen smiled and waved and, in the cool air of a sunny day, delivered a short speech thanking the donors and promoting the museum as the way to remember and learn from history. Justik suppressed a guffaw at the thought that a museum collection would prevent the coming invasion.

He was sure the man next to Queen Mercerio was his father. The man could be Justik's mirror image, but older and better clothed. I do indeed mirror my father, he thought, but only vaguely like my half brother Prince Meru, who must be the younger man. The prince, who was almost his age, seemed smaller than Justik. And bored.

Justik had no claim to any position in the Zell. Not like his half brother. But he must be due something. He could get money as a payment for keeping quiet about his bastardy, but he had plenty of gold. He wanted recognition and acceptance.

Prince Meru was not bored but concentrating. He had noticed Justik in the audience because of his appearance and what he emanated. Meru could feel something wrong, a darkness and a threat. Meru felt the same alarm when the wolf confronted him and Danilla in the forest. He'd summoned some force to subdue the animal, a force he didn't understand and never felt again. Will I have to do the same here? he wondered, knowing no way to summon any power. The prince stared at the stranger and continued to feel disturbed, but the stranger did nothing but stand and watch. There was no reason to alert his mother or father.

The next day Justik attended a public session presided over by Justi in a cavernous room that could be a museum or a temple. Walls held mounted swords, pikes, chains, and helmets, but religious symbols of the god Li marked several panels. High windows cast natural light on everything, including the raised platform in front. A chest-high, polished, carved wooden railing separated the dais from backless benches that filled the space. About five tens of Zellish, mostly men, occupied the seats. Justik settled on a seat a few rows from the front, intent on studying his supposed father to learn if the years had sapped his vitality.

A white-bearded man in a blue robe entered carrying a staff with a gilded, gnarled top that loomed above his head. He banged the staff on the floor and called out, "Gather here and be heard by the queen's representative, Justi of Ortun."

The chamberlain chose who spoke. He pointed to a cadaverous man clutching a red hat a row behind Justik. "Be heard and be brief," the chamberlain said.

Red Hat sidled forward and stood at the rail. "I seek the crown's help in regaining water for my herd. My neighbor has diverted the stream that used to flow on my land. My sheep are left to die of thirst."

"Why have you not brought this to a judge's attention?" Justi asked.

"He will not hear my claim because I cannot produce a deed. The land has been in my family for three generations and was left to me by my father."

A murmur of conversation rippled through the temple causing the robed man to bang his staff. Justi turned to the scribe who was taking notes. "Tell the magistrate the crown wishes him to consider this man's situation regardless of a missing deed. There must be witnesses to his claim of possession. If he owns the land, he owns the stream and cannot be deprived of water."

The crowd voiced approval at this pronouncement, and this elicited another thump of the chamberlain's staff. The deedless man muttered a thank you, donned his red cap, and backed away.

Justik realized what was going on. The gathering gave citizens a chance to opine on issues and petitions that might have to be decided by the throne. Justi heard two more cases, remedied one man's trouble, and agreed to present another's petition to the queen. So Justi was the filter for what deserved the queen's attention.

The chamberlain called on a sad-faced, rotund man sitting beside a substantial woman. The man stood and walked resolutely to the rail. "My lord," he said in a thin voice, "The issue is my daughter, my missing daughter. She is but ten and six years and has vanished. The sheriff claims she has run off and will return. But my girl was not one to run off. The day she disappeared, a trade caravan from Abantazar arrived, and near dusk she went to investigate its wares. She said she would be quick, but she never returned."

Justi had leaned forward during this recitation of woe. He pointed to a large, seated woman and motioned her to rise. "Madam, are you the girl's mother?"

"Her stepmother, my lord. What my husband said is true. Our daughter would not run off, and the sheriff refuses to even check the caravan, which is about to depart."

Justi sat back and said, "Chamberlain, have the sheriff detain the caravan until he searches it and questions the merchants. I want to hear what he finds out."

The well-fed couple muttered their thanks and waddled toward the exit. They pushed open both great doors and the daylight encouraged a bird to dive from the rafters toward the opening. It sailed over the woman, who screamed and flapped her hands over her head. Several, including Justik, stood at the commotion and watched the bird escape as the embarrassed husband shove his wife through the door. When Justik turned back to the front, the chamberlain pointed at him.

"Come forward, young man, and present your issue."

Justik hesitated, reluctant to reveal his true purpose. But he saw an unexpected opportunity. He stood and faced the chamberlain. "I have no issue for the queen's representative, but I would request a meeting in private. I have something important to say that cannot be said in public."

Justi had been examining a scroll as Justik spoke but lifted his head to hear the last.

"It is for your ears only and has to do with your son," Justik said.

Justi wondered what this young man could know about Prince Meru. He studied the speaker, and slowly his face transformed from a judicial calm to surprise. It was as though he gazed into a mirror of time. The man bore a remarkable resemblance to Justi's younger self. He felt a connection and knew he must hear more. Without preamble he said, "I will grant you private session. We will meet at the palace in one hour. The chamberlain will direct you."

A burst of chatter ensued with questions about who this man might be to be given such a boon. That he might know something about the prince fueled more comment, which continued, despite the chamberlain's thumping disapproval.

Justi disposed of several more cases and cut the session short. He went to hear from Justik, admitting how his voice and mannerisms were eerily familiar and that the stranger exuded confidence and power that both attracted and repelled.

The chamberlain told Justik to find a sally port in the north wall of the palace. Two guards removed his knife and guided him across a substantial courtyard past a barn and to a palace door. The men ushered him into a room with four padded chairs and a polished circular table. A fireplace occupied one wall and royal crests of the current and past rulers of Zellingon decorated another. Tall narrow windows provided abundant light and a view of the courtyard. He waited.

Justi entered to find the young man seated in a relaxed posture. A bit taller and more muscular than Meru, but of the same age, the visitor wore the worldly air of the traveler, perhaps one who held some valuable secret. Justi stood by the fireplace. "Greetings. What is your name?"

"I am called Justik."

Justi stared at the visitor. "That is the name your mother gave you?"

"As I said. And you know my mother."

Justi knew no woman in Zellingon with a son like Justik. From elsewhere, perhaps, or from the past. "When? From where?" He wasn't sure he wanted to hear more.

Justik half smiled, but his eyes remained hard. "You knew her well in Abantazar, my lord. So well that she bore me nine months later. Provani is her name and you are my father."

Justi stumbled back, his face pale, and placed his hand on a chair to steady himself. The scene years earlier in the Abantazar Inn flooded his memory. But he rejected the notion that this man was his son. How could he know the truth of the young man's assertion? His appearance proved little.

"Your claim is hardly credible," Justi said. "Yes, you are blond with blue eyes, but your mother was a redhead who had many men, some blond. I think you imagine we are related." He ignored his sense that this young man harbored some great strength. "Even if you believe your own story, why do you come to me now?"

Justik waved at the empty table. "Might we not share a drink, Father? I have been hours without refreshment."

"Do not call me 'father.'" Justi went to door and spoke to an attendant in the hall. A moment later, the man appeared with a flagon of wine and two cups. He poured the wine and left.

"This is quite civilized, Father. Something I could grow to like." Justik sampled the wine. "A far better vintage than the sour stuff I have tasted in pubs."

Justi, his wine untouched, sat in another chair and studied the boy. Perhaps he felt kinship, but something held him from acknowledging it. His acute sense of justice said he should act as a father, but he also detected something foul, an evil like the one he'd felt in the Tantrocan lieutenant who tried to assault his mother in Ortun, or in the assassin Ukor who'd attacked him in the Ortun forest.

"What do you want? You have no proof, other than your face, of this claim."

A cart rumbled past in the courtyard and Justik turned to gaze out a window. Nearby horses whinnied. "Proof. Oh, I have proof, but not something you want to see. I think you know to what I refer."

Justi suspected this man claimed to wield the Justice Power, the ability to cast flame. The power might be the same, but there would be no justice with it. Justi would not want to see that power.

"What I desire is position, one of influence here in Zellingon in my rightful place alongside my brother Prince Meru."

"What are you talking about?"

"I know I cannot enjoy the prince's royal inheritance, but I can serve as his advisor. We can share rulership of the Zell. That seems fair. I am his older brother and, from what I've heard, possess a far greater strength than the Withered Prince."

"You speak as a fool. Queen Mercerio rules the Zell and will do so for many years. You have no rank here, regardless of your claimed origins. I have heard enough."

"Perhaps not, my lord. If we cannot come to an agreement, I will be forced to tell my story to the queen. I'm sure you do not want that."

Justi stood. "Now you play the fool as well. The queen may not know about you, but she has met your mother. Did Provani not tell you she was dragged to Fathom to tell Mercerio her story. Your threat is impotent."

His mother had never spoken of Mercerio, but Justik had another threat. "You deny that I possess your burning power but know in your heart that I do. Know that I would have my boon, or I will use it."

Justi squeezed the back of the chair and felt his hands warm. Somewhere in the distance a bell rang. He spoke carefully, "I do not think you want to do that, Justik. Even if it be true that you have power like mine, I have not given up that gift. Mine is older, more mature, and more controlled than yours. It has become even more powerful at four tens of years than it was when I was your age. Do not test me." The last was a bluff, for Justi had had no occasion to use the Justice Flame since the escape from Fathom. He might not even have the ability anymore. "I will not have you bothering my family or the court. Here is what is going to happen. You will leave Zellingon and not return. Your future does not lie here."

Justi strode from the room and gave orders to the guards.

As darkness descended, two uniformed giants escorted Justik from the palace grounds. "We've been told to escort you to the city gate, so march," the bald guard announced. His partner lit a torch and pointed toward the town wall.

The process went smoothly until the bearded soldier shoved Justik. "Move along. We have better things to do."

Justik stiffened and his hands warmed. He fought to contain the urge to kill and managed barely to quell the impulse. The group reached the main gate and Justik strolled into the gathering gloom, his jaw clenched.

The guards reported success, and Justi felt he'd handled the visitor correctly. He could not be sure that Justik was his son, but his heart said it was surely so. If there had been only supplication and no demand and threat, he might have acted differently. But he had more than himself to protect. There were Mercerio and Meru and Danilla. And the dignity of the royal house.

When the two guards who'd hustled Justik out of Zellingon went missing, only to be found dead in a back alley with throats cut, Justi was shocked. The fact that the men were not burned could mean that Justik had not killed them. Or that he lacked the power he claimed or didn't want to make his power known. Alarmed, Justi knew he had a problem.

In Anchor, Caldir's plan unfolded. In the vast, cold expanse on the east of Tantroc Island dwelt a tribe of hunter-craftsmen known as the Ice. These neighbors were generally darker and shorter than the Tantrocans but faster and more agile. If Tantrocans were elk, the Ice were deer. Over the years Caldir had resolved disputes over hunting rights in border lands and crafted agreements to get meat, furs, and weavings from the Ice in exchange for Tantrocan metal goods. In these affairs he dealt with Fospe, a senior advisor to the Ice chief.

He sent a message to Fospe, claiming he had a matter of state to discuss. He intended to propose in King Brosun's name a united effort against the Zell. Acceptance of his plan depended on two things: the Ice desire for status and Princess Ranera's hunger for power.

The last Ice king had died and left no heir. His people bemoaned the loss and felt incomplete without a ruler of royal blood. Why they lacked the intelligence to create a new line was hard to understand, perhaps expecting Dar to give them a new king or queen. Both peoples worshiped Dar and expected the god to provide. Since the Ice and the Tantrocans were once one people, the Ice would accept a Tantrocan of royal lineage as legitimate. Of course, such a person would wed an Ice leader.

That was the opening Caldir would use and where Ranera came in. Caldir had become the princess's confidante, and he would now convince her to wed a suitably virile hunter to become the Ice queen. Her need for power would be satisfied.

Weeks later, the parties met near the Tantrocan border a league from the nearest village. A breeze from the south swept the sparse grassland and warmed the pleasant spot. At the hunting hut, Caldir ordered his guards to roll up the hides covering windows in each wall. The light and view almost made the crude shelter comfortable.

Fospe arrived with two guards. Caldir viewed Fospe as a fox—an image fed as much by his pointed, whiskered face as by his sly thinking. Caldir and Fospe exchanged gifts of potent native fermentations.

"Why are we met?" Fospe asked after he'd sipped the Tantrocan liqueur.

"I have a proposition that benefits us both."

Fospe frowned. "Is this a riddle? Not the riches of the southland again? We don't need the Tantrocans to help in raiding the south. Certainly not to share the booty."

"Yes, I speak of the southland but not just raids and a boatload of plunder. I'm talking about acquiring the land, ruling there, enjoying the greater warmth." The hut creaked in a stiffened breeze.

"We worship the same almighty Dar and should have his rewards," Fospe said. "But there is distrust between our peoples."

Caldir sampled his beverage and watched Fospe taste his. "That was not always so. The priests say we were once one people under one king. We must remember that and forget all squabbles over who can hunt where."

"We speak of much more than hunting. The Tantrocans occupied the southlands for two tens of years without Ice help. Why seek alliance now?"

"Surely you've heard of the Zellish champion who throws fire?"

"We do not believe those stories."

Caldir leaned forward. "A strange rejection from a people who rely on magic enchantments to defeat their enemies." The ability of Ice priests to fog the minds of warriors, making them forget where they were or what they were about was known. "But the story of the Zellish wizard is true," Caldir continued. "His power is why we were driven from what is rightfully ours. I am offering the chance for an easier life in a warmer place."

"We are not as discontented with our land as you are with yours," Fospe said, "but we do want to hunt the herds that roam across eastern lands beyond the water."

"Together we can have what our people desire," Caldir said. "With Ice power to control minds and Tantrocan fighting skill and numbers, we can easily take the north coast towns of the Zell."

Fospe shook his head. "Let me correct your thinking about magic enchantments. Our priests are powerful but few. And their sphere of mind control is small. They could not affect the outcome in large battles."

Caldir smiled. "Think, Fospe. Your priests need to enchant but one enemy, the one called Justi."

Fospe rose, scratched his vulpine nose, and walked in a circle about the shelter. "More sun is not worth the death of our young men," he said. "The Ice do not share the Tantrocan lust for Zellish women, slaves, and bloody sacrifices to Dar. We prefer to remain alive and will not see our men killed to satisfy your need for vengeful conquest."

Caldir found these words unsurprising. He smiled. "I offer a far greater boon than warm weather."

"What boon?"

"Tantroc can give you royalty, what the Ice need to have a leader again."

"What? You propose that the Ice accept your king as ours? I have heard Brosun is but a petulant child who happened to be available when his father died suddenly. And suspiciously, I would add."

Caldir shrugged. "Men die. Brokul was not young. But my proposal has nothing to do with King Brosun. He has a sister, the Princess Ranera, who is uncommonly lovely and seeks the power of a throne. She is willing to take the Ice as her subjects."

Fospe examined the snowcapped peaks visible to the north. "And this princess is willing to wed an Ice man?" I suppose she mimics a fur seal."

"She has the seal's liquid eyes, but her form is tall, athletic, and very much a woman's. She is the same age as her brother and ready to be wed."

"But she hates men."

"Quite the opposite," Caldir said, thinking of the constant traffic to and from the princess's chamber.

While Fospe thought, Caldir was patient, content to observe a herd of elk in the distance.

"Why would Ranera want to wed a rough hunter," Fospe asked, "and live in land that does not enjoy the warming breeze from Sea West?"

"The princess will do what her king commands. And she appreciates men of strength," Caldir said, thinking the rougher the better, "but she does not intend to live in a cold climate. A Zellish coastal town will suit her just fine. This is your chance to give your people a queen."

Fospe turned his gaze toward the coast and said, "I will convey your proposal to our leader, but I doubt it will be accepted."

Alarmed, Caldir said something that sounded too desperate. "Fospe, this is good for both our peoples. You must convince your chief."

PART IV
Dar's Might

Dar's disciples prepare for conquest.

25
Dark Champion

Justik struggled to contain his rage as he was shoved through the north gate. He controlled the impulse to burn the life out of the two guards and slipped into the forest along the Zelar River where he plotted revenge.

The men who'd manhandled him had made a mistake: they talked about their favorite tavern and plans to meet that evening. From his pack Justik took a razor and at the river's edge scraped off his beard. Nearby grew a tall, red-stemmed bush thick with inky berries. He picked the grape-sized fruit, stained his fingers, and used the berries to darken his hair. Then he donned a hooded cloak and set out for the west gate of Zellingon.

"Hail, friend," Justik greeted the guard on duty, an older man with weary eyes. "Is there a tavern nearby where a traveler can get a drink before continuing his journey?"

The man folded his arms and blocked the way. "It is too late to enter Zellingon. Find water in the forest for your travels."

"It's hardly late, friend. I will be but a short time and return to leave before the gates are locked." Justik made a show of pulling a coin from his pocket.

The guard eyed the silver and said, "Remove your hood."

Justik complied and stroked his now hairless face as the man examined the blackish hair.

"Blue eyes with dark hair. Unusual. Have you been to Zellingon before?" the guard challenged.

"No, but I've heard good things about the town and its inns. Can you point me to a drinking hole?" Justik held out a coin.

The guard took the bribe and smiled. "Try The Sunken Inn. Straight ahead. We lock the gates at the tenth hour."

Justik strode through the gate and headed for the tavern his escort guard had named. He found the small place and peered through a front window. The guards were drinking with two women, which might be a problem. He waited, imagining he would be trapped in Zellingon. He had considered burning the nighttime drinkers, a message that Justi would understand, but decided it was too risky. A flame, even a narrow white beam, would attract attention in the dark. Better to let his father wonder about his son's power until it was too late.

Two things happened in Justik's favor. First, the queen's men decided to leave. Second, the women stayed behind. When the guards stumbled from the tavern and turned down an alley, a dark figure holding a knife followed. The men walked unsteadily, clucking like fattened chickens about what they fancied in a woman.

"I can give you that," said a female voice from deeper in the alley.

Justik froze as a woman emerged from the blackness. He wondered if he would have to kill the prostitute along with the guards.

The second man, slower than his companion, lurched into the wall and stopped as if surprised to find it in his way. He burped and answered, "I'm sure you can, but we cannot tarry to find out. Perhaps—"

Justik's knife slashed the man's throat and cut off the words. Blood sprayed and the other guard turned to take the second deadly cut. The woman saw this and backed away, silent, her hands held out. Justik grabbed the woman's arm. "Scream and you will die."

She ran. Justik dragged the bodies deeper into the darkness, leaving red smears on the paving stones, and wondering why he hadn't killed the witness. He rationalized the woman avoided the town authorities and, if forced to speak, would only confirm his black hair. He left by the same west gate, tipped the guard another gold coin, and asserted his thirst was quenched.

Under a half moon, Justik followed the Zelar River bridge to the lake south of Manwark. He entered that town as the sun rose and found a small inn. The next day, rested and resupplied, he continued north and crossed the River Wark southwest of Pale as the sun warmed the cold fall air. The solitary trip gave him time to think about his situation. He was the bastard son of the queen's consort, and Meru was his weak half brother. Meru seemed a mild dandy, probably with a feeble brain to go with the feeble hand. More than one resident claimed the boy had never shown any evidence of inheriting his father's power. By some trick of nature, Justik alone had inherited the power to burn.

His only doubt arose days later. Justik chose the path through hills between the River Wark and Fathom because it shortened the trip to Fathom, even allowing for the climb and descent. After a day of pleasant temperatures, a stiff sea breeze hit him when he reached the top of a hill and began the descent. His steps down the north-facing slope led to a forest glen where, in the distance, he glimpsed fire and decided to investigate. A campfire burned in a cave entrance. A tall man with head and face surrounded by amber hair emerged into the falling light.

The man's clothing was patched, but his belt was rich leather. He seemed twice Justik's age and yet had retained his muscles. Large hands grasped logs to stack neatly at the cave entrance. The hairy man saw Justik and in a strong voice called, "Hail, traveler, it is good to see a human face in these parts. I haven't encountered another human since my last trip to Maduk." The fellow waved Justik toward him. "Will you join me for a meal?"

Justik wondered what meal might be offered. Had to be better than the cold cheese, jerky, and bread he carried, and the flickering fire offered a haven from the cold. The man's speech suggested he had some education and might provide an entertaining tale.

"Hail," Justik said. "A meal sounds good as it grows dark and cold. What be your name?"

The man's eyes grew large and his mouth opened. It took long seconds to produce an answer. "I am not sure. You see, I hit my head. After waking, I had no memory. Sometimes a name comes to me, but I cannot be sure it's mine."

"What name is it?"

"Panthis."

This cave-dwelling hermit was indeed Panthis, the father of Breel, who'd never made it back to Zellingon and never returned to Pale. After leaving Credo, he decided to avoid the usual route to Zellingon. He was a hunter and chose to scout in the woods for signs of deer, not realizing he was observed. Then he made the mistake of waiting too long to establish camp the first night. Exhausted, he made a poor fire that went out soon after he fell into a deep sleep.

He woke to find a hoarwolf, a black giant with frosted fur on head and neck, standing over him. He had no time to grab his sword before great fangs sank into his neck and shoulder and dragged him from the bedroll. The wolf shook its catch and Panthis lost consciousness.

Surely the man's neck would have snapped in the next shake, but a dog as massive as the wolf erupted from the trees and barreled into the wolf. The animals rolled in a snarling mass, teeth bared, fangs seeking purchase. The creatures separated, circled, growling, eyes aglow, and then charged. The dog sidestepped a maw aimed at its throat and clamped the wolf's shoulder. The hoarwolf howled in pain as blood spurted. The pair rolled until the yelping wolf dislodged his adversary, hesitated a moment, and then with a half-hearted growl, bounded into the trees.

The dog turned to the human. Panthis remained unconscious as the dog licked the shoulder and neck wound. The creature kept watch until a dazed Panthis woke, and then the dog slipped away. The messenger from Zellingon had no idea where he was or why. Moments later he faced a worse truth: he did not know his name or where he came from.

"Fine, we'll make Panthis your name," Justik said. "What about that meal?"

Panthis waved his guest into the cave, which opened into a wide chamber. The white limestone walls glowed in the firelight, and a vessel suspended over the flame exuded an aroma of rabbit stew. To one side lay a torn sleeping roll, a ratty blanket, and a gleaming Zellish longsword.

As they finished their meal, Justik said, "Your sword is the type used by Zellingon guards. Have you been there?"

Panthis wiped bits of stew from his beard with a rag. "I suppose, but not since I woke. I do all my trading of rabbits, squirrels, and coons for supplies in Maduk. They don't ask questions but give me news of the kingdom. Have you come from Zellingon?"

"Yes," Justik said, seeing no reason to lie. "I saw the queen, her husband, and the prince."

"What about the princess?"

Justik glared. "What princess?"

"Danilla, Meru's twin."

Justik wondered why he had heard nothing of another royal child. Was she kept hidden for some reason? Perhaps because she had a power worth hiding.

"What do you know of this twin? Is she like her brother?"

"I've heard that she is strong-willed."

"Has she some . . . talent?"

Panthis scratched his beard. "Do you ask if she has inherited her father's power? I have heard nothing about that."

None of Justik's drinking companions had even mentioned Danilla let alone hinted she might have power. She was likely as weak as her maimed sibling. Maybe crippled herself. He would have to learn more of Danilla, but for now, he focused on Justi, sure his own power was as great as any his father used against the Tantrocans. Whether Justi retained that ability today was another question. After the Tantrocan war, no one reported seeing Justi burn anything. Perhaps age had sapped his father's power.

In the morning Justik broke bread with Panthis and bid the hermit goodbye, leaving behind a few gold coins. "This will help with winter supplies," he said, filling his lungs with cold, sea-tinged air.

Once alone on a forest trail, with noisy birds and squirrels as company, he wrestled with the thought that power waned with age. Justik might have to face such a fate. Now he could get what he wanted by force, but what about in the future? It would be wise to secure a position like Justi's, one where power was not needed to live in a palace and be called lord. Justi had proven himself when he was young. Now the man strutted about as a judge and savored the rewards of a gift he might no longer possess.

Justik concluded he had to be the Tantrocan champion and employ his power now to assure his position forever. Fortunately, he'd already inserted himself as an integral part of Tantrocan plans to reconquer the Zell. He'd kill for the northerners and seize his reward: honor and power. What he deserved.

With his mind settled, he found the stretch of shore where he'd hidden his boat. There was no boat. The brush Justik used to hide the vessel was tossed left and right. Not pushed in one direction as the wind would do, he thought. The rope that tethered his craft to a lone tree was missing. The thief had been lucky enough to stumble on the hiding place but stupid enough to leave boot prints that marked his arrival and departure dragging the boat to the sea. Justik couldn't follow into the water, but he could find out where the thief came from. The deep, distinctive impressions led Justik into the dense bushes that grew near the coast. He trekked on a flat, coastal trail to a creek wide and deep enough to float the missing boat. The prints led up the creek to a squat, thatched-roof cottage. Moored to a post was the stolen boat. Trees crowded the site, so he arrived unseen, but crows protested his presence. The building remained silent.

Justik could have quietly untied the boat and guided it back down the creek to the sea. But anger drove him to the cottage door. He pounded. Nothing happened, and he pounded again.

"What be yer business here?" a deep voice bellowed from the west side of the house.

Justik turned to see a black-bearded man twice his size standing bare-chested a dozen feet away. Muscles bulged his arms and chest as he lifted a large axe with one hand. His belly was as flat as his large forehead. His wide, flat nose, bushy brows guarded unfriendly eyes as black as his beard.

"I am here to get my stolen property." Justik pointed at the tied-up boat.

The slits holding the beady eyes became narrower. The man spat words that Justik finally understood as a claim that the boat was his, that Justik was a pig's ass, and that his life was over.

"I do not intend to leave without the boat."

"Then never leave." The giant thumped forward, scattering leaves.

Reasoning with the fellow was not going to work. Justik's hand became hot and he was about to kill the ogre when the knife appeared, as if from air. The blade grazed Justik's shoulder and drew blood. Justik winced and shot a weak flame that caught the axe handle.

The flames leapt at the man's arm and he screamed and dropped his weapon. Spouting a string of curses, the giant backed away, holding his singed forearm.

Justik grabbed his bleeding shoulder and prepared to send his adversary to a painful, scorching death. But the man had ducked behind a wood pile and began heaving chunks of split firewood. One bounced on the ground and caught Justik's knee. He tried to ignore his pain and summon fire. A narrow lance of white flame exploded from his outstretched arm and sailed over the woodpile to where the giant's head had been. But was no more. His target had vanished.

Justik cursed and briefly considered chasing his attacker. He put that idea aside and limped to untie the boat. He found a rag in the vessel and tied it around his wounded shoulder. When he got the craft into a wider part of the stream, he boarded and let the water flow carry him toward the Gulf, using his good arm to work the rudder. He wondered why he'd let the peasant live. The man would recover and undoubtedly talk. Having such a tale in the north of the kingdom would enhance Justik's reputation. That might be good, he thought, though it would alert the Zellish about his power. Caldir would not like that.

When he entered the Gulf, Justik set the small sail. The passage to Ankor was uneventful except, when he slept, the passing of a dark sea creature almost capsized the vessel. Justik grabbed the gunnel and held on until the waves subsided. Warily, he gave up on sleep and continued northwest, relieved at last to spy the lamps along the Ankor mooring platform. He docked and climbed the stone steps to the palace, warming in the process. Two guards greeted him at the entrance gate and informed him he must see Caldir immediately. Justik was told to go to Provak's chamber.

The high priest's quarters impressed Justik. The large main room designed for eating, study, and perhaps entertainment had a comfortable feel. A large hearth on the outer wall was fronted by two padded chairs. To one side a narrow window framed a view of the rocky beach, and a goat-hair rug with a flame pattern covered the plank floor. Mosaics of religious symbols adorned the walls along with bookshelves and a substantial wine rack. The sleeping area was separate.

Caldir, second in rank of priests, rose from a wooden table in an alcove where he worked with scrolls. He pointed to the fireplace chairs. "Provak is with a temple acolyte, a pretty one. He will be busy for some time," Caldir said, taking a seat. "I welcome your return. I began to worry."

"I had business," Justik said and sat. "In Zellingon."

Caldir studied Justik's blackened hair and scalp and the missing beard. "Business."

"Justi of the Zell is my father. Of more importance to the Tantrocans, Prince Meru has inherited no power from his father. He is a weak and ineffectual boy and will pose no threat."

Caldir acted as if this were news to him. Justik knew the priest had spies in Zellingon, all of whom had reported the same thing about the prince. And probably about the princess.

"How did you learn these things?" Caldir asked.

"I questioned people. I listened. I observed the royals in a ceremony."

Caldir nodded at Justik's blood-stained shirt. "What happened?"

"A scratch from the sail boom."

Caldir's fingers drummed on the chair arm. He rose. "Refresh in your quarters and I will have food and drink waiting in the meeting room. I will join you there."

Justik washed and donned clean clothes. By the time he reached the meeting room, the fact that he hadn't eaten since dawn was foremost on his mind. He set to work on pieces of beef and pork. The inky wine pleased him. Caldir sipped, licked his lips, and watched.

When Justik sat back, the priest said, "So you observed in Zellingon and left. Did Justi see you?"

"No. I remained hidden in the crowd," Justik lied.

"Good. Our purpose would not be served by giving the Zellish any warning about your existence or, worse, your power. In your absence I have enlisted the Ice in our mission. These hunters inhabit the eastern islands and will assist us."

"Really. What is their price?"

"Princess Ranera."

Caldir explained the agreement and spoke of the Ice enchanters. He also told of the princess's devotion to physical pleasure that made an alliance with an uncultured brute acceptable to her. "You must understand what we are about. A combined force of Tantrocans and Ice priests and you will overwhelm the Zellish. Ice priests can cast enchantments to confuse and weaken warriors. You must eliminate the wizard Justi."

The idea of a priestly spell to disable warriors worried Justik. What if such magic impaired his own power? It could leave him vulnerable. "I should clear the way for your great force by taking care of this wizard before you attack."

Caldir's face whitened. "That would alert the enemy. Better they know nothing of your power until it is too late."

"And then Justi will come out of hiding and I will have no advantage. I could be injured." As he spoke, Justik realized he'd erred by letting Justi see him. It would be better to get close to his father and attack without warning.

"Do not worry," Caldir said. "Justi will be held by the priests. You will face an impotent foe with Tantrocan warriors at your side."

"I don't need warriors at my side," Justik said, ignoring the pain in his wounded shoulder. *And I am not happy to rely on priestly mumblings.*

Mobilization began immediately, and within weeks the followers of Dar had moved in force to the coast with ships ready to transport the army. They intended to gain control of several coastal towns and Fathom. In this campaign the Tantrocans would take no care to hide their actions, confident that Justik would clear the way by eliminating the wieldier of the power that had saved the Zellish two tens of years earlier.

* * * * *

Justik's decision to kill Justi thrilled the Miasma. *The servants of Dar had tried many times to kill the gifted one, first by sending a maddened boar after the pregnant mother,* *then with a tainted cat to attack the infant in its crib, then a rabid dog, and then with enchanted wolves. These had failed, but the Miasma had not given up. The Tantrocan high priest had been persuaded to unleash a master assassin, and an Abantazar thug had tried a poisoned knife. The last had almost succeeded. Now he would die at his son's hand.*

*****

Caldir entered Provak's room as the high priest ate his evening meal. The hedgehog was stuffing a slab of meat into his jowly cheeks and signaled with his finger that his apprentice was to sit. Caldir took his place and tried not to watch as Provak finished his plate in his usual porcine manner. King Brosun tolerated Provak, for his mother liked the man. The young king would not go against his mother, leaving Caldir to suffer under this narrow-minded, overcautious blowfly.

Provak eyed Caldir as he sipped dark red wine. "Tell me what you heard from Fospe."

"I presented my plan for an alliance—"

"Despite my objections."

"I felt it could not hurt to establish contact and find out where our neighbors stood. Fospe met with me and listened."

"Listened?" Provak said, lifting the wine glass and then putting it down without drinking.

Caldir had to admire the man's restraint, for he knew how much Provak liked his wine. "He agreed that his people covet land across the Gulf and conceded that raids yielded little."

"I find it hard to believe that these dumb hunters would join us without some incentive other than plunder and a bit of land. What else do they want from us?"

Caldir dared not tell Provak of his offer of Ranera as the prize. "Military alliance," he said.

Provak reached for his wine glass. "How did you leave it?"

"I will meet with Fospe in two weeks and hear what he learned from his chief."

"I must inform the king of what you are doing. He may not be happy."

"King Brosun wants to return to the Kingdom of the Zell as much as you and I do," Caldir said.

"He will not act unless there is prophecy that predicts success."

"But there is such prophecy. The Dark One will counter the one called The Gifted. You know that."

"That is one interpretation. I have not shared it with the king. And I don't intend to. You will have to tell this Fospe that it is not the time for an alliance."

Caldir's face grew hot as he watched Provak finish the wine.

"This is an extraordinary wine," Provak said, studying the empty glass. "I acquired it from a southern merchant for twice the gold his good wines command. Yet it was worth it. The wine has the unique taste of grape mixed with exotic southern fruits and a smooth, pleasant feeling on the tongue. I'd offer you a taste, but the wine is too precious to me." He pointed to his wine rack in the corner. “Those are my last bottles, and they will last but a month.”

“You alone share in this wonderful vintage?” Caldir asked as the germ of an idea took root.

26
The Ice

Fospe did not go directly to the central Ice village. He traveled over the grassy plain along the coast. He was in no rush, and the grass was a treat the horses savored. When the party turned toward the mountains that formed the backbone of Tantroc, the trail grew steeper and the air colder. Fospe maintained a slow pace that gave him time to ponder Caldir's proposal. When he presented it to Thal, the Ice chief, Fospe would have to advise, weighing the pros of new hunting grounds, warmer villages, and a queen versus the cons of battle, defeat, and death.

The Ice tolerated life in the cold north, but they, like the Tantrocans, craved land in the Zell, south of the Tantric Gulf. Currents of ocean and air made the Zell warmer than the island of Tantroc. The Ice sent hunting parties to the sparsely populated plain in eastern Zell, but Markul rangers often found them and attacked. It was difficult to hunt with armed men in pursuit.

Fospe signaled his men to halt in a glade near the first narrow mountain pass. The men set the animals to graze and went in search of firewood. Fospe climbed to a nearby promontory and viewed the distant river plain to the east. As he watched, several deer led by a great buck crossed. A beautiful sight, he thought, but the herd was small. The hunters would be hard put to add to the winter meat supply. A breeze from the snowcapped peaks to the north forced Fospe to gather his fur cape about him. Having milder hunting grounds across the Gulf might be worth fighting for.

Caldir's proposal to use Ice priests worried Fospe. Ancestral spirits had granted power to their holy men to serve as a defense. Now Caldir wanted priestly talent for offense, to conquer another land, to confuse Zellish men while the Tantrocans killed them. Spirits might not allow such use. Who knew what disaster might ensue?

Seated on a cold stone as his men coaxed a fire from the meager pickings of fallen wood, Fospe toyed with the second part of Caldir's proposal, restoring the Ice royal line. Would Princess Ranera leave her life in Ankor, wed an Ice man, and bear their next king or queen? Seemed like being sold in a slave market. Yet Caldir claimed the woman wanted a queen's power, something she could not have in Ankor without killing her brother. Taking an Ice chieftain to bed—perhaps Thal, more likely his son—was probably easier than regicide.

Thal, chief of the Ice, stood outside his house in the main village, a vast collection of wood buildings of good size and complexity. The tallest stood three stories high. Using hardwoods from foothill forests, skilled Ice carpenters crafted spacious, comfortable structures, all gathered behind a pike-filled pit wider than a horse could jump. Thal watched as Fospe passed over the bridge and approached.

"You are a day overdue. I hope that means you have learned something worth the trip," Thal said. The Ice leader was in his fourth decade, bearded and dark-haired, as wide as a barrel with arms as thick as most men's thighs. He'd used his strength to claw to the top of the Ice ranks, proving his skill as a hunter and then as a manipulator of men. He now had the power of a king among his people with no title other than chief. Thal had authorized Fospe to find out what the Tantrocan priest wanted for two reasons. First, the bickering over where the Tantrocan-Ice border lay and who could hunt where was a drain that left men dead or wounded and did nothing to feed his people. Second, solving this conflict would augment Thal's position. His status as leader was uncertain, and more than one man wanted his position, a recipe for conflict and bloodshed.

Thal led Fospe into a large dwelling where a fire warmed the air near an inviting seating area before the hearth. Pelt rugs covered the floor. Fospe sat on a padded bench near Thal's giant chair.

"What did Caldir want?" Thal asked.

Fospe related Caldir's proposal of an alliance to invade the Zell, using Ice priests to enable easy victory.

Thal's eyes widened. Fospe's report was not what he expected. "How does this Caldir know of the enchantment power? Our priests keep hidden what they do to distract enemies."

"I suspect he's known for some time."

Thal had to acknowledge that possibility. The Tantrocans and Ice had a long relationship involving related peoples who skirmished many times over territory, trade, and hunting rights. The Tantrocans could have figured out the Ice priests. "That gift has been used for defense. Why would Caldir think it could be employed in aggression? Did you point this out?"

Fospe lowered his eyes and shook his head. "I did not. Like you, I was surprised Caldir knew about the priests and did not want to tell him more. Besides, we cannot be sure that enchantment works only in defense. We might warn Caldir of this possible limitation at the next meeting."

"Or not," Thal said. Outside, shouts arose. Thal investigated and found a group of children playing with a ball of hide. Soon they will play with balls of snow, he thought. Short, cool summers and long, dark, icy winters made the northland a tough place to live. He considered the prospect of acquiring land in the Zell where the warm season was longer and the winter shorter. "How does Caldir explain their defeat across the water?"

Fospe brought his fingertips together. "He claims that the tales of a flame-throwing Zellish warrior are true and suggested our priests would have to distract only that one man."

"So like his father, King Brosun seeks conquest. And Caldir proposes to use our priests."

"He wants our warriors as well," Fospe said.

Thal waved off a strand of smoke drawn into the room by the opened door. "Why should we trust Caldir? The Tantrocans want more than land in the Zell. They are obsessed with their view of Dar as a cruel god who requires sacrifices. Human sacrifices. They would slay us in temples if we were weaker."

Before Fospe could answer, Thal's son interrupted. The big youth named Sathal poked his head into the room and announced he would spend the night with a group of youth in a hunting blind. They would hunt in the early morning.

"May the great spirit guide your hunt," Thal said, thinking how, in contrast to the Tantrocan belief, the Ice believed in ancestral spirits that guided the tribe. Sacrifice was not required.

Sathal grabbed a pack, his fur, and his bow and quiver, and left.

Thal circled the room. Joining the Tantrocans, not in conflict, but in cooperation to achieve what both wanted—a place in the warmer regions—was appealing, but not worth the lives of young men like his son. Fospe would know that. There must be something he wasn't seeing. "What more did Caldir offer for our help?"

Fospe cleared his throat. "The Tantrocan priest proposed that Princess Ranera would be willing to assume the Ice throne and serve as our titular ruler."

Thal stopped circling and massaged his jaw. Caldir's offer of a queen, one whose Tantrocan lineage qualified her to rule the Ice, intrigued him. "What do we know of this Ranera?"

"Caldir claims Princess Ranera is driven by two desires: one for power and another for strong men. I suspect that he has nurtured both these impulses."

Thal stood near a richly carved wooden chair, the work of a Tantrocan artist. The piece had been handed down for generations for use by the chief advisor to the Ice king. Thal held that title even though there was no king. If this Ranera became queen, even in name only, it would unite and satisfy his people. To bind this princess to the Ice, however, would take marriage. Sathal was the logical choice for such a union, but Sathal had romantic notions about the interactions of men and women. That would complicate matters.

"I will think on this," Thal concluded.

Sathal was a youth of ten and nine years who did not resemble his father. The son was tall with a long face, high brows, thin lips, and straight brown hair. He lacked Thal's thick muscular build but had a wiry strength that often prevailed in the wrestling contests enjoyed by young men. He had added flesh in the past year but lost none of the quickness that gave him victories.

"What is it, Father?" he asked as he entered the chief's room a day after his hunting expedition.

Thal motioned his son toward a bench. "The Tantrocans propose an alliance to take land across the Gulf. Their proposal involves you. Not you exactly, but a young man eligible for marriage."

Sathal's mouth opened, but it took him a long moment to find words. "It sounds as if I am to be sacrificed."

Thal folded his hands. "Let me speak plainly. The Tantrocans are offering the Princess Ranera to become an Ice royal."

"In exchange for what?"

"Our help in conquering the Zell."

"Why does this Ranera need to marry to be declared our royal?"

"To be accepted as one of us, she must have a connection," Thal said, leaning forward and examining his son. "That will be achieved by marriage."

"This sounds foolish, Father. Who is this woman? Is she pleasant to behold? What if I can't stand to be in her presence?"

"Then you can have separate bedchambers. Ranera, I am told, is a year younger than you, and we will see her before the deal is done. If she needs it, you have strength and resolve to tame her."

My son needs a woman, Thal thought. In the past year, he had avoided women, almost as if the taste for such companionship had fled. That was not good, for without a woman, a man was incomplete. Of course, both he and his son would have to see this Princess Ranera, and if she turned out to be a witch, the proposal could not stand, at least not for Sathal. But if she was tolerable and had the shape a young woman should have, it was Sathal's duty to his people to wed her. Here was a chance for great service—to provide the Ice with a true royal and then with an heir to the throne. *It would also secure my own position.*

Sathal waited. When the older man held his peace, Sathal said, "So what am I to do?"

"Prepare to travel. And choose something clean to wear. Shave. Tie your hair back. We will leave on the morrow. The Tantrocans are anxious to get on with things."

When his son left, Thal dispatched a fast messenger to Ankor and ordered his chief warrior to visit the five major Ice villages to collect fighters and priests. The Tantrocans did not expect much muscle from the Ice. They were mostly interested in the enchanters. And willing to use Princess Ranera to get them.

27
Seer's Lament

When Justi was of ten and three years, he traveled to a nearby village to learn more about his power. He met Rakur in a decrepit cabin. The unsavory hermit was reputed to be a learned collector of prophecies, but Justi found a bug-eating, sharp-tongued grump who spouted obscure information. Rakur did reveal there was another child of the gift. That turned out to be Mercerio, who as queen rewarded Rakur with an appointment as a scholar in the royal library.

Justi had to admit that Rakur deserved the reward. Besides pointing to Mercerio and her mercy gift, he—his dog—had inadvertently revealed Justi's healing power. The injured dog Foot had forced Justi to pet it and in the process mend its leg. Rakur had also saved Justi's family from a pursuing killer when they fled Ortun. Later, when Mercerio was held hostage, Rakur had found Justi, lost, discouraged, and depressed, near the Swamp of Snakes and sent him to Fathom where he rescued the princess. These services merited reward indeed.

Rakur's quarters in the royal city were a marked improvement over his Ortun house. His clothes were clean and unpatched. Even he had transformed—his fringe of gray hair was trimmed and his skin was pink. He dressed like a queen's scholar and was able to spend time in the Zellingon library without alarming patrons, who would have fled from the odiferous, unkempt scholar Justi had faced. Somehow, he'd managed, after the war, to acquire his personal collection of old texts, some of which were rare and not found among the library's holdings, and that earned him status in the scrollish class.

Rakur had a space in the library, a yellow stone building that faced the central square opposite the palace, and that is where Meligo, the queen's advisor, found him, poring over a new scroll. Meligo remained lanky with thick black hair, now touched with gray. He didn't so much walk as glide in with his usual grace, wearing the white smock he favored. Meligo had been Prince Meru's tutor and now served as advisor to the prince and his mother. Since acquiring that position, he had started wearing a blue sash across his chest and a gold chain and amulet about his neck, adornment with no official meaning but possibly daunting to the gullible.

"I see you arrive with the puffery of authority," Rakur said.

"I see your grumpiness has not waned. Let us discuss what the Tantrocan preparation means."

The short Rakur rose from his desk and embraced his visitor, assuming a ridiculous position with his head on Meligo's chest. The two had become friends, not just because they were both scholars, but because they shared an irreverent view of things. With his appointment to royal service, Rakur had toned down his language and improved his manners. In Meligo's presence, however, there was slippage in both departments.

"I thought the discussion was over," Rakur said as he backed away. "The barbarians plan to invade again. It seems as simple as that."

"But the Tantrocans have not multiplied. Why would they risk another defeat?"

"Perhaps they are fools."

"Nothing in this conflict is so simple, you old raccoon. It is the next chapter in the larger conflict—Li's followers against Dar's, the good against the evil, the very thing you fret about. It is the scenario foretold in all these scrolls you hide beneath."

"I don't hide beneath them. I study them for clues, but I find only scant reference to this second invasion." Rakur sat at his desk and pointed at a padded armchair for Meligo. "See if you can fit yourself into that without disturbing your sash and jewelry."

"Don't be literal as you read the texts. The invasion may be but one scene in a great play. Driving the Tantrocans back across the gulf two decades ago was less important than the introduction of Li's gift and the unification of Justi and Queen Mercerio."

Rakur grunted.

"And the job is not done. The sundered gift is not unified merely by the fact that Justi and the queen are joined. Justi's power is tempered by Mercerio's mercy, but that does not make the gift that Li intended."

Rakur blinked, closed his eyes, opened one, and said, "I suppose you expect the gift to be unified in their child. A reasonable, if simplistic, notion, but one belied by a cruel fact: Prince Meru has shown no evidence of any power." Rakur opened the other eye and took on a toadish look as if he'd skewered a dragonfly.

"The prince is but ten and seven years. He has time yet to show his gift."

"Justi's power was evident at ten and three years," Rakur said.

"It may await some reason to appear."

"One would think that just getting to ten and seven years would provide abundant provocation and reason to singe someone."

"A prince of the realm leads a sheltered life."

Rakur waved his hand as if he were dispersing a foul odor. "So you insist that Meru is the true recipient of Li's gift in the absence of evidence."

"There is evidence," Meligo said. "Lord Justi claims that all his life he has been accompanied by a hawk that shows up whenever he summoned the Justice Gift."

"So?" Rakur said, moving a scroll from his desk to a shelf.

"Well, I noted a hawk often accompanied the prince when he was young—"

"And then disappeared."

"True. I've seen nothing of this bird since the cat Lyra arrived. Expand your mind, Rakur. Lyra is a replacement guardian."

"Maybe the animal watches Meru, but she belongs more to Danilla."

Both men frowned and together stroked their chins. Rakur stared at the elegant man in the chair near the window. Posed, as if he were having his portrait done. A beam of sun stabbed through the pane illuminating motes of dust. Somewhere close a muleteer yelled encouragement to his team.

Rakur tapped a finger on his desk. "You imagine that because the feathered guardian of Justi, who may in fact be nothing more than a pesky hunter, became the guardian of Meru for a time, that the boy has some piece of Li's gift?"

Meligo, who seemed almost to have melted into the piece of furniture, said, "Exactly. With the addition that the form of the guardian has changed from avian to feline."

In the year Meru reached ten and seven, his grandmother, the Queen Mother Melsin, died after a short illness. The kingdom mourned her death, which was followed by an elaborate state funeral. In fall under a bright sun, Melsin's body was placed in a grave beside her husband King Bronte, who'd died in battle during the Tantrocan attack on Zellingon. Before the barbarians overran the town, the king's body had been secreted in a hidden plot in the town cemetery. The plot, now marked with a large stone, was accessible at times to the public.

After the ceremony, a subdued Meru, holding his right hand in his left, led the way back to the palace. Danilla, trailed by Lyra, followed. Justi and Mercerio, after speaking to several mourners, also left the cemetery, sad but at peace with the idea that the woman they both loved had not suffered long. Queen Mercerio recalled how her mother had kept the secret of her own and her daughter's royalty for many years in Abantazar, the town to which she'd fled after the loss of Zellingon. Secrecy protected both queen and princess from unwanted attention from both friends and enemies of the kingdom. It was Melsin who summoned the new Zellish army to liberate Zellingon. Most importantly, the queen mother had guided Mercerio as she matured and then when she wore the crown.

"I will miss her," Justi said when they reached the privacy of the royal rooms.

"Yes, but we must focus on the future. That was always her lesson to me," Mercerio said as she tossed an outer cloak on the bed, shed her boots, and commenced to remove her public dress. "You can serve as my maid. Unbutton this thing, please."

"I am pleased to serve," Justi said and helped Mercerio out of the blue and white garment. He stood holding it as his wife rummaged in a wardrobe. She came out with something green, stepped into it, and turned her back to him. He deposited the first garment on the bed and buttoned the new one.

"That's better. Have you thought further on when our son will be king?"

Justi glanced at his own hand before speaking. "Yes. His weak hand means nothing for assuming the throne."

"Perhaps two good hands aren't needed by a king, but the psychological effect of his weakness will matter. He perceives himself as defective. What's more, he acts as if the weakness increases."

They had hoped that Meru would ignore his minor disability. The royal physicians could find no physical basis for the weakness in the prince's right hand and expressed the hope that he would outgrow the condition. When his hand seemed to grow weaker, a court physician raised the possibility that the weakness stemmed from something in the young man's mind. Mercerio had refused to consider that until recently when her son complained about increased weakness.

"I have decided to consult with Credo. Although she has no skill in treating the mind, I have received reports from Pale that her daughter Breel may."

Justi wrestled with several thoughts. Meru's weak hand meant he had not inherited his father's power. But Provani's son claimed to have the power. Could it be that only the first-born son held the gift? Should he tell Mercerio about the encounter with Justik? What wife wants to hear of her husband's bastard child?

"Did you hear what I said? About Credo's daughter?"

Justi spoke carefully. "I wonder if poking at Meru with a new healer would do more harm than good."

Mercerio stood with arms akimbo. "We have to try."

"How old is Breel?"

"Why, she is Meru's age," Mercerio said as she slipped on a pair of soft leather shoes.

Justi sighed. "That may make her probing of our son either more painful or more pleasant."

A month after Justik had appeared in Zellingon to confront his father, Credo arrived from Pale. She had aged gracefully and still held the beauty that had so enchanted Panthis. Breel, daughter of Credo and

Panthis, and her dog Bib accompanied her mother. Breel was a few months older than Meru and Danilla with Credo's black eyes and hair, each with a hint of green, and tallness from Panthis. Credo introduced her when they were brought before the queen.

Queen Mercerio smiled. "It's wonderful to see you again, Breel. Last time you were here, you were starting to walk. You have grown into a beautiful woman."

"I am happy to greet you, Your Highness." Breel said. "And I am excited to see Zellingon."

Mercerio assessed the large dog who sat at Breel's side. The dog's muzzle showed white, and he exuded dignity and intelligence. "Your dog is as welcome as you, Breel. We will have to make sure there is no problem with Lyra."

"Who is Lyra, Highness?" Breel asked.

"Danilla has acquired a giant cat who might object to a canine."

"Oh," Credo said, with a lifted brow.

"We will keep them apart," Mercerio said.

Her idea foundered when Danilla entered the room with Lyra alongside. Bib stood, his fur bristling, and barked. Breel commanded him to sit. Lyra did not seem in the least perturbed, even when Bib darted across the room and slid to a stop. In fact, the cat took a moment to lick her paw before dealing with the dog. Standing almost as tall as the dog, Lyra reached out her paw and touched Bib's nose. Eyes big, Bib sat. Then both animals settled on the floor and seemed content to watch each other.

"That is strange," Mercerio said. "I guess they don't have to be kept apart."

Breel went over and put her hand on the dog. "Bib seems to have come to some sort of acceptance. I sense he is more than calm. He's almost serene."

"This is my daughter, the Princess Danilla," Mercerio said.

The girls smiled and greeted each other, their eyes reluctant to leave their pets.

The queen made a motion to an attendant waiting at the side of the room. "I will have a servant show you to your rooms and let you freshen up from your travels. There is time to rest until dinner."

Prince Meru sat in the garden petting one of the three resident, normal-sized cats with his left hand. Queen Mercerio entered and said, "We're having one of your favorite dishes this evening: roast pig."

"Great," the prince said. "I'm hungry already."

"We'll start dinner early. We have two guests, an old friend, the healer Credo from Pale, and her daughter."

The prince stopped touching the cat. Mentioning a healer meant that it had something to do with his hand. He was sick of physicians. He wanted to be left alone. But mention of a daughter caught his attention. He turned to his mother. "How old is this daughter?"

"Your father asked the same question. About your age I believe."

Meru entered the dining room wearing a brown doublet that made him confident, even bold. He found his sister talking to a dog. Rakur and Meligo with goblets in hand spoke quietly in one corner. A servant hovered near a door. Justi and Mercerio stood near two beautiful women, one older, one a teenager. Meru knew Credo but not the younger one. The queen waved him close.

"Meru, you remember Credo, the healer from Pale." Mercerio said. "This is her daughter Breel, who also has such skills. Ladies, this is Prince Meru."

Meru flinched at the word "healers." Was he to be humiliated before two women at the same time? He gritted his teeth and managed a smile. When the girl glanced at him, Meru noticed green in her black hair. She has great beauty, he thought, but doesn't flaunt it. *Maybe she is just shy.*

Dinner was announced, and the guests went to assigned seats. Meru found that Breel was seated next to him. When they were sampling the starting bowl of mushroom soup, Meru finally felt uncomfortable enough with his silence to say, "I have never been to Pale. What is it like?"

It took Breel a moment to answer, as if she'd missed that the prince was talking to her. "It is a much smaller place than Zellingon," she said. "There is farming, herding of goats, fishing, and, of course, hunting. And we have a couple of merchants plus an inn. Just a normal small town. But I'm sure people are the same in Pale as they are here. You know, just normal."

Meru scanned the dining room. "I'm not sure I encounter many normal people here. Most are dressed to impress and seem to be on stage when they visit the palace. And all seem to want something."

Breel's green eyes widened slightly. "Yes, I can see that. I am hardly acting as I would at a meal in our own small cottage. I feel that I have to be careful not to do or say something that might offend."

"Offend whom?"

"The royal family—the queen, your father, your sister, and you. You are the prince, after all."

"Yes, I have that title, but I don't offend easily. But I understand. And every dinner with even one guest seems to be an official function."

"Exactly," Breel said. "One has to be careful."

Meru finished the last of his soup and waited until a servant removed the bowl. Breel indicated that she'd had enough, and the man took her plate as well. Other servers appeared and placed the second course— a rack of ribs, a potato dish, and a new vegetable imported from the southlands. Dull, red, and round, it added color whether edible or not, Meru thought. Even Bib received chunks of meat not elegant enough for human fare. Water glasses were refilled and a new wine served. Conversation continued only after everyone had sampled the offerings and found them acceptable.

"I know why you're here," Meru said, deciding to get the whole healer matter out in the open. "It's my hand."

Again, the greenish eyes grew large as Breel studied the young man next to her. "Yes, it's true, but I really know nothing about it. My mother just told me I should come in case I could help."

"Can you?"

"Perhaps. I would have to know you better."

Meru felt heat in his face. "Know me? Why? Can't you just examine my hand?"

"But I need to know how you use your hand."

Meru found himself on a long, leather-clad bench with Credo and Breel seated on either side of him. Being that close to Breel made him a bit uncomfortable, but he summoned all his princely dignity to endure it. Credo asked questions about whether Meru's hand ever hurt (it didn't), whether exercise ever helped (not much), and if he wanted the hand to be normal (of course). Then she asked what he felt when he tried to use his hand. He said he felt nothing special.

"When was the first time you noticed a change in the hand, the greater loss of strength?" Credo asked.

"When I was about eight or nine."

"What was happening at that time?"

Meru had to give that some thought. Finally, he said, "I was studying with Meligo every day and hardly had time to do anything else. No, wait, that's when my sword-training began as well. I remember because I couldn't hold the sword in my weak hand. I had to practice backwards."

"What were you studying with Meligo?"

"History. Of the Zell and the great conflict with the Tantrocans. How the Zellish prevailed, drove the barbarians back across the Tantric Gulf, and restored the kingdom."

Credo asked permission to examine the prince's hand and did so. She said it felt normal and then closed her eyes. Meru could feel her strength and the sensation made him even more aware of how different her grip was from his own. She asked him to squeeze and he made a weak effort. At last, she let go his hand and sat back.

"I sense nothing wrong within your hand. Just as the physicians could see nothing wrong from the outside. Do you mind if Breel touches you?"

That alarmed Meru, not sure where or to what extent the young girl meant to do her physical examination. "No. I guess not."

"Fine, Prince Meru. Breel's talent works best without distraction. I will leave you two alone and talk to the royal physician." Credo smiled and left.

Breel said, "I only need to sense what is going on in your head as you move your hand. It won't hurt."

Meru straightened his back and inflated his chest. "I am able to abide whatever pain you must inflict."

Breel slid closer to Meru, pressing her thigh against his. "You'll have to roll up your sleeve."

Meru exposed his forearm. Breel frowned.

"Maybe it's better if you remove the shirt, for I must sense how your entire arm works."

Meru reddened. "Is this really necessary? I have nothing beneath this shirt."

"It's warm in here," Breel said. "And I promise I'll just be feeling."

Credo heard the outcome of her daughter's examination and arranged to see the queen.

"What did you learn of the prince's condition?" Mercerio asked.

"There seems to be nothing physically wrong with the prince's hand. All muscles are fine and capable of contraction and receive healthy blood."

"His weakness is not real?"

"It is real to Prince Meru, but not real to his arm and hand."

"I do not understand," the queen said.

"Something within his mind is blocking the flow of intention. I agree with the suggestion made by the royal physician that the problem may be in the prince's mind." Credo did not seem upset by her diagnosis.

"What about Breel? Can she not treat the mind? Are you saying nothing can be done?" Mercerio's seemed sad and grim at the same time.

Credo took time to formulate her answer. "I did not say that, Highness. My daughter thinks that with time she can help, but Prince Meru must be ready to receive help. He needs to believe and really want to conquer this weakness."

"How can I make that happen?" Mercerio asked.

"Sometimes just having more responsibility works. Also the passage of time. When Breel does try to treat the prince, there is something she can use to free Prince Meru's mind. I have found a plant extract that relaxes and opens the mind. Breel has used it several times to treat difficult cases in Pale."

"Where is this extract?"

"The extract comes from plants that grow only along the shore. An old chemist in Pale has experience in the precise steps of preparation. We will return to Pale, tend patients who need us, and create enough supply of this drug to treat the prince. This will give the prince some time to accept both the need for, and the possibilities of, Breel's treatment."

Mercerio sighed. "I will tell my son nothing of this until you return."

Credo shook her head. "You must tell him everything."

28
A New High Priest

Caldir decided Provak was more interested in good food and drink than in interpreting Dar's commands. He acknowledged the Tantrocans needed slaves, sacrifices, and wealth, but advised against the very thing that would bring all three treasures: war. He had to be removed.

Caldir's first choice was poison, like the kingsbane he'd given to Prince Brosun. Unfortunately, King Brosun had outlawed kingsbane and destroyed the black market that supplied it. Probably in fear of his sister. Caldir's suppliers had not seen any kingsbane since the ban. The priest paced, considering how to proceed without the toxin. He debated using a knife on Provak and dismissed that as undignified and messy. Blood turned Caldir's stomach. He imagined luring Provak to a high place where a push might teach him to fly. But the man was short and wide and no fool. He would not put himself in such a danger and might take Caldir over the edge with him. An assassin would do the deed, but then Caldir would have to kill the killer. His plan to become high priest needed something else, something effective and secret.

Over a mug of wine, Caldir considered a different poison. A traveler from Abantazar had been noted because he acted rich, gambled, dined well, and hired expensive women. Caldir sent his servant to find out about this visitor. A prostitute claimed the man boasted of selling mushrooms from the Swamp of Snakes, mushrooms that yielded a substance that could affect the mind and the body, even kill. Caldir's servant knew of an amulet and potion dealer, a chemist, who bought new and exotic plants and elixirs and told Caldir where the shop was. The priest then feigned disinterest and dismissed his servant. A drug that could kill was exactly what Caldir needed.

Late in the day, the priest darkened his cheeks with a berry stain and donned a black, hooded cloak. Satisfied he wouldn't be identified, he headed to the Ankor marketplace. The cold air did not keep crowds from the shops that sold fish, meat, cloth, implements, antiquities, and oddities.

Caldir found the potion shop on a back street. Inside the cramped space, wall shelves held vials and bottles with a rainbow of liquids and pills. A wooden counter was covered with trinkets. Hardly the sort of display if you wanted customers to browse to find the right talisman or potion. The air, tainted with dust and chemicals, made Caldir's eyes water.

An old man in a stained tunic came from a door behind the wooden bench. He greeted his customer and asked what manner of charm was needed. Caldir got a brief view of a workbench filled with stoppered flasks the size and shape of crabapples.

"Not a charm. I have a friend in dire need of something to relax his mind," Caldir said.

The shopkeeper tried unsuccessfully to smooth the tufts of gray hair that rimmed his mottled head. He squinted first at his visitor and then at his vials. "I have a potion with the mark of Dar that can do that. Perhaps along with an herb."

Caldir sized up the man. "No, this is a more serious case. I need something potent, even dangerous, that can be given to shock my friend's system."

"Perhaps a chemist—"

Caldir's hand shot out and he grabbed the shopkeeper's garment at the neck. He pulled the startled man half over the counter. "I know you sell such potions, even kingsbane, so let us be frank. I want something and can pay for it. You want the money and life."

The chemist's eyes widened. "I have no kingsbane."

"Something like it? To be used in a minute amount, of course, for benefit."

"Sorry. I can't help you."

Caldir tightened his grip and revealed a blade in his other hand. He brought the knife to the man's throat. "I said this is urgent. And most of your remedies are meant to trick the mind. I suspect several poisonings in Ankor have relied on your products. You wouldn't want the guards rummaging in your back room for evidence, would you? So. think hard, friend, and find something. I know you just paid a man from Abantazar a goodly sum for a bag of mushrooms."

The merchant made choking sounds as he grabbed Caldir's hand. "Let me breathe."

Caldir released the man but kept the knife in plain sight.

"The traveler you speak of brought me black-capped mushrooms found near the Swamp of Snakes. He included the recipe for extracting a substance called morcin that strongly affects the mind. He suggested it might, in small doses, have some use as a medicine. I assure you that was my interest."

"Where is the extract?"

"I have not yet prepared the drug. I have the mushrooms and a recipe." The chemist reached below the counter and lifted a sack. "I have no experience with this concoction and getting it may be dangerous."

"Why?"

"Because extraction concentrates the agent in the fungus and concentration means more effect."

Caldir studied the chemist. "What are you not telling me? Speak or you will pay a severe price." Caldir flicked his knife.

The merchant flinched. "The seller told me of a killer who used morcin to eliminate a rich merchant. Twice the recommended dose of morcin caused vomiting that the intended victim attributed to bad lamb. The killer then administered half that dose, and the victim sickened but recovered. The persistent assassin gave a dose and a half. The merchant grew ill and stayed so. With another half dose, the man's mind clouded, and he experienced fearful hallucinations, and then a paranoia. Justified, I'd say. Later, the man lost the ability to speak. His mind snapped. In the final stages, spasms and agony set in. Finally, the brain shut down and the merchant perished."

Caldir opened the sack and found the document that described the preparation of a green substance called morcin, a substance used in the south for treating diseases of the mind. In larger script it warned of the dangers of excess morcin. "Useful," he muttered.

"What is the recommended dose the man mentioned?"

The chemist slid a metal spoon across the counter. "This volume is an apothecary standard. You must extract the morcin precisely as described and dissolve the end powder in ten and two of these volumes."

"I'll take the mushrooms," Caldir said.

"If you take them, you must risk the extraction. I do not recommend it. I can prepare the morcin and deliver it."

"I will handle it." Caldir dropped several coins on the counter and backed away with the bag. Before he opened the door, he said, "Who else knows of these mushrooms and the poi . . . drug they contain?"

"No one except the man who sold them to me."

"Keep it that way. Do not mention this transaction to anyone."

Back in his room, Caldir studied the extraction instructions. Tedious, he thought, then turned his attention to morcin's effects. A single, precise apothecary dose cleared confusion and agitation. Multiple doses led to progressive weakness and loss of speech. Excess amounts produced insanity and death. A dozen mushrooms yielded a dozen doses of morcin.

Before he began extracting the poison, Caldir summoned a man thought to be the son of Ukor, the assassin who served the deceased high priest Aduk. This man handled unsavory tasks, such as removing people in ways that appeared accidental. "The keeper of an amulet shop behind the marketplace has a loose tongue," Caldir said. "I did business with him yesterday and do not want that known. Do not kill him—we need our chemists after all—but make him understand that talking about his customers would be unwise."

Extracting the morcin was not difficult—something any priest could handle—but it took a day's work. He collected a green sludge on a paper filter and dissolved it in water to get a green liquid. With a flask of the tasteless liquid, Caldir entered Provak's apartment while the high priest counseled the king. Caldir uncorked a bottle of the priest's special wine, poured out a tiny amount, and replaced it with enough morcin to provide, according to Caldir's calculations, what the assassin had used to slowly kill the rich merchant. Caldir resealed the vessel and treated the other three bottles in the same way and moved them slightly forward in the rack. He added a bit of dust to match adjacent containers that held lesser quality wine. Provak would consume his favorite new wine first. Even one bottle might send him into a downward spiral. Opening the second bottle would ensure it. Caldir would tend his ailing superior and use a second bottle if needed.

Late the next day, Provak summoned him. He entered the man's chamber and noted the mostly empty wine bottle on the table. Provak huddled in a chair with a blanket wrapped around him, and his eyes, normally steady, darted from Caldir to dark corners. The high priest's shoulders twitched.

"I do not feel well," Provak said with a hoarse voice and then breathed deep as if air were scarce. "I hope it passes by tomorrow, but I fear that it is not something so benign. I am being besieged by spirits of evil intent. If I close my eyes, I see them flying at me in bizarre garb of many colors, with lights flashing about their bodies. When I stand, I am unsure of my balance. I find it hard to think."

"I am sorry to hear this," Caldir said solicitously as he considered the size of the hedgehog and wondered about the bulk of the merchant. "Is there anything I can do?"

"You must be ready to answer the king's summons if I am not well. I would call the physician, but I have no confidence in that bumbling idiot." Provak threw the blanket over his legs. "I will sleep and see how I am tomorrow."

"Perhaps a glass of wine will help?" Caldir asked, having calculated that Provak was an oversized man who needed a larger dose of morcin.

Provak hesitated and then said, "Yes. There's bread and cheese to go with it. Perhaps you will have a glass with me."

The offer of wine shocked Caldir and made him wonder if the unusual generosity was a side effect of the morcin. How could he refuse the offer without raising suspicion? Drop his cup? Provak's beady eyes watched too closely. He had to drink. Maybe a small amount would do him no harm. He smiled and poured most of the remaining wine into Provak's mug and a swallow into his own. He raised his cup and drank.

"You sip as a child would, Caldir."

"I do not have your palate for fine wine. This one seems, I don't know, a bit earthy."

Provak's brows lifted, but before he could speak, a servant arrived announcing the king's summons. "I am not well," Provak said. "Caldir will go in my stead."

Caldir served Provak his meal, patted the man's shoulder, bade him farewell, and fled. In his chamber, feeling lightheaded and nauseated, he vomited and then rinsed his mouth and wiped his face. With unsteady steps he sought King Brosun.

Provak lingered. For two weeks he was unable to leave his room. He began to speak gibberish that morphed into an angry bellicosity when he perceived he was not understood.

Caldir ensured that recovery would not happen. The court physician administered several foul-smelling, useless concoctions with which Caldir served wine. Caldir kept King Brosun informed about Provak.

"How fares my high priest?" King Brosun asked.

"Alas, sire, the man seems no better," Caldir said sadly. "Worse, in fact. And the physician is not optimistic. He says it is like nothing he's seen before."

"Quite strange. Provak always seemed healthy as a stag."

"Or a hedgehog."

The two men stared at each other.

"Well, such is fate," Brosun said. "But I need Dar's representative as a guide."

When Caldir remained silent, the king continued, "Your time as apprentice is over, Caldir. You must now become high priest and serve this court."

"Is that wise, my king? Might not some think it hasty?"

Brosun stared at Caldir for a long moment. "Perhaps you are right. There are many ready to criticize my every move. I will announce that Provak has two weeks to recover, after which I will be forced to fill his position with someone familiar with the enigmatic words of prophecy as we contemplate invading the Zell."

The two weeks passed without Provak's recovery, an outcome assured by additional doses of morcin. The man no longer even tried to speak and seemed to have entered a world that existed only in his head. His sleep, marked by labored breathing and tremors, lasted most of the day. He was forced to wear diapers and eat only liquids, liquids that Caldir made sure he was there to administer with a bit of wine. When Brosun appointed Caldir his new high priest, Provak conveniently succumbed to his morcin-induced ailments and left this world.

Caldir was told of the death and hastened to the man's chambers. He asked the servant to give him some time alone with his master. When the servant left, Caldir emptied the remaining bottle of wine contaminated with morcin. He rearranged the wine rack so that there were no large gaps. He left with the empty bottle concealed beneath his garment.

An elaborate state funeral honored the departed high priest. Caldir's eulogy, delivered in the full ceremonial robes of the high priest, was considered by many to be touching and heartfelt. The funeral pyre was spectacular.

*****

The dark spirits were happy to see Caldir become the Tantrocan high priest. *With Caldir advising King Brosun, invasion would unfold. I wondered if the Justice Flame might again be called on to save the kingdom. And that could mean danger for Justi and his children.*

29
A Path to Power

Justik was summoned to Caldir's room where the new high priest welcomed him with a platter of cheese, butter, and dark bread. A fire burned in the fireplace to ward off the chill. Justik watched as Caldir made a show of opening a bottle of wine. Clearly something was afoot, for his host was not prone to throwing parties.

"Sit," Caldir said. "I want to share my vision of the invasion. It is more than a military exercise."

"How?" Justik asked, filling a mug with wine and buttering a piece of bread. "That's exactly how I see it."

"You need a history lesson. This conquest marks the ascendance of Dar's people over Li's misguided followers."

Referring to a table full of scrolls and several leather-bound notebooks, the priest covered the initial invasion that destroyed the trading post of Maduk and conquered the walled town of Fathom. He related how the Tantrocans marched undetected to Zellingon, which had been left unguarded when King Bronte led his troops to Fathom. By the time the Zellish army reappeared in the royal city, the Tantrocans possessed Zellingon. In the ensuing battle, King Bronte was slain, Queen Melsin fled, and the Zellish army scattered.

"For ten and eight years, we ruled the northern regions, finding it a rich source of slaves and sacrifices to Dar," Caldir said.

Justik listened, not seeing how this recount of a past military venture made the new invasion anything different. He gazed out a window where a few snowflakes drifted. "So no warrior with strange powers opposed your conquest of the Zell?" Justik asked, hoping he might learn something useful about Justi.

"Not for the invasion." Caldir hesitated, as if thinking of something new. "But from that time came a report of Tantrocan soldiers who encountered what might be a strange power. A woman was captured briefly near Maduk, but she escaped. As she did, she killed one of our men by what appeared to be magic."

"Magic?"

Caldir held up a red, leather-bound notebook. "A term for a power not of this world, at least not until Justi arrived. And now you, of course. The woman apparently burned a crater in the soldier's chest."

Justik thought of the wound he'd inflicted on the girl in Vok Boorl. "If this woman had power, why did she not join the fight?"

"Our scholars concluded the power did not belong to her. She is thought to be the mother of Justi and was pregnant at the time of the incident. She used her son's power to escape."

Justik found this story interesting and wondered if Provani had ever felt power when he was in her womb. "So how did the Tantrocans lose their foothold in the south?"

"You know the answer," Caldir said. "An unnatural power defeated us. By the time we decided to extend our control to the southern lands including the rich city of Abantazar, a new Zellish army, composed of old military men, young adventurers, farmers, shopkeepers, and boys, formed under the leadership of the newly discovered royal heir, the Princess Mercerio."

Caldir poured a mug of wine before continuing. "The Zellish army marched north as the Tantrocan army left Zellingon intending to take Abantazar. The two forces met in a narrow valley near the Swamp of Snakes. Our troops retreated to Zellingon with a prize: the kidnapped Princess Mercerio as a hostage. That should have disheartened the Zellish and stayed their hand. Instead it brought forth the power of Justi,"

Justik straightened, interested at last. "Tell me exactly what happened."

"The unnatural power was part of a gift to two children. Justi wielded a killing flame against our soldiers, burning and maiming."

"But the Tantrocans were behind the walls of Zellingon."

"The flame thrower led a small band through a secret tunnel below the castle, the same passage used by Queen Melsin to escape when we took the town years earlier. Justi found the princess, and in the process of escaping, opened a gate that admitted a squad of seasoned Zellish fighters. He joined them and turned the tide of battle."

"What did Justi do?" Justik asked, spearing another cheese chunk.

"His sword spewed flame, burning swaths through our men. Our army fled to Fathom, but a mistake was made."

"What?"

"The high priest Aduk, as he fled, encountered the princess with an old adviser outside the walls of Zellingon. He killed the adviser and grabbed Mercerio, intending to use her as bait to get Justi under his control."

"How was that a mistake?"

"Justi came after the princess and was captured. But that brought the Zellish army down upon Fathom and, in the attack, Justi escaped with Mercerio, burning his way out of the town."

Another story of my father's power, Justik thought. However, it was the first time he'd heard of the second gifted child. "Who was the other child?" he asked. "And what was the gift?"

Caldir took his time answering, content to stand in front of the scrolls, poking at them with his long fingers. At last he said, "The Queen Mercerio is rumored to have been the second gifted child. We are not sure what her gift is, but in some way it completed the power of Justi. Provak's theory, and that of Aduk before him, was that the god Li meant the gift to reside entirely in Justi, but it was split by Dar."

"Has this Mercerio killed anyone?"

"No. She has no killing power," Caldir said, "but helps Justi control his gift when the two are near."

Justik selected a soft cheese from the west coast of the Zell known for its offensive odor but rich flavor and smeared it on bread. He poured more wine. "So both Justi and Mercerio remain and are closer together than ever. In fact, they are man and wife. Yet you think you will be successful now despite the defeat. Is this not foolishness?"

Caldir stiffened. "We have you. And the Ice priests."

Justik grunted, thinking that unknown hazards plagued Caldir's plan. The Tantrocans were making assumptions. Only one action would favor their venture: he must eliminate Justi before the invasion.

Justik met the Princess Ranera that evening at a dinner in the great hall where her brother King Brosun presided over a group of advisors and military men. Ranera entered in a long scarlet garment that left exposed a line of flesh from her neck to the gold inlaid leather belt at her waist. She had dark, intelligent eyes and a sensuous mouth in a pleasing face framed by long black hair. She spotted Justik and smiled.

He returned her smile, bowing slightly. The princess motioned for him to sit beside her and he complied. Their conversation at first touched on nothing of substance, but eventually focused on the looming conflict with the Zellish. Ranera had been told Justik had agreed to fight for the Tantrocans and that he had some power akin to the Zellish champion's.

"What hand do you use for this power?" she asked.

Justik smiled, put his fork down, and slowly lowered his right hand to his lap. Ranera took Justik's hand in her own and examined it, causing him some embarrassment.

"It does seem large and powerful," Ranera said, holding his hand for far longer than necessary. "Much of you seems large and powerful. So how will you give us victory in this invasion?"

"I will counter Justi."

"That seems nebulous and risky. You have never seen his power. You could be countered."

Ranera's thought echoed his secret fear and confirmed he must kill his father before any confrontation.

30
Betrayal

The next morning Justik dressed and packed a bag and found Caldir in his chamber. "I am leaving," Justik announced.

Caldir grabbed Justik's arm. "Why? Where are you going? We are almost ready to invade and need you." The high priest held on as if by his will alone he could detain the younger, bigger, and determined man.

Justik shook off Caldir's hand. "Calm yourself, priest. From what I see, you are far from ready. I will return or meet the Tantrocans on the Zellish coast when they arrive."

Justik's unyielding expression backed Caldir away. He said no more, forced to watch in silence as his weapon and key to victory left the castle and strode to the pier.

A two-masted ketch, narrow of beam and swift, awaited. Two hired sailors took advantage of brisk winds to make an overnight passage across the Tantric Gulf to Pale. Late the next day, Justik stood ashore and shed his cloak in the noticeably warmer air, pleased that this side of the Gulf was free of the clouds that marked fall in Ankor. Avoiding contacts in Pale and skirting Manwark, Justik journeyed to Zellingon, his pace rapid and expression grim. He'd had time to think on what he was about to do and wanted to get it done.

Justik spent a cold night outside Zellingon, in the same forest where he'd hidden before sneaking back and killing the two guards. In late morning on a carpet of gold and red fallen leaves, he shivered as he donned an Abantazar robe and a straw hat that hid his blond hair. The colors and smells of fall and chimney smoke were not part of his experience growing up in Vok Boorl, and neither was the cool fall air. At the town gate he waited until a large caravan was cleared to enter, blended in, and made it through the portal, trailing close to the last wagon. He left the caravan and wound his way through back streets to the palace where a guard heard his request that he deliver a message to the queen from an old friend.

"Really," the gray-haired soldier said. "And why would you expect such a thing?"

"Because I am asking."

"Clear out before I call the sergeant."

Anger warmed Justik's face and hands. He worked to calm himself and extracted a coin from his pocket. "I would be most happy to pay you for this service. This is but a portion of what I will pay. He handed over the piece of silver. "Please get this message to the queen. Tell her in private that I am the son of Provani of Vok Boorl, a friend of Queen Mercerio, and I bear a message for the queen's ears. Believe me, she will be grateful to hear this."

The guard regarded Justik, and perhaps something in the intensity he saw made him take the coin and agree to deliver the message. "Fine. I will send your words to the queen."

"Only to her. The queen would not like this message known. If the queen admits me, you will have another coin." Justik pointed to The Sunken Inn across the square. "I will be at that tavern."

When Justik left, the guard summoned a servant. "I have a task for you," he said. "You must give the queen a message. Tell her a young man of less than two decades claims to be the son of Provani of Vok Boorl and wishes to tell her something."

"Why would you even consider such a request?"

"I am not sure," the guard said.

"You seem upset. Your hand shakes."

"The man was intense, filled with some power. He may have important information."

The servant shook his head. "Did you sense danger? What is his name?"

"Danger? No . . . but the man had hard eyes. He did not give a name but wore southern clothes, and I glimpsed a strand of bright blond hair under his hat."

Queen Mercerio, Princess Danilla, and Credo sat in a small garden near a lit brazier. The Pale healer had arrived earlier in the day for a visit and to report progress securing the seaweed-based compound that was supposed to help Meru. Lyra, savoring the warmth from the fire and rays of afternoon sun, open her eyes and stared at the arriving servant. Mercerio wondered what the cat might do if the visitor had not passed inspection. The servant delivered the message as soon as he was allowed to speak.

When Mercerio heard a name she'd not thought about for ten and eight years, it unleashed memories of the beautiful, red-haired girl who'd visited her when she was Karabandor's prisoner in Fathom. She dreaded seeing this messenger, but her curiosity was aroused. What possible message could the man have for her?

"Who is this Provani?" Danilla asked, giving Lyra a calming stroke.

Mercerio lifted her eyes to the cloudless summer sky before answering. "Just someone your father and I knew many years ago."

The queen turned back to the servant. "Is this man waiting?"

"No, Highness. He left word with the guard where he would be."

"That's impolite," Danilla said.

Lyra growled.

"His appearance?" Mercerio asked.

"I'm sorry, but I did not see him. The guard said he was young, not yet two tens of years, and might have blond hair."

"Anything else?"

"The guard mentioned hard eyes and a southern robe."

Mercerio pondered a bit before she said, "I will see him."

When the servant left, Danilla asked, "Shall I get Father?"

Mercerio again studied the sky, finding a single, dark cloud creeping from the west. "No," she said in a firm voice. "Do not trouble him. I will tend to this."

Lyra rose and growled. Danilla stroked the animal that trembled at her side.

Justik surrendered his knife and was escorted to a large room on the south side of the palace where he and a guard waited. Three small windows high on one wall admitted sunbeams. Wood burning in a large fireplace warmed the air and hot wax from burning candles in two alcoves emitted a pleasant aroma. The usual swords and shields decorated the paneled walls along with a large painting that portrayed a confrontation in this room. Men emerging into this room from a portal with a thick wooden door and black metal latch faced Tantrocan soldiers. One of the arriving men, presumably Justik's father, held a glowing sword. Justik scanned the walls and polished floor that bore no evidence of the flames Justi had used to win that fight. Justik examined the black-latched door for a moment, and something, perhaps the past use of power like his own, made his skin tingle.

After making Justik wait for a suitable period, Mercerio entered. Two guards took positions outside the open door. Mercerio studied the well-muscled man, perhaps a year older than Meru and Danilla. He seemed a double of the young Justi. The same blond hair, blue eyes, and set of his jaw. When he introduced himself as Justik, her mind raced. She had given scant thought to the consequence of Provani's seduction of Justi, but now it was clear what that might be. This was Justi's son. She grew angry, then felt disappointment and dread.

"You know it is true, Queen Mercerio. I can see it in your face. I am Justi's bastard son and half brother to your son and daughter. My countenance is proof."

Mercerio settled into a chair and tried to compose herself. She studied the polished wood as she said in a low voice, "You make a bold claim. But what is your purpose in coming to me? What do you want?"

"I want to be acknowledged."

"By whom? How? You make no sense." Mercerio summoned the guards. "Take this man to a waiting room. And provide him food and drink." To Justik she said, "I must think on this. We will speak again."

Mercerio summoned Justi, who arrived seeming puzzled. When Mercerio related what had just happened, Justi's faced turned red. "You say he calls himself Justik and resembles me. Yes, he could be my son. He arrived a few weeks back, and I sent him away. In fact, he was escorted by armed guards and told never to return."

"And you told me nothing of this?"

Justi hesitated. "I was going to, but Justik's guards were found later in a back alley, their throats slit."

Mercerio paled. "I know the men you mean. Are you saying Justik was responsible? Isn't that more reason to tell me?"

"I wanted to find out who killed the guards first. What does Justik want?"

"Acknowledgement," Mercerio said.

"Surely not a public announcement. And he already turned down money. What is going on?"

"We must find out." Queen Mercerio sent the guards to bring Justik back.

The moment the guards came to return him to the queen, Justik felt he'd won. With a surge of power, he wondered how he could get Justi to join them when he found his father in the room with the queen.

"Why are you back in Zellingon, Justik?" Justi asked in a cold tone. "I thought we agreed this was not the place for you. You said you were leaving."

"I did leave. Now I'm back."

Princess Danilla, intrigued by what her mother said in the garden, decided to listen in on the meeting with the rude visitor. She approached the chamber, nodded to the guards stationed there, and peeked in. She could see a large man about her age, who claimed in too bold a voice that he was back. Lyra glimpsed Justik and rumbled. The princess shushed her. Neither the queen nor Justi could see Danilla, for their backs were to the door where she stood. Justik, however, had a view and smiled. Again, Lyra signaled her displeasure.

Justik spoke softly. "I wanted to meet my family, all of them: my queen, my half brother, and my half sister. Sorry the prince and princess are missing." Again, he flashed a glance toward Danilla, who moved out of sight.

Prince Meru found his sister spying. "What are you doing?" he hissed.

"Listening."

He frowned, stepped around her and into the room.

"My prince," Justik said and bowed.

Meru studied the young man. Nothing seemed amiss, except for the unusual southern garb, but something about him alarmed the prince. The man's hands, blue eyes, and especially the fierce smile struck Meru as strange. His head began to throb. Something was wrong.

"You claim to be my husband's son," Mercerio said, "and you have the appearance that some might say is akin to Justi's. But many young men have blond hair and your facial lines. We have no way of knowing if you speak the truth."

"But there is a way of knowing, Queen Mercerio," Justik said.

Meru's vision became misty, as if a green haze were in front of him. The haze moved, reaching out toward the visitor. His headache vanished and he found himself willing the haze to touch Justik.

Justik hesitated and then thrust out his hand. "My power is your power, old man," he yelled, and a diffuse yellowish flame blasted toward Justi.

31
Preparation

Light flared from Justik's balled fist, caught a chair, scorched the wood, and ignited the blue cushion. Half the flame seared Justi's side and set his shirt on fire. He screamed, hunched his shoulders, and tried to lift his burning arm. His face contorted in pain as he thrust his hand toward his attacker. Nothing came forth. There was no Justice Gift in the face of clear injustice. The smoky tang of burning fabric and flesh fouled the air, and Meru's green haze grew thicker as Justik aimed a second beam toward his father. The mist-dimmed flame struck and Justi fell.

Queen Mercerio screamed as Danilla grabbed the table covering and smothered the flames eating at her father. Meru stepped toward Justik and was thrust aside by two guards, who rushed at the assassin, swords drawn. Lyra leapt at Justik who overturned a chair, dodged, and darted out the room's rear door, slamming it closed with the cat trapped inside.

Danilla and Meru knelt beside the unconscious Justi. Both had tears on their cheeks as they tried to assess the damage to their father. A white-faced Mercerio touched both. "Danilla, summon the physician. Pray Li that the burns are not deep."

Justik raced down a hall and, once away from the meeting room, stopped. He shook his head as if to free it from some confusion and turned. The guards ran at him and he sent precise, narrow, white lances that penetrated each man. Justik slipped from the palace. He had arranged a hideout with a thief formerly in the employ of Farsik, the Abantazar crime lord who'd used Justik as a loan collector. The man was not enthusiastic about harboring someone hunted, but he'd seen what Justik could do and wanted no demonstration.

When the frantic search died down, his reluctant host put Justik in a wagon beneath hides that had been poorly cleaned. Wall guards let the wagon pass after a cursory examination.

Outside the city, Justik left the wagon and retrieved his travel pack and sword from the woods. He changed clothes again, then traveled to the coast to await the arrival of the Tantrocan invaders. After several days, he decided he had to see Caldir, thinking his information might hasten the invasion and be of use in staging the attack. A fisherman took him across the Gulf to Ankor in a boat that he soon shared with several giant fish.

* * * * *

In the spirit realm, Mewissio, the seventh order male Adamanti, sensed great danger *after Justik's attack. The gift in Justik might be stronger than Justi's original, purer version. How could that be? "If the Tantrocans retake the Zell, Dar's servants become stronger and we become weaker. Justi lies near death. If Justik has the power, why would not Meru?" A white cloud swirled over Mewissio, then washed away in a new thought. "Perhaps the gift only passes to the first son."*

* * * * *

From a palace balcony, Caldir watched the Ankor pier as a small fishing boat drew near around midday. Justik stepped from the vessel, paid the fishermen, and climbed the wet steps slowly. At the palace entrance, the guards saluted and stood aside as the high priest rushed from the door.

"Are you all right? You move slowly," Caldir said.

"Only weary."

"We will speak in my chamber."

The pair climbed several flights and Caldir opened the door. The room contained a new rectangular table that was covered with documents, including scrolls and a map. Justik sat in the chair by the hearth. "I killed the Zellish champion," he said. "He was, as I expected, slow and unprepared."

Caldir stepped back. "Are you sure you killed him? Are you hurt?"

"He fell burning and didn't move. Even if he did not die immediately, his death will follow shortly. I would have finished the job, but I was distracted by sword-wielding guards intent on taking my head off. They both died."

Caldir straightened the mess on the table and brought a second chair close. He sat but leaned forward as if to make sure he was heard. "Too bad you can't guarantee that Justi, too, is dead, but grievously wounded amounts to the same thing. I hope a lone assassin is not viewed as the prelude to an invasion. Our attack must come as a surprise."

"No one would see me as a Tantrocan agent."

"Fine. We will complete our preparations and move on Pale." Caldir pointed to a spot on the map. "You must come with us."

"Oh, I intend to. I liked the warmer air of Zellingon, and the palace seemed like a nice place to live."

"We will cross as soon as the Ice join us."

Justik stroked his cheek. "That gives me time to visit the princess."

That statement alarmed Caldir, who'd not quite sealed the deal with the Ice. Nor had he told Ranera her role. Sathal, the Ice chief's son, demanded to see the woman who would be his bride. He refused to take a harpy to bed, even if royal.

Caldir found King Brosun enjoying a hearty midday meal in his quarters. The king held a large ceramic tankard in one hand and waved Caldir to a seat with the other.

"Sit," Brosun said. "Will you try the new beer? It's dark and bold."

"Water is fine," Caldir said, wondering how much sampling the king had done.

"What do you have to tell me?"

Caldir selected a chunk of bread and some cheese. After a moment, he took a slice of roast. "I have heard from the Ice, my king. They are not opposed to our proposal but must examine the princess to determine if she is suitable. It is time we informed Princess Ranera of her part in this."

Brosun sighed. "I suppose we must." He called for a servant. When the man entered, Brosun said, "Tell the princess her king summons her."

Ranera arrived with a frown on her face. "What is it, Brother? I was quite busy."

"Busy with what? I thought you lived a life without duties or bother except when we entertain court guests."

"In fact, I was discussing state business with your new champion, Justik. He has interesting news of his adventures spying on the Zellish."

"What news?"

Caldir rushed to answer. "This was one of the things I wanted to discuss. Justik says he successfully attacked Justi."

Brosun's eyes widened. "What does 'successfully attacked' mean?"

"Justik said he struck the man with his own flame and left him unconscious on the floor, with lethal injuries."

Brosun pointed to another chair, but the princess remained standing. "I told you to sit, Sister. That was not a suggestion. What did Justik say to you about this?"

"The same." Ranera marched stiffly to the chair and sat.

"And Justi did not fight back?"

Ranera grabbed a piece of cheese and stuck it her mouth before answering. "He struck by surprise. The man could do nothing."

"And he just walked away?"

"He killed two guards to escape," Ranera said. "I require wine."

Brosun raised his hand and the servant presented a mug of red wine to the princess.

As Ranera drank, both the king and Caldir sipped their beverages, content to let the silence grow over the news of the first successful battle of the second war.

At last Brosun asked, "Is there anything in the prophecies that speak of this fate of the gifted one?"

Caldir tented his fingers. "One passage says the gifted one must die but is not specific about who or when or how."

"Is this some part of your great scheme to re-conquer the Zell, my king?" Ranera asked, leaning forward, suddenly interested in the conversation. "Has the time really come to stop planning and talking and start doing?"

Brosun also leaned close. "What if it has?"

"Then I say good. I'm sick of dreaming. But why am I here? Don't you men like to just plan these things and tell the women afterwards?"

"Actually, dear Sister, I want you to be part of this. Indeed, you have a role to play."

That widened Ranera's eyes.

"You have made it clear that you are bored playing the idle sister with no power and nothing to do, other than cause trouble. You now have a chance to change that."

"What are you talking about?"

Brosun pointed at his high priest. "Explain the important role the princess will play to help our victory. And the great honor she will earn."

Caldir glanced nervously from his king to the princess and then began. "To conquer the Zell, we must defeat the larger, well-trained Zellish army. We have taken the first step by removing their unnatural weapon, the flame-thrower Justi. We have our own weapon, Justik."

"He refuses to engage in common battle," Ranera said, her tone dismissive.

"We'll see about that," Brosun said and speared a chunk of meat.

"Even with Justik," Caldir continued, "the greater numbers of Zellish might evade his flame. Or he could be killed. We need something else, and I have found it. Our neighbors, the Ice, have often thwarted our attacks by their own strange gift. Their priests can reach the minds of enemies and freeze them. We need their enchantment power."

"And they agree to join us?" Ranera asked.

"They will share the spoils, of course," the king said, "but we offered them something they greatly desire. That's where you come in,"

Ranera frowned. "I don't understand."

"The Ice will fight with us in exchange for a boon," Caldir said. "They lost their royal line in a freak accident and need to reestablish it."

Ranera seemed uncomprehending.

"You will reestablish it, Ranera," Brosun said.

Silence filled the chamber. Ranera rose and went to the open window overlooking dark waters. She watched a gull dive and emerge with a fish in its beak. Other gulls screeched after it. At last Ranera turned to her brother. "So I am to become queen of the Ice just like that? I will have to rule over a tribe of hunters who do not know how to construct a palace." Her voice was not as scornful as it might have been. She returned to the table and wrapped both hands about her wine mug.

"You can command them to construct a palace, but you don't just become queen," Caldir said. "You must marry the chief's son and produce a royal heir."

Ranera's face transformed from slightly bored to angry. Her eyes flashed at her brother. "You can't be serious. This is idiocy. I am not some palace whore to be abused at will and then removed. I will not do this."

"Focus on the positive," Brosun said. "You will gain a title and power. You will be revered. You will do as you are told."

Ranera reddened and her hand shook. "I am to be sold like a piece of meat to some . . . some smelly, furred goat," Ranera said. "I will not. I will not." The princess shattered the wine vessel against the fireplace and rushed from the room.

Brosun said to Caldir, "The princess needs time to think on this. She will grow to understand her role."

"I hope so. The Ice party is on its way."

Brosun gave his sister an hour to throw her tantrum. He then went to her chamber where she had sequestered herself. The king dismissed the maid and entered.

Ranera sat stiff in a chair at a table with a mug of wine and a dagger before her. Brosun approached and picked up the weapon.

"You enjoy yourself too much to end your life, Sister. Let us talk of what is bothering you."

"I don't want to talk. You are a pig, my king, and your proposal is piggish."

Brosun took Ranera's hands. "It is your duty to serve the kingdom. Besides, you have tolerated all sorts of men in your bed, tall, short, young, old, bald, and hairy. Not all of them smelled of a perfumery. It should be no problem to perform for a furred goat."

"I choose who I sleep with."

Brosun walked slowly around the chamber. He examined the pieces of jewelry left on a bedside table. "Think of this as a grand opportunity. It will get you out of your empty life. It will give you purpose, something you always craved. It will make you an important part of Tantrocan history."

"I will hate you for this, Brother."

"Perhaps, but that will give you focus. The Ice emissaries will be here in a few days. They are coming to inspect you."

"Inspect me? I will not be inspected as a breeding cow."

"Of course not, Sister. Just as a breeding princess. I suggest you prepare and be on your most pleasant behavior."

The Ice delegation arrived at the Ankor stronghold a week later, on a day when autumn weather turned pleasant. A warm breeze pushed from the south as if to remind both Ice and Tantrocans of the comfort and wealth that awaited them across the Tantric Gulf.

Ranera heard the signal that the group was near. From her chamber window, she watched nine men approach. In the midday sunshine they wore leather vests rather than the usual furs. The garments left muscled arms bare. The guards were easy to identify by their spears and knives, scanning eyes, and positions around the perimeter of the group. Ranera identified Fospe from Caldir's description and figured another man with white in his beard must be the Ice leader. She wondered about the younger man, a tall one with black hair. He obviously had rank, for he was close to the leader.

As the party entered the palace, Ranera ran to a balcony above the great room where she could observe without being seen. Below, King Brosun awaited on his throne, flanked on each side by three rather than the usual one guard. He wore his crown and the largest jeweled amulet in the royal collection. A carpet had been laid before the throne.

The Ice advanced the length of the room and stopped. Caldir spoke briefly to Fospe before he announced the visitors. "My king, this is Thal, high lord of the Ice. He is with Sathal, his firstborn, and Fospe, his advisor."

"Welcome to Ankor," Brosun said.

"We come in peace and for a purpose," Thal said.

"You have had a long journey. I suggest you take time to refresh. Then we can share food and discuss our business."

Thal nodded and said, "And meet the Princess Ranera."

"Of course."

Ranera cringed.

The Ice party returned to the great room an hour later. To Ranera's surprise, they had changed to decorated garments. It was almost civilized behavior. The young man now wore a shirt and breeches with patterns of red stitched into the end of sleeves and pants. The princess studied his chiseled features and very dark eyes. Was this the one she had to marry to become their queen? she wondered.

At the end of a meal, Thal said, "So this proposal to unite for the sake of gaining land across the Gulf hinges on our acquiring a person of the royal line. Let's get on with this, Brosun. Show us this Princess Ranera and we will judge her value."

Brosun nodded to a waiting servant, and moments later, Ranera, dressed in a green gown and wearing her royal tiara and gold necklace with the Tantrocan emblem done in red stones followed the guard into the throne room. The gown was low-cut and showed the pleasing shape of her young breasts. She held her head high and gazed frankly for a moment on the old visitor and then fully on the younger one. She had no smile.

"My sister Ranera, princess of the Royal House of Ankor, first in line to the Tantrocan Throne," Brosun said with a casual gesture.

Thal and Sathal studied Ranera as they would examine a herd animal before deciding which one to kill for dinner. Thal rose and walked around the princess. Ranera wondered if he would lay his hands upon her to assess her musculature and her teeth, but the Ice leader was content to just examine.

"Speak to us, Princess," Thal said. "What do you think of the proposal that makes you our queen?"

"She is intrigued," Brosun said.

"I will serve my people in doing my duty," Ranera said.

Sathal stood. "I will speak with the princess alone, King Brosun."

In the small adjacent room, Sathal and Ranera stood facing each other. Both were doing the sort of inspection that would be rude in other circumstances, but now seemed part of the horse-trading ritual imposed on them.

"I am Sathal, son of Thal. That puts me in the same position as you."

Ranera laughed. "Hardly. I am of the royal Tantrocan line. You are but the son of a hunter."

"I at least am sure to rule one day," Sathal said. "You are but decoration." As if to show his superiority, Sathal flopped into a chair, leaning back, legs stretched.

Placing her hands on her hips, Ranera said, "Commoners do not sit in the presence of royalty unless asked to do so. I could have you whipped."

"Tantrocan commoners, perhaps. I am Ice. But let us get to the point. You and I are to marry to seal this alliance between your people and mine. Neither of us is happy about this. Our best course is to put aside worthless pride and get on with it. I have been told to do this, provided you are not ugly and have proper woman parts. Clearly you are not ugly."

Ranera smiled. "Nor are you."

"A queen must bear children to continue the royal line. I see from your bosom and the flare of your hips that you are likely a breeder."

Ranera leaned over with her hands on the top of a table and brought her shoulders forward. Her low-cut gown softened, giving Sathal a view of her cleavage. "I have proper woman parts. I hope you have proper man parts. At least your hands and feet seem large."

Sathal found himself staring at Ranera's chest. At last he forced his eyes to hers. "Fine, we are equipped in body for this role we must play. But I must know your mind, Ranera. Are you the spoiled vixen witch they say you are?'

"Probably."

"Then know this. You will be queen of the Ice, but I will be the ruler. You will listen to me in making all decisions. I know my people and you do not."

Ranera stood with a smile on her face. She smoothed her gown, running her hands slowly down each hip. When she spoke, it was not a direct response.

"Where are we to do this ruling of the Ice? Not in the frozen north, I hope."

"We expect to occupy a part of the Zell along the northern coast," Sathal said. "I'm sure you would find that more to your liking."

"Good. Then let us say we have come to an understanding."

Thal and Brosun agreed that the actual marriage of Ranera and Sathal would occur after the successful invasion of the Kingdom of the Zell. Summer warmed the northern island when preparations for invasion started. As fishermen, the Tantrocans had many boats for transporting soldiers to the mainland. As hunters, the Ice had few, but their chief contribution to the invasion force was their priests who would be distributed among the boats carrying Tantrocan fighters. In the ensuing weeks, Ice priests arrived in Ankor along with hunters. Weapons, extra clothing, and food were loaded into the Tantrocan fleet.

This activity did not go unnoticed.

PART V
Li's Might

The children of Li find strength in strange forms and places.

32

A New King

A stunned Prince Meru asked. "Why didn't Father defend himself? Does he no longer possess the Justice Gift?" Meru had doubted tales of his father's actions during the Tantrocan war, thinking more than once the stories exaggerated, but this demonstration from someone who might have inherited traits from Justi was hard to dismiss. "But Justik's flame was weak, more yellow than white," he said with more hope than certainty.

"We don't have time for this now," Queen Mercerio said, kneeling over her husband.

"But the war journals say that injustice should have ignited a response," Meru insisted.

"Enough. Help me here." As Mercerio picked bits of burned cloth from Justi's arm and leg, he twitched. "Thank Li he lives," Mercerio said.

Meru laid his hand on Justi's chest. He leaned to steady Justi, realizing he had grown larger than his father. As another spasm started and Justi moaned, the prince said, "I will calm him."

"Hold his shoulders," Mercerio said as she peeled away charred cloth. "This Justik's power is like your father's." As she picked pieces of burned fabric from Justi's arm, Mercerio chattered nervously, her words running together, leaving no room for a response. "Your father had the power to heal . . . that is what is needed now." Her eyes fixed on Meru. "I have always thought your skill mending injured animals was like Justi's. You even seemed to help your sister when she twisted her ankle—at least she stopped screaming. Perhaps you have inherited healing from Justi. Can you feel anything of Justi's injury?"

Meru remembered how he'd felt mending animals and his sister, thinking it might be a gift but knowing it wasn't healing. He could calm so recovery occurred. He grasped his father's head, placing his strong hand on one temple and his weak hand on the other. At the same time, he spoke to Justi—not aloud but in his mind—telling him to be calm and quiet. He tried to form an image of Justi's seared arm and leg.

"Close your eyes," Mercerio said to her son.

When Meru shut his eyes, he could see nothing of Justi's injuries, but he could sense the pain assaulting his father's brain. Meru's response was instinctive. A faint green haze spread from his hands to Justi's head as he flooded his father with a sense of calm and peace. Justi relaxed, his eyes closed, and the tension on his face drained away. He no longer twitched as Mercerio cleaned his burns.

Meru opened his eyes as Danilla arrived with the white-haired physician, an overconfident practitioner who'd served the crown for years. The doctor examined Justi and helped Mercerio cut off the remains of the sleeve and pants leg. The flesh on both appendages was melted. Meru watched, thinking that Justi himself had been able to inflict this damage. If Mercerio was right—that his father had been able to heal such damage in both men and animals—Meru hoped Justi could repair himself.

Credo arrived with fresh bandages and laid her hands on Justi. "His blood reacts to the injury as it should, so it will support healing. Somehow the tissues must repair the injury, something beyond my skills. But I have a salve that will help."

Mercerio turned first to her husband, whose eyes were closed, and then to her son. "At least he seems calm."

"He is near sleep, mother," Meru said, still touching Justi's head.

The physician finished cleaning Justi's burns, cooling the tissues, and covering the area first with Credo's poultice designed to block the loss of moisture and then with clean cloth. "We must keep close watch that the arm does not turn foul," the doctor said. "Let's get him to his bed."

Justi did regain consciousness, but he did not recover. In the week after the attack, his arm hardly moved, his appetite vanished, and his health diminished. He walked about his apartment, grimacing with each step. When his daughter arrived with Lyra, he managed a smile. The cat approached Justi and sniffed, then raised a large paw to his thigh.

"How are you today, Father?" Danilla chirped. "It's time to change the dressing."

"Must I deal with the doctor again? He has the personality of a mule."

"He is just making you do what you must," Danilla said, picking up a blade. "I will replace the bandages. Lie down, Father, and close your eyes. A nap would not hurt you."

"I do feel tired these days, though I do nothing." Justi settled back onto his pillow and moaned as he positioned his arm and leg.

"You don't eat well."

Lyra sniffed at Justi's arm and leg, made a rumble of disapproval, and turned large feline eyes on Danilla, as if urging her to do something. The princess removed the old dressing, seeing the burned flesh for the first time since the injury, and suppressed a gasp. Justi's arm and leg were red masses pocked with bits of black. The color was wrong, and no signs of healing were evident. Justi moaned again.

Lyra leaned against Danilla's leg, and the girl felt a strange urge. She wanted to touch the raw redness. Her father's eyes were closed, so the princess dared to gently lay her hand on the discolored forearm flesh. As soon as father and daughter were physically connected, Danilla envisioned tissue deep below her hand. She sensed the burned arm as a gnarled mass where tissues were in chaotic conflict over what belonged where. Damaged muscle fibers, misshapen blood vessels, and jangled nerves competed for place and dominance. She visualized with increasing clarity what was amiss.

Lyra grumbled and a gust of wind rattled the chamber panes. Danilla glanced at her feline companion, who seemed to nod. The princess shut her eyes, and her vision of the damaged arm grew clearer.

Without knowing how or exactly what she was trying to do, she mentally manipulated the burned mass, forcing it to mimic healthy tissue. Her mind worked without conscious thought, and she sorted tissues of different types and recruited the few undamaged skin cells to move to the surface. Lyra rumbled again. Once things were in the correct position, Danilla willed nerves to quiet, tissue to heal, and skin to grow. A faint ripple surged over Justi's arm and leg.

Danilla was uncertain how long this process took. She opened her eyes to find Justi asleep. When she released her father's arm, he did not waken and seemed more peaceful than he'd been since the encounter with Justik. Then she examined the injured arm and blinked. The arm seemed less angry and the unnatural crook that held his elbow at an angle had relaxed. She eyed the burned upper leg. Even as she watched, the skin color turned pink, and Danilla caught her breath. No doubt she had caused healing, though she had no idea how. The thought she had some unnatural power thrilled and scared her. Never before had the possibility even crossed her mind. If this was her father's gift, why should she inherit it?

With trembling hands, Danilla applied a new bandage. The skin she covered seemed even more normal, more healed. Had she really fixed her father? Who should she tell? Rising, she stared for a long moment at her own hands and then tiptoed from the bedchamber. Lyra followed and seemed satisfied.

Justi slept for a day, a peaceful slumber without the whimpers of pain and spasmodic movements that had disturbed his rest. Credo checked on him and pronounced him better. When he finally woke as sun splashed the bed and birds bickered raucously from the inner courtyard, he rose gingerly, amazed there was no pain, and went to the looking glass. His face was free of the grimace that had marked it since the attack. His arm and leg felt pain free. Mainly they itched.

He stood for some time, letting the sun warm his hands and marveling at his sudden, rapid recovery. He had no sense of having regained his healing power and wondered if he'd healed himself while sleeping.

The nurse arrived and at first was speechless. Then she spoke excitedly of burned skin that was no long red, of how the entire burned area seemed to have new skin. She summoned the physician who examined Justi and smiled as if he had done something.

Justi moved his arm with care, flexing it. "I couldn't move it at all yesterday." He bent his knee and straightened it. "The leg works as does my arm and is without pain." Justi's stomach growled. "And I am starving."

Observers posted along the northern coast of the Zell reported unusual Tantrocan activities. Fishermen who dared sail close enough to see things through spy glasses noted gatherings of men, equipment, and ships along the shores of Tantroc. Among the materials being loaded onto ships were catapults.

"How do you interpret these things, Meligo?" the queen asked her advisor.

Meligo had arrived with Rakur, who'd hobbled into the throne room with a walking stick. The pair had been consulting old prophesies about conflicts between the Zellish and the Tantrocans.

"This could be the start of the second war that some have read into obscure signs in the old texts," Meligo said, fingering the black beard that fell halfway down his chest.

"One does not need old scrolls to conclude invasion is in the making," Rakur said, obviously exasperated. "The new fact in front of us is that the Ice were seen helping to load ships."

"What difference does that make?" Mercerio asked.

Rakur plopped down in a soft chair. "The Ice priests are enchanters. They distract soldiers long enough for swords to be run through them. Gives them a bit of advantage in a fight, I would think."

Meligo circled Rakur as if to contain the old curmudgeon. "Enchanters could help, especially if the Tantrocans have yet another weapon, something else we must consider."

"Tell me," Mercerio said.

"They may have Justik with them. A man of his description was seen on the road north of Zellingon after his attack on Lord Justi. There was another report of a young, blond stranger glimpsed near Pale, and one of our fisherman spies observed a Tantrocan boat embark a passenger of this description near Pale. The boat was fast, but the fisherman followed it to Ankor."

"So Justik may be with the Tantrocans," Mercerio said. "Do the scrolls say anything about his role?"

"No. But one prophesy seemed to hint that the conflict might be brief," Meligo said.

Rakur thumped his stick and harrumphed. "The conflict could be brief, but the occupation very long."

Queen Mercerio knew it was time. Even though Justi had recovered physically, Justik's attack had taken a mental toll. Leadership in time of war must fall to someone younger. Mercerio decided that Prince Meru would assume his rightful position as king.

"I am not so sure," Justi said. "Perhaps, we should wait until he is older."

Mercerio listed Meru's qualifications. "You and I were commanding the Zelslish army at the same age Meru is now. The boldest way to make him that leader is to make him King Meru. A crisis reveals a leader, and that is what we face. He will make mistakes for sure, but we must not interfere."

Mercerio simultaneously stepped aside and appointed Meru King of the Zell. In a short, but official coronation ceremony, Meru was crowned. The new king hosted a celebration dinner. Meru then turned his attention to countering the Tantrocan threat, something that had remained dormant for all the years of his life. His first task was to ready the Zellish army, but was unsure whether the army leaders, all young without combat experience, were prepared for war. He asked Justi for advice.

"I recommend you appoint one experienced in fighting the Tantrocans to prepare the army," Justi said. "Ask Drenkiri for his help."

"Why?" Meru asked.

"Drenkiri was the military strategist who liberated Zellingon and drove the Tantrocans from our land. He knows their tactics."

"I thought you were in charge."

"Only in name. Drenkiri knew what to do, how to position troops, what to do with archers and swordsmen, when to attack, and when to withdraw. He has seen war and defeated the Tantrocans."

Knowing that his father, despite great power, still needed advice and guidance from experienced military men boosted Meru's confidence. He asked Drenkiri to serve, and the old soldier accepted the appointment as military advisor. Drenkiri had aged well, and beneath snowy hair, his mind remained sharp. He doubled the number of fishermen spying on the enemy.

Reports that a fleet of Tantrocan sat on the coast of Tantroc across from Pale precipitated Meru's first crisis. Thinking of Pale as the home of Breel and Credo, he ordered citizens to retreat. Residents complied reluctantly, but when a week passed and no wave of barbarians came across the Tantric Gulf, villagers drifted back.

Meru realized he'd made a mistake. The decision made him seem ill-informed and a bit foolish, leaving him unsettled, questioning his readiness to be king. Justi convinced him that errors were a part of leadership, and Meru resolved to learn from his mistake.

Both military preparations and the missing Justice Power occupied the new king and his advisors, Rakur and Meligo.

"Perhaps we are mistaken about what is coming," Meligo said. "The Tantrocans may intend yet another coastal raid."

Meru shook his head. "No. My half brother has chosen to be their champion. This means full-scale attack. What have your agents learned about Justik?"

Meligo related that Queen Mercerio forbade questioning Provani, but messengers from the southern regions uncovered horrible stories of torture, destruction, and death indiscriminately meted out by a creature many called Vengeance, reputed to possess Justik's power. More than one account mentioned a flame.

"That could be Justik." Meru said. "But the question is whether I have any power."

Rakur spoke. "Justi showed his power before birth by saving his mother from the Tantrocans. Then the power lay dormant for years. He showed the gift when he lived in Ortun and confronted a bully. Later, its use was the reason for fleeing to Abantazar after he saved his mother from rape and killed a Tantrocan lieutenant."

"How does this help us?" Meru asked. "My father's gift was never missing. When he rescued my mother and got her safely out of Zellingon, he used his flame to defeat the Tantrocans."

"True," Rakur said. "But why not in the first battle? Justi says he does not know."

"Maybe it wasn't needed," Meru said. "This fragmentary history hardly helps us. If the Tantrocans now control such a power, Li must have conferred on us something to oppose it."

Meligo scanned the high ceilings of the throne room as if he were seeking answers. "Is it not logical that, if your father's gift passed to your half brother, it also passed to you?"

"It is also possible," Rakur said with a wave of his hand, "that there was only one gift to pass on. Justik is older than you. That makes him the first-born. He received the gift and you got nothing."

Meru stared at the old scholar, knowing he shared Rakur's suspicion. He did not believe the theory that the power lay dormant within him. Maybe some other power but not the killing flame. It was whatever he used to calm the dire wolf, direct a green mist at Justik, and ease his father's pain. "Rakur could be on the right track," Meru said, struck by a notion. "We need to know more about my father's gift. Someone alive at the time of restoration of the Kingdom must have written more about what controlled the power. We must find that document."

33
Discovery

Breel scoured the shoreline seeking the plants containing the drug revonal. The plants had become scarce, thwarting the search for ripe pods and forcing Breel far from Pale. After searching for a day in the dunes, Breel reported the delay to her mother as the two prepared the evening meal. "Mother, you should travel to Zellingon and assure the queen that we have not forgotten her charge," Breel urged, stirring the stew. "I will follow when I have enough revonal."

Credo frowned. "I don't like your wandering alone so far from the village. There are dangerous animals, including humans."

"You worry too much, but I will pay some village boys to come with me. They can be both guards and pod hunters."

Breel hired two lanky boys, each a head taller than she, and on their first day, they stumbled on a cluster of plants on an inlet half a day's trek from Pale. That patch produced several sacks of seed pods. Breel's helpers bore the sacks to the chemist who would extract the revonal.

Unfortunately, the old chemist fell sick and died, leaving a young apprentice who had never extracted revonal and seemed averse to trying. Breel pointed to the detailed recipe he could follow, one created by the old master at Credo's insistence. Those directions helped, but the young man, who made Breel think of a toad because of his half-closed eyelids, was a slow learner. His first attempts to prepare the drug failed, and his fiddling used all the pods.

Breel barely contained her anger and frustration and returned to the plants herself, filled two sacks, and delivered the pods to the chemist. "I must have the extraction done at once. I know you can do it. Just follow the instructions." She left with a smile of encouragement.

Late the next day the drug was still not ready. "What is the problem?" Breel asked, watching the young man's nervous movements.

"No problem," he said. "I heeded the directions and processed but a few pods first, just to practice. Unfortunately, it was so small the extracted drug was invisible. But I'm sure it was of good quality. I will now start my extraction with the rest of the pods."

From the first, Breel detected an unnatural hesitancy in in the toad's reaction to this task. She stared at the bottles of drugs directed at all parts of the body, including the brain, then pointed at several magenta compounds that caused more profound changes in thinking than the sea marsh drug. "Did you prepare those drugs?"

Toadface squinted at the shelf. "Oh, no. The master did those. He said they were dangerous."

Breel sensed fear. "You admitted last week you felt some anxiety about this preparation."

The man's sagged and sighed. "Yes. I fear being affected by the finished drug. I don't want to hurt my brain. I need all of it."

Breel couldn't deny that notion. She focused on the warty-faced chemist. "I can help you with your anxiety."

Toadface lifted his eyelids and backed away. "How?"

"No drugs. Just a touch. You will feel better." Breel held out her hands, palms up. Her treatment soothed the nervous man enough that he completed the preparation of the revonal.

With the revonal, Breel accompanied a trader to Zellingon. A light spring snow coated the northern regions of the Zell, but black graze beasts rooted to find new grass beneath the white. Breel considered how she might approach the task of treating King Meru's hand. She would have to know more about his condition. In Zellingon Breel and Credo presented themselves to Mercerio.

"Good news," began Credo. "My daughter has the drug to treat the king."

Mercerio considered this statement for a long moment before speaking. "You both have received the gift of healing from Li, and Breel's power over the mind may be exactly what's needed. There's been no change in the king's hand, but I sense he works to hide his anxiety over it."

Meru heard of Breel's arrival and was torn between not wanting more medical probing and desire to see Breel. When she appeared as arranged in the king's chamber, Meru was again struck by her beauty. Her hair seemed more lustrous, eyes larger, her form more pleasant. Even her smile seemed brighter. His new status as king should have made him less self-conscious. It did not.

Meru gazed at Breel for a long moment and then asked, "What do we do now? What can you do that your mother could not?"

Breel sat on the low-backed couch next to the king. "My ability is more in the mental realm."

Meru smiled. "You still think this is in my head?" He lifted his hand and attempted to tighten his fist. "My arm on the weak side seems no less muscled than the other. But I feel little strength. I cannot hold a sword, I cannot squeeze a filled wineskin, and if I were to try to punch something, I'm sure my hand would break."

"May I, Your Majesty?" Breel asked, pointing to Meru's hand.

Breel studied the offered hand. "Are there other areas of weakness?"

Meru felt his face warm. "My other hand is fine. My feet are fine. All other parts work as they should."

"What do you sense when you try to use your hand?"

"Nothing hurts, but my hand does not work. It is almost as if something is blocking me." What he said next surprised him. "I feel as if I am forbidden from using the hand."

"Who forbids it?"

"I do not know."

Breel closed her eyes for a moment, which gave the king a chance to study her, to think how nice it would be to kiss her.

"To assess your hand, I must feel the impulse from your brain to your shoulder to your arm to your hand. With your permission, of course."

"Well, I gave permission before, so why do you need to ask again?"

"That was when you were Prince Meru. Now you are king, and it seems a bigger imposition. What's more, my exam may take longer this time, and it will include your head. Is this possible?"

"It is quite possible, improper as it might be. Shall I call a servant to act as chaperone?" Meru smiled, thinking he'd like to experience the impulse that traveled in Breel's body as she moved.

"A witness would distract, my lord."

Meru dropped his upper garment on the couch.

"The king's arm and chest seem . . . healthy," Breel said in a clinical tone belied by a smile. "Muscles seem well-developed on both sides." Breel circled behind Meru. "Squeeze your shirt to a small size when I ask. First do it with your good hand." When the king was ready, Breel placed her two hands on the king's neck. "Squeeze."

Meru reduced the wad of cloth into a ball. Breel touched Meru's shoulder and repeated her request. Then she moved to the upper arm, the lower arm, and the strong hand. Each time Meru squeezed the cloth into submission.

"Now we must do this for the other side. Meru's effort to squeeze the shirt into a ball largely failed. Breel also laid her hands on her patient's pectoral muscle before moving to the upper and lower arm.

"Do you sense the block?" she asked.

"I do."

"I must do one more thing. It requires my hand on the royal head."

Meru nodded and Breel pressed Meru's temples. After the test, Breel asked when Meru first noticed his weak hand and what his mother and father had done about it. She also wanted to know about Meru's travels, who was in the party, how far he'd gone, and for how long.

"I must consult my mother," Breel said, "and do some research in the palace library. Then we will begin your treatment, using a drug to help."

"Why can't we just do it?"

"I need to understand your problem better to be of help."

"I become impatient."

Breel found her mother in her room arranging small glass vials of rainbow-colored liquids and powders. Breel poured herself a cup of tea. "There is nothing wrong with the king's hand or arm or shoulder or neck. The impulse from his brain to use his fist on the weak side starts strong but ebbs before it reaches his hand. The muscles of the hand are fine, just unused. Meru said something surprising: he feels blocked. It will help to know the source of the blockage."

"Can you free Meru from this block?" Credo asked.

"Chances would be better if I understood what was blocking him. I tried no cure today."

"We must tell Mercerio."

They found Mercerio in a meeting room talking to Meligo. Bright sun streamed in to warm the chamber. The queen smiled and Breel reported.

Meligo asked. "How can you find out what blocks the king?"

"I hoped the queen might have an idea about this."

Mercerio frowned. "Unfortunately, I do not."

Meligo seemed to mull that over. "This discussion echoes with me. The king himself suggested finding such an answer in the history of Justi's power. We want old accounts on how Justi eventually used his power."

"These are two different items, it seems to me," Queen Mother Mercerio said. "One deals with my husband's use of the Justice Fire. The other deals with my son's weak hand. What are you thinking?"

"Getting Justi to use his power in combat could be viewed as removing a block. Now Breel says Meru is blocked." Meligo cupped his chin, his thoughtful pose. He nodded at Mercerio and Breel. "Perhaps, if the healer can restore a normal hand, she can unblock a more-than-normal hand, one that holds some power."

Veta, an old woman who'd served as Queen Melsin's attendant, overheard Meligo's comment about old texts and remembered Melsin's diaries in which the-queen wrote entries each night, even during the march and battle to retake Zellingon. Queen Melsin often talked with her daughter about controlling Justi's power.

Veta took the stairway to the subterranean storage areas. A torch lit her way to a chamber crowded with boxes and chests. Veta surveyed the collection and worked her way to three similar cases in the middle of the room. She willed herself to ignore the scratching and scurrying sounds and opened the first box. Moving the lid stirred dust. No diaries.

In the second case were more clothes. In the third, beneath pictures lay a green cloth that covered the diaries. Veta lifted one thin volume, clad in red leather with gilded page edges and opened it. The first page contained a date range, which corresponded with the great war. The first entry started at the time Melsin told her daughter Mercerio that she was a princess. That seemed irrelevant and Veta wondered if her notion about the diary being useful was wrong.

The she found Melsin's account of Mercerio's concern that Justi's power was unharnessed and dangerous and Veta's eyes widened. She would deliver the diary to Meligo. Immediately.

"Thank you, Veta," Meligo said when he received the diary. "I should have thought of this." Surprise and a smile took over when he read of Mercerio's tempering Justi's gift, a notion he had not heard before. Melsin used an interesting word to describe Mercerio's contribution to Justi, something her daughter thought of as adding a missing component. Melsin called the component mercy.

Melsin's diary also mentioned Meru. Besides all the expected notations of a grandmother for her grandson, one thing was clear. The prince never manifested his father's gift. Meru had his mother's temperament.

Meligo marked all references to the Justice Power, including comments of Zellish seers about its meaning and nature, and took the book to Meru. He found the king with Breel discussing prospects for healing his hand. Meru asked her to stay and began to read the marked passages in his grandmother's diary. Meligo watched in silence, perhaps wondering whether there might be within this man, whom he'd known since birth, some killing force.

"I don't see how this is of use," the king said.

"It might be," Breel said. When Meru nodded, she continued, "We now have a clue as to what might be blocking the king's use of his hand. Let me ask a question. Have you been away from your mother much?"

Meru frowned. "No. What are you thinking?"

"Your mother influenced your father's gift when she was close. Maybe she unconsciously suppresses any power in her children. I propose that we move some distance away and repeat my tests."

Meru considered the notion. "I guess it is worth a try. We could travel to Manwark. That is a day's distance."

"Going to Manwark would not be wise," Meligo said. "You would have to take the army with you."

"No. I will not make the mistake of my grandfather King Bronte, who left Zellingon undefended when he went toward Fathom. A small force will suffice for me as a bodyguard. I will pretend to be a commoner."

Meligo seemed doubtful.

34
Healing

I observed Meru and Breel leave Zellingon at dawn and head into the forest. I stole from Danilla's room and slipped from an open window to the rear courtyard. In the early hour, a hawk settled on a tree branch and eyed the stable chickens. As the oblivious fowl continued their early morning pecking, my Marget spirit leapt from the lynx and possessed the bird of prey. It took a moment to recall how one controlled a feathered body, but I was soon flying north to accompany King Meru.

*****

Meru had assembled six skilled swordsmen and archers, sworn them to secrecy, and left from a rear sally gate. The party entered the forest to follow a game trail and proceeded at a leisurely pace until the sun splashed the turf at the horses' feet. When the trail widened, the king brought his horse alongside Breel's and broke the silence.

"You are my age," Meru said, "but different from other girls I've encountered."

Breel wrinkled her brow. "Different? What do you mean?"

"You seem confident, self-assured, in control."

"Women should always be in control, especially around men," Breel said.

"But aren't women supposed to defer to men?"

Breel laughed. "I don't know how you learned that—your mother is the queen and defers to no man."

Meru considered that rejoinder. "So you want a man to treat you as an equal." It was not a question.

"Hardly. Women have their separate roles, but they should always be respected and have a say."

"I agree. We have come to know each other well enough to be comfortable. I have grown to like you, Breel. A lot. Our relationship is more than that between a king and a subject."

"Thank you, Sire. I am only your subject here to solve a problem."

"You are also my friend."

Breel said nothing, and before the conversation could unearth more controversy, a small black creature with a white stripe darted across the path. The horses shied and reared. When the animals settled, Meru said, "Skunk. Maybe a bad omen."

They forded the Zelar and circled west halfway around Lake Manwark. At noon Meru ordered a break to rest and graze the horses. The men guarded the perimeter as the king and Breel ate a light meal. When a hawk swooped into the clearing and settled on a high branch, Meru told the story of his father's protective bird that seemed to accompany him everywhere. "Rather impossible for the same bird to dwell for years in Ortun, then leagues distant in Abantazar, and finally in Zellingon," he added.

"But if your father's gift came from Li, would it be unusual for him to have such a guardian?"

Meru watched the hawk lift from the branch and circle above them. "If the same guardian is watching over me, the bird has lived four tens of years."

"Could be different birds with the same purpose," Breel said. "One red hawk appears like any other. And if it's now your guardian, you must be worth guarding."

"And that is why we are here—to cure my hand problem and perhaps see if I possess anything worth guarding," Meru said, "How shall we proceed now that we are away from Zellingon?"

Breel rose and studied the hawk for a long moment before turning to Meru with her arms crossed. "Roll back your sleeve." Without asking permission, she placed two hands on his forearm. "Force your hand to relax and then form a tight fist."

Meru first relaxed the slight tension that pointed his fingers toward his palm and then tried to form a tight fist. The hand relaxed but could manage only a loose fist. "That's more than usual," he said.

"I detect the block," Breel said, "but it seems diminished. Putting distance between you and the queen may be having an effect, but either we are not far enough, or it takes time."

The pair strolled toward a grassy clearing dotted with a few infant pines. In the center, fringed by taller grass, lay a flat rock whose smooth surface gleamed in the midday sun. Breel headed to the stone.

"The power may come after we restore your hand," Breel said, waving her own hand over the bright granite surface. She froze. "I heard something."

The something was the rattle of a diamond-patterned snake coiled on the warm surface in a depression. The creature's wide triangular head danced far too close. Meru carefully stepped forward and extended his weak hand with an almost flat palm. The rattler followed the movement and hissed as the rattling intensified. A green mist flowed from Meru to engulf the snake. The rattling ceased and the creature slithered back.

"Back away," the king said. "Slowly."

When Breel flinched, the rattling resumed, and the snake coiled to strike. The hawk plunged, swooshed over the rock slab, and caught the surprised snake in its talons. The bird flapped its wings strongly and carried off the heavy prize, dragging it along the ground. A moment later, the heavy reptile broke free of the claws and flopped at the clearing edge.

Meru, his face pale, stared at the red hawk lifting over the trees in the breeze. Then he examined his hand, willing it to stop shaking.

Breel took the king's arm, drawing him away from the rock.

"Perhaps you are right about the bird," Meru said.

They reached Manwark late in the day. Meru called a halt when the town's walls came into view. "When I do not return today or tomorrow, Queen Mercerio will become alarmed. She will come after me. I would not want to openly oppose her will. Furthermore, she will come because the burgher of Manwark will recognize me and tell her. He is her most loyal subject. Soon I will be closer to my mother, not more distant."

"We could try your treatment here," Breel said.

"I would prefer more privacy," Meru said. "I propose we camp here overnight and proceed to Pale in the morning. My visit would be a goodwill gesture after I forced them to leave their town. I want to encourage defensive preparations. And Pale is your home, Breel. I would like to see it."

Queen Mercerio found it farfetched that Breel's treatment required a hunting trip. Meru should not stray from the palace. After fretting and waiting a day for the party to return, she investigated, learning that Meru, rather than the head of security, picked the guards, men who lacked special hunting skills.

Meru's valet confessed the king had taken enough clothes for a week. Credo checked her daughter's things and reported the same. Even the stable master remembered a bag with a large quantity of grain being loaded on one horse. Now convinced that this trip was meant to last more than a day or so, Mercerio sent experienced trackers to locate her son.

When Meru and Breel reached Pale the next evening, the stunned gate guard stuttered, bowed, and at last jumped to open the portal. He summoned the town leader, a gnarly, gray-haired, former fisherman named Riff. He welcomed his guests, begged to know what the king required, but did not dare ask the obvious question of why the king was in Pale.

"We will rest after our journey," Meru said. "Then you and I can discuss the Tantrocan threat. What are the most suitable quarters for my party?"

Riff directed them to the largest inn, the House of Sails, in the center of Pale. "I will, of course, come with you to make sure they treat the King of the Zell suitably. They have a fine stable behind the inn for the horses."

The royal party occupied the entire second floor of the House of Sails. A guard kept watch at the stairs and others at the inn entrances.

Meru's room was meager by palace standards but comfortable enough with a bed, table, and a fireplace. The window overlooked the town square decorated with ship mementos including large wheels, nets, statues, and a mast. The last was mounted in the center of a planted garden and featured three crossbars. Meru saw a hawk settle onto the highest crossbeam and stare at the House of Sails.

Breel refused to take a room at the inn, intending to go to her house. Meru sensed that he was close to a breakthrough and wanted to get on with the procedure. "Before you leave, we must complete my treatment."

Breel nodded. "This is a much better place than in the open or in a tent to do what must be done."

Meru thought that sounded ominous. "You mean another test?"

"I mean an attempted cure."

Meru removed his shirt, feeling less self-conscious about it. He balled the garment, prepared to squeeze it as a test. Breel watched as the king tried mightily to crush the shirt. Not much happened.

"I sense that the block is fainter," Breel said. She studied Meru's eyes and continued; "Now I must do more than sense. I will probe and clear your head. It will be uncomfortable."

Meru only half-heard Breel's words. He marveled at the depth of her eyes, the beauty of her skin, the warm tone of her voice. When she placed her cool hands on his skin, he was startled at the feelings that flooded through him.

"Did you hear me, Sire? I said there will be some pain."

Meru shook his head as if to wipe away a cobweb. "If there is any chance of changing the Withered Prince into the mighty king, I will endure it. How will it hurt?"

"It won't be a physical pain, but your brain will struggle."

"What do you want me to do?"

Breel presented a vial. "First, take the revonal. It will relax you and open your mind to suggestion."

Meru downed the liquid, followed by water. "It has a salty, fishy taste."

Breel nodded. "The drug acts rapidly and you may feel lightheaded. You should close your eyes."

Meru felt the room spin about him and sat down. He closed his eyes, sensing Breel standing before him, her face next to his. She smelled of wildflowers, sweet and evanescent. He placed his good hand at her waist.

"I must touch you again, this time your head, for a longer time to feel what is happening. Then I will intervene and alter the way your brain reacts when you try to use your hand."

"How can you do this?"

"It is my gift." She touched the king's temples and leaned her forehead against his. She closed her eyes and said, "Slowly try to squeeze."

Meru had to be told again to squeeze and realized she meant the shirt. The pressure increased on his head, both outside and in, making it feel as if a weight like a large flat river rock would crush his skull. The pain stopped his breathing and he tried to jerk back, but Breel held him.

"Breathe. Squeeze."

Meru blinked and a tear ran down a cheek. Warmth suffused his weak hand, and he began to compress the shirt. As his hand responded, the weight on his head grew lighter. "I can do it. I can close my weak hand. It feels strong."

"Squeeze."

Without thinking Meru dropped the shirt and placed his renewed hand on Breel's waist. He gently squeezed. Breel's eyes widened and she started to back away. Meru's hand went to her neck and brought her face back to his. He kissed her fully on the mouth.

When Breel managed to back away from the long kiss, she said, "Meru, this is not part of the procedure."

"I know."

Hours before dawn, Justik stood alone in the bow of a ship sailing east from Ankor. The time for planning and preparation had ended. Justik's vessel sailed in the darkness amidst broad-beamed craft, each laden with armed men and supplies. The ships hugged the Tantroc coast as they plowed in a steady breeze, leaving vanishing furrows in the calm black sea. The quarter moon provided meager light, but clouds and a light fog hid the armada. Justik pondered his role in the battles to come, confident he was the key to victory, that his power would decide the struggle, that he would realize his destiny. The crew and Tantrocan soldiers, aware of the power he possessed, left him alone.

Caldir had ordered the night departure to thwart witnesses like Zellish fishermen. To further ensure surprise, the high priest set the fleet's landing in the wilderness east of Pale, beyond the Zelar and away from any settlement.

*****

Spirits noted the Tantrocan ships and Meru's departure from Zellingon. *The male high spirit Dar-nuk projected, "The first son sails with the invaders as the second son leaves the protection of the palace. Perhaps the two will meet, and Justik can eliminate Meru."*

"We should help the Tantrocans," Dar-cor answered. "Before the first invasion, we used animals as well as humans to thwart Li's worshipers."

"And we failed to kill Justi's mother with a wild boar or the boy with a cat and wolves."

"But Meru is less powerful. An animal can kill him."

"Is he?"

*****

The next day Meru told Riff he would survey the defenses of Pale. The arrival of the captain of the town guard with alarming news made it urgent. "Sire, I have heard from a lone fisherman who spent the night on his small boat near the Tantroc coast. He had let his lantern go dark as he slept in calm waters, a sleep interrupted by the wake of a large boat. He woke to the slap of oars as ship after ship ploughed east. The fisherman remained quiet until they passed and then hoisted sail and made for Pale." The captain pointed to a young man with thick, muscled arms who accompanied him. "Then this Markul ranger brought news."

The ranger bowed to the king. "I am a farmer, Sire, as well as a soldier and was tracking a lost cow as the sun rose. East of Markul I saw smoke and investigated. The thin cloud originated beyond the Zelar River, so I tethered my horse, crossed the stream, and climbed a rise."

"Why the caution?" Meru asked.

"Instinct. We have had to deal with raiding parties before, although never beyond the Zelar. The smoke arose from a fire where many armed men had gathered. Others toted sacks from the direction of the coast. I returned to my horse and went closer to the sea. There, with the help of my glass, I observed many masts, some at shore and some approaching."

"Any idea of the number of ships?" the guardsman captain asked.

"Many, but a fog obscured the water. I raced my horse to Markul to warn the ranger post and then rode here at top speed. By Li's will, the horse was young and strong and speedy."

"So this report is but hours old?" Meru asked.

"Yes, my lord. The rangers will follow after me, for it would be suicide to try to defend Markul from such a horde."

Mercerio's trackers arrived and told Meru that the queen mother demanded a fast rider report to her once they found him. Meru eyed the indicated messenger. "You will take fresh horses and leave immediately for Zellingon. Report the Tantrocan invasion east of Pale to the queen mother and Drenkiri. The army must be made ready to march. How long will the trip take?"

The man was young, small, and would hardly be felt on the back of a horse. "With a fresh horse and taking the eastern path through the mountains near Manwark, I can be there in a day and a half."

"Leave now."

As soon as the man departed, Meru ordered the smallest of his guardsmen to carry out the same mission but travel to Zellingon by the western route.

35
Attack

Meru ordered scouts to confirm the Tantrocan landing and assess the enemy force. He then surveyed Pale's fortifications, finding a poorly maintained stockade and an undermanned guard. Again he regretted his hasty decision to order evacuation of the town. I should have commanded these people to harden their defenses, he thought.

Meru told Riff to assemble the village council and the guard commander in the town hall.

"Would tomorrow be suitable?" Riff asked.

"Now would be suitable. There's work to be done if you want to live."

After Riff darted off to fetch councilmen and the town guard leader, Meru's party proceeded to the village council hall, a building of stone and weathered oak with a cavernous room. Banners celebrating victories over Tantrocan raiders and gilded sconces adorned the dark walls. Somewhere above in the high rafters a small bird flitted and chirped to interrupt the church-like silence. Village officials arrived wearing expressions of annoyance. They stood before the king until he pointed at seats around the council table. They sat.

Meru surveyed the group, wishing they were younger and showed more worry than irritation. "Pale will be attacked soon by a large force of Tantrocans," he began.

"We perceived that when you ordered an evacuation of Pale, my lord," Riff said, casting his eyes at councilmen as if to remind them that no invasion had occurred. Murmured conversations began.

Meru rose and closed the distance between himself and the town leader. "Yet the town is not prepared." His loud words silenced the group. "Your defenses may be adequate to repel small raiding parties, but not an army. The penalty for being unprepared is defeat. With this enemy, that means death." Meru allowed silence to grow before he began issuing orders.

"You will reinforce the weak parts of the stockade with whatever materials are at hand. I want to see more weapons and arrows. Every able-bodied man is now a member of the defense force. Scouts will range beyond the wall to warn of the Tantrocan approach."

The king issued other orders and his presence changed Pale's attitude about defense from lax to urgent. Masons and carpenters fortified the walls, blacksmiths multiplied weapons, and children crafted arrows. Fisherman, hunters, and farmers hauled foodstuffs within the walls and then joined shopkeepers and youth as part of the town guard, Rangers trained the new recruits.

"But we cannot hope to resist attack from a large force," Riff whined.

"The Markul Rangers are in command of Pale's forces. You will resist while the army marches from Zellingon."

Meru knew he must leave Pale. He ordered his guard to prepare for immediate travel and left to find Breel, who had departed as soon as she finished treating his hand. Meru reached Breel's residence as she returned from visiting patients.

"I am pleased to see you," Meru said, astonished at her garb. Instead of the usual dress, she wore breeches with a smock, brown with green trim, and her hair was tied up. The green echoed the hints of jade in her hair. *How can she still be so beautiful in such different clothing?*

He declined her offer of tea and said, "I must go to Zellingon and return with the army. You should come with me to join your mother."

Breel hesitated, casting her eyes to the ground, before answering. "You must go, Meru, for you are king of the Zell. But I am needed here, especially if war is upon us. You have done much to strengthen our defenses, but if we are attacked, people will need healers. That is what I am, and these are my people."

"But you will not be safe," Meru said.

"We will be safe if Li wills it. You can be back here in days with the army, maybe even before the Tantrocans attack."

Demon curse, thought Meru. He considered commanding Breel to obey him. Instead, he thanked her for her help and promised to return quickly. He wanted to kiss her, but she kept her distance and seemed to have developed an inordinate interest in the floor.

Led by a hawk above them, the king's party left as the day faded to night.

The party pushed the horses through half the night, rested briefly until dawn, and then rode hard. In two days, they reached Zellingon. The messengers sent earlier had delivered the king's commands, so preparations were well underway. Mercerio's unhappiness about her son's secret trip dissipated when she learned the success of Breel's treatment and realized the Tantrocan threat.

Full-time soldiers formed the core of the king's army, which was now reinforced by the standby militias, men who earned a living as craftsmen, farmers, hunters, and merchants. Drenkiri, a veteran who witnessed the atrocities committed by the Tantrocans in the first war, joined the new fight as a senior advisor. The white hair and sunbaked skin added an aura of wisdom to anything he said.

"The army should move immediately to Manwark," Drenkiri announced, "to prevent the Tantrocans from taking that larger town. Manwark is well fortified and we could safely assemble behind its walls."

Meru shook his head. "No, we go to Pale. That is where the enemy is. And we cannot wait for other recruits."

Meru and Danilla, with Lyra nearby, watched the final preparations.

"I must leave, Sister. Breel refused to come with me and is in danger. Send the eastern contingent when it assembles. If we fail to stop the Tantrocans, you must protect our parents. And yourself. Flee to the south. How is Father?"

"He has grown much stronger and his mind has returned in full," Danilla said.

"Good." Meru kissed his sister and left.

Even without Justik, the Tantrocans expected an easy conquest of Pale. Their spies painted a picture of a coastal town with few defenders, a weak town where Tantrocan troops could get food and prepare for the battle with the main army of the Zell.

The Tantrocans crossed the Zelar on a misty morning and advanced to Markul. The ranger station had been abandoned, but the Tantrocans left a contingent to ensure the rangers did not return. The rest of the horde continued to Pale, dragging with them several catapults. The rumble of the machines alerted the Pale defenders of the arrival of the enemy and brought defenders to the fortified walls. War drums thundered and a dust cloud formed, as the Tantrocans approached the eastern gate. Pale archers waited until the enemy came within range and loosed a volley of arrows. Many found a target. Tantrocans screamed with chest wounds. Those with neck wounds didn't scream.

The Tantrocans retreated beyond the range of archers. The defenders took in the enemy: men in battle leathers, carrying swords, pikes, and shields. Some were digging out rocks and hauling them toward the catapults. The dust drifted over Pale and obscured the sun. The message was clear: Tantrocans far outnumbered the Zellish. Pale had no hope. The town would be taken.

An hour passed. Then two. A contingent of Tantrocans approached the west gate with a white flag. In a gruff northern dialect, the leader offered Pale a chance to surrender. He offered assurance of safety for everyone.

Some on the Pale council wanted to accept the offer.

"The Tantrocan assurance of safety is worthless," Riff said. "These are Dar worshippers who glorify human sacrifice. Our king orders us to defend Pale and inflict damage on these barbarians. Honor demands we do nothing less. We will fight. May Li be with us and hasten the king's army."

Hours later the Tantrocans catapults pounded rocks against the walls. Boulders splintered timbers, throwing Pale guardsmen from their positions. Tantrocan archers sent flights of arrows to keep reinforcements at bay as their soldiers rushed forward with scaling ladders. Pale defenders tossed incendiary pots on the invaders. Then came burning oil. The Tantrocans fell back but returned in greater numbers that were able to swarm to the top of the stockade. Fierce fighting by young guards led by Markul Rangers drove them back. Pale archers fired accurately and took out reinforcements. The Tantrocans retreated, leaving dead and dying men behind.

Darkness was pierced by the occasional flaming arrow aimed at a thatched roof inside the walls. Residents scrambled to douse the flames. That, and the cries of dying men, kept the men and women of Pale awake, leaving them unrested as they prepared for a repeat assault. In daylight, the enemy changed tactics. Men without weapons led the soldiers and began to chant. A feeling of lethargy and confusion gripped the Pale guardsmen and archers. They lost their focus on the enemy and seemed unsure of what they were to do.

The Tantrocans charged in great numbers, threw up scaling ladders, and clambered onto the wall. The invaders pushed back the now listless defenders. Many died as the intruders took control of the town gate and opened it. Tantrocans poured into Pale, pushing back a resistant band of fierce fighters.

Justik entered through the west gate. Although his power was not needed, he found an excuse to demonstrate it. Caldir had encouraged a plan designed to send a message. Justik would show his ability and allow a few from Pale to escape. They would deliver the story of his unnatural strength to the Zellish.

A dozen men of Pale were the victims. As they backed away from the advancing Tantrocan army, Justik came to face them alone, his sword drawn. A Markul ranger, perhaps thinking this was a foolhardy act of a neophyte, advanced and thrust his sword at the foolish man. Justik raised his hands, and a spear of flame crossed the space. The explosion of light and power burned a crater in the man's chest, leaving behind a foul smell and a dead man.

Other Pale fighters rushed forward and met a similar fate from immense blasts of hot light. Women tending wounded men witnessed the slaughter, and one turned her head in Justik's direction as the flame erupted. She screamed and fell, not burned, but blinded. Her companions dragged her away as more Tantrocans arrived. Justik held the soldiers back.

"Let them go," he said. "They will make excellent witnesses of my power."

The women were pushed toward the west wall by eager, probing Tantrocan hands. The groping victims stumbled away from the bloody bodies and heard cries of other women being gathered as ripe fruit by hungry soldiers. Most shocking were wails of children as they were torn from mothers. The expelled witnesses stumbled from Pale and somehow found the strength to flee toward Manwark.

*****

The Miasma relished the Tantrocan subjugation of Pale, *accepting Justik's cruelty as balance for Justi's killing of Tantrocans decades back.*

"Dar's people have a champion," Dar-cor said.

Dar-nuk agreed. "Events favor ascendance of Dar's power in the human realm, and we must act further to ensure this event."

"What?"

"We can confront Li's servants in our realm."

*****

The Zellish army west of Manwark was pounded by rain as thunder rattled and lightning flashed. Meru took shelter in his tent. The Pale refugees arrived and Entor and Meligo, the king's advisors, brought the leaders to Meru. Both women, wet, maybe in shock, bowed before the king.

"I am Cheyla, apprentice to the seer of Pale, my lord. Pale has been taken by the Tantrocans."

Meru tensed. "Tell us what happened, Cheyla."

Cheyla described the attack on Pale and how the Tantrocans were able to get past the strengthened defenses. "Our defenders were strong enough to hold the wall," she said, "but something strange happened. Men dressed in odd robes were with the Tantrocans. They did not fight but began a mesmerizing chant. Our soldiers ceased fighting and were cut down by Tantrocans who clambered over the walls."

"Sounds like the Ice enchanters," Meligo said. "The power had never been observed and was only rumored. The Ice have raided some Zellish coastal villages, but never used anything like enchantment to plunder."

"The Tantrocans have another weapon, my lord," Cheyla said. She described the actions and power of a young man who'd killed with fire. "He let us leave to testify of his power."

The second woman tugged on Cheyla's sleeve and whispered. Meru watched and waited for Cheyla to speak.

"This man's flame blinded one of us," Cheyla said hesitantly. "She is Breel, our healer."

The blood drained from Meru's face. He jumped up and said in a choked voice, "Where is she? I must see her."

He found Breel sitting with the group under a canvas sheet rigged between two trees. She must have heard the approaching footsteps and reached to a companion. "What is happening?"

"The king is coming."

Breel stiffened when Meru embraced her.

"Breel, I am so sorry," Meru said, feeling her reaction and realizing there were witnesses. He held her away and examined her face. "Can you tell what is wrong?"

Breel shivered and her voice broke as she answered. "I am fine, my king. It is just that I cannot see."

"I should have commanded you to leave Pale with me. This is my fault."

"There is no fault, sire. It was my decision. We cannot see into the future."

"I could have insisted . . . more," Meru said. "I should have commanded."

Breel crossed her arms. "Not everything can be commanded."

"Well, if I had, you would not be sightless. You must go to the Manwark healer."

Breel departed, guided by Entor. Meru felt guilt, sadness, and longing as he plodded toward his tent. A commotion arose from the south. A thousand Zellish had joined the camp. Meru was confused to see the flags that accompanied this army. One was the Zellish banner and the other was his sister's. For some reason Danilla had decided to risk her life.

She soon appeared. "Greetings, Brother. I have brought reinforcements."

"They are much needed, but why are you here? This is no idle outing. War means danger and death.

No place for a royal. If I die, you will become queen. That alone is reason to stay in Zellingon."

"These late-arriving conscripts did not think they were needed, despite explanations from the military men you left behind. Drenkiri feared the men might leave. Royal leadership was needed. I let the recruits know we faced a threat to the entire kingdom. They seemed moved by my words. I commanded them to follow me as representative of you, their king."

"Thank you for doing this, but only one of us should face the dangers of war. I will lead our one army."

Danilla crossed her arms and remained silent.

Meru found Breel in the Manwark Inn after she'd consulted the town healer. She seemed to be developing a sense of her surroundings and knew he was in the room before he said anything.

"Thank you for visiting, Meru. It grows lonely sitting here with no sight."

"What did the healer say?"

"My eyes are undamaged. He became quite foolish when he started to talk about something in my brain, a self-imposed blindness. I pointed out that I am also a healer and specialize in mental ailments. He suggested I might regain some sight with time, gave me a stick, and wished me well."

The king came close and said, "I can attest to your ability, Breel. I have had normal use of my hand since you applied your skill." Meru flexed his left hand. "Too bad your cure did not uncover the Justice Power. We sorely need that gift to fight the Tantrocans."

Breel laid her hands on Meru's. She bowed her head as if searching for some elusive hint. "Think of this Justice Power. Picture it." Meru summoned the stories he'd heard of Justi and painted a picture of the battle to reclaim Zellingon in his mind. Breel went pale. "You have a great power within you, my king, and it seems to be in turmoil."

"But how do I invoke this force?"

"I am not sure. I have heard that Justi had to have a clear picture of need, a threat to the innocent, or to the righteous, posed by evil, to exercise his gift. It may be that you, too, will find your power only when it is needed."

"I would hope to discover power before my half brother kills me."

Danilla arrived with Lyra and announced that scouts were reporting in. Meru went to talk to his commanders, asking his sister to stay with Breel for a while. "Perhaps you can discuss my missing power, given your scholarship in the old prophecies."

"You must lead the army to Pale. I will keep my friend company," Danilla said with a smile, "and we will discuss what we want."

36
Revelations

Zellish scouts reported the Tantrocans marched on Manwark. Meru rejected facing the invaders from behind Manwark's walls. The Zellish would confront the enemy on the open plain north of Manwark.

The plain along the River Wark had escaped the rain, so dust clouds revealed the approach of the Zellish and Tantrocan armies. The opposing forces halted, separated by more than an arrow's reach, and stared at each. Rumbles of voices and the clang of weapons broke the silence as soldiers waited.

As night fell Meru paced in front of a small fire, processing the reports delivered by scouts. Around him, as far as the eye could see, fires marked locations of Zellish and Tantrocan soldiers, separated by a stretch of vacant plain. In Meru's imagination the dark expanse seemed hungry for human blood. The ground would feed at dawn.

The young scholar Entor asked the question foremost on everyone's mind. "Do you feel the power, my lord?"

The king turned his back to Entor and debated several possible answers. He chose the truth. "I feel no such power but have been told by the Pale healer that I possess it. It may appear when needed. But we outnumber the Tantrocans—the fires prove that. We shall defeat them."

After Meru left Danilla and Breel in the Manwark Inn, the princess said, "Breel, your condition saddens me as much as it does the king. I am so sorry this has happened. What did the Manwark physician say?"

"That nothing is wrong with the structure of my eyes."

Dropped crockery crashed in the kitchen beneath Breel's room. A woman's angry words lambasted the clumsiness of a servant, calling him or her a "stupid child." A second outburst ended with another sound of disintegrating pottery.

"Come to my chamber," Danilla said. "It's on the third floor and quiet, and guards will assure our privacy." As Danilla guided Breel to the stairs, she continued, "I saw Justik attack my father, and I nursed Father as he recovered from burns." Danilla suspected her father's recovery was due to more than just nursing, but she kept that possibility to herself. If it wasn't her imagination, it meant she had inherited a healing gift from her parents. Or at least from Justi. His healing fixed damaged body parts, like a dog's sprained foot or a man's head bruise. *Maybe I can't help Breel if her eyes have normal structure.*

Danilla ignored the knot in her stomach. "Father's sight was not affected, perhaps because Justik's flame was less bright." Another possibility occurred to Danilla. She recalled a green haze from Meru. It may have dimmed Justik's light.

Danilla took Breel to the bed, the only place to sit. Lyra had been napping there. The cat stood up, stretched, and stepped over to Breel. When she heard the cat purr a greeting, Breel reached out and stroked the furred creature.

"I know you from your large head and pointed ears. You met me and my dog Bib in Zellingon. Why are you here?"

"Lyra has been my friend since before I was of ten years," Danilla said. "She is more a companion than a pet and decided to come with me."

"Well, Lyra, I wish my Bib were here as well," Breel said, scratching between the animal's ears.

"Did you leave him behind in Pale?"

"No. The dog went to a distant farm before the Tantrocans attacked."

Danilla walked about the room, finally sitting in a window seat. "Tell me what you know of Meru's condition."

"I sense he has inherited a power."

Danilla pondered why she should inherit healing without her brother also receiving some gift. "My mother believes her mercy component of the gift tempered my father's power. You cured Meru's weak hand by getting him away from Mother. He is distant now, so we can't blame Mother for his inability to cast flame."

"I would not say 'blame. Perhaps the gifts of Li manifest only when they are needed."

That idea appealed to Danilla, who realized her own healing gift appeared only when Father needed her help. But it was a risky belief to rely on power that arose only when danger threatened. Justik did not seem to feed on danger. He was the danger. "Enough on Meru. We are here to deal with your blindness. Did you find Justik's flame very bright?"

"Yes."

Lyra growled, leapt off the bed, and went to Danilla. The cat put her paw and a bit of claw in the royal knee.

"Stop that," Danilla said, pushing the paw away. "What do you want?"

The cat returned to Breel, placing a paw on her knee, this time with claws sheathed. She yowled again and did something most unusual. Lyra clamped her mouth on Breel's wrist.

"Ouch. Stop that."

Danilla rushed over and placed her hands on either side of her cat's head.

"Wait, she's not really biting, just holding," Breel said.

"What do you want, Lyra?" Danilla spoke softly. "You have my attention. Release Breel."

The cat rumbled, not a growl, but clearly a disagreement. Danilla tried to reposition her hands to separate the cat's jaws and, in the process, touched Breel's forearm. Both women gasped.

"Your touch tingles and warms my arm." Breel said. "It is not unpleasant."

Danilla brought her other hand to Breel's arm and closed her eyes. A sense of the human body, its complexity and form, filled her mind. Lyra opened her jaws and backed away.

The princess let her mind travel, knowing her target. She eased through spaces, going from arm, to shoulder, to neck, and at last into Breel's eyes. There, at the back, where light is gathered and its signal sent to the brain, she found stunned cells and disconnection. Without knowing exactly what she was doing, Danilla soothed and repaired. Breel kept her eyes closed and trembled as the probing continued. After minutes of concentration, Danilla released her grip and sank onto the bed. Lyra licked her cheek.

"I sense light," Breel said. "Dare I open my eyes?"

"Do it with care."

Breel's eyelids rose slowly. "I see dimly…now more." She turned her head, eyes fully open, and surveyed the room. When she was able to focus on Danilla, her breath caught. Reaching to touch Danilla, Breel asked, "Are you all right?"

Danilla sat up and shook her head as if to clear a fog. "I just feel exhausted, as if I'd done a great labor."

"I think you did. I can see. You have a healing power. Did you not know it? Have you not used it before?"

Danilla knew she'd cured Justi. Now she'd healed Breel. "I repaired my father's injury after he was burned."

Breel rose and went to the window. "My sight is as keen as it has ever been," she said, smiling. Then she turned her head toward Danilla, and the cat sprawled beside her on the bed. "And Lyra must have some kind of power."

Danilla gazed at her companion animal who, with hooded lids, seemed to smile. "Two children of Justi have inherited his gift or parts of it. Justik can cast flame, a power Justi used only to protect the innocent and punish evil, but Justik uses for his own evil purposes. Father could also heal, which I seem able to do. Why shouldn't the third child of Justi, my brother Meru, inherit a power?"

In the distance came the sound of marching men. Breel said to Danilla. "I am the one who sensed King Meru's unused power. I may be of assistance in bringing it forth. I should be near him."

Danilla nodded. "We will follow the Zellish army.

The Zellish had slept fitfully in face of what had finally become a reality: the battle to defend the Zell. As gray light crept over the Manwark Mountains, shooting stars streaked the western horizon. The darkness faded to reveal two armies facing each other, each writhing as if they were great chained beasts. The sun crested the eastern peaks and swept the dawn gray aside. The beasts grew silent in still air and the chatter of birds faded.

Meru surveyed the scene with Entor. "What are they waiting for?" the king asked.

"Perhaps they are still assessing the situation and are considering withdrawal," Entor answered unconvincingly.

Before more speculation, a horn bellowed and there was movement in the Tantrocan lines. A single man advanced, joined by robed men who carried no weapons. A lone drum pounded as other Tantrocan soldiers in battle leathers carrying either pikes or short swords followed the strange leaders.

Meru watched the enemy advance and issued his command. "Sound the attack."

* * * * *

The barrier between the Lihoch and Darhoch spirits was breached. *The Miasma thrust darkness at the stunned Adamanti. Powerful Adamanti countered the invasion and halted the collapse of their personal spheres. Li-nom of lesser status contracted. The conflict rocked the spirit world, engaging each spirit in a titanic struggle. Human scholars would claim the shooting stars seen at dawn marked this conflict.*

Li-nom cringed in a small puddle of the infusion, where they struggled to restore the light. The Seventh Order Adamanti Mewissio raged at the High Lord. How could Li permit his servants to suffer this humiliation, this loss of power?

Pofay burst in on her cohort's anger. "The Li-nom were created equal to the Dar-nom. We can resist and drive the Miasma back. But who wins depends on what the humans do. The Zellish cannot succumb to the Tantrocans if we are to prevail."

* * * * *

The first Zellish troops to reach the lone man charged, swords extended. When they got near enough to slay the fool, Justik directed explosions of flame that punctured bodies and roasted hearts. The lances of killing yellow fire picked out large Zellish first, as if

Justik sought to demonstrate his might by killing the strongest foe. The morning air erupted in brief, sharp screams of death. Away from Justik, Zellish skill with the long sword drove back the invaders, but this brief success soured when the Tantrocans collapsed in a tight phalanx behind Justik. The attacking Zellish who came within range of his fire were slain. On either side of Justik, priests of Ice began to sing a dirge-like, monotonal chant that rose above the cries of the wounded.

"What are they doing?" yelled a Zellish swordsman.

"Some kind of incantation. Probably invoking Dar's blessing," his comrade replied. "Ignore it."

That proved impossible. The Ice enchantment enveloped Zellish forces, sowing confusion and sapping the will to fight. Affected men, clearly befuddled, dropped swords to their sides and backed from the fight. Justik burned and Tantrocans stabbed the helpless Zellish. Screams of those who survived Justik's fire were silenced, impaled on Tantrocan pikes. As the sun rose higher and heated the valley, corpses littered the grassy field and blood fed the ground.

Above the song of the robed priests, Meru heard anguished wails of his soldiers and he grew angry. Something stirred within him, the onset of a rage that transformed to a feeling of power. Confused, Meru did not know what was happening or what the power might be, but it grew stronger within him as the barbarians and their fire-caster slayed more Zellish. Meru charged toward Justik, alarming his guard who were intent on retreating.

"You will die, my lord," a guard yelled.

Meru heard nothing but the screams of dying men as he spurred his stallion forward. When he drew near Justik, he had no doubt this was his half brother, the man he'd seen briefly in Zellingon. Now Justik seemed larger and more muscled than Meru remembered.

Meru reined his steed to a stop on a rise above his enemy. "I am Meru, King of the Zell. Cease your attack and withdraw and we will let you return to the North Lands. We far outnumber you."

Justik folded his arms across his chest, palms flat. He leaned forward and glared at Meru. "Hail, Brother Meru, King of the Doomed Zell. I am Justik, soon to be King of the Zell. Why should we withdraw when we prevail?" He spread his fingers and closed them.

Meru forced his eyes away from Justik's hands to his face. It struck him that his half brother was not just posturing but seemed fatigued as if the killing of so many took a great effort. Perhaps using the power came at a price.

"You shall not prevail." Meru said, his rage growing as he saw the carnage of battle. He willed his anger to become his own Justice Power.

"You are a fool, Meru. You have seen my power and know that there is nothing to oppose it. Take your pitiful army and flee. Perhaps some of you may survive."

Meru raised his sword and invoked whatever power he had to strike Justik. He saw a green mist leave his sword hand, run up the blade, and expand to a cloud.

The cloud raced forward, becoming thicker and darker, and enveloped Justik and the Ice priests.

The Ice priests ceased their incantation. Justik coughed and staggered back, thrust both arms forward, and sent flame at King Meru. The flame, dimmed to dull yellow, lost its sharp focus and went wide, burning nearby Zellish soldiers. They retreated, but Meru held his ground, and a second blast from Justik struck the king, spinning him from his horse.

*****

As Meru challenged Justik, the seventh order Li-nom grew stronger. *Lesser Adamanti fought back the encroaching darkness, confusion, and chaos. The resistance slowed but did not stop the invasion. Some of the lesser spirits succumbed to darkness and reduced to feeble points of consciousness.*

Mewissio could not understand how the Li-nom were losing but realized loss on the spirit plane mirrored loss by the followers of Li on the material plane. He grasped the notion that faith was needed. He must believe in Li. The Zellish must believe in Li. Meru must believe in his power.

*****

Meru fell awkwardly, breaking his left arm. The pain blinded him, and his effort to evoke his power evaporated. He fought the urge to give up. A more intense green glow flared toward Justik and the men around him. The cloud had an effect. Justik bent, as if a boulder were laid on his back. His face reddened and he panted. The Ice priests remained silent, and the confusion of the Zellish soldiers lifted. These men burst into action, raised swords, and pushed the enemy back. As his men advanced, Meru groaned and lost consciousness.

Perhaps Justik had felt Meru's mist, something later scholars decided was directed at the mind. Justik was clearly affected, and his flame was dimmed. When the Ice priests lost their ability to confuse Zellish soldiers, Justik and the Tantrocans retreated. The Zellish let them go. Both armies took their original distant positions. The dusk settled on a large area filled with bodies, both dead and wounded.

The Tantrocans did not follow their usual practice of scouring a battlefield to make sure the wounded would not rise again. This deviation saved Meru's life, for he lay in the dark with burns and a broken arm. The fire cauterized, so when the king regained consciousness, he had not lost much blood. He ignored the piercing pain in his arm and shook his head, attempting to clear his clouded vision. He could see bodies around him in the moonlight, some groaning in agony, most blessed with the painless stillness of death.

The shock of failure hit Meru. He'd tried to exercise the power, but the result was pitiful. He tried to rise, but the pain in his arm almost made him pass out. What was the point anyway? His thoughts became blacker as he imagined the destruction of the Zell, the slavery and human sacrifice. Anger at the injustice of the world gripped him, and he pounded the ground.

Hours passed before Danilla and Breel arrived with a group of healers, mostly women who traveled with a supply of bandages, ointments, potions, and skills to mend wounded troops. The princess and Breel donned the scarlet hood worn by these special women and men. Even the Tantrocan warriors would not harm those who wore such hoods.

"Even with a bit of moonlight, the field is dark. How will we find the King?" Breel asked.

In answer, a hawk screeched and dove toward the mound where Meru lay.

"Such birds do not fly at night," Danilla said.

Breel ran to the place the bird had indicated. "Princess, here he is. He's alive." Breel knelt and assessed his injuries.

"You have sight," Meru muttered.

Danilla also laid her hands on her brother.

"Why are you here?" Meru gasped.

"I am here as a healer."

"But—"

Danilla put finger to Meru's lips and cut off his questions. She closed her eyes and searched for his injury, finding it in a broken bone and burned tissue. A sphere of silence engulfed both patient and healer as Danilla invoked her power. She forced the cracked bone to seal and soothed surrounding tissues. Still concentrating, Danilla healed damaged tissue as she'd done for her father. The intact cells replaced the burned skin on Meru's arm and neck.

When she finished, she breathed deep and bent her head. Meru stared.

Danilla opened her eyes. "I have Father's healing power," she said. "I restored Breel's sight."

Meru nodded and turned to Breel. "You claimed to have sensed some gift in me after you healed my hand. Maybe you were right, but my power seems weak."

"We must get you out of here."

"But what is the point in saving me?" Meru said. "I'm the only hope against that monster and have failed."

The hawk swooped low over the trio. "Surely a sign," Breel said. "And I am struck by a thought that Meru's problem may be faith. A lack."

"Faith? Faith in what?" Meru asked in a quiet voice.

Breel answered with a burst of words. "In good, in the ultimate dominance of Li, in yourself. You see only the here and now. There is more to the world than the mundane affairs of men, and until you have some belief in the greater meaning of life, you cannot invoke the power."

Meru stared at the healer with a strange expression. "Do you have this faith, Breel? Even after being blinded by an evil being?"

"I can see, thanks to your sister. Even if I remained blind, my faith is not shaken, my Lord, and I wish that I could share it with you. But you must find it yourself."

The women helped Meru to his feet and made their way to the Zellish camp.

37
Prophecy

At the end of the battle, Justik spoke to Caldir. "Meru seems to have a power," Justik said, subdued. "He casts a mesmerizing green halo that affects the mind. I felt it as confusion, a loss of will. Something akin to what the Ice priests do."

The high priest considered Justik's theory. "If true, it is a meager power. Your power is far greater. Concentrate and attack first with the Ice priests. Give Meru no time to cast a fog. Burn the flesh from Zellish bodies. If Meru appears, kill him."

In the Zellish camp, Meru marveled at Danilla's healing skill. The break in his left forearm was mended, but the royal physician insisted the limb be splinted. The next morning, as the sun licked the valley floor, the Tantrocan and Zellish armies closed the gap between them. Despite his splinted arm, Meru declared he would lead his men into battle.

"You should be in the rear," Drenkiri insisted.

Meru gazed at the old man. "Was my father in the rear when he fought the Tantrocans? I must lead. I felt some power before Justik struck. It will be stronger today." When Drenkiri shook his head, Meru added, "I will not fight, but I must be present."

Justik led his army toward the Zellish. Shouts of soldiers and clangs of pommels on shields accompanied the march, and stomping boots raised a cloud of dust and insects. Zellish horses snorted and crows cawed against the disturbance. Justik, flanked by guards, emerged from the ranks and stood in a shaft of sunlight. He raised a hand and the Tantrocans quieted. The warm breeze vanished, flags drooped, and crows muted.

Meru stepped from the Zellish ranks and gestured at the army behind him. "My soldiers far outnumber yours. We will prevail despite your power."

Justik stepped closer. "You have unwisely chosen to stand exposed before your troops," he warned. "Your death will strike fear in their hearts." He signaled the Ice priests, and the clerics began their monotonic invocation, louder and more vigorous today in an archaic language no soldier understood.

Meru breathed in, concentrated, and acted. From his right hand billowed a thick green haze, visible to all as it raced along the ground toward Justik, the Ice priests, and the Tantrocans troops. When it reached the front line, the cloud whooshed up as if animated and rolled over the soldiers. The song of the Ice priests faltered, and the mystics shrank back.

Justik expected more boasting before battle, so Meru's quick action surprised him. The green emanation was more visible, moved faster, and swallowed him. The dazed Ice priests seemed to have lost their voices. Justik felt sluggish and distracted, his mind wandering. He resisted, focused on his own power, and willed his arm up. He searched for his power but was distracted by movement behind Meru.

Behind the Zellish king, a tall woman with a red cap appeared. Why would a healer endanger herself on a battle scene? Justik wondered. Then he recognized his half sister, the princess. Her presence confused and annoyed him. If she appeared on a battlefield, she could witness her brother's death. Maybe that is what she wanted: Meru's death and her coronation. Another thought struck him. He could remove a whole generation of Zellish royalty at once. That would surely stun the Zellish and assure Tantrocan victory.

Danilla had followed Meru and heard the words of Justik and Meru. *Why is Meru putting himself in harm's way?* She saw Meru's green cloud settled on the nearest Tantrocans and Justik raise his arm. Danilla grew angry, her hands heated, and her hearing faded, blocking out sounds of shifting men. Then came a roar as her hair glowed.

Justik seemed startled at his half sister's transformation. "Only a trick of light," he muttered, squinting in the sunlight. He faced Meru and aimed his hand in the king's direction.

Danilla raised both her hands and willed action. Later she would admit not knowing what action, remembering only a hawk screeching, the sound, and a narrow lance of white light that struck Justik's outstretched arm.

He screamed and slapped the flames dancing on his garment. Then, with more fear than arrogance, he aimed his reddened hand at Danilla. "You are my enemy, Sister, and will pay the price. Die."

Meru blasted a narrow, intense green fog at Justik, who swiped it from his eyes. That gave Danilla an opening. She directed a second spear of flame, brighter, thicker this time. It reignited Justik's arm. He swiped at the flames and stumbled back, holding his burned hand. He screamed another string of invective that somehow became an order to soldiers to attack.

Zellish and Tantrocan fighters watched the display of unnatural power. "The Zellish possess magic," one Tantrocan yelled. When the green mist dissipated, the Tantrocans charged toward Danilla.

Meru ordered Danilla back. She ignored him and stepped toward the fighters who were slashing and killing each other with swords. In close quarters where finesse with a long sword was less important, the generally larger Tantrocans had an advantage. The Zellish fell back but Danilla stood her ground, then directed a swath of white fire across the approaching Tantrocans. Bodies of those in front were sliced in two, and men behind sustained black burn holes, many lethal. Wounded survivors fell screaming and the momentum of the enemy faltered. An arrow sailed at Danilla and she exploded it in a shaft of fire. More flame raked the enemy, and the Tantrocans fled back along the River Wark. From a nearby stand of trees a great flock of starlings rose squawking and flapping and darkened the sky over the fleeing Tantrocans.

"You are the one," Meru said in an awed tone. His face was pale and his eyes wide. "You have the gift."

"I have some gifts, Brother, but you have another," Danilla said as she felt the effects of her power. "The halo you cast is as unnatural as my flame. We must accept what Li has granted." There had never been a hint she'd inherited her father's power, and she felt no control over it. It was almost as if the power had used her.

Drenkiri, who'd watched the abrupt Zellish victory, asked, "What are your orders, Sire?"

Meru's eyes darted to Danilla. "Have the army follow the Tantrocans, but at a distance. I suspect they may be fleeing to the coast, and I don't want to prevent that. We've seen enough death."

Meru, Danilla, and Breel went to the royal tent. Entor offered wet cloths to clean the grime of the battlefield. They wiped their faces, but the cloths did nothing to ease their anxiety and excitement. Only time would do that. Meru ordered wine and a meal, not because he was hungry, but more as a distraction. The women left for Danilla's tent, claiming they would feel better with clean clothes.

Meru removed his battle vest while Entor poured wine. Meru drained the mug before speaking, more to himself than to Entor. "The Tantrocans have witnessed an event that changes their thinking. They may return with a new plan. They could recruit more Ice priests with stronger enchantments. Perhaps I could stop them. Apparently, my gift is one that affects the mind and nullifies the Ice priests. But Justik could make himself less vulnerable. Regardless, the Tantrocans continue to need sacrifice and slaves. They will invade again."

"You mentioned an event?" Entor queried.

"Their flame-throwing champion encountered our own champion, one with a power like his own. He will not want to face my sister again."

Entor opened his mouth, but no words emerged. Wind billowed the tent sides and thunder sounded.

"What is that scrap you seem so busy with?" Meru demanded.

"Meligo gave it to me," Entor said, his forehead wrinkled. "He found it in a stale archive of Manwark. Before the archivist became senile, he'd sorted documents by age. In a drawer labeled 'Very Old,' Meligo found this text that appears to be part of the *Book of Signs,* a late canticle. It contains this passage: 'Peace will flourish when the dark and light unite, when royal houses bond.'"

"What does that mean?" Meru asked.

Entor placed the paper on the table. "Meligo suggests that 'royal houses' can only refer to the thrones of this kingdom and of the Tantrocans. He says that 'unite' and 'bond' were used by ancient writers to signify marriage."

"When is that supposed to happen?"

"Prophecies do not give dates," Entor said. "Scholars usually say that something will happen when everything is ready. For example, you and Princess Danilla are unmarried as are King Brosun and Princess Ranera in Ankor. One might argue that everything is ready."

Stunned, Meru sat, his mind awhirl. *Could the price of peace be marriage?* He tried to recall what he'd heard of

Ranera. She was portrayed as willful, stubborn, and, by some accounts, a libertine.

Entor added, "Meligo would argue this notion is the key to peace. Not just a short peace, but one that flourishes. I would give no advice to your majesty. But it may be worth thinking on. I am sure you've heard the old lore that says that the Tantrocans and the Zellish were once one people. Drenkiri told me that is what protected the then-princess Mercerio when she was held captive by the Tantrocans. They respected her royal status."

Danilla and Breel entered, each in garments more suited to a palace than to a field tent. the princess had found something in her wardrobe suitable for Breel, who wore a deep green gown of some light fabric that left her shoulders bare. Danilla had chosen a red dress of similar material with a bodice that revealed more breast than Queen Mercerio would approve of. Meru smiled and pointed to wine and cups on a table. The women sat as their meal arrived, and the three consumed day-old bread, rabbit, and a vegetable Meru did not recognize.

Meru found it hard not to watch Breel and had to yank his attention back to Entor's notion. To marry for reasons of state. It had certainly been done before. The prize of lasting peace was not to be dismissed. Even when the barbarians were not invading the Zell in great numbers, the northerners regularly conducted raids on coastal towns, costing lives. That had to stop. Perhaps a trade deal could be struck if there were some force to link the two peoples. Marriage might be that force.

Meru thought again of Princess Ranera, but his eyes were on Breel. Her long hair was tied back with a white ribbon, and she seemed more knowing with her regained sight.

"Of course, this uniting could refer to Princess Danilla," Entor said, raising his voice over the rain. "She could wed the Tantrocan king or even the Tantrocan champion. Surely he has a high place of honor in that court."

"The last cannot be," Meru said. "If this man is my half brother, he is Danilla's. I suppose Brosun's a possibility."

"What are you talking about?" Danilla said with heat in her voice.

Meru answered. "Sorry. Let me explain. Entor and Meligo have interpreted a new verse from the *Book of Signs.* It tells how to create a lasting peace between us and the Tantrocans. The price of that peace is a bond between the royal houses of Ankor and Zellingon. Apparently 'bond' means marriage." Meru tasted a chunk of vegetable and frowned.

Danilla crossed her arms. "Yes, you should have had me here if you are speaking of selling me."

"Not selling. Just listing possibilities. You are one possibility. I am the other."

Danilla turned to Entor. "Where is this text?"

The young seer read the lines aloud.

Danilla drummed her long fingers on the table. "I understand this King Brosun is a pig. The Princess Ranera, on the other hand, is a vixen. Comely, but a vixen. Neither of us would fare well having our lives forfeited for the kingdom."

Breel asked, "How would you pursue this interpretation of the text, my lord?"

The rain ebbed and stopped completely as Meru pondered the next step. He figured this would require a delegation to Ankor, something far too dangerous. Maybe a neutral site. "As soon as I am sure that the Tantrocans have returned to Tantroc, I will send a proposal."

Danilla, hands on her hips, inspected her brother. "Breel and I will talk in private."

Breel and Princess Danilla walked past women tending injured soldiers, getting them ready to travel. The brief rain had cleaned the air and cooled it. Breel pointed out the renewed bird sounds, but other than that, the women were silent until they entered Danilla's spacious tent.

"I think this notion of buying peace by selling oneself is insane," Danilla fumed. "The benefits of peace should sell themselves. To base this scheme on a dubious interpretation of a line of old text is foolish. From what I've heard, Princess Ranera would accept a proposal from Meru if she thought it brought her power. Meru would be wise to keep knives out of their bedchamber."

The princess sat at a small table while Breel served the tea.

"What do you think," Danilla pressed.

"Arranged marriages are done all the time."

"But what about this arranged marriage?"

"It is hardly my place to question my king."

"Breel, we've spoken before. I know you have feelings for my brother, and I saw your reaction when Meru first spoke of marrying Ranera."

Breel put her cup down and stood, walking somewhat stiffly to the tent door where she gazed for a long moment. Without turning around, she said, "I admit that this does not seem suitable for Mer . . . the king. I have gotten to know him as I treated his hand. Not really know him, but we talked, and I learned he is a handsome, mild soul. He is not suited for a sham marriage with such a woman." Her voice grew soft. "I would, I mean he would be happier if he found true . . . true . . . love."

Danilla rose and faced Breel. "Your cheeks are wet. Admit it. You love him."

In their retreat to the sea, the Tantrocan force was joined by the contingent left behind in Pale. With these reinforcements the fleeing army twice mounted attacks, but the greater numbers of Zellish held them off, but did not press to destroy the enemy. Justik remained out of sight. Finally, the surviving Tantrocans fled to their ships as the pleasant late summer weather broke, and ominous, dark clouds gathered over the Tantric Gulf. By the time the ships departed, the clouds covered the whole region. The occasional breeze became a constant wind with gusts that bent small trees and swayed tops of tall ones. Distant thunder growled and black clouds crept toward the coast. The sail from the north coast to Tantroc was not pleasant.

The Zellish army returned to Zellingon while King Meru pursued his plan to alter the relationship between the long-time adversaries. He'd consulted his advisors and several seers with expertise in ancient documents. The latter confirmed that the scrap of the *Book of Signs* was authentic, and the interpretation of the text about joining of royal houses was in keeping with the old writer's use of terms.

The advisors were dubious about making peace with the Tantrocans by proposing a marriage between Meru and Ranera, but none actively opposed the scheme. Meru dictated an official message that started by enumerating the advantages of peace and offered to allow trade if the Tantrocans agreed to a treaty. It cited the newly found text from the *Book of Signs,* a source the Tantrocans knew and respected. The scribe copied the fragment into the note. Meru left the notion of a marriage to ensure peace to Brosun's imagination or the perceptiveness of his high priest. Even if he didn't get it, his priests were capable of translating.

After the message had been dispatched, he asked Breel to visit him. The healer was busy visiting patients and did not get the king's invitation for hours. She found Meru pacing before a cold fireplace.

"Breel, thank you for coming," he said. "Please sit. I want to talk about us."

"Us? What is there to say, Sire?"

"To you I am Meru." The king hesitated as if collecting his thoughts. At last he went to a bamboo table brought from Abantazar by his grandmother Melsin, a memento of the many years she spent there after the fall of Zellingon. He poured a cup of wine, took a breath, and continued. "I wanted you to know that I have grown fond of you. I would take it further, but I am forced to something that is larger than my feelings for you. It is important to me that you hear of this before others and that you understand what is happening."

Breel frowned. "I'm not sure I understand your words. Speaking of fondness, taking it further, and feeling is what a diplomat might say. Please talk plainly."

Meru sighed, approached Breel, and held her green-tinted eyes. "I think I love you, Breel, everything about you. I hope you feel the same about me."

"What is this something larger that blocks going further?" Breel asked, ignoring what she knew from the discussion with Danilla.

"It is a matter of state. Prophecy claims that peace between us and the Tantrocans will come about if we are linked by a royal marriage. I must bring this about for the protection of my people. I will propose union with the Tantrocan Princess Ranera. Alas, this is my duty."

Breel turned her back to Meru. "You must do what you must. I too have felt the attraction between us but could not speak of it. You, after all, are the king, and I am but a commoner. I will return to my home and put our relationship out of my mind. What you have said just makes this easier. I hope you are happy with the . . . barbarian princess."

She bowed and marched stiffly to the door, turning to ask, "Am I permitted to leave, my king?"

Meru nodded, not trusting his ability to speak.

38
Travel

A swirling wind raised little sand devils on the Ankor beach while King Brosun waited on a high palace balcony for the fleet to enter the harbor. He watched the vessels struggle through chop, tie up at the long pier, and disgorge soldiers, who glumly climbed the stone steps. The Tantrocan defeat hit home. Brosun couldn't fathom why his conquest of the Zell failed, but wanted to find a scapegoat. When Justik appeared on a boat ramp, the king frowned and pursed his lips as if he'd sucked on a persimmon. He would have questions for the champion. And for Caldir.

Brosun found Princess Ranera lounging on the king's throne. It was not unusual for her to seek firsthand accounts of events, but she seemed overdressed for this news. Her tan gown was complemented by gold chain circling her waist, a gold band about her hair, and a gold brooch with a bloody gem around her neck. Brosun scowled and Ranera vacated the throne.

"Know your place, Sister. You may lust for power but placing your royal backside on the royal seat does not confer it. Your little amusement has become tiring."

Ranera settled on a smaller chair to the side of the throne. "I see my king is in a foul mood. I was only making sure the throne suited me in case an assassin finds his way to your heart. But why are you so upset,

Brosun? Messengers have already told you what happened."

Brosun indeed knew both the good and bad news. Defeat was bad. Having an intact army was good. The Ice priests' ability to mesmerize the Pale defenders and Tantrocan soldiers at Manwark was good. King Meru's mysterious mist was bad. The killing power of Princess Danilla was very bad.

Justik was another matter. His failure was responsible for defeat. Brosun suspected that Danilla's maiming took both a physical and psychological toll. For the first time, Justik had been thwarted. The king stared glumly at his sister. "Just because the bad news is known does not lessen its impact or meaning."

"What is the meaning?"

"Perhaps that Dar is displeased." Brosun waved a servant close. "Tell my high priest that I want him here. Now."

The man hurried off, and soon Caldir stumbled into the throne room. He seemed to have lost his cunning arrogance. His eyes were red, his face unshaven, and his hair as messy as an unfinished basket. Brosun smelled alcohol. Caldir used a chair for support and sat only when the king settled onto the throne.

Guards swung back the heavy doors, and Justik entered accompanied by a large soldier in -sweat-stained battle garb. Both advanced to the throne, their heavy steps thumping on the slate floor. When they stood before the king, who nodded permission to speak, the soldier gave his report.

"Our invasion surprised the enemy," he said, his deep, gravelly tone echoing in the high, raftered space, disturbing a bat that sailed from its roost near the peak and disappeared where a chimney pierced the roof. "We crossed the gulf at night and, undetected, assembled in unoccupied lands. Pale fell quickly with the help of the Ice priests and Justik. We expected similar success against the Zellish army, even though that force turned out to be far larger than our spies reported. But the Zellish possessed strange, unexpected powers."

King Brosun turned his attention to Justik. "Speak. Why did this happen? What became of your great power?"

Justik jerked his gaze from Ranera and stiffened. "My power removed Justi before the fight. But spies made more than one mistake. They miscalculated the size of the Zellish army and claimed Justi was the only one with power. Based on that, I ignored my half brother and half sister."

"You ignored them. You made a mistake."

"My instinct said they must die, but Caldir claimed three deaths would give the Zellish warning of the invasion."

Brosun glared at Justik. "So you blame Caldir. Why did you not kill them both in battle?"

Justik held up his burned arm. "I was surprised and my power was impaired by injury."

The king pointed at his high priest. "Your spies failed, Caldir?"

Caldir breathed deeply. "No, Highness. Reports were accurate. The size of the Zellish army doubled at the last moment. Meru and Danilla displayed no power until they were called forth by battle."

When neither Justik nor Caldir had more to say, Brosun glared and said, "So a minor burn sent you fleeing, Justik, like a cur with your tail between your legs and you, Caldir, did not press your spies. Both of you have failed."

The commander cut off Justik's response. "The Ice priests were rendered useless by the spell cast by the young Zellish king. We were left facing a larger army. I thought it wise to retreat before sacrificing more men."

"You have all failed me. You will find a way to overcome this disruption of my plans or pay a dear price," Brosun screamed.

In the principal Ice village, Thal heard the same story from his stunned priests. He gathered his advisor Fospe, six skilled warriors, and his son Sathal to travel with him to Ankor. Sathal protested the pact his father had signed and hoped defeat voided the deal. Even after seeing her beauty, sparkling eyes, and alluring curves, Sathal had no desire to have Ranera as his wife.

Sathal brought his horse beside his father's on the path to Ankor. "The pact with the Tantrocans is dead. We have not gotten warmer hunting grounds."

"We provided Ice priests. We deserve a queen," Thal answered.

At the gate on Ankor's eastern wall, Fospe paid the guards a routine bribe, something required even of diplomats, that eased access to the stone fortress. The party approached along the slope that overlooked the harbor where white-caped waves slapped against the sides of anchored vessels. The sun slipped behind clouds, and Sathal and his father wrapped their cloaks about themselves.

Caldir welcomed them and suggested they rest and take refreshment.

"I must speak with Brosun," Thal insisted. "Your military failure will not get him out of his agreement."

Caldir led the party toward the throne room. Outside the royal hall, the palace guards refused entry until Thal's guards agreed to remain outside the door. Thal gave them orders to wait and he, Sathal, and Fospe were admitted.

"Hail, Thal," Brosun said, as the Ice leader swept into the chamber. "I hope your trip was pleasant."

"Greetings, Brosun. What say ye of this failed invasion?" Thal asked.

"I say we encountered forces not of this realm. First, King Meru exudes a vapor that your priests did not stop. Then the Princess Danilla cast a white fire. Both powers were unexpected."

"So the princess rendered your champion useless? He could not respond?"

"Could not or would not, I am unsure which. At any rate, when an ally fails to provide what was promised, there is defeat."

"But our agreement stands," Thal said, giving his words a force of fact.

Brosun sat back and did not answer at once. Finally, he said, "Our agreement said your priests would help defeat the Zellish. They didn't. So our pact is null." Brosun listened to further arguments from Fospe for how keeping the agreement in place would benefit both the Tantrocans and the Ice, including the notion of giving Princess Ranera a ruling role away from Ankor. That idea seemed to interest the king, but all he offered was a promise to think it over. He pointed at a large table set for dining. Brosun sat, his guests followed his lead, and a stream of servants emerged from a side door carrying trays of bread, meats, and vegetables imported from the Zell. Brosun was about to eat when a messenger arrived and whispered in the king's ear. Brosun excused himself and left the room. He remained an inordinate time with the messenger, and his return raised eyebrows. After the meal, King Brosun let Thal and Fospe know that he had made his decision. The agreement between the Tantrocans and the Ice was ended.

Fospe and Thal were angry. Fospe wanted compensation. Thal wanted a unifying royal. Only Sathal seemed content when Brosun insisted the Princess Ranera would not be bound by a marriage pact. King Brosun did his best to be sympathetic and diplomatic in bidding the delegation goodbye the next morning. Then he summoned Caldir.

"I have another role for my sister, something better than rutting with a goat," Brosun said.

Caldir squinted as if in thought. "Does this come from the message you just received?"

"Yes. King Meru offers a peace proposal and includes the possibility of a marriage to seal the treaty."

"Why?"

"Some new prophecy."

"And you are considering this idea?"

Brosun smiled. "A peace negotiation is a way to learn more about the new Zellish powers. It may give us a chance to destroy Meru and his sister. You will have to convince Justik to act."

"He may resist," Caldir said.

"He has already attacked his father. I will provide the chance to remove his siblings. You will see that he does what I want."

Brosun accepted King Meru's proposition, claiming interest in a lasting peace. He said he accepted the new fragment from the Book of Signs, which the Tantrocans recognized as prophecy, and offered his sister as queen of the Zell. *An excellent way to ensure the peace alliance,* he wrote.

Brosun extended a formal invitation to Meru, Princess Danilla, and Justi to meet at a small island halfway between Ankor and Fathom. The crust of land called Bentnord was large enough to erect tents but small enough to preclude large numbers of troops. Neither kingdom paid much attention to this island, making it a neutral place for talks. Once Brosun dispatched the message, he summoned Justik and Ranera and told them their roles. Ranera was not enthusiastic.

In Zellingon, Meru met with Danilla and his father to discuss the response to King Brosun's invitation. Lyra accompanied the princess and settled on a cushion kept in Meru's room just for her. She rested her head on her paws but her pointed ears remained erect. Her eyes followed the conversation. Only Danilla thought she had any ability to understand what was being said.

Justi was against the whole venture. He had to admit, however, that he abided by the words of prophecy when he fought to restore the Kingdom of the Zell. "Surely, you cannot think that marrying Princess Ranera will change barbarian behavior?"

"We will agree to terms of interaction with a treaty," Meru explained.

"What title do you offer her?" Danilla asked.

"She already has a title. Here she can be called 'Lady.'"

Danilla puffed disbelief. "That title will not suffice for Ranera."

Meru muttered something unintelligible. Then he said, "Perhaps the prophecy foretells your union with King Brosun. Then you could be the Lady Danilla."

Danilla's face paled. "That will not happen, but if it did, I would be queen."

"Fine. Ranera can be queen," Meru said. "It is only for show."

Justi shook his head. "Some things between men and women are not just for show."

"Have you spoken to Breel about this proposed marriage?" Danilla asked. "And did she approve?"

"Not exactly. More like she understood. But enough. I have decided and the Tantrocans have agreed to a conference. Father and I will travel on a fast ship from Fathom. I will take six of our best guards. King Brosun also extends an invitation to you, Danilla, but I see no reason for you to be there."

"Really? Given what I did to end the invasion, you see no reason?"

"But Father's power is the same as yours. If anything goes amiss, he can protect us. Isn't that right, Father?"

Justi studied his son and daughter. After a few seconds, he spoke carefully. "In truth, I have not used my power for years. I am not sure I have the ability any longer."

It was Meru's chance to think, which he did as he paced the room. "Breel had a theory that my hand problem was caused by Mother's influence. Just as she controlled your power, she unconsciously suppressed mine."

"That's a nice theory," Justi said, "but I'd hate to find out it is wrong when Justik decides to kill us both."

Lyra yowled and rose. The princess patted the cat and told her it was all right. "There is an easy solution," Danilla said. "I will travel with you. I can counter Justik. We will all be safe as long as I am there." The words were confident, decisive, and ended with a rumble from Lyra.

Both men stared. Meru said, "You may be right. We have no reason to trust the Tantrocans, and an attack is possible. We will be prepared."

Lyra rose and rubbed against Danilla.

"Now I'd like to have some time with Breel," Meru said.

"I think not," Danilla said.

"Why not?"

"Breel left for Pale this morning."

Meru seemed stunned. "I thought we had an understanding. Why didn't she tell me? Why didn't she say goodbye?"

Danilla held both pity and disgust on her face. "Why indeed."

39
Bentnord

Peace between humans threatened the balance in the spirit realm. Forcing Ranera to marry Meru might soften the northerners and draw them away from Dar. A god with fewer human adherents meant the god's spirit followers were diminished.

Dar-nuk offered his analysis. "Li's divided gift is shared by four humans. Justik follows Dar's will. But the other gifted humans do Li's bidding. They stand in the way of Tantrocan conquest. We must try to remove Li's gifted humans."

The female angel Dar-Cor rippled the darkness about her. "How?"

"We have compelled creatures in the human realm to do our will. As have Li's angels. I have touched an intelligent beast – what humans call the Megadarch. The Megadarch – part reptile, part squid, part shark and as large as a sailing ship – has learned to savor the taste of human flesh. It will do my bidding."

* * * * *

Bentnord, an uninhabited slash of rock in the western Tantric Gulf, was a spring, sea-bird rookery equidistant from Ankor and Fathom. To get there Meru intended to sail from Pale, but Danilla objected.

"Pale makes no sense," she said. "It lacks boats to accommodate us and Fathom is closer to Bentnord. We will be less exposed to the sudden storms and wild seas that plague the Gulf in the fall." When Meru shook his head, Danilla added, "Besides, Breel will not want to see you as you sail to meet your bride."

Meligo told Mercerio of the trip and she fumed. She questioned the interpretation of the prophecy and was alarmed about the meeting. "A trip to a barren rock in the middle of the Tantric Gulf is dangerous," she said.

"Prophecy requires it, Mother," Meru answered.

"The interpretation seems ridiculous. Marriage should mean more than a bargaining chip in a peace negotiation."

"I agree," said Danilla. "And the Tantrocans can't be trusted. They enslaved our people for ten and eight years, sacrificed our children to their evil god, raped our women, laid waste our farms and cities, and slaughtered our wildlife. If Father hadn't driven them out, we would still be crushed by their cruelty. What they did in Pale shows they have not changed."

Meru tilted his head back, eyes closed. "Bentnord is a small rock. No room for troops. Just two small parties, and Father, Danilla, and I are not without power. The meeting is a formality."

"A formality where you acquire a wife of fearsome reputation," Danilla said.

"Traveling with but a few guards is perilous," Mercerio said.

Meru sighed. "We shall pose as humble visitors to Li's temple in Fathom and sail from there. No fancy clothes, no banners, no polished golden emblems."

The group mounted horses and left Zellingon quietly at dawn. They crossed the Zelar and followed the River Wark toward the coast. On the second day, they camped north of the Manwark Mountains where a cold wind from the northern glaciers blew. Meru and Danilla had already fallen asleep under woolen blankets while Justi confirmed an adequate guard was posted. Satisfied that the surrounding area was empty, he retired.

At dawn Meligo and his student Entor emerged from their shared tent to assess the weather. Meligo faced south into the breeze. "The warm air augurs well for this venture."

Entor yawned. "Do ventures depend on the weather?"

Meligo examined thin clouds stained orange by the rising sun. "More misadventures are blamed on weather than you imagine."

The group broke camp and proceeded through hilly terrain to Maduk, finding a breakfast of fresh fish and eggs at an inn. Afterwards, they made good time to Fathom, reaching that port city in late afternoon. The restored Fathom Inn, where then Princess Mercerio had been held captive, had rooms waiting. King Meru, Princess Danilla, and four guards went to the temple to provide an excuse for being in Fathom. Meligo and Entor visited the town seer, and Justi with two guards went to locate Nar, the harbormaster. They found him, a grizzled man with wrinkled, sun-browned skin, puffing on a briar pipe and fussing with the sail of a decrepit vessel that seemed more suited for fish than a royal party.

Justi introduced himself and said, "I hope this is not the ship you expect us to use."

Nar shook his head. "Your message made it clear what's needed. I have something that will please the gentleman." He walked along the creaking dock to a clean craft of sleek lines with a cabin and a single mast. A fish hawk swooped over the water, landed atop the mast, and eyed the visitors. "This one be called *The Golden*, my lord. Built for speed."

As Justi inspected, the harbormaster studied Justi's face. "She will be takin' your lordship anywheres you want in good time and comfort," the old sailor said, smoothing his grey hair. "What be your destination?"

"That's my business," Justi said.

Nar folded his arms. "I see. Then I cannot be renting this vessel."

Justi considered how to get around this obstacle. "Naturally, we will compensate you for the uncertainty. Just good business, I suppose. And we will do all in our power to return your property unharmed."

With a disgruntled face, Nar watched the hawk fly from the mast to a nearby piling. He sucked smoke from his pipe and blew it toward the bird. "Will ye be needin' a crew?"

"No," Justi answered, gesturing to the two guards who stood a way off. "We have men who know how to handle a ship."

The old man tapped out his pipe on a bollard. "You hide your destination and reject a crew. Only a fool would take such a deal and I'm not a fool. Find a fisherman who will sell you a ship." Nar glared at Justi and then his face softened, as if he'd discovered the hidden image in a painting. "I feel I know you. Maybe from years back. Might we be meetin' during the war?"

Justi realized that most men Nar's age would have served in the Zellish army that took Zellingon. "Perhaps. I fought to drive out the Tantrocans."

Nar's face lit up, and he spoke without his salesman argot. "I was King Bronte's scout in the party sent to Fathom. We found not a soul alive, bodies burnt." Nar sighed. "We saved a boy and his dog."

Justi had heard the story before. "The boy was called Jandaral," Justi said.

Nar dropped his pipe. "How would you know that?"

"My father led that party."

"Rocley? Rocley is your father? Then you must be . . ." Nar's mouth hung open.

"I am and you must keep this to yourself."

"Of course, my lord. Scouts know how to keep our mouths shut." Nar turned back to the boat as if The Gifted One who'd restored the kingdom was not standing on the dock. "Aye, you will have this craft," he said, "but take care. The Gulf can be gnarly this time of year, and storms can pop up." He pointed to a line of wispy clouds on the far horizon. "How long will your trip last?"

"Perhaps a few days. I will give you enough gold to cover a week. Plus extra for the sake of good business. We should be back before any change in weather." Justi turned toward town and the hawk jumped into the air and sailed barely over his head. He ducked and watched the bird land on a smaller ship moored beyond *The Golden*. Justi's eyes took in the boat and an idea formed. "Might that vessel also be available?" he asked.

The harbormaster's forehead wrinkled, and he scratched the bushy beard that hid his chin. "That be my son's ship, *The Silver*. He doesn't use it much anymore. It could be available."

"Fine. I would take it. And I will need a crew for her."

"My sons can handle *The Silver*. Maybe with a friend. That will give them something to do besides pesterin' the barmaids at *The Reef*. It will cost more gold."

"We leave tonight."

Nar shook his head slowly and then sighed. "My sons and their friend will be ready to cast off at dusk."

The party reassembled at the inn. Meligo reported the resident wise man claimed there was nothing in local lore or writings about nearby islands, including Bentnord. Justi told of procuring two ships, the second one a diversion and a backup. He was uneasy about engaging the harbormaster's sons, but it had to be done. Meru agreed with Justi's plan to make the crossing to Bentnord at night. Sailing in the dark was dangerous, but it kept them hidden and prevented a surprise attack. It also meant the Zellish would arrive at Bentnord first, the better to foil treachery.

The group boarded *The Golden* at sundown and, joined by *The Silver*, pushed from the dock. At the harbor mouth, Justi waved *The Silver* within hailing range and told Nar's sons and their friend the destination. The young men shrugged and led the way, tacking with skill in the western breeze.

Because they sailed at night, sleep was necessary. Danilla took one cabin and Meru and Justi shared the other. The guards unfurled hammocks while those with sailing experience shared navigation duties. Once the lights of shore disappeared, the ship moved rather blindly on an indirect course to Bentnord, dealing with choppy seas with occasional swells the height of a man and the westering wind.

The Silver held a truer course in front of *The Golden*, leaving behind a gentle wake of luminescent sea life, tiny glowing creatures. The white wakes made each ship's location obvious in the pale moonlight. Justi hoped the two lanterns showing two ships would ward off any sleepless pirates seeking for a lone target.

An hour out of Fathom, the weather changed. The wind dropped, and the sea became a gentle swell. *The Golden* drifted. *The Silver*, smaller, lighter, and manned by experienced sailors, sailed on in the meager breeze. Sleeping Zellish were roused and put to the oars, moving the ship west over black waters. A greenish-faced guard who was hanging over the starboard rail and moaning saw the white splash first.

"A fish," he murmured. As he gazed, the water surface swelled until it seemed an island. He hoisted himself up and yelled, "Hard to left…port."

The cry woke Entor, who'd been dozing on a coil of rope in the center of the deck. He jumped up and, as the ship veered left, fell back onto the rope.

"There is not supposed to be any island here," Entor grunted. "Have we drifted far off course?" He struggled up and watched the dark mass undulate. "It is not an island," he yelled. "A monster. Large."

The blob drifted closer and then submerged. Entor sucked in a great breath and said, "Maybe it's gone. Thank Li."

The Golden regained its course as oars dipped and the deck creaked. *The Silver* had returned and sailed a stone's throw from *The Golden.* Wisps of fog snaked over the dark water, creating a sense of peace, peace that vanished with a thudding crash, a lurch, and the sound of splintering wood. Meru's guards stared at *The Silver*, which sat at an odd angle, its bow too low.

"What's happening?" Bargaron, the guard captain, demanded, pulling on a leather vest.

The Silver rotated and lurched closer. Moonlight revealed a greenish tentacle over the bow. Nar's sons screamed and hacked at it with short swords and daggers and the blows seemed to anger the behemoth. The appendage lashed fore and aft, smashed the deck rail, caught the third sailor, and tossed him into the sea, then wrapped about the mast and snapped it off. The bow and stern of the ship lifted and collapsed on the center deck. Water sloshed over the midships, and Nar's sons flew overboard. *The Golden*'s crew watched as *The Silver* disappeared in a tangle of wood and tentacles and churning dark water.

"Men to arms," Entor yelled, grabbing a harpoon with a blade as long as his arm. He could barely lift it.

As *The Silver* went down, Justi and Meru rushed onto the deck, followed by a barefoot Danilla pulling a dark jerkin over her night dress. Meru stared at where the other ship had been.

"The other ship has been dragged under by . . . by a sea demon," Entor yelled.

"Are there such things?" Meru asked.

"There is the answer, sire," Entor screamed, pointing at the frothing waters. "It's called the Megadarch."

A sailor from *The Silver,* the friend, surfaced off the starboard bow. He thrashed toward *The Golden,* and Entor grabbed a rope attached to a cleat and heaved it at the swimmer. It fell short and the swimmer splashed to the lifeline. Beneath him loomed a greenish mass, then a gaping hole filled with white, pointed spikes. The man's screamed once as the mouth closed and the creature sank beneath the pink-stained, fluorescent sea.

"Its mouth is as wide as this vessel," Justi said. "Dar's curse, can our blades hack enough flesh to drive it off?"

Danilla put aside her panic and summoned her power. The heat came and intensified, and darkness retreated from her glowing hair. A tentacle slapped onto the deck, and the ship shuddered. With a thunder boom, Danilla's hands exploded in a beam and sliced through the thick monster arm.

The stub recoiled, then snapped, flinging ichor at a sailor. Danilla stepped toward the deck rail and aimed at the reptilian mass at the water surface. Her beam frothed the water and drove the beast deeper. Another thump rattled *The Golden*. "The creature stays below the surface," she yelled. "I can't reach it."

Meru pulled his sister back as a second tentacle slithered toward the stern. The king furrowed his brow, and a green glow spread from his hands. The colored mist billowed over the water and penetrated the churning sea, lighting the Megadarch's body. The creature, longer than the ship, writhed against the wooden hull. Timbers creaked as tentacles wrapped tighter. Danilla, horrified and fascinated, watched, sure that, regardless of powers granted by Li, she would perish.

The tentacle that twitched on the deck oozing crimson blood seemed to absorb Meru's vapor. Then it snapped back and slipped into the water. The creature sank. Danilla lost sight of it until, moments later, a thick flat tail wider than their sail slapped the water off the stern and sent a swell that rocked the boat.

"It is gone," Meru said.

"How can you know that?" Danilla asked.

"Because I touched its mind and freed it from whatever dark influence controlled it. It had been driven to find us, told to destroy this ship. It will not be back."

"Men overboard," Entor yelled.

The harbormaster's boys clung to a floating spar, their eyes darting about, searching the water around them. Guards on *The Golden* tossed a float and hauled once the men swam to it. A splash in the darkness made the guards pull faster. Once on board, the survivors from *The Silver* spat water and coughed. One with a bloody head seemed dazed. As men wrapped blankets about the brothers, Meru touched them, calmed their fears, and made them sleep.

"This is Dar's work," Justi said. They do not want this meeting to happen."

With the Megadarch's departure, a breeze developed, and the guards shipped their oars. The sail billowed and propelled the ship with enough pace to reach the waters off Bentnord by first light. None of *The Golden*'s crew had had much sleep, and Justi decided to drop anchor far enough from the island to avoid rocky shallows and wait for full light before using depth soundings to approach. The harbormaster's boys might be awake then and able to give local guidance. There was no sign of the Tantrocans, so the weary men were able to catch a few hours of sleep.

A ship larger than *The Golden* arrived after sunrise and pulled alongside. A man with a crown stepped to the rail. "I am King Brosun," he said.

Meru introduced himself and his sister but did not call attention to Justi. Brosun brought his sister to his side and announced Ranera. The Tantrocan princess seemed to study first Meru and then Danilla. Finally, she smiled and bowed her head.

"A cove with a sandy beach lies on the north side of this island," Brosun said. "A rock shelf protrudes into deep water and forms a natural pier. I suggest we moor there. My men will set up a covering and we brought a few provisions. Once refreshed, we can get to the business at hand." Brosun spoke quickly. His smile did not reach his eyes.

The Tantrocan vessel rowed away and *The Golden* followed. The cove and rock pier were indeed suited for docking two small ships. King Brosun's sword-bearing men spread a canvas for shade and placed chairs and a table. Justi left the ship first after counting the Tantrocan party and noting it seemed twice as large as agreed to. That made him wary, but at least Justik was absent. When the site was ready, Meru and Danilla left *The Golden*. Brosun welcomed them and presented his high priest, Caldir. King Meru introduced Meligo as his advisor.

After wine and cheese were served, Brosun said, "Let us proceed."

"We have both lost good men," Meru began. "Despite the warfare, the Zellish and the Tantrocans find themselves in the same place as before. But prophecy has revealed a way to end our enmity. This newly discovered text from the Book of Signs tells us how to replace hostility with accord."

"Perhaps we can change the course of history," Brosun said, sounding pleasant.

A commotion arose outside the tent. A guard posted outside the tent entered and announced the arrival of a ship. "It is an Ice vessel, my king."

"They were not invited," Brosun said, casting his eye first at Caldir and then at Meru.

Danilla watched two men disembark and walk to the conference site. They resembled each other, perhaps father and son. Both were tall with black hair and wore animal skin garments. The younger, well-muscled man had a square jaw and wide eyes.

"I am Thal, leader of the Ice, and this is my son Sathal," the older man said. "This treaty, whatever it is, seems to concern my people along with yours, Brosun, and yours, Meru. I want to hear what new thing the Tantrocan king plans to do with his sister, since his pledge to marry her to my son has been forgotten."

Danilla figured the newcomers were more a threat to King Brosun than to King Meru. Sathal frowned when he saw Ranera, but he smiled at Danilla, a transformation that seemed to change his whole personality. He bowed before turning back to his father.

"This agreement hardly concerns you, Thal, but you can be a witness," Brosun said.

Danilla was glad that Thal and Sathal arrived with no additional guards. She was concerned enough with the men around Brosun. There were too many of them and their faces, partially hidden by leather helmets, could not be read. She sensed something was amiss.

Brosun turned to Caldir. "Give us the heart of the document."

Caldir stood in front of the Tantrocan guards, where he blocked Danilla's view of a man she wondered about.

"We agree to peace between the Tantrocans and the Zellish in exchange for trading rights throughout the kingdom," Caldir said. "Tantrocans will be able to transit for trade. Tantroc will allow unhampered fishing in the Tantric Gulf. The guarantor of this treaty will be the union of Princess Ranera with King Meru."

Brosun turned to Meru. "Does this summarize things?"

Meligo whispered in Meru's ear, and the Zellish king said, "Peace means an end to coastal raids, invasions, and attacks on fisherman. Travel restrictions are defined in the document. You have summarized satisfactorily."

"Then we should allow my sister and you to meet. We have set aside a table over there for your private discussion." Brosun pointed to an alcove.

"What treaty requirements do I make clear?" Meru whispered to Meligo.

"Just confirm with Ranera that this is a state marriage with obligations on both sides. She must reside in Zellingon during the winter months. And produce an heir. Assure her we do not abuse women."

Meru and Ranera walked side-by-side to the table set away from the group.

Ranera thought Meru seemed young to be a king, quite unlike her brother who was the same age. She struggled to put a name on those differences and settled on the thought that Meru was too nice.

"I hope you will find this arrangement tolerable, Ranera. It is for the sake of both our peoples. It is our duty."

"Don't be pompous, Meru. You may find some noble motive to justify an arranged marriage, but I will do it because I was ordered. A month ago I was to be sold to an Ice hunter. Now you are the buyer." Ranera smiled thinly.

Meru stuck to his script. "You will be required to live in Zellingon during the winter. And act with royal decorum."

"I will keep my clothes on, at least in public." Ranera said with a fuller smile. "Are we required to sleep together?"

"Peace between our peoples will require an heir." Meru waited as Ranera adopted a predatory leer.

"Then we are ready to sign the document."

The pair rose and rejoined their delegations. Ranera glanced at Meru as he spoke to King Brosun. Too nice, she thought.

Danilla had been watching one of the Tantrocan men when the couple rejoined the meeting. The man stiffened and whispered to the guards next to him. To the casual observer, nothing had changed, but Danilla tensed. The Tantrocans seemed more alert and a wisp of too-bright blond hair slipped from the suspicious Tantrocan's leather helmet, hair that reminded her of her father's.

No man should have hair that bright, she thought. The man disappeared behind two guards. Danilla poked Meru.

Meru reacted, casting a blanket of calm over the assemblage. It slowed Justik's movements, but he shuddered like a wet dog and advanced. His hand glowed as he headed toward Princess Danilla. He aimed his unnatural gift and prepared to destroy the one who had injured him before.

Meru's power slowed Danilla. She backed away, exposing herself even more. As Justik's hand rose, the princess grabbed a round metal tray with wooden handles. The shield, twice her width, took Justik's blast, bouncing the heat away. But the force threw Danilla, still clutching the tray, backward onto the sand.

When Justi saw his daughter fall, he transformed. The Justice Power, so long dormant within him, stirred, and he thrust a fist at Justik. No Justice Gift ignited, and no flame of righteous vengeance came forth. Justik smiled, and Justi tried again. This time thunder roared, and a great rush of air lifted the canvas from the poles and flew it toward the water.

The noise accompanied a flame from Justi that drove Justik back. He ducked behind guards who charged forward. As a soldier raised a gleaming sword to strike Meru, Bargaron threw a knife. The blade pierced the man's chest and dropped him. Zellish men with long swords drawn ran at Tantrocans. Justik and Tantrocan guards fell back to form a shield around King Brosun.

Bargaron ordered retreat. A guard lifted Danilla over his shoulder and carried her as Meru and Justi ran from the fighting. Brosun, perhaps understanding that he'd lost the element of surprise and not sure of the balance of power, also ordered retreat.

40
Megadarch

After natural and unnatural power disrupted the peace conference, the Zellish and the Tantrocans retreated to rocks at opposite ends of the cove. Justi watched his adversaries as wind kicked up and a distant cloud bank flashed lightning. Sea mist crept over Bentnord, obscuring the view.

"We can't stay here," Meru warned. "They could use this cover to get closer."

Justi put his hands on Danilla's shoulders as he tried to regain his breath. He felt unsure of what they faced and imagined the Tantrocans were also uncertain. "Justik was thrown to the ground as was Danilla," he said. "He may not have his power."

"We should use the fog cover to reach the ship," Bargaron urged.

Meru turned toward the rock pier that lay closer to their end of Bentnord. He touched Danilla arm. "How are you feeling?"

The princess seemed dazed. "Is the meeting over?"

"There was treachery," Meru said.

"What happened?"

"Justik attacked you. That tray shielded you, but you were thrown back, unconscious."

"Did I kill him?"

"No. We fled. You had no chance to respond."

Danilla struggled to her feet, "Unfortunate," she said in a weak voice.

Justi examined his daughter's eyes. "Her eyes do not focus. We must get her to a healer."

"Stories tell of you having a healing power, Father," Meru said.

Justi shook his head. "I fear it is as weak as my ability to summon fire. I dare not try to use it. I might do more harm than good. Bargaron is right. Time to move." He eyed the distance to the pier. "The Tantrocans may be uncertain about Justik's ability. I didn't see any archers. The fog is lifting. Let's make sure they see Danilla standing upright and moving on her own. If they think she is unharmed, they will fear her power. Even Justik."

"I can help," Meru said. "The green cloud I command will confuse them and dampen thoughts of attack."

Danilla stepped higher on the rocks and examined the Tantrocans long enough to be sure she was seen. Then Meru put his hands palm to palm and aimed his mind-numbing cloud toward the Tantrocans. As the view along the beach dimmed, the Zellish broke to the pier, Justi and Danilla leading. Unfortunately the calm changed to a clearing breeze and the Tantrocans could see what was happening. They shouted and loosed a volley of arrows. One caught a guard in the neck, and he fell. Another guard, a giant, hoisted the wounded man to his shoulder and ran.

Bargaron positioned himself behind his king as they both darted across rocks. "The Tantrocans had more than a peace conference in mind," Bargaron hissed.

Another arrow staggered a second Zellish guard, but he pulled the shaft from his shoulder and held his hand to stem the blood. The Zellish rushed to the anchor rock as the wind pelted them with sand particles. Waves sloshed against the ship's hull and made the deck a moving target, but all managed to jump aboard.

As the last man thundered onto the deck, the harbormaster's older son yanked the ramp, loosed the mooring rope, and shoved *The Golden* from the rock. He ran to the wheel as his brother and a guard unfurled the sail. The growing wind billowed the sheet and pushed the ship toward open water.

As soon as the Zellish ran, the Tantrocans abandoned their wounded and charged after them like wolves after a wounded prey. They boarded their vessel and got underway. Archers sent arrows at *The Golden*, hitting the deck and ripping through the sail. The sheet slackened, but *The Golden* escaped the shelter of Bentnord, and the island disappeared as rain began.

Justi ushered Danilla into a cabin and returned to tend the injured guards. The man with the neck wound needed no care. He died as the ship got underway. The man who took the arrow in his shoulder needed pressure on the wound. Justi stemmed the blood flow and assessed that the man's life was not in danger. Justi touched the guard and past sensations flooded his mind. He saw in his mind where the tissue and vessels were torn, and he forced repair, soothing the damaged area. The guard relaxed, his bleeding stopped, and the pain on his face faded. Perhaps I haven't lost Li's gifts after all, Justi thought.

Meru pointed to the stern where through the rain the Tantrocan vessel loomed, picking up speed, drawing closer. The wind filled the mainsails and both ships raced east. "Demon curse," Meru said, gripping the deck rail. "They have a faster ship, and it's coming after us. They want us dead."

As the Tantrocan ship drew closer, Justi could make out men standing at the prow. One was Justik. *The Golden* nosed into a high wave and shuddered, and Justi realized their chance of outrunning the Tantrocans back to Fathom was slim.

The Tantrocans plowed closer under full sail. Justik felt his rage grow. Twice he had been thwarted in his attacks on his family. He would have revenge.

"Why do we pursue?" Ranera screamed.

"Because they vex me," Brosun said, pacing the deck. "Dar has promised us rewards for our devotion. We tasted those rewards once and I want them again."

"You've lost the element of surprise, Brother. Weather is closing in. Don't be a fool. Return to Ankor and regroup."

"We follow," Justik screamed. "This is my chance. I saw no flame to smite us. My father produced only noise and wind. I knocked Danilla unconscious, and she had to be carried off as a doll."

"But we saw her walking," Ranera objected.

"Still woozy. She cannot do anything in her state. The only weapon at their disposal is whatever Meru does. Some sort of distraction I can ignore. We can crush the only power that can oppose me. I will slay them all."

The beast lurked beneath the waves near the spot where it had destroyed the Fathom boat and tasted the flesh of man. Some force had quelled the hunger and driven the Megadarch off. That had dissipated and now the hunger, an unsatisfied craving stronger than before, returned. The Megadarch sensed vibrations.

The disturbance made by two human vessels running under full sail excited the creature. The ships seemed small, small enough to be grasped and dragged under. Quivering in anticipation, the Megadarch flexed its giant tail and swam toward the prey.

Justi ordered crates stacked at the stern and tried to summon anger and outrage, but mostly he felt fear. This confused him, for the ingredients of injustice and a threat were clearly present. Surely Danilla would detect these elements, but he doubted her ability to respond. She'd emerged from the cabin and slumped on a crate, her head bowed. Meru could affect the minds of the pursuers, something Justi suspected would not be enough in the mist-clearing wind. The Tantrocan vessel crept closer leaving a frothy wake. *The Golden* slogged on in the rough sea, while the larger Tantrocan ship plowed on, less unimpeded by the swells. In moments the two ships would be close enough for Justik's attack.

At shouting distance Tantrocan archers launched arrows aimed at the crew of *The Golden*. The Zellish were able to duck the whistling shafts, aided by an erratic wind that misdirected the arrows. Meru aimed his mist at the archers and the rain of projectiles ended, replaced by sprayed flame. Justik's attack hit the wall of crates and ignited the rope that lashed them in place, but the rain and waves doused the flames.

"Any closer and Justik will be able to burn people," Meru said.

Danilla struggled up and almost fell as *The Golden* crested a swell. She lurched to a railing and anchored herself as heavier rain pounded the deck and drenched her. She breathed deeply and closed her eyes. When they snapped open, her hair blazed yellow and her eyes seemed focused.

Justi saw helplessness, danger, immense injustice. His fright began to change, morphing from fear to anger. Abruptly the anger snapped into rage against the threat to his innocent children. Heat enveloped him from head to foot and blazed bright as a solstice fire through to mist.

Justik crouched and shouted warning. The Tantrocan vessel lurched to starboard as Justi the Gifted unleashed a white, narrow beam of heat at the bow. Justik jumped, but the hot lance caught his upper arm, searing flesh. The dark champion screamed and sprayed flame along the side of the Zellish vessel.

The flame licked Justi who cursed, grabbing his shoulder. The shock and sudden motion of the boat sent him over the rail and into the sea. The water quenched the flame and probably saved his life.

As Bargaron luffed the sail, Meru jumped in after his father. He battled several swells, grabbed his father, and held his head above water. A sailor tossed a rope and float to the pair. Danilla stumbled to the rear of *The Golden,* heat growing in her head, her heart, and her hand. The two vessels heaved closer, bringing Justik and his half sister face-to-face. Justik, his hair glowing, raised his fist. Danilla was faster and cast a beam toward the Tantrocans just as the deck dipped. Her power ignited the side of the enemy ship, and flame licked toward the rail until the next swell extinguished it.

Meru snared the rope as the ship passed. Somehow, he held on, and a guard hauled the King of the Zell and his father closer. Rain smeared glowing hair into Danilla's face. The hair lost its glow and her shoulders sagged.

Justik grimaced. "Victory will be mine," he spat. "I alone will possess the gift. Nothing stands in my way." His hair began to glow. A crash of thunder shook the air and rain pelted the deck.

"Finish them," King Brosun shouted at Justik. The king leaned over the rail, a hate-filled gleam in his eyes as he squinted into the rain.

Justik anchored himself. Eyes glowing reddish blue, he saw Meru and Justi as they were hauled onto *The Golden*. The power pulsed within him and he let it grow, imagining an eruption of fire that would consume the wallowing Zellish ship and all aboard. His hand opened, and as if nature itself could sense the force he controlled, the deck rose beneath him.

The Megadarch thrust from the abyss beneath the Tantrocan ship and heaved it almost clear of the sea. Justik fell back, banging his head on a hatch cover. King Brosun sailed overboard. A tentacle wrapped about the sputtering Tantrocan king, choking his cry of anger to fear. The sound died as the maw of the Megadarch sucked in the entire royal body in one gulp. Princess Ranera clung to a mast rope and witnessed her brother's fate. Perhaps her soul softened when Brosun's wail was chopped off, and perhaps she felt a certain pity for a brother she once knew with fondness, but the sentiment, if it existed, was short-lived. Her attention was directed to the craft on which her own life depended. The attack of the creature had shoved the Tantrocan vessel far from *The Golden* and left it wallowing in choppy seas.

"Princess Ranera, what should we do?" a sailor asked.

Ranera stood taller. "Turn toward Ankor, you idiot. And you will address me as Queen Ranera." As an afterthought she added, "And see to Justik. Bring him below to my quarters."

The Megadarch was not done. Perhaps because the king of the Tantrocans was particularly tasty, the monster focused on the nearby ship. *The Golden* was trying to get the wind back in its sail when the tentacle rose from the sea and grasped the stern. Guards yelled and hacked at the monster's slithering appendage, but the tentacle spasmed and knocked men away. With creaks and an immense groan, *The Golden*'s bow rose high as the stern was dragged below the sea.

Wind, waves, and the slanted ship deck cast humans overboard. Danilla clutched a crate as she went into the sea, and the box became her raft. She saw *The Golden* split in two and watched both halves sink, soon replaced by floating chunks of wood. Half a dozen men who were conscious when they hit the water grabbed anything that floated. Meru and Justi surfaced near a piece of floating deck. Danilla felt the sea heave beneath her and imagined none of them would die by drowning. Her fear became reality: a sailor screamed as the Megadarch's jaws took him. The princess waited for death.

Lightning flashed over the desperate survivors struggling to stay afloat. A blinding, white discharge struck the Megadarch's tentacles, scorching flesh. The wounded tentacle twitched and steamed, and the creature regurgitated a mangled human body, floated a moment, and finally regained enough control to swim away. The monster's tail rose and pounded the water as if in farewell.

The sea settled, leaving the remains of *The Golden* wreckage and survivors clinging to jagged timber. Bargaron yelled orders to men draped over a large spar tangled with pieces of rope. The sailors kicked and paddled and rode the downside of a wave to bring the spar near the others.

Stunned, Meru and Justi swam toward Danilla, pushing themselves and the princess closer to the spar. The sea calmed, and survivors steered bigger pieces of flotsam together and lashed the debris with ropes into a raft.

"What good does our power do now?" Meru yelled. "We're surely dead."

Bargaron answered. "We must stay together. Someone may be in the vicinity and find us."

"Not much chance of that in this storm," Justi said.

His words were contradicted by a hull emerging from the mist. The oddly shaped ship loomed high above the makeshift raft, threatening to crush the few survivors.

41
Unarranged

The broad-beamed, low-riding mystery ship loomed over the Zellish. Meru was sure it would crush the flotsam raft and everyone clinging to it. Already exhausted and immobilized by the cold water, they were helpless. Meru screamed, but the rain and mist dampened the sound and he lost all hope.

"There are survivors," a male voice boomed from above. "Loose the sea anchor." Then the prow rose and the vessel ceased forward motion. Water swelled over the spar, and lightning illuminated the floating refugees.

The Tantrocan dialect chilled Meru, and he wondered if King Brosun had returned to finish his treachery. Meru summoned his power and found nothing.

Bargaron, clinging to a plank, rose on a sea swell and yelled, "Help."

Lanterns appeared along the ship's hull, casting light on the water through the gloom. A blond-headed man with a rope tied around his waist leapt into the water and swam strongly toward the makeshift raft. Bargaron grabbed the line from Sathal and tied it to a jutting hook on the spar. The line grew taut and drew the flotsam closer to the rescuing craft.

Sathal swam to Princess Danilla and lifted her higher in the water. She seemed small in his muscled arms. He supported her, saying something Meru could hear but not understand. The raft banged against the heaving ship where two rope ladders hung. Sathal boosted Danilla and guided her foot onto the first slippery rung. From above a sailor lifted her aboard. Men tossed lines to other swimmers and hauled them to the ladders. All made it onto the deck.

Danilla collapsed on a chest, gagging and gasping. She'd spit out enough brine and cleared her breathing when Sathal wrapped an oilskin about her.

"She will be all right," Sathal said to Justi, handing him his own skin. Justi stayed near his daughter, still protecting his burned arm, as Sathal distributed blankets to each man taken from the sea. Finally, he wrapped one about himself and returned to Justi.

"Might there be a bit of grog for the princess?" Justi asked.

Sathal shouted to a deckhand, who ducked below deck and returned with cups and a cask. He poured and served the Zellish.

Meru shivered on the wet deck and watched the Ice leader Thal approach. Meru decided the Ice had no part in the plot that used the peace conference as bait. "How did you find us?" he asked over the creak of the rocking boat.

Thal drained his cup. "One flash of lightning revealed your ship, and a second showed it gone."

"Thank Li you were near. But why were you near?"

"When the Tantrocans attacked you," Thal said, "we boarded our ship and rounded Bentnord in time to see the Tantrocan ship pursuing you. We had to find out why."

"Most fortunate for us. What happened with the Tantrocans?"

"They abruptly ceased their attack and headed north, probably to Ankor. The vessel passed some distance from us as the rain began." Thal pointed at the debris in the water. "What destroyed your vessel?"

Meru considered how to explain. He started with a question. "Do the Ice have any knowledge of a sea monster in these waters."

"You mean the Megadarch? We dismissed the stories as fables."

"Not a fable. A creature enormous enough to wrap a tentacle about our ship dragged it below. We survived only because lightning struck the monster."

A sailor approached and spoke to Thal. "Chief, we have found two other men, floating on a piece of broken deck. They are being brought aboard now."

Meru recognized the pair. "We cannot return the two vessels to Fathom's harbormaster, but we will deliver what is more important. Those are the man's sons."

Danilla patted the chest on which she sat, and Justi eased himself down next to her. She lifted and examined Justi's arm, seeing angry red and black skin. Meru had calmed Justi's mind and eased his pain as they clung to the spar, but he winced when Danilla gently covered the burn with both her hands and closed her eyes. She sensed injured tissue and swollen cells, felt the extent of the damage, then began a process of restoring what could be saved and recruiting cells to replace those beyond saving. Nerves soothed and Justi's grimace eased and he even smiled.

"My arm no longer hurts. The redness has vanished. Daughter, your gift is much like mine. I was able to heal both men and beasts. Well, a dog. And your mother. You seem more capable of healing than I ever was."

Danilla pursed her lips. "Mother told me how she saved your life when you were poisoned. She thinks her talent is to fix ills of the blood, while yours repairs tissues. As you said, Father, my talent is like yours."

Sathal returned with a brown woven gown that he handed to Danilla. "You can use the second cabin below. Danilla left and Sathal examined Justi. "Your arm seems suddenly well."

"My daughter has talents as a healer."

A crewman opened a new jug of something alcoholic and offered drinks to the nearly drowned Zellish. All took it and emptied the mugs.

"Can you take us to Fathom, Thal?" Justi asked the Ice leader.

"I am not familiar with this area of the gulf, but if I am shown the way, this craft will carry us safely, even if the wind grows stronger and the waves higher. Ice ships are built for stability, not speed."

Justi pointed to Nar's sons, who were being treated with a second helping from the jug. "Those men call Fathom home. They will know the way."

Thal went toward the young sailors, and Meru, holding the oilskin close around him, gazed at the choppy seas. "I have failed, Father," Meru said. "There will be no peace. The new writing from the *Book of Signs* was wrong."

Meligo was seated on a barrel nearby. "Or wrongly read."

"Don't berate yourself, Meru," Justi added. "You took action you thought was right. The evil is too firmly embedded in the Tantrocan spirit. They do not value peace. We should have crushed their invading army. Now you must return to Zellingon and rule with confidence. Coastal defenses will have to be strengthened, in case the Tantrocans invade again."

Meru pondered that for a moment. "They were driven back by Danilla, but she did not kill them. They may think her power is no longer a threat." Meru watched his sister. Danilla now had Sathal's strong arm around her and rested her head on his chest. "They may attack again."

Thal returned and pointed at the harbormaster's son. "The older one says we sail southeast. We must find a great rock just east of Fathom that maintains a signal fire. We will use it to guide us in . . . if the rain is truly spent. If not, we can wait until daylight to dock."

They found the signal fire and then Fathom. Night had come, but lights from a dockside tavern streaked the mooring area. When the ship drew close, two patrons stumbled from the barroom and shouted. Nar, the harbormaster, came from his house pulling on an oilskin. He sprinted to help moor the strange vessel and then spied his sons huddled in the bow. He whooped, leapt on board, and embraced them both.

"We lost both boats, Father," the boys said in unison.

"I see," Nar said. He turned to Justi and said, "I am filled with gladness to see my sons, but this vessel is neither one you rented. What happened?"

"Father, we were attacked by the monster," the older boy answered, "and both ships were crushed."

Nar's mouth fell open and he stood for a moment speechless. His eyes moved from his boys to the Ice ship and back to Justi. "I'm thinking we have to renegotiate our deal, my lord."

Justi smiled and helped Danilla from the boat. The Zellish guards assembled on the wooden pier as Meru and Meligo disembarked. Perhaps assessing the conditions of all the passengers including his offspring, Nar did not pursue the question of his missing property.

"That grog shop has food and drink," he announced, waving at the tavern where several patrons stood watching the arrival. "But I be thinking you might prefer we go to the Fathom Inn where rooms await."

Meru felt solidity beneath his feet and, despite the pervasive fish smell, gave thanks to Li. "Is there another inn where we are not known?"

Nar pursed his lips. "The Harbor Inn is not as fine, but the rooms are clean and the food good."

Meru saw Thal watching the departure. "Will you join us, Thal? The inn will be warmer than this chill air and we have things to discuss."

"I agree. Let me make sure my crew is settled."

"There is no reason to reveal who we are. Please tell your men."

"The food is hearty at the tavern," Nar yelled.

Thal and his son followed the Zellish toward the inn as the Ice crew headed for the tavern, leaving a sole, unlucky man to guard the boat.

Nar led them the stone's throw from the dock to the Harbor Inn, a two-story wood-and-stone building that faced a rock-strewn beach. The structure was fronted by a wide plank deck with a dozen or so chairs. Meru bumped one and was surprised that it moved back and forward. He could see that it had legs attached to bowed runners. Meru had never seen anything like it.

They entered a large room lit by oil lamps that emitted a pleasant, aromatic smell. A gentle fire hissed in the black stone fireplace. After the cold, wet voyage back, the warmth radiated by the yellow flames was welcome. Nar headed toward a roundish, red-faced woman wearing a green apron.

She stood, thick arms akimbo, quiet until the last man cleared the door. "You can stop right there. I'm about to close. What's going on?"

Nar smiled and said, "Why, Tari, these be guests for ye. Just rowed in. They have battled the storm and need a place to rest. I immediately thought of you, my sweet."

"Did ye now? When you think of me, it means trouble." Tari scanned the wet entourage, and, when she spied Danilla, sighed. "I suppose I have space. Hang your wet garments on those pegs near the hearth, and I'll see what rooms I have. I suppose you'll want something to eat."

"That would be kind of you, ma'am," Meru said.

Justi took Nar's arm. "I want you to summon the Fathom healer. My daughter needs to be examined."

"The healer is a crotchety sort. Does not abide coming out at this hour."

Justi handed the man a gold coin. "Tell him he will be well paid, but he must come forthwith."

The group found accommodations on the second floor. Each room had a fireplace that allowed them to dry their clothing. Tari provided towels for all and a dressing gown for Danilla. The princess took advantage of both while the men seemed content to stand near the ground floor hearth to dry their damp garments.

As food was being prepared, Thal and Meru sat at a corner table drinking rather good beer. "What can I offer to thank you for rescuing us, Thal?" Meru asked.

The Ice leader leaned forward and kept his voice low. "Let me start by saying that we had nothing to do with the attack. That was Brosun. Or perhaps the idea of the Tantrocan high priest, a man called Caldir. He is the one who proposed using the Ice priests to confound the minds of the Zellish in the invasion. I did not know you possessed enchantment."

Meru took another swallow of beer.

"At any rate," Thal continued, "the conflict that exists between peoples on opposite sides of the Tantric Gulf concerns the Ice. We are excellent hunters and fishermen, and some would like to hunt in the Zell where game is more plentiful. Zellish are great craftsmen. Our people should trade. What are your feelings, Meru?"

Nar and a whiskered man with a limp burst into the inn. Nar introduced Nool as the finest physician in Fathom. The healer scowled and thumped his walking stick on the plank floor, obviously unhappy. Meru sensed the tension between the two men and did not ask how many physicians existed in Fathom.

"The patient is upstairs in a room at the end of the hall," Meru said, wondering how the physician's mental state might affect his ability to assess Danilla. He added, "A guard will escort you. We are grateful you could attend us and will reward your service."

Nool's frown vanished. Meru waited until the healer disappeared and then turned back to Thal.

"I want peace," Meru said. "We could welcome your visits, but our game is not so abundant that my kinsmen would welcome competition."

"But I know of an area where you do not hunt even though the game is plentiful."

"What are you talking about?"

"The east beyond Markul and the river you call The Zelar has been visited by small bands of Ice hunters for many years. We never arrive by day and never with many men, fearing to attract the attention of Markul rangers."

Meru pondered the idea of foreigners hunting on the kingdom's lands. "That area is indeed populated only by a few fisherman and hermits. Yet it is territory traditionally a part of my kingdom. What are you suggesting?"

"I am suggesting an agreement in which the Ice can create hunting lodges and go after the game. In return we promise no coastal raids, no attacking fishing boats. The game we harvest over our needs could be traded to residents of Markul and Pale."

"The Ice should offer more than a share of our own animals," Meru suggested.

Thal thumped his forefinger on the wooden table. "We can also provide the thick, warm skins of the Tantroc deer to your coastal residents. And we can agree not to use our priests in any fashion against the Zell."

"I'll have my advisors delve into this," Meru said. "Perhaps my people might use the hunting lodges as well. And we could collect a nominal fee for use of the land." He glanced at the door leading to the kitchen. "Meanwhile I smell inviting aromas coming from the kitchen and here come the others. I don't know about you, but I am hungry."

Justi opened the chamber door to admit a man with a gaunt face, high cheekbones, and large ears made comical by his thinness. The man announced his name and profession. Justi pointed to Danilla in a chair near the fire.

"Who is the patient and what seems to be the problem?" Nool asked.

"My daughter—she is called Dee—suffered a fall and has a knot on her head. I want you to tell me her state and what we should do."

"Could this not have waited till the morrow?"

"No," Justi said with full authority.

Nool let out a sound that sounded like a muffled cow belch and went to Danilla. He found the knot and was surprisingly gentle in determining its size. He then checked Danilla's eyes, asking her to follow his finger. He held a candle first to the side of the patient's head and then directly before her eyes. He repeated the test from the opposite side. Nool felt Danilla's wrists and had her hold her hands out. He asked her to stand and walk and then return to the chair. "How to you feel, Dee?" he asked.

"I am tired, hungry, and have a headache. But my vision is fine."

Nool circled without his stick around "Dee," favoring one foot. "When did this fall occur?" Nool asked.

"Half a day back," Justi said.

"Hmm. Was she unconscious?"

Justi hesitated. "I think not. Dazed and quiet, perhaps, but able to speak."

"Was she able to do things after the fall?"

"Yes, she moved well and reacted well," Justi said, thinking that surviving a shipwreck qualified as being able to do things. He also remembered Danilla healing his arm.

Nool took his stick and thumped around.

Justi allowed this to go on for a minute.

"What is your diagnosis, healer?" Justi asked, his tone impatient. "What should we do?"

"My diagnosis? She has hit her head. Has she been resting since the accident half a day back?"

Justi had to think a moment before answering, perhaps wondering if a sea voyage interrupted by attacks, flames, rough seas, a sea monster, loss of the ship, and falling into the sea might be called resting. "No," he said. "She has not had a moment's rest since the . . . fall."

Nool folded his arms, his large ears seeming to bend forward, and pronounced, "The girl is fine. Her eyes are focused, her heart rate is normal, she has no tremor and walks with balance. What she needs is time to recover. Being kept awake after the accident was good. She can sleep now."

"That's it? There is nothing you can give her?"

"You should put a cold cloth on her lump. She is young and healthy. Natural sleep is what will help. Now, I could offer you some herbs to ease her into sleep if you desire."

Justi inspected his daughter and then stood, handing the healer a coin. "With the coin Nar gave you—"

"What coin? Nar offered no coin,"

"Really. Perhaps my intention was unclear. I will speak to the harbormaster." Justi handed over another coin to Nool.

Nool took his payment, bowed, and left the room.

Justi directed Danilla to the bed. She shook her head.

"You heard the diagnosis. I am fine, only tired. More important, I am famished. I will clean up and see you in the dining room."

Justi and Meligo joined Meru and Thal in the dining room. The hostess had summoned young girls to handle the emergency. They distributed drinks, loaves of brown bread with seeded crusts, and butter. Everyone was into their second round of drinks when Sathal accompanied Danilla down the stairs and to a table by themselves. The princess wore the dressing gown secured at the waist with a wide red belt. A girl brought them drinks and then disappeared into the kitchen. Moments later she reappeared followed by other servers with platters containing fish, mutton, and the red vegetables Meru had encountered before. Wine and mead mugs were refilled, conversation buzzed, and utensils clattered. The Zellish had eaten little since break of day, and all proclaimed the food delicious.

On the morrow Justi compensated Nar for his lost ships, less the gold he'd stolen from Nool. The man grumbled about the ruinous nature of the deal, but since the amount of gold was probably more than he'd ever seen in one place and exceeded a shipbuilder's fee, his grumbling was insincere.

Meligo, Danilla, and a guard bought replacement clothing, weapons, foodstuffs, and travel packs. They returned to The Harbor Inn with these materials on the back of a small burro.

"Our horses await, rested and fit," Meligo said to Justi who stood on the deck of the inn.

Justi eyed the burro. "You borrowed this animal?"

"The fellow was for sale at the stables and had been for a while. He paid attention to the princess, nuzzling her hand, making eyes at her, and cooing. She decided he was cute and bought him. He can carry our food."

Inside the inn King Meru bid farewell to Thal, promising he would communicate by messenger about the proposal they'd discussed. Meligo bade farewell to Entor, who needed more time to recover from his near drowning. Fortunately, a maid had volunteered to nurse the young man until he could return to Zellingon on his own. The goodbye between Sathal and Danilla took place in private, and the princess and her bodyguard were last to join the party.

The burro refused to be tethered at the rear of the line of horses. He insisted being close to Princess Danilla and trotted beside her horse without being on a rope. Once they had passed beyond Fathom's walls, Meru announced they would travel east to the River Wark, not southeast through the Manwark Mountains. "We have but three guards left," he said. We don't want to meet the robber bands near Maduk. We will be safer paralleling the coast to the river."

The party stayed near the coast until they veered south and stopped midday in a hilly, forested place. When they did, ten sets of eyes watched the approach of the royal party. The eyes belonged to rough men armed with throwing knives and daggers who made their livelihoods "taxing" travelers. Usually they conducted their affairs near Maduk, but today they watched the coastal trail, a route that usually offered few prey. The chief ruffian had awakened with a vision that spoke of gold. He'd roused his decrepit band and hustled them out of the Manwark Forest across the grassy space to the hills near the coast. They'd lain in wait for hours, growing irritated at seeing nothing. One called Tok trained a spyglass on the road, and he alerted his comrades to the approach of Meru's party.

"I see seven," the thick-jawed, thick-limbed Tok said. "Only three carry swords. The other four don't appear to be fighters. Oh, wait, I see a prize. One is a young girl, a pretty one she is."

"Where's the gold?" the leader asked.

"A heavy purse sags at the waist of the older man. And the burro is toting bags."

"Fine. We take out the three with swords first, kill the other men, and grab the gold. The woman we can share."

The robbers drew their throwing knives and waited where the trail came close to the hills.

The Zellish were about to pass the hills when the burro bounded in front of Danilla's horse and planted his feet. The horse shied when the smaller animal bared his teeth and brayed.

"What is that foolish animal doing?" Meligo asked.

Justi was quite familiar with such behavior, having dealt with a diving hawk more than once. "It is a warning."

Meru raised a hand. "I thought a saw a flash of light in those hills. Maybe a reflection from a blade."

Bargaron stepped close and scanned the area. "That one hill looms over the trail. If I were planning an ambush, that's where I'd do it."

"Shall we flee?" Danilla asked.

"We prepare for attack," Meru said.

Bargaron signaled the two guards to move in front. As they did, men sprang down the overhanging hill, five toward the guards and the rest to circle Justi, Meligo, Meru, and Danilla. Knives sailed at the guards and the most forward man caught a blade in the thigh and fell from his horse. Bargaron and the other man dodged the knives but could not close on the robbers without risking a second volley.

"Drop your weapons and we will let you live," Tok said. "We want the gold."

"I have our money," Justi said. "Take it and go."

A robber snatched the purse tossed by Justi, opened it, and confirmed it was filled with gold coin.

The leader of the band grabbed the prize. "I am grateful for your cooperation, but you'll excuse me for not believing this is all you have. We'll just have to check. Kill the men." The robbers raised more knives.

That was a mistake. The threat provoked Justi and Danilla, who cast white lances of flame. A boom sounded as Justi slew three men near him. His fiery shafts were not well aimed: necks, torsos, and bellies burned. Danilla's lethal pulse centered on the chests of the robbers near Bargaron and killed them. The remaining shocked ruffians screamed and ran until dropped by wider white-orange sheets of fire. After the violence, the silent cove reeked of burned flesh and the animals shivered.

Justi grabbed his purse. "We should flee. There may be more."

Bargaron wrapped a cloth around his companion's knifed thigh and helped the man limp to his horse. The group rode, slowed somewhat by the burro who seemed unconcerned about what had happened. When they'd covered a league without signs of pursuit, the party stopped and Justi tended to the knife wound. His healing powers were obviously intact, for after he laid his hands on the leg and closed his eyes, the man no longer grimaced in pain and was able to walk with a gait that favored the mended leg.

They reached the River Wark late. Dark overcame dusk as Bargaron coaxed a fire to life. The limping guard unpacked the burro and tried to attach him to a tree with a long tether. He gave up after the stubborn animal nipped his good leg, sending the man away hoping the animal would wander off. The burro brayed, drank from a pool of standing rainwater, and chomped on the abundant river grass. The other guard set up the tent for Danilla.

"We must watch through the night in case we are followed," Justi said. "I will stay awake until the moon is high, then Bargaron can stand for three hours, followed by the sergeant."

The night passed without incident, and after a meager breakfast, Meru announced that they would cross the river and head to Pale. "We will spend the night there in comfort. With decent food. I see that the guard's thigh is still bleeding some. He should stay in Pale until the healing is complete."

"So rest and a meal," Danilla said dryly. "Is that your only reason for taking this detour?"

"Fine," Meru said with an exaggerated sigh. "I want to talk to Breel."

Danilla smiled.

Fall warmth favored the trek to Pale, and they arrived late in the day before the gates were closed for the night. The large Pale Inn had rooms, good food, and a stable that gave the horses and burro care and the company of two other burros. Danilla's pet had to be housed separately after braying made it clear he did not view companionship as a boon.

At Danilla's insistence, Meru sent a messenger to Breel to announce his presence and his desire to meet with her in the morning. "That will give the girl a chance to prepare," she said.

After a fish-and-eggs breakfast at daybreak, Meru and Bargaron walked to Breel's house. The king's knock brought Credo to the door, who immediately bowed before the young man she'd known as a baby.

"How big and strong you have grown," Credo said. Without hesitation, she hugged her king and then grasped his once weak hand and squeezed. "And your hand seems normal. I am so glad to have you here."

Meru stood back from the healer. "I have come to see your daughter."

"Yes, yes, of course. Breel will appear shortly. Who is this with you?" Credo asked, noticing the tall, muscular guard who stood back from the door.

"This is Bargaron, the head of the royal guards."

"Please enter, Bargaron. I will prepare tea and you can tell me of your adventures while the king and my daughter . . . consult."

Breel entered the room wearing a simple green dress and a white jacket. Her dog Bib, now showing a bit of gray on his muzzle, accompanied her. The animal leaned forward toward Meru and had to be held back by his mistress. Without smiling, Breel said, "Greetings, King Meru. We are honored to have you visit our lowly dwelling."

Meru's breathing quickened. He sensed something different and stood there rather stupidly trying to figure it out. Finally, he blurted, "Your hair is different."

"It is longer."

"That's not it." Meru walked to Breel's side, movement that caused the dog to growl.

"Hush, Bib. It's all right. The king is our friend."

"It's greener."

Breel frowned. "Why are you here, King Meru?"

"Breel, please. I am Meru to you, the poor patient who needed your help to gain control of his hand."

"Fine. This is Bib in case you don't remember. He has been my companion since I was of ten years and can be protective. I will get to the heart of this conversation. Are you now pledged to wed Ranera, Tantrocan Princess and soon to be queen of the Zell?"

"Can we go somewhere more private?"

Breel led Meru to the rear garden where tall leafless trees cast shadows. A table and chairs surrounded by red and white, late-season flowers provided a meeting place. When Meru sat, the dog came closer and sniffed. Apparently satisfied, Bib allowed the king to touch the dog's head. Meru scratched while Bib sat with his eyes closed.

"There is no wedding agreement," Meru said. "The meeting was a ruse to attack us. It almost succeeded with the help of . . . a sea creature I wouldn't believe if I hadn't seen it myself."

"Did you find the Tantrocan woman beautiful?"

The question befuddled Meru, for he could not fathom its significance. He decided on honesty. "Yes, she was quite lovely. But not to my taste. Too brazen. Too tall. Too—I don't know—threatening."

The answer seemed to please Breel. "What will you do now?"

Meru drew a deep breath and began. "I will pursue the woman I love, a beautiful angel, a delight to be with."

It was Breel's turn to be befuddled. "What do you mean? Who is this woman?"

Bib laid his big head on Meru's thigh and directed his brown eyes toward the monarch as if to reinforce Breel's question.

"Oh, did I not make it clear enough? Let me add that the girl has intriguing green hair and green eyes. It is you, Breel. You are the one I love. I am asking you to be my wife."

Breel's hand went to her mouth and she stood. She backed away and it took her several long moments before she could speak. "I cannot leave this village. They need me."

"But that doesn't answer the real question: do you love me?" Meru left the chair and went to one knee. "Will you be my wife?"

Bib seemed to like the idea of the visitor being closer to the ground. It brought Meru's head level with the dog's, and Bib planted a big lick on Meru's ear.

"That is two questions."

"Choose one to answer."

"Fine, I love you."

Meru rose, came close, and put his arms around Breel, and they kissed. Bib pushed between the two.

"It's all right, Bib," Breel said. "We are just being friendly."

"Not friendly enough," Meru added. "What about the second question?"

"What was that one?"

Meru stared at Breel, frowning.

"I told you, Pale needs me here."

"Didn't you tell me about a pupil of yours, the girl with the scar on her forehead? What's become of her?"

"Oh, you mean Cheyla. She does have great healing talent."

"Then it is settled. She can serve in your absence. And Pale is only a few days' travel from Zellingon. You can visit here as often as you like. With the children, of course." Meru smiled.

Bib woofed softly and leaned into Meru. As the king scratched the hound's back, Bib thumped his tail and seemed to grin.

Breel put her hands on her hips. "I'll think about your proposal."

42
Reign of Peace

When the Megadarch's tentacle swept the foredeck of the Tantrocan ship, Justik was knocked unconscious and King Brosun was swept overboard. Ranera witnessed this event and stifled her fleeting grief after the Megadarch swallowed her brother. *Serves him right for selling his sister.* She made sure the captain knew who was in charge and ordered the ship back to Ankor. Then she retired to her cabin.

She found Caldir using his limited medical skills to assess Justik's breathing, his pulse, and the lump on the back of his head. Ranera thought he was doing a credible job. "What do you think, Caldir?"

"He is young and hale. He should recover."

"When?" Ranera asked. "We need him now. What if that monster returns?"

"I could use a stimulant, but it might harm him in this state."

Ranera balled her hands before her mouth and closed her eyes. "Do it."

Caldir uncorked a vial near Justik's nose, delivering a whiff of a tincture designed to wake the dead. Justik moaned and opened his eyes. "He is still groggy, my queen. A real physician should see him in Ankor."

The title of queen pleased Ranera. She would see that a coronation ceremony occurred quickly to make it formal. The Tantrocans did not like power vacuums.

When the ship moored, Caldir stumbled onto the pier and, still green from seasickness, threw up again. "We left Ankor with a king and a princess," Caldir muttered, "and returned with a queen. We started out with a champion who killed with shafts of fire but came back with . . . something less."

Ranera disembarked with Justik. She took some comfort in seeing Justik able to walk on his own. In the castle she ordered the court physician to evaluate Justik. It didn't take the man long to report that the patient would recover. "See that he stays awake," the physician said.

Ranera took the first vigil with Justik, thinking that if he was impaired in any way, she wanted to be the first to know.

Ranera got to sleep after midnight and, the next morning as she dressed, received her maid's report on Justik. She said he seemed alert, pain-free, and hungry. The queen-to-be went to her private dining room and found Justik eating grapes. "How are you feeling?" Ranera asked.

"Quite fine, I think. These grapes are sweet."

"You realize what happened, right?"

"What happened?" Justik asked, wrinkling his brow. "Where? When?"

"Yesterday."

Justik's face went blank, then his brow furrowed. At last he said, "Strange. I remember nothing."

Ranera offered a few prompts that failed to spark Justik's memory. He seemed to have forgotten Bentnord and the Megadarch attack. His first memory was of regaining consciousness as they docked in Ankor. An even more significant loss became evident when Justik seemed baffled by any questions about his power. He seemed far more interested in knowing whether the two of them had slept together. Ranera decided she needed to speak with Caldir.

King Meru waited for some response from Breel. Danilla found him staring glumly at the town square from his second-level room at the inn.

"You seem a bit upset, Brother," Danilla said.

"Breel has not yet sent her answer. It has been hours. How long does a woman need to make up her mind? I am the king, am I not? She has received a proposal to wed from the most powerful inhabitant in the Zell."

Smiling, Danilla said, "Most powerful, maybe. If you exclude our dear brother, who was born in the kingdom, our parents, and me."

"What are you saying?" Meru said, picking up his cloak.

"I'm saying you may or may not be the most powerful. At least you are the most influential, since you wear the crown. But in the end, you are but a man and one who knows little about women."

"What makes you think I know little about the not-so-gentle sex. I may have consorted with all sorts of girls for all you know. How can you be sure I have not?" Meru tangled the cloak as he tossed it around himself.

Danilla laughed. "Because I have watched you like a hawk. You are as social as an albatross."

Meru watched two crows bickering in a swaying tree, thinking his sister was right. He was not acting like a king. He poured himself a cup of water, drank, stomped around a bit, and asked, "So what should I do?"

"Here is what I suggest," Danilla said. "You could send Breel a gift of some sort with a card saying you are thinking about her."

Meru's face brightened. "Yes, good. And I could include a big bone for her dog."

Danilla shook her head. "Take the bone with you when you visit later."

"Right. A second visit."

"And when you go, listen to what Breel has to say. I know she has feelings for you, Brother, but the prospects of marriage to the king of the Zell may be overwhelming. You may have to be satisfied with not having an answer for a while."

"That's it? You advise patience?"

"That . . . and you may want to turn that cloak to the right side."

Meru sent flowers, then followed up with a visit. He carried a grazebeast bone with a tantalizing bit of meat attached. Breel herself opened the cottage door with Bib at her side. The dog seemed to recognize he human who'd petted him earlier and wagged his tail. When Meru presented the bone, Bib grabbed it and disappeared.

"You are wooing both me and my dog," Breel said with a smile.

"As it should be," Meru replied.

Credo appeared. "The garden has been warmed by the fall sun. I will bring refreshments."

Bib chose a sun-lit depression in the garden to work on his gift. He gnawed on his bone with an eye on his mistress and Meru. Meru and Breel sat together on a bench while Meru thought furiously about how to begin. He didn't want to start with pleasantries and irrelevant topics when his mind screamed to know what Breel thought. On the other hand, he didn't want to seem blunt.

Breel solved the problem. "The flowers were lovely, Meru. I suppose you have returned for an answer."

Meru held up his hand. "After a night of sober thought, I want to say that I really do love you and want you to be my wife. But I realize that you may need time to think on this. I accept that. And your desire to visit Pale is understandable. We can certainly travel to the coast and elsewhere—"

"I accept," Breel said.

"—in the Zell. What did you say?"

"I will marry you, Meru, on one condition."

A stunned look came over Meru. Had he heard right? How stupid would he seem if he asked again. He breathed deeply and smiled. He took Breel's hands in his. "That is wonderful. I think I have loved you since you first assessed my weak hand. I will love you and give you no reason to ever regret this decision." Breel's last phrase finally made it into his head. "What condition?"

Breel stood, pulling them both to their feet. "That Bib can come as well."

The king glanced over at the large dog who'd removed all scraps of meat from his bone and now seemed interested in cleaning his teeth against it. "Well, yes. We have dogs in Zellingon."

"And Bib likes to spend the night indoors."

"That shouldn't be a problem. We have nice stables."

"With me."

Meru sighed. "A servant can certainly handle a dog." He considered Bib. "A large servant, I think."

Breel smiled, stood, and added another part of her one condition. "My dog likes to sleep with me."

Meru stood. "But I will be sleeping with you . . . all night. A king is supposed to produce an heir, many so there is no shortage. For that we must share a bed. I want to share your bed."

"But Bib . . ."

Bib's ears straightened and he dropped his bone. The dog trotted over to the humans and shoved Meru forward into Breel. The king wrapped his arms around Breel and they kissed. Bib thumped his tail, woofed, and nosed between them.

Breel pushed back. "A shortage is hardly a reason for many. And Bib will need a royal dog bed."

After promising to send a suitable contingent of armed men to escort Breel when she decided to come to

Zellingon, Meru prepared to leave Pale. The guard with the knife wound had developed an infection and was mending slowly, and Credo forbade travel. He stayed behind under her care. Meru, Justi, Danilla, Meligo, Bargaron, and another guard formed the travel party. Without incident they reached Manwark before nightfall. The inn was comfortable, and the next morning, breakfast was tasty. Unfortunately, the second day of travel featured a cold, driving rain on the road to Zellingon. When they reached the royal town, the warm room waiting for them was all the cozier.

Mercerio had wine, bread, cheese, and apples waiting and insisted on hearing every detail of the failed diplomatic mission. Meru let Meligo describe the trek to Fathom, the procurement of two ships, the attack of the Megadarch, and the events on Bentnord.

"I knew my children were both gifted," Mercerio said to Justi. She was unhappy that Danilla had been rendered unconscious by the blast from Justik. And upset that Justi had been tumbled into the sea and barely rescued by Meru as they were about to become food for some sort of monster. "My premonition was right," Mercerio said. "So why did the Tantrocans do this?"

"Because they could or thought they could," Meru said. "They wanted to destroy the Justice Power. We became easy targets for Justik. Not only would they eradicate our power, but they would wipe out Zellish royalty.

"What became of Justik?" Mercerio asked.

Justi put down his mug of wine and said, "Last I saw he was sprawled on the deck. I think he hit his head. Our spies will learn his fate."

"All right," Mercerio said. "I am glad that you were not much hurt, and I am sorry that guards and the hired sailor died. I assume you informed all families about the burial at sea."

"All received the king's honor," Meru said.

"Any other news?" Mercerio asked, surveying the sweet cakes.

"That is the whole story," Meru said, rising. "I will rest before dinner."

Danilla cleared her throat. "Perhaps there is one other thing that might interest you, Mother. The king is to be married."

Mercerio dropped her pastry. "What do you mean?"

Cornered, Meru related his successful courtship of Breel. Mercerio took a moment to digest the news. A smile grew as she did so.

"I knew from the first that Credo's daughter was special. This is wonderful news and much more important than sea adventures. You should not have kept it from me. I will invite Credo to help plan the wedding day. We will make it a celebration of union and peace. And I want to hear more from you, Meru, on how this came to be."

Meru excused himself, repeating his need for sleep.

Meru found Meligo in the library with a gray-haired, sun-browned man. The man bowed before the king and excused himself.

"That is one of our fisherman spies who do business with the Tantrocans," Meligo said. "He has an interesting report. Ranera is now queen. Justik suffered a blow on the head and lost consciousness. He has been nursed back to not-quite-perfect health, and Queen Ranera is keeping him at the palace."

"Kept as what? A personal guard of unnatural power?"

"More as an adornment, a toy."

"Well it could have been worse. I assume that King Brosun did not survive being eaten."

Meligo took on a confused look and then smiled. He then reported that Justik remembers nothing that happened before he was knocked unconscious. "Caldir, the high priest, is said to have tested your brother and found no power."

"Perhaps Justik's power will return with time," Meru speculated.

Princess Danilla had wandered into the library with Lyra. The great cat, yellow eyes catching the slanting rays from high windows, padded silently beside her mistress. When Danilla stopped near Meru, Lyra yowled.

"Be patient, Lyra. I want to say something to the king," Danilla said and turned to Meru. "I have heard of the Ice proposal to have a settlement in the far eastern lands along the coast. Have you decided?"

Meru considered his sister's question. "Thal wants hunting rights there. It will be more a trading post and less a settlement. In exchange for these rights, the Ice will offer furs and meat for sale. How did you hear of this?"

"From Sathal."

"When did you have chance to talk to him?"

"At the Fathom Inn. He came in after the haphazard healer Nool examined me."

"Really? After Justi left?"

"Sathal wanted to see I was all right. Then we talked at dinner. Is there a royal decision?"

"Not yet."

"I urge you to sign such an agreement. For one thing it makes use of those regions and its herds. The coastal people are more fishermen than hunters. They will benefit from the new source of meat and hides. And most important, it drives a wedge between the Ice and the Tantrocans."

"You've really thought on this. I didn't know you had such an interest in statecraft. I blame Sathal."

Danilla spun away and followed Lyra to the door.

A servant arrived holding a scroll. Meru nodded in his direction and the man said, "I have just received this from an emissary of Queen Ranera of the Tantrocan Kingdom."

Meligo scanned the several inked lines, "The message is addressed to you, King Meru. It reads as follows: 'I wish to convey, in a spirit of peace, my regrets about the incident on Bentnord. It was the doing of undisciplined members of the royal court, who have been punished. I had nothing to do with it. My consort and I convey our congratulations on your betrothal to Breel, the healer of Pale, daughter of Credo and Panthis.'"

"This is a remarkable amount of information held by our enemy," Meru said. "Obviously, they have their own capable spies. Who signed this?"

"It is signed and sealed by Ranera, Queen of Tantroc."

"Intriguing," Meru said. "Can 'spirit of peace' mean we are relieved of the Tantrocan threat?"

"Perhaps for now," Meligo said.

"Did we know Ranera had a consort? Who could it be?"

Meligo shrugged.

"She is reported to have taken many lovers," Meru continued. "Perhaps she has settled on my brother. If so, then we have in a way fulfilled the words of prophecy that said peace would flow from a bond between royal families."

Meligo frowned. "Justik is not royal, but he certainly has a strong link—one could say bond—to the Zellish royal family. I must research this possible interpretation. Maybe Rakur can help."

Meru rose and stretched. "Perhaps he can fathom what a bond is. I will be in the garden discussing the notion with my sister. This sort of thing may interest her, given her new hobby of statecraft."

In the spring, Breel traveled from Pale to Zellingon. Mercerio's communications with Credo produced wedding plans and Breel's measurements, which the royal dressmaker used to create an elegant wedding garment.

As Breel and Credo settled into a suite of rooms in the guest wing of the castle, Meru fretted. "I have asked Breel to see me in the conference room and have ordered refreshments," he told Danilla. "Does this seem suitable?"

Danilla gave Meru her exasperated expression. "You are just going to talk with her. You have already proposed and Breel has accepted. If she had second thoughts, she would not have made the trip. Relax."

"I am relaxed. Don't I look relaxed? It's just that we haven't seen each other for a while. Can you tell her I will be waiting and am anxious to see her?"

Princess Danilla cast her eyes to the rafters, then went to Breel's room. The pair hugged as Bib and Lyra renewed acquaintance. Lyra pushed her head into Bib's shoulder, and the dog settled onto the floor and laid his head on his paws. The cat stretched out near Bib. And that was that. The animals turned their attention to the humans.

"Perhaps they understand that they are about to become kin," Danilla said.

"Bib has always acted smarter than any other dog I have ever encountered."

"The same for Lyra. A cat smarter than other cats, that is."

As the future sisters-in-law spoke of Breel's journey, the wedding preparations, and who would attend, a servant arrived and reminded Danilla that the king was waiting with refreshments.

"Oh, yes," Danilla said. "I forgot that was why I came. You had better go, Breel. Meru has been pacing around ever since you arrived. He worries that you have come to tell him you have reconsidered."

"Oh, I have reconsidered every single day. But what counts is where I wind up."

"You better tell him that."

The women left together, walking arm in arm. Lyra and Bib followed. In the small parlor, it took some convincing by the princess to get Lyra to leave with her so that the two lovers could have some privacy. Bib said goodbye with a gentle woof as the orange cat departed. Meru had been clever enough to include a bone treat on the snack table. That comforted Bib and gave Breel and Meru a chance to talk and talk and talk.

Representatives from all over the Kingdom of the Zell, from Raeel in the west to Abantazar in the south to Fathom and Pale in the north gathered in Zellingon for the wedding. The spring day was sunny but mild and filled with the promise of renewal. Thal of the Ice sent his son Sathal to represent the northern tribe and presumably push for a settlement of the treaty with the Zellish. After thanking Queen Ranera of Tantroc for her words of peace and congratulations, Meru, despite his sister's objection, had invited her to attend his wedding.

She had demurred but sent her high priest Caldir to represent her.

The throne room had been transformed. Its everyday brown appearance vanished, replaced with gold and blue and white. Long white banners edged in gilt with royal crests in the center hung from high rafters. Chairs were covered in blue drapes decorated in gold borders. Vases overflowed with white, pink, and lavender blooms. Oversized containers with ferns and lilies flowers made the throne area a magical garden.

The white-haired high priest of Zellingon had his own coterie of support, priests from the temples of Li throughout the kingdom. Their job was not only to decorate the ceremony in robes of white and scarlet, but to observe and report back to their people details of the marriage of Meru and Breel.

Trumpets sounded and King Meru in his most ceremonial outfit emerged from a side door and went to the dais. He stood beside the cleric on the platform. After a suitable pause, another single horn signaled the start of more mellow sounds of lutes and assorted stringed instruments. The royal court entered.

Princess Danilla wore a sky-blue dress with sheer sleeves and a gold tiara. She was escorted by Sathal in what amounted to well-brushed deer hide. Several young women from Pale in sea-blue gowns followed Danilla to places on the raised area at the front. Mercerio with Justi at her side followed a royal guard down the center aisle. Mercerio was in a deep blue gown, and Justi wore a high-necked brown jacket with gold buttons. At his waist was a sword in a shiny leather scabbard. They sat in the front row next to Credo, who wore a white outfit with pink stitching at the bodice. These processions seemed to please the dignitaries who filled the seats and commoners who stood along the walls.

When the aisle was empty, the musicians switched to the Zellingon wedding tune. The standing crowd waited for the bride-to-be to appear but were kept waiting. After a single horn sound, the strings changed the song, choosing one popular in the north country as a wedding melody. A young boy appeared at the throne room door. He carried a tray covered with a gold-stitched blue cloth. Behind the lad walked a dog whose head was at the same level as the tray-carrier. Bib, who wore a blue ribbon with a bow around his neck, moved with rather stiff steps toward the throne. Next to the dog glided a golden cat.

Breel appeared in a white dress decorated at the bodice with gleaming diamonds. She wore a matching veil and carried a bouquet of green sprigs and white flowers. Lyra gave Bib a gentle swipe with claws half extended and the animals sat on the dais. Breel stepped up and Meru joined her.

The wedding took place as weddings often do, ending with two young people married and facing a life of learning about each other. On cue, the royal trumpets sounded a royal fanfare as the young boy with a tray covered with a fringed blue cloth advanced. He offered it to the high priest. The man whipped away the cloth to reveal a thin golden crown. With the words of celebration, the priest placed the sign of royalty on

Breel's head. Music played as Meru took Breel's arm, and the royal couple, man and wife, king and queen, strode past their cheering subjects.

About the Author

Robert R. Brooks, a native of New Jersey, writes fantasy, mystery, and science fiction novels and short stories as

R.R. Brooks. He has fiction training from several schools, including The Great Smokies Writing Program of the University of North Carolina. His publications include a dozen short stories and two novels. His epic fantasy novel, *Justi the Gifted,* was published by Leo Publishing in 2015. A mystery, *The Clown Forest Murders* (co-authored with A.C. Brooks), was published by Black Opal Books in 2018.

Bob is a member of the Blue Ridge Writers Group and the Appalachian Round Table, has served as a judge for the Brevard Little Theater Annual Play Competition, and is now a reader for the Eric M. Hoffer Award for self-published and small press books.

Retired from the pharmaceutical industry, he lives with a wife, two cats, and beagle in Western North Carolina. A science fiction, thriller novel of Chinese espionage, *Clean Copy,* will be published by Black Opal Books. Under the guidance of his large black cat, Bob is poking around in the cozy mystery-paranormal genre. His website is www.brooks-authors.com.

www.ingramcontent.com/pod-product-compliance
Lightning Source LLC
Chambersburg PA
CBHW070752280626
47162CB00016B/162

9781734675078